The Address of God

The Address of God

Gourahari Das

Translated from Odia
by
Manoranjan Mishra

BLACK EAGLE BOOKS
2020

 BLACK EAGLE BOOKS

USA address:
7464 Wisdom Lane
Dublin, OH 43016

India address:
E/312, Trident Galaxy, Kalinga Nagar,
Bhubaneswar-751003, Odisha, India

E-mail: info@blackeaglebooks.org
Website: www.blackeaglebooks.org

First International Edition published by
BLACK EAGLE BOOKS, 2020

THE ADDRESS OF GOD
by **Gourahari Das**

Translated from Odia by
Manoranjan Mishra

Original Copyright © **Gourahari Das**
Translation Copyright © **Manoranjan Mishra**

Cover Art: **Tarakant Parida**
Interior Design: Ezy's Publication

ISBN- 978-1-64560-064-0 (Paperback)
Library of Congress Control Number: 2020933271

Printed in United States of America

Foreword

Some paintings are executed with broad brush strokes on a large canvas. They explore stately themes that awe and impress viewers by capturing the immensity of great events. But others adopt a humbler approach to the task of defining and presenting human experience through colours and lines. The pointillist technique of the famous French neo-impressionist painter Georges-Pierre Seurat comes to the mind here. In his paintings, innumerable dots or points resolve themselves on a canvas into fascinating figures or patterns which deftly convey a deeply nuanced and profound understanding of and response to reality.

Gourahari Das's *The Address of God*, which is, at first sight, a collection of columns written on different occasions to reflect upon or make sense of particular incidents experienced or witnessed by its central character reminds one of a pointillist painting. Each piece in this volume can be seen as a dot on a richly complex canvas which, in combination with other dots, illuminates the shifting contours of a moral and social universe in flux. Apparently unconnected with each other and recounting seemingly isolated events in the lives of ordinary, unremarkable characters, these pieces cumulatively create a living mosaic of impressions that helps one pierce to the fundamentals of existence.

Sidharth, the character who features in all the pieces included in the volume provides it with some kind of unity. The dilemmas he faces in the course of leading a humdrum yet stressful life, the experiences he goes through in the rapidly expanding small towns and decaying villages in Odisha, the places he visits outside his state and the characters he comes across or copes with lend the volume a deeper unity. Everywhere in the narrative, human beings, even animals and birds, engage in a tense negotiation with each other and a world growing harsh, unfeeling and indifferent. Several pieces in the volume are awash with a corrosive nostalgia for the simplicity of a lost rural world, its rivers, orchards and unpaved paths. The narrator mourns the decay and death of human values in a rat race for success devoid of significance. A melancholy witness to a familiar cultural landscape growing disconcertingly unfamiliar, he contents himself with recording and celebrating small acts of mercy and unemphatic gestures of kindness and intimacy. Eschewing everywhere the temptation to introduce the dramatic or the unexpected, the narrator yet succeeds in lighting up the narrative with unforgettable images. How can one, for instance, forget the child picking up the bananas offered to a roadside deity by bus drivers and melting into the gathering twilight? Who won't keep being haunted by the faces of old men and women trooping to the government office in the dark to receive their pension after enduring silently an oppressively long lecture by a political leader? Equally unforgettable is the cat with whom a customer can have coffee at a certain Japanese restaurant. One feels intensely for the dog that gets run over by a speeding truck when it runs out of his master's house to savour the freedom of the highway. A child's protest at her father trying to stop two birds from building a nest in his drawing room where they can lay eggs continues to resonate in the mind of the reader. It poignantly illustrates how, turning against nature, man has lost his essential humanity.

The text of *The Address of God* is studded with such luminously evocative images, which lead us to the rich texture of the meaning underlying the deceptively ordinary surface of the pieces. They disclose the inscrutable wisdom of the heart to which petty calculations of human intellect are utter strangers. The volume draws its intensity from the unobtrusive mastery with which the author employs these images. They stay with us long after we rise from a reading of the narrative Gourahari Das has expertly woven from fragments of everyday experience.

The translator, Dr Manoranjan Mishra has deftly rendered these columns written in Odia into English and his sensitive and lucid translation has successfully captured the nuances of the original.

Jatindra Kumar Nayak

Translator's Note

It was the summer of 2017. One Sunday, I went through a vignette written by Dr. Gourahari Das which was published by in the Sambad. Enchanted by the deft treatment of the subject matter I decided to translate it into English and mailed the translation to the author. In the mail I introduced myself as a teacher interested in research and as a published translator. I had requested the writer to make a critical evaluation of the translated text, for who other than the author of the original could judge if I had done justice to his text?

Of course, I did not expect an eminent author like Dr Das to respond to my mail.

The following week, another vignette was published. This time, too, the translated text was sent to the mail box of the writer.

However, the much awaited response from the writer still eluded me. Though disheartened, I consoled myself saying that I should not expect a reply so soon.

A few weeks later, another vignette was published and I translated it. This time I wrote, "I feel I deserve a comment". At long last, my patience and perseverance paid off. The response came. Dr. Das informed me that he had sent the translated vignettes to Prof. Jatindra Kumar Nayak for his comments. Prof. Nayak' response to the translations was encouraging and enthusiastic. With this came the offer to translate a few hundred vignettes so that a book featuring them could be brought out. This was how the idea of *The Address of God* was conceived.

What's more remarkable is the fact that my associations with Dr Das and Professor Nayak brought me some more translation projects including one from Central Sahitya Akademy and another from Black Eagle Books.

Friends, you may ask me what exactly it was that attracted me to these vignettes. I am sure, any reader who grew up in rural Odisha would relate to the experiences so vividly narrated in these. The protagonist, Sidharth, could be anyone ... you, me or someone else. The experiences may have been enriched by imagination but are never outlandish. The writer makes ample use of the flashback technique to transport us to the enjoyable and delightful days of the past. At the same time, he contrasts it with the dearth of humanity that impoverishes and disfigures the present generation.

I would request the readers to critically evaluate the text and e-mail their opinions at manoranjanmishra74@gmail.com

Manoranjan Mishra

Contents

The Address of God

"Are you not keen to have a *darshan* of God?" Narpat Panwar asked Sidharth in surprise when he learnt that the former had been to Udaypur but hadn't paid a visit to the 'Gautameswar Mandir' nearby. Sidharth didn't know how to answer that question. Frankly speaking, he had never expected to meet Narpat Panwar again. He looked around and discovered his co-traveller Raghunath standing in front of the 'Patwaris Haveli' and listening to a *ghazal* sung by a Rajasthani singer. His other two co-travellers, Manoj and Chandraprakash, were busy discussing the title *"Shravana bandhi nelani padare ghungura"* (Shravana has tied *ghungroos* to her feet) published in the morning newspaper. Rain in the Thar desert of Rajasthan is a rarity. That's why the local newspaper had carried a news item related to rain in Jaisalmer occupying eight columns. While getting down the verandah of the Haveli with his group of tourists, the tourist-guide, Narpat found Sidharth, murmured good wishes, and put the question to him.

Narpat Panwar is a popular guide of Jaisalmer city. He says, "The unsuspecting tourists suffer losses because of deceitful guides. Such guides themselves don't know anything about Jaisalmer; what information will they give the tourists? The tourists, before choosing their guides, should ask whether the government of Rajasthan has provided them I-cards for that job. Needless to say, Narpat always dangled the Tourist-Guide I-card provided by the Rajasthan Government.

Narpat said, "This time, you have brought the rains with you; otherwise rains and Jaisalmer are strangers to each other. You came here in March and experienced the intense heat yourself. March, April, May and June: during these four months we guides have almost nothing to do." Then with a feeling of hurt blending with anger in his voice, he said, "I had given you my card but it seems, you forgot all about it."

"No! No! I had come to Jodhpur on an urgent work. These friends of mine insisted on our visiting Jaisalmer."

Sidharth looked at his co-travellers. Raghunath was still standing near that singer, listening to his songs. Manoj was buying some toys and souvenirs for his family. Chandraprakash was busy capturing the beauty of Jaisalmer in his camera.

When Sidharth had visited Jaisalmer along with his family on the previous occasion, they had heard about three wonderful places of pilgrimage in Rajasthan. The first one is the "Karanimata Mandir" of Bikaner. The speciality of the temple, established by Maharaj Ganga Singh, is that visitors have to pass two thousand black rats and a few white rats on their way to the goddess. Goddess Karanimata persuaded Lord Yama to let her sons take rebirth; that's why the pilgrims coming here offer milk as *bhog* to the rats and pray for the long life of their own children and family. The second one is the "Bullet Temple," lying on the way between Jodhpur and Jaisalmer. In this temple, one finds a motorcycle instead of a god or goddess. On the night of December 2, 1991, a young man named Om Singh Rathore met with an accident while travelling from Bangdi to Choutila riding his bullet motorcycle. Om Singh was killed in that accident. The next morning, police brought his motorcycle to the police station. However, in the evening, the motorcycle was found missing from the police station. It was seen parked at the accident site. The surprised policemen took it back to the police station. They drained out the petrol from its tank and kept it chained, so that nobody could take it away. But, next morning, the motorcycle had disappeared and was found parked, as on the previous occasion, at the accident site, which lay some twenty kilometers away. After this, numerous attempts were made to keep the motorcycle in the police station, but in vain. News about the strange incident spread far and wide like wild fire. People, thereafter, started worshipping the motorcycle by offering garlands and burning incense sticks and *diyas*. This is now being worshipped as "Bullet baba". People strongly believe that the soul of Ombaba rests here and it protects the worshippers from all dangers. During his last visit, Sidharth had seen that place on the way while journeying from Jodhpur to Jaisalmer. The third temple, in which Narpat was intensely interested, was more amazing than the first two. Narpat said, "Man commits many sins during his lifetime, either knowingly or unknowingly. To be absolved of the sins, it is most important to visit the Gautameswar Shiva Temple in the district of Pratapgarh near Udaypur. Not only are the sins cleansed if one takes bath in the tanks of the temple, but the temple also provides certificates stating that you have been absolved of your sins."

"Certificates! What are you saying?" asked Sidharth unable to control his laughter. He knew that banks issued

'No Dues Certificates' when loans were paid off. He heard for the first time that certificates on absolution of sins were also issued.

Narpat explained, "The Gautameswar Mahadev Papamochan Tirth" in Arnab tehsil is a famous place. The temple office has records of all the visitors who have received certificates since independence. After taking the 'sin-washing bath' paying ten rupees, one has to pay an additional one rupee to receive a certificate.

Standing on the verandah of the Haveli, Sidharth was still thinking about what Narpat had said and absolution of sins. Intelligent men have made different arrangements at different places of the world. The most fascinating among those is the system of absolving one's sins by paying one rupee. Narpat then said, "You must go there. You can have a *darshan* of God in that temple."

Sidharth remembered what his high school teacher, Rammohan sir had told them once: "The source of the two main causes of man's misfortunes is man himself. The first one is religion and the second one is God." Alluding to a philosopher's words he had said, "Do you know why God exists? Because, fear exists in the mind of man. Had there been no fear in men's hearts, God would have bidden goodbye to this earth long ago."

Narpat had gone off. What was the fault of the poor man? It is the job of the tourist guide to highlight the significance of different places of his state to the tourists; he had only done his job. Sidharth hurried up. They had to visit different places by four o' clock so that they could go to the desert to watch the sunset. He was going to call Raghunath. He found that the singer, sitting by the compound wall and playing the harmonium, had started singing another song. While listening to the song he felt that the answer to the question that lurked in his mind could be found in the song. The meaning of the first line of the *sufi* song that the singer sang was, "While searching for God I found I had discovered myself, and while searching for myself I found I had reached God."

The golden glow of rain-drenched Jaisalmer now appeared even brighter to Sidharth. He felt that if the meaning of those two lines found its way into the soul of man, there would be no need for running here and there to have a *darshan* of God.

Arjun Babaji's Pond

Arjun Babaji had departed for his heavenly abode but Sidharth did not know of this. It was, for him, the most distressing news. Of course, Babaji wasn't such a renowned political or historical figure that T.V. or newspapers would broadcast the news of his death, but this didn't mean that Sidharth would remain unaware of the happening. Last year, the tamarind tree in Sidharth's backyard was blown down in a storm; Sidharth got the information after two days. On an earlier occasion, Sridhar's blue bicycle had broken; Sidharth got the news after a week. (Dear Readers, Sridhar's blue cycle was the first in our village) However, no one thought it necessary to send him news of Arjun Babaji's death.

Sidharth's eyes grew moist. Arjun Babaji was a part of his consciousness just like the cool shade of the dense tamarind tree growing in his backyard, the delightful rides on the blue bicycle, and the multiple hues of Baguli's pet parrot. Without Arjun Babaji, what value the adventures of youth that Sidharth and a few of his classmates had! Those days, Arjun Babaji's pond, its crystal clear water, and its stone steps were the main attraction for Sidharth and his friends. It was a huge pond with a lamp stand in the middle.

In the water one found white and red water-lilies; and around it stood babul and *krishnachura* trees. The entire morning was spent watching bunches of red flowers on the *krishnachura* tree, and the kites stuck in the thorns of the babul tree. Then they would slide into the pond like buffaloes. After that, would commence, long nude swimming, backstrokes, plucking of water-lilies, and catching of fish. Sidharth and his friends would be oblivious of the presence of Arjun Babaji. By the time they came to the bank, he would be standing there. One found it impossible to look directly into his fiery eyes. His necklace of beads would always stir—no one knew whether in anger or because the wind shook them. Sidharth would slowly come up to the bank like a thief caught by the police, pick up his pants like a kite picking up its prey, and scoot. Arjun Babaji's words of abuse would follow them. Who cared for those? Perhaps the *krushnachura* flowers or the *Chaitra* wind or the *Baisakh* wind that blew on the banks cared for him and heard him.

Arjun Babaji lived alone in the *math* that he had constructed on the bank of the pond. He had relinquished family life years ago before being initiated at the *Karamala Math*. When evening fell the surroundings of the math would resonate with the *mahima bhajans* that he sang in his quivering voice as well as with the sound of the *khanjani* that he played. His ascetic world consisted of this pond, the garden adjacent to it, some sandalwood-smeared photos of his *gurudev* and *guru-brothers*, and a few articles of worship. He harboured a great fascination for this pond. Just as a cow tended its calf, similarly Babaji was extremely possessive about the pond. No one was allowed to take bath using soap or to wash clothes, or to wash their cattle, or to wash themselves clean after relieving themselves. For people like Sidharth and his friends, this prohibited area under

Babaji's protection held a strange fascination. How would one experience the same delight of swimming in this cool, shady pond in other ponds full of muddy water?

One day, under the leadership of Sidharth, a three-member committee decided that they would surely take bath in Arjun Babaji's pond. The simple reason was that the pond, like the playground and the school, was a public place. No matter how much the Babaji shouted, they would never run away. Everybody including Sidharth agreed that their fearful flights made Arjun Babaji extremely bold. A novel yet conspicuous method of defying the law was invented. Three pieces of soap were either purchased or procured cunningly. They also collected a fish-net. Then they started their forward march towards the pond. Sidharth's heart beat very loudly that day. But he was not supposed to express fear. Besides, was not there something called leadership? When they reached the banks, they heard the sound of the tinkling of bells. Very good. This was the perfect hour.

The tinkling of the bells suddenly stopped. Nothing needed to be told to the group-shunner, Nakhia. Before the tinkling sound seized, he got up hurriedly and left the place saying, "My father is searching for me." Another followed suit immediately. On hearing Arjun Babaji's loud 'Who is it?' even the female crane flew away, a couple of *danduri* fish in its mouth. On the lonely bank of the pond, stood the nude soap and Sidharth. He also held the fish-net in his hand.

What an angry look Arjun Babaji gave him! With a stick in hand, he rushed forward taking long strides. Sidharth realized it was the last scene of his play. Babaji would shower on him a heap of abuses. He would pull him to his parents, holding him by his ears. He would be at the mercy of his father's stick that always stood ready to discipline him, as well as his mother's advice. There was no escape for him... today.

Babaji stood in front of him. He looked into Sidharth's eyes like a tiger. He asked, "Are you not studying somewhere, outside?"

"Yes."

"Reading nonsense." Tell me, what does this line mean? *"Olatabrukshye kheluchi lotanipara."*

This was Ojha sir's formula. Prior to punishing someone, he would keep his mind and hand prepared; only he would ask a question just for the sake of it.

Sidharth looked down with a bent head.

What shamed and offended him more was the retreat of his friends than the rage of Arjun Babaji.

He touched his eyes, ears and nose and swore that he would never come to the bank ever again—at least to take bath or catch fish. Babaji was somewhat relaxed that day. Hence, he was pleased with his begging an apology, and took the matter no further.

Many years had passed in between. Sidharth had moved far from Arjun Babaji's pond; so far that he would find it extremely difficult to remember either Arjun Babaji or his pond from that far. At times he would hear about Babaji, his *bhajans* and his practice of religion. Who else but a group of half-educated and poor women heard those from him? Towards the end, Babaji became extremely greedy. He started lending money to the needy charging interest. His way of doing that business was completely novel, Baguli had informed him.

He would place currency notes among pages in between the tenth and eleventh chapters of the Bhagavad. If some needy debtor pleaded with him, he would close his eyes and respond in that meditative posture, "Open at page fourteen, fifteen or twenty-four." The debtor would open the book. He would inform the Babaji about the presence of a ten rupee or twenty-rupee note. "That much is God's grace for you." Saying this, Babaji would lend him the money and ask when he was going to repay the debt along with the interest. In the holy atmosphere of the *math* and the Bhagavad in hand, no one dared tell a lie. The debtor would pay off the loan amount, either by selling rice or mortgaging ornaments, on the promised date.

For a very long time, memories of Arjun Babaji lingered in the consciousness of Sidharth, like the memories of the mighty Durvasha. No discussion was complete without a mention of him. Despite Arjun Babaji's prohibitive orders, no feast tasted delicious without catching a few fish with the help of a net. Arjun Babaji and his pond were a sheer challenge; a forbidden pleasure that taunted them like an unconquered rival and a vain boldness. There was a pride in getting crushed.

Arjun Babaji passed away two years ago. Sridhar wrote that the pond now looked like a helpless widow. There was now no hindrance, no prohibitions. Goats, cows, and devilish as well as decent human beings enjoyed free access to it. Everybody did as they wished, without any hesitation. All of a sudden, the bearded face of Arjun Babaji and his pitch-dark pond flashed before Sidharth's eyes. Would that person have thought such misfortune would ever befall his own pond after his demise?

Unknown to Sidharth, his eyes grew moist. Had one looked closely at him, he would have surely noticed, then and there, a reflection of the pious memory of his youth—a pitch-dark picture of Arjun Babaji's pond.

Arrogantly humble

By the time the minister reached the village, it was 10 o'clock at night. Usually, in a *mofussal* village, people should have gone to bed by now. However, the attraction of four or five petromax lights and a microphone of the Information Department had kept the people including young men and children sitting awake in the field, at one end of the village. The minister reached the spot, made his speech, and vowed to lead the country to the twenty-first century, and the village to the zenith of civilization. The place reverberated with applause of the people. The meeting came to an end.

After the meeting was over, the minister was taken to the Dak Bungalow, some distance away from the village. The local Revenue Inspector had run his office at the Dak Bungalow for the last few years. The minister was going to be served dinner there. For this reason, the eight member preparatory committee under the chairmanship of the Revenue Inspector had been working tirelessly since morning.

On a table covered with a white cloth were served, in a marble plate, *basumati* fried rice, dal, chicken, fried fish eggs, date *khata*, fried vegetables, *raita*, salad, papad and rasogollas. Eight chairs were laid out for the minister and his associates. "Come, sir. Please come. What can we serve you in this poor village? Just have a little food" said the local leader whose unnecessary humility made him look strange.

The honourable minister got down his vehicle and reached the table but he was so overcome by grief and regret that for more than five minutes no philosophical observation came out of his mouth. He cast one glance on the items of dinner placed on the table covered with a white cloth and cast another at the fifty government officials and commoners who had gathered there and in a voice choked with emotion said, "What have you people done?"

The Revenue Inspector and his companions, who were unusually busy and anxious since dawn about the preparation of the minister's dinner, were not prepared for this question. The minister's private secretary, who was expecting a promotion and therefore displaying more obedience, inhaled the aroma of the pure ghee in which the food was cooked and spoke on behalf of the hosts in the manner of a gentle explanation, "Sir, it's a village. You have to manage with the food."

Without keeping the spectators and audience in suspense, the honourable minister spoke in a voice laden with emotion, "By serving fried rice and chicken for me, you have not only offended me but you have also offended lakhs and lakhs of poor, hard-working brothers and sisters of the country. As a social worker, I didn't expect such behaviour from you. I have just returned from a meeting with the poor brothers and sisters of this village. I have tried to listen to their problems. By feeding me such food, kindly don't make me a partaker of sin. I would rather return without taking any food."

The audience present on the spot stood stunned and flabbergasted. Some started sympathizing with the minister. What a kind-hearted human being! The minister was just like a father and mother to the poor, as benevolent as *dharmaraj* Yudhisthir. This is the state where the Utkalmani was born. The minister was not only a divine soul but also an ascetic.

The hosts were trying to explain, "Sir, we are sorry for the mistake. If you go back on an empty stomach at this hour of the night, we will feel very sad. The name of our village will be tainted. How will we allow the guest to leave on an empty stomach?"

The minister relented and said, "OK. I will keep your request. But I won't eat this food." Keeping the index finger of the right hand stretched out, which he normally did while addressing public meetings, the minister said, "You have to bring *pakhala* and fried *saga* for me. I can't sit on this table and chair. Please arrange a mat of palm leaves. These plates and glasses are meant for kings and monarchs. I will eat out of a banana leaf. If you bring me a bowl, I'll drink a bowlful of rice water."

Such was the request (order) of the honourable minister, who empathized with the suffering masses of Odisha; and who was a beneficent human being as well as a lover of his country and humanity. To carry out the order, all eight workers mentioned previously went out immediately, a petromax light in hand. It is immaterial to mention here that by the time coarse rice was collected and cooked; the cooked rice was mixed with lemon water to make *pakhala*; saga was fried; and a good-quality banana leaf was collected from the regularly storm-ravaged village it was two o' clock at night. However, the noble-minded minister requested the others who had accompanied him to eat the fried rice and chicken served earlier, and they acceded to the request. It was a memorable sight for all those who had gathered there— the followers and assistants were eating the delicious dishes served on the table whereas, some distance away, donning a white *punjabi* and silk cloth, sat the portly minister on a mat and ate *pakhala* and fried *saga* off banana leaves. Who would say that the country lacked people who sympathized with the poor?

After saying this, Sudhodan fell into silence for a while. Sidharth failed to understand why Sudhodan was saying this. He only wanted to know who the person was, who had created a dramatic scene a moment ago, while drinking tea from the tea shop.

"The gentleman is a member of the Rajadhani Sweeper Sangh; he is a foremost figure of the present-day politics of Odisha. Irrespective of whichever shop he drank tea from, he would keep the glass on the table and look around to find whether there were any lady-sweepers. If required, he would wait till the tea went cold. If he found a lady-sweeper crossing the way, he would call her affectionately, "Oh, dear. Please come and dip your finger in the tea-cup." The excited woman would dip her finger in the tea just as the mother-in-laws in the villages dip their toes in bowls of water meant to be drunk by their daughter-in-laws. Holding aloft the tea-cup into which the lady-sweeper has dipped her finger, the leader would create a dramatic scene and conquer the heart of the spectators, without even fighting a battle."

"How would he behave at home?"

Not letting Sidharth complete what he was saying, Sudhodan said, "He was a conservative Brahmin. His house was like a temple; entry without prior permission into it was prohibited. These are their masks; not faces. They are just like elephants that have two sets of teeth- one for display and the other for chewing.

Sidharth thought that these 'arrogantly humble' were more dangerous than those who are really arrogant. Some people, over the years, had turned their masks into a part of their personality to such an extent that they would shy away from showing people their real faces. The simple people of this poor country feel happy when they see the masks. They think, there are leaders to tackle their problems and ministers to solve the problems they face.

"Oh my God! Even Sita had once mistaken a live deer for a deer made of gold," concluded Sidharth.

The Loop of Poison

They were returning from Puri. The cold breeze made Sidharth feel drowsy. The entire afternoon had been spent on the beach. The calm and beautiful beach always seduced him and he felt more intimate with it than he felt with the Srimandir. The crowd, the hustle and bustle, and the uncomfortable formalities that one had to follow in the Srimandir were absent on the beach.

A sudden call of his friend jerked him out of drowsiness. Sidharth sat straight, and asked, "What happened? Why have you stopped the car?" By then the driver had parked the car by the side of the road and switched off the engine. His friend answered, "A gentleman is sitting in the dark at Dhauli square with his wife and child. Perhaps he is repairing his scooter. Poor man! Perhaps, his scooter has gone out of order. Shouldn't we help him?"

Sidharth looked back through the window of the car. He could see blurred outlines of the scooter and three people. Despite the best efforts of the gentleman, the engine of the scooter was not starting. He was compelled to make the child sit on the seat and push the scooter forward. His wife was trying her best to lend a helping hand; she was holding her *saree* with one hand and with the other, pushing the scooter with all her might.

Sidharth could not immediately decide what his duty was under such circumstances. If the gentleman's scooter had run out of petrol, they could lend him some, but they had not mastered the art of repairing a scooter. The friend suggested, "They are going to Bhubaneswar. Let's take his wife and child with us and drop them at their home. The gentleman can get his scooter repaired at any garage and return later."

The proposal appeared acceptable to all. By then, they had pushed the scooter till the car. Sidharth took his face out through the window and said, "Sir, perhaps your scooter has gone out of order. If you desire, we can drop your wife and child at Bhubaneswar."

Surprisingly, instead of being delighted, they paid him no heed and crossed the car hurriedly. Sidharth suspected either they were not able to hear him or they took the proposal amiss. He shrank within.

When the friend's wife guessed Sidharth's mental state, she said, "Perhaps they are not able to trust male members like you. Let's go near them and ask them once again. If I ask them, they may trust my words."

That was done. They had gone a few meters ahead. We reached them once again. The driver stopped the car. My friend's wife told very politely, "You see, there are small children and women in the car. We are going towards Bhubaneswar. If you want, you can come with us." Since the gentleman had already pushed the scooter over a long distance, he was gasping. While breathing heavily he replied, in no uncertain terms, "We are going to a nearby village. Thank you very much for your kind offer. But, we can walk there. You may go now."

There was now nothing more one could do. So, they started the vehicle and drove off.

Out of curiosity, they pulled up the car near a shop at Samantrapur and waited. After waiting there for quite some time, they saw the gentleman and his wife approach. They pushed the scooter and gasped for breath. They also had a lot of luggage with them. Since the child was feeling sleepy, he was dozing on the seat. His mother had to wake him up frequently. They stopped near a garage and tried to catch their breath.

Sidharth and his friend got out of the car and asked the gentleman, "You crossed such a long distance pushing the scooter. We requested you two times to send your wife and child by car. Had you wanted, you could have sent them with us."

The gentleman felt a little ashamed by this question. He did not tell anything in particular but said a few lines in favour of the decision he had taken. A look at his face revealed that he was not able to express his feelings clearly and openly. If we had asked him to open his heart without any hesitation, he would have said, "Please go, sir. Don't try to act smart. You could have kidnapped us or blackmailed us in the middle of the night and destroyed our peace of mind. We have seen many gentlemen like you."

After returning home, Sidharth thought about the feelings of that gentleman for a long time. He tried to calculate the weight of the doubt as well as the lack of faith in him. He then consoled himself, "Why should one blame the gentleman? In reality, they have already erected a world of distrust around them, where human beings trust anybody other than a human being."

On the first page of the newspaper, lying on the centre table, the words of the Prime Minister were printed in bold letters. Those read, "We have to prepare ourselves for the twenty-first century." Sidharth was busy drawing an outline of the twenty-first century in his mind.

Bizarre Manifestations of Democracy

The golden hue of the setting sun enlivened the dilapidated buildings of Nalanda. The place was surrounded by sprawling green lawns, and dotted with multi-hued bougainvillea here and there. The tourists from foreign countries were enjoying the sight of the historical fifth century B.C. site. Sidharth had collected some information from his books about Nalanda University of Bihar. He found, to his amazement, that the real beauty of this place was much more enchanting than what the books described. There were times when renowned personalities like Harshvardhan, Chandragupta, and Hsuan Tsang were educated here. The University enjoyed unmatched reputation in the entire Asian continent. Today, most of the buildings are in a dilapidated condition. The plaster of history had peeled off from the layers of red bricks. Despite this, the tourists were filled with a sense of wonder the moment they set foot on this spot.

The taxi driver who had accompanied them from Ranchi had grown tired by the time they reached Rajgiri.

So, he decided to park the car near Makhadam hot spring and take rest, instead of going up to the aerial ropeway. Sidharth and his friends hired a tom-tom and visited Rajgiri. The aerial ropeway of Rajgiri was famous in India. When one travelled about three kilometers over mountains and jungles, hanging from the rope, both the feelings of fear and wonder sprouted in him. Ropeway was also existent in Nandankanan of Odisha. Fear gripped all the four or five people that travelled at one time. At Rajgiri, one had to sit alone on a single chair and travel. Sidharth marked that the faces of all the travellers who had descended from the top, were ridden with deep fear. He himself felt scared while going up the mountain. If by chance someone fell from that height, death would surely embrace him.

The plan to pay a visit to Bihar was a sudden one. If Sidharth had been asked to visit it alone, he would never have come. Bihar was infamous for train dacoities, murders and goondaism. Hidden behind the façade of these, there was a calm and quiet bazzar at Jhumartaleya, acres and acres of coal mines at Hazaribag, miles and miles of potato and wheat crop fields; an outsider would never find it possible to imagine this. He could experience the richness of Bihar's history when he remembered the episodes associated with Bimbisara. He was also reminded of the famous story "Pita Putra" By the celebrated Odia Story writer, Surendra Mohanty. The palace there was once the Capital of Jarasandha of the Mahabharat days. Sidharth asked his friends, "Will you find it difficult to accept if I tell you that this place was once the richest place in the whole of India?"

His friends laughed loudly. It was evident that through that laughter they were trying to hide their fear. The owner of the tom-tom was startled to hear that laughter. Even, the lady who was travelling by another tom-tom also felt scared. Sidharth said, "We have already spent much time here. On the way back, we also have to visit Pawapuri."

Ranchi was situated at a distance of three hundred kilometers from Nalanda but it was only a hundred kilometers away from Patna. Had they got that information earlier, they could have gone to Patna first, and hired a taxi from there. But, there was no use thinking like that. It would be better if they reached Ranchi by midnight.

The taxi driver, while introducing himself, sounded like a character in a Hindi film, "My name is Dillip but I am popular in Ranchi as Pappu mechanic." There was no way one could know whether he was famous or infamous, but he was surely insistent. At times on the way, without information, he would stop the car, go outside, and buy something. Pradeep was getting irritated. Just to keep their attention diverted from the car and the driver, Paresh was telling one funny story after another.

While travelling during the morning, they had come across hundreds of mango trees full of mango blossoms. Just as on the way from Tata to Ranchi one would find hundreds of dhak plants, similarly while travelling from Ranchi to Nalanda one would find a large number of mango and *simili* trees. Honey bees would settle on the branches of the *simili* trees. On both sides of the road, spread fields of wheat. At places, the dhak flowers glittered like flames. All of them silently watched the spectacle.

But, time didn't allow them to watch the spectacle any further. Very soon, darkness descended on the earth and, by the time they crossed Hazaribag, it was twelve o' clock. Even at this hour of the night, the driver stopped the car at one place. During the onward journey, he had passed the message that he wanted to buy two bags of coal at a cheaper price. Sidharth and his friends were astonished at this. A bare-chested man really waited there to sell coal at twelve o' clock. In a manner of offering a certificate to himself, the driver said, "Sir, the price of a bag of coal is thirty rupees here, but when it reaches Ranchi, it sells at one hundred and twenty rupees. So, when I travel by this way, I take home a bag or two."

Pradeep became angry once again. He told Sidharth, "Do you remember what the Hazaribag jailor had told us in the morning? The sooner we reach Ranchi the better."

He had hardly finished talking when the car suddenly stopped in the middle of the road. Paresh was dozing; he woke up when the driver applied brakes. More than a hundred people were sitting on the road in front, blocking it. Some twenty-five or thirty cars or trucks were parked on either side. Donning the dress of leaders, some people were trying to pacify them; those blocking the road were not listening to them at all. They were repeating one thing, "You can take the buses wherever you want to take, but only after providing us some mode of travel."

All the evil things I had heard about Bihar came back to the mind at once. Pradeep rolled down the window screen and asked, "What happened? Why have they blocked the road?"

The driver went to find out what had happened, came back and reported, "The local leader of the Janata Dal had seized the buses plying on that road for a rally. The travellers had blocked the road in protest. They argued, some of them had purchased tickets to go to Patna and some others wanted to go to Rajgiri. If they were asked to get down on the way in the middle of the night, where would they go?" But the leader did not pay any heed to their argument.

Pradeep and Paresh were startled. What a surprising

thing! Rallies and meetings were organized in Odisha also. Party leaders reserved buses and trucks for the purpose. But, no one forcefully made people get down in the middle of the road and captured the vehicle. Sidharth was taking pity on the people who had been forced to get down the vehicles in the middle of the night. Where would they go at such an hour? They had women and children with them. What alternative would they think of in the darkness, with the bags and baggages in hand? Sidharth's own problem, and not the problem of the travellers, presented itself to him as a threatening prospect. They had started the journey at five in the morning; it was more than twelve at night. They felt very tired as they moved from place to place throughout the day. If they had taken rest for an hour or two in the guest house, they would have felt fresh. But, that seemed a distant dream now. They travelled over such a long distance without any mishap, but to be stuck at a place only seventeen kilometers from their destination! Perhaps this had been decreed by their fate.

Looking out with fearful eyes, the friends asked, "What will happen now? Whether any alternative roads to Ranchi existed on the right or left? What should we do now?" The driver answered their fearful questions with more ruthless answers, "Anything might happen. There may be hurling of stones, brickbats, or even, firing of gunshots. There was no road along which they could escape."

They had to pass time in the company of mosquitoes, fleas, and a warm weather. No one knew how many hours had passed. They at once saw that seven or eight gun-totting men had arrived to take the buses to the place of the meeting. Sidharth trembled in fear and excitement.

The gun-totting people ran threateningly towards the people who were blocking the road. They spoke in manner of issuing warnings, "We can't wait any more. We have to take the buses. We don't have time to think where you would go or what you would do. If you don't clear the road, we will not be responsible for the consequences."

The inner beings of those helpless people shook with fear and terror. On the one hand, they had to face difficulties in that sleepless, dark night. On the other, there was the question of saving their lives. Can someone give up his life for such a meager cause! Only to remain alive one faced so many difficulties, worked so hard, and journeyed through so many obstacles. While submitting themselves to their fate, cursing the evil hour when they had started their journey, hurling abuses at democracy and the administration, they moved away, one by one, from the road. The rally buses left the place one after another under the strict supervision of the gun-totting people. Road blockade, peaceful protest, slogans asserting the rights of travellers – everything now appeared utterly futile.

While leaving the helpless and unknown people in the darkness and moving towards Ranchi, Sidharth was reminded of what the Hazaribag jailor had told them in the morning, "Forget about the law and order situation of the place, it will be enough if you return to Odisha unharmed."

Sidharth was unable to think of anything else. He felt as if a terrible form of democracy was superimposed on justice, morality, peace, tranquility represented through the structures of undying fame built at Nalanda, Rajgiri, Boudhvihar, and Shantistupa. Even he himself shuddered at the sight of that terrible form.

Blind Pride

At first, Sidharth thought Kamalakant would be building his house somewhere in the city. But his scooter had already crossed Khandagiri and the Kalinga Studios and had moved two kilometers in the direction of Sampur but there was no sign of the house anywhere. On both sides of the road spread bare patches of land. On the right side, some trees had been planted by the forest department. Some institution had put up huge signboards proclaiming, "We want to spread the beauty of greenery here".

In reality, the construction of the building of Kamalakant had not begun; only the boundary wall was being constructed. Kamalakant was very careful with money. He never spent a pie on friends. From the very beginning of the year, he would encircle the holidays on the calendar. Optional, casual and medical leaves would be planned carefully after or before such holidays. When second Saturdays and Sundays were added to these, he managed to obtain leaves as long as Puja holidays, on seven or eight occasions in a year. During the time he spent in the office, he would talk more about insurance companies than about things related to his office and job. His wife owned an agency named "Anuj". To take care of it and seek its prosperity, was his prime objective.

Despite all this, Kamalakant was valued by his friends. He possessed little technical competence but was always surrounded by those who were eager to construct houses. It was as if Kamalakant would teach them ways of earning lakhs over night; and equipped with the wisdom provided by him, they would march forward. Taking advantage of the situation, Kamalakant would easily sell his ideas and arrange policy holders for his insurance company. Kamalakant didn't talk only about insurance companies; he gave advice about Share Certificates, Time Share, Unit Trust lottery, life insurance, Peerless and the Hanuman lottery that was organized in the area where he lived. For him, earning money was the be-all and end-all of life. His philosophy of life was that any method employed to earn money, other than theft, was perfectly acceptable. He would advise people like a sage, "The ways to Goddess Lakshmi are many, but Goddess Lakshmi is unique."

Sidharth felt restless. He asked, "How much further do we have to go?" Kamalakant immediately responded, "It is very near. We will reach there in two minutes." Sidharth shot back, "Does anyone construct a house in such a far-off place?" Kamalakant shook his head in the manner of granting pardon to a foolish question and said, "You are a fool. I bought land at one hundred rupees for a decimal here. When houses are constructed in Kalinganagar and private houses come up in the vicinity after five years, the price of this plot will go up to one thousand per decimal. A profit of ten times cannot be made even in gold business, forget about the share market. Besides, what is the need of a house for me now? I have been provided accommodation facilities by the government. I have constructed two additional rooms there. There I have kept two cows and eight chickens. I don't require visiting the market even for things like *saga* and drumsticks. I have also applied to B.D.A. for a house at Chandrasekharpur."

Sidharth had no patience to hear the story. How calculative Kamalakant was! How was he getting time to do so many things? In order to make Kamalakant happy he said, "You are very fortunate, the favourite of Goddess Lakshmi. Are we so lucky like you?"

Kamalakant felt happy. He proposed, "Why don't you buy some shares? There is no harm at all…" Sidharth didn't allow him to complete his sentence. He said, "We will talk about it later" and looked at the watch. He had left saying, "Coming from the canteen" but in the meantime forty minutes had elapsed.

"Here it is". Kamalakant switched off the ignition key and got down his scooter. Sidharth saw a narrow footpath that ran from the left side of the road. Four people were working there, including men and women. The boundary wall was being constructed drawing water from a narrow well.

Kamalakant was going to say something, when he suddenly flew into a rage. Forgetting about Sidharth's presence, he rushed forward. An old man was smoking a *biri* sitting in the shade of a eucalyptus tree. Kamalakant rushed towards him.

Sidharth saw three tiffin-carriers hanging from the forked branch of a bare tree. It was clearly understood that they carried food for the three labourers. The two female labourers had already reached the place of work with ends of their *sarees* turned into rings. The mason was washing his hands after taking lunch.

Sidharth heard Kamalakant scolding that old man in a loud voice, "You, bloody cheats! You will turn a man into a pauper. It is not even two o' clock; you have already had your lunch break. In addition, there is the break of half an hour for smoking."

Sidharth had no business to interfere in this matter. But, he was not able to accept Kamalakant scolding that old man. "Wait a while. Let him smoke a *biri*. He will go back to work after that."

Kamalakant turned towards Sidharth and said, "You don't know these people well. They would be ready to leave for home, duly washing and cleaning themselves, even before four thirty. They will demand thirty rupees as wages. It is for people like these, the country hardly makes any progress."

Even after so many words were said, the old man did not respond. Sidharth failed to understand how these people could be so irresponsive and indifferent. The old man inhaled the last puff and while going to the place of work said, "No, Sir... I have arranged the stones, so that the mason won't have to wait for me!"

"Ok, ok...go...go. The mason won't have to wait! To hell with the work you have done! You have not smoothed the corners." Kamalakant went on behaving like a school master.

Sidharth's interest to see the plot of Kamalakant evaporated. He said, "We are getting late. Someone might ask for us in the office."

Throwing a carefree glance at Sidharth, Kamalakant said, "Who will ask for us? Let him search for us. We are working in the office but that doesn't mean we have sold ourselves to it." Sidharth was not ready to listen to his jabbering any more. Kamalakanta said, "Ok... let's go. I'll drop you at the office and come back. The work has to be completed here anyhow."

Sidharth knew Kamalakant had signed the register in the office. Most of the days, he would sign in the register and leave; today also he would go and remain present at the construction site. He said, "Why don't you take two days leave and complete the task?" Kamalakant looked at Sidharth. His look reflected his cunningness. He said, "Why should I take leave unnecessarily? If I sell them at the end of the year, I will get three or four thousand rupees extra."

Sidharth remained silent. He wanted to turn back to have a look at that old man. In the bright sunlight of April, the four labourers were disappearing from his view like four black dots. The silver tiffin carriers hanging on the branches of the eucalyptus tree were not visible anymore. However, he could distinctly hear the words of Kamalakant reverberating in his mind. The country was hurled into hell if that lean and emaciated old man sat in the shade of the tree for fifteen minutes to take rest; but how was the country not affected if a government servant earning five thousand rupees a month simply put his signature in the attendance register and remained busy doing insurance business, buying and selling shares, or supervising the construction of his house? He wished to say, "Kamalakant, if you are so much concerned about the progress of the country, please do your duty responsibly from tomorrow. Please don't kick others simply because you are in an advantageous position."

Boat Riding Netas

At times, stories of man's grief, misery and helplessness described in story books and novels prove insufficient when compared to the reality. The imagination of a poet and the ability of the story-teller fail to delineate reality truthfully. This truth dawned on Sidharth vividly when he wandered across the flood-ravaged area. Large areas were inundated by flood waters as the bank had caved in. In the darkness of the night, water rushed in from all sides like hungry tigers. Some people had already gone to bed, with their wives finishing up the night's chores in the kitchen. When a man's wife rushed to find what the loud noise was all about, she found herself encircled by the water. Carrying the two children, sleeping deeply on his shoulders, and holding his wife's hands in his own, the man must have run until he found a safe high land. Man finds it extremely hard to detach himself from his ancestral homestead land — though it might be a one-roomed-hut. It is precisely for this reason that man finds himself entangled in his family affairs; he braves hardships just to experience the pleasures of life.

One found hundreds of huts built with palm leaves

and bamboo mattings. Built by the side of the blacktopped roads, these resembled haystacks. Their walls were made of wet *sarees* and *dhotis*. The poor men of the flood-ravaged areas sat in those, their heads bent. They were surrounded by flood waters swirling all around them; besides, they had to face the rain of *Shravan* from above. Everything had gone wet—the palm leaves, the road, earthen pots and pans, clothes and everything else. Sleep eluded everyone at the thought that their houses, in the village, might have been damaged; their fields might have been submerged by flood water. They had no thoughts of the present or the future; they lived a despicable life and let out sighs. Not even a crow flew in to console them.

The small child was eating a handful of *chuda*. His mother had carried some tied in a wet *gamchha*. When she opened the little bundle, she found a line of black ants. Sidharth felt giddy when he looked at the helpless, small human being separating sand, mud, and ants from that handful of *chuda*. It is in India that everybody, starting from leaders to gods, proclaimed, "Children are the future of the country." Sidharth considered it a crime to stand there, helpless and decided to return to his boat. A sob rose within him.

On the way, while returning, Sidharth heard that the political leader of that area was going around the area. Let him come; he must observe the grief and suffering of the people. There was no wood to light a fire; no rice to cook. They were surrounded by muddy water from all sides. The stranded villages looked like abandoned islands. The leaders had the power to do anything they wanted. The Utkalmani was born in this district. Highlighting the misery and misfortune of the people of the state in the assembly, he had awakened the conscience of the administration, lost in a deep slumber. This present leader was born in this area. He would not be unaware of the problems and concerns of the people of his area. He would surely bring them food and water; the helpless people would get some respite.

The following day's newspaper carried extensive news about the said leader's visit to the flood-affected areas. Along with the news were published photos spreading over three columns. Sidharth shrank within in shame, regret and anger when he saw those. The photo contained the palm leaf hut and its helpless inhabitants on the background. The leader was shown visiting the flood affected areas by boat. The face of the leader looked bright with a smile spreading on it. His hands were folded in supplication. Some powerful people in white clothes flanked him. They exhibited much eagerness to come to the front so that they could be shown clearly in the photo. The morning had turned disgusting for Sidharth. The hungry figure of that small child of the flood-affected area flashed before his eyes; the long procession of naked people, who waited for a brighter morning, followed. How could the leader flash a smile amidst such misery and helplessness? Sidharth now had no doubt that the leader, who could flash a smile, had considered his visit to the flood-affected areas as a joyride in a boat. Under such circumstances, it was foolish to think that the leader would sincerely do, or wish to do, anything worthwhile for the flood-ravaged area. The boat-ride of the leader was nothing but heartless betrayal of the helpless people ravaged by the flood.

Several days ago, Sidharth had witnessed such a shameful sight. In a meeting of the Relief Committee at the State Guest House, a group of leaders, munching cashew nuts and gulping soft drinks, was busy discussing shortage of rice in the State. Sidharth had considered each of them an incarnation of the Buddha, and his kindness and sympathy. But, very soon, he was proved wrong. One of the leaders, on the way home after the meeting, was heard asking his driver, "What is the price of coarse rice today? You must have some idea." Sidharth gaped in surprise and amazement. What was the leader, elected for the first time as a legislator, doing in the Relief Committee meeting? If he was unaware of the price of rice, then what did he know of the hungry population? Moreover, such people were responsible for the planning; they would decide how much rice, wheat and oil the state needed!

Sidharth threw away, in disgust, the newspaper that contained news and photos about the leader's boat-ride. Amidst increasing cheating and treachery, the crocodile tears of the leaders for poor Odisha, growing weaker day by day, seemed nothing but a sheer deceit.

Brightened Darkness

Sidharth had never realized earlier that that city life can be so subservient, dependent, and helpless. After waiting for the approach of the water tanker in his colony from morning till eleven o' clock and casting a glance at the lusterless face of Malati who had gone without food or water since the previous night, he thought, if he had been in his village, he would not have to face so many difficulties to have either a cup of tea or a bath. He had not realized till then that behind the façade of a sophisticated existence, there lurked a sinister reality in the city.

For the last thirty-six hours electricity supply to the colony had been disrupted. Water pipes had been rendered useless. Petrol in the scooter had been used up. The petrol pump workers would not operate the petrol pump manually, lest they should supply more petrol than the customers paid for. Besides, there was the problem of water. How difficult it was to manage without water! But what was to be done? The electricity department officials were on strike. That was their democratic right. If fifteen or twenty lakh people suffered while they exercised their democratic right, why should they bother? Their strike was not limited to only non-cooperation; they had drained out oil from the transformers; wrecked the supply cables; and damaged electricity supply equipment. Sidharth failed to comprehend why the buses and trains, government buildings or transformers or water supply equipment bore the brunt of the agitators' anger every time there was a strike. The methods employed before independence were still being traditionally employed even long years after independence. The methods employed to drive away the British Government once were still being used to damage government property today. In the land of Mahatma Gandhi, violence has been used as the main weapon during every strike.

Sidharth had hoped that perhaps the condition would improve by the evening. There was no strong ground to harbour such a hope, but it was only a way of consoling himself. He hoped perhaps electricity supply would be restored and pipes would carry water. The candle procured for two rupees had got exhausted long ago. Long queues were found in front of the Control Shops for kerosene. Sidharth had stood in the queue for some time before giving up angrily. Now, he seethed with only useless anger. Sidharth didn't know at whom the anger was directed. He felt as if his and his family's existence was dependent on a few individuals.

It was eight o' clock. Sidharth was walking alone with measured steps. From a distance he could see a patch of the sky lighted up. It was as if that lighted patch of sky, appearing dazzlingly bright, was making fun of the surrounding area which was enveloped in complete darkness. Had electricity supply been restored in the city? With curiosity writ large on his face, Sidharth proceeded towards the spot.

Sidharth had never seen a more vulgar display of power and affluence. Electricity supply had not been restored. The members of an affluent club of the city were playing badminton under flood light. When the entire city was in the grip of darkness; when for a little kerosene or a candle people had been fighting with each other in front of the shop; where from the members of a club arrange enough light to play badminton? It was true that they had hired a generator, but on a day like this, could not they have managed without playing the game? Sidharth felt anger swelling up inside him. This careless attitude of the affluent was a mockery of the misery of thousands of helpless people of the city. This game of badminton under floodlight played by a few prosperous human beings when the entire city was plunged in darkness was no less vulgar than a minister being invited to a sumptuous banquet in the *dak* bungalow after his visit through the flood-affected areas.

The country where some opportunistic people utilize the power in their hands in this way while some others hijack the happiness of lakhs and lakhs of simple innocent people, is named 'Bharatvarsa'.

Chakravyuh

Like every other day, Sukadeb stood in front of Bablubabu's school and kept on gazing at the world inside. A tall, huge, yellow building stood there. A wide variety of fruit and flower bearing trees adorned the space in front. The place also sported a clump of tall deodar and eucalyptus trees. The mosaic verandah glittered in the sun. Many kids like Bablubabu ran helter skelter, with long steps, dressed in sky blue shirts, grey pants, school shoes and tie. On their shoulders were hung water bottles whereas on their back, they carried the school bags bursting with red and blue books, notebooks and the tiffin boxes. Sukadeb would have stood some more time watching what went on there. He liked to watch Bablubabu's school and garden standing there like that. Raju, sitting on the carrier at the back of the cycle said, "Let's go, Papa. I'm getting late. My teacher will once again make me stand at the front of the class." Sukadeb put his feet on the paddle.

Sukadeb, residing at Bhubaneswar, was a group four employee of the state government. He was peon to the Under Secretary, Mishrababu. He had got the job by the grace of Mishrababu; he stayed in his garage. Mishrababu didn't possess a four wheeler. Sukadeb stayed in the garage with the four members of his family. In the morning, Sukadeb visited the milkman and fetched milk for Mishrababu. After returning from there, he would go to Unit-1 market to bring vegetables. At nine o' clock, he would carry Bablubabu, Mishrababu's son, to his school and drop him there. On the way to office, he would drop his son Raju at the lower primary school of the colony. He would fetch Bablubabu when his school closed for the day and drop him at home before leaving for office once again. His son Raju would walk back home from school.

The other day Bablubabu handed one of his old picture books to Raju. Raju danced in joy when he saw it. Throughout the morning, both Sukadeb and his wife watched the colourful pictures it contained. How wonderful the pictures really were! It was as if the picture elephant and horse were really living ones. The following day Raju was insistent; he wanted such books, like the ones that Bablubabu had. He would go to Bablubabu's school; he would put on shoes, socks, and tie. Sukadeb was taken aback.

Sukadeb knew that Mishrababu sent hundreds of rupees to Bablubabu's school through him every month. In the month of *Phalguna*, Bablubabu was enrolled in the school. Mishrababu said that a fee of rupees fifteen hundred was required to be paid. Last year, during his sister's marriage, Sukadeb had taken a loan of four thousand rupees. One and a half thousand rupees a month! Was it within his reach? No. He wondered why thousands of rupees was required for small children like Bablubabu! He purchased a balloon worth ten paisa from the nearby shop and made him forget his demand.

Sukadeb deceived Raju quite easily, but he failed to

deceive himself. Sukadeb knew that in Bablubabu's school students learnt English. There they were trained to become *baboos*, Secretaries and Commissioners. The people who sent their children to the lower primary school were like Sukadeb or of a slightly higher grade. None of their children was expected to be a Collector or a Secretary.

Sukadeb was acquainted with the happenings in the Secretariat. The officers' chambers were air-conditioned. They commuted to and from the office in cars. They had telephones both at home and office. They went on tours to Delhi, Mumbai, England and America. They didn't eat *bada* or any other fried eatables during the recess hiding their faces behind files; nor did they eat *rotis* and *santula*, if they had stomach upsets, and wiped their faces with pieces of paper. They went for lunch at one thirty only to return after four pm.. Guards, gardeners, peons, attendants waited eagerly to serve them. For their stay, huge decorated mansions had been provided that looked like a king's palace.

Once Raju grew up, he would become a clerk, surrounded by papers in racks that looked like pigeon holes and heaps of files. He wondered if a clerk's job would be available easily then. For him, arranging twenty-five or thirty thousand rupees was like paying a visit to heaven and returning from there. Would Raju, then, become a peon like him? A mere peon? Sukadeb would find it difficult to aim higher than this.

However, one thing never entered Sukadeb's head. After India gained independence, the British left the country and went back to their own. Everybody was proclaimed equal. How, then, there were different schools for different people? In one type of school, English was taught; these schools produced Sahibs. On the other hand, in the thousands or lakhs of schools in the villages, only peons or clerks were produced. A teacher of the village school visited them a few days ago. He told that the government had formulated a new policy; Odia was going to be the official language. Even college education would be provided in Odia. One who scored twenty or twenty-five in English, would pass the examination. Sukadeb asked the village teacher about Bablubabu's school. The village school teacher looked at him with wide eyes. The eyes had no answers hidden in them, but only questions. Sukadeb understood that this was the cunning of the sahibs. Their children would be educated in English medium schools. They had the ability to spend thousands of rupees. Would their children fail in the interviews? If fewer students came to these schools, it would augur well for them. They would climb greater heights very easily then. They would get good jobs; they would manage big companies.

Sukadeb could understand everything easily. Everybody was not equal. The kings and princes went; they were replaced by ministers and *baboos*. What changed? Where? How? The fate of thousands and thousands, even crores of people was crushed under the heavy weight of stones, like his own fate and the fate of his son, Raju.

Despite all that, Sukadeb, after dropping Bablubabu in his school, would stand for some time watching the tall building, the tall compound wall, and the eucalyptus trees in the compound. A sob would rise in his heart—had he enough money with him, he would enroll his son Raju with Bablubabu.

Did a poor person like Sukadeb have the courage to jump over such a huge compound wall and break into the *chakravyuh* of the sahibs?

Change is Inevitable

Sidharth's face shone like a newly bloomed flower. Displaying the facebook page on his cellphone before his wife could ask him anything he said, "See, how brave my student Ayushi is! She has won everybody's acclaim by slapping the uncivil conductor who misbehaved with girls in a jam-packed bus. Ayushi said, "We must register our protest, irrespective of the consequences, instead of tolerating such insult every day keeping our mouth shut. For any human being, preserving self-respect is the most important thing." This was posted by one of her friends.

Arundhati snatched away the phone from her husband's hands and read the news herself. Sidharth said, "Today, I have to leave for college a little early. I have to honour Ayushi in front of other students."

Sidharth Jena was the principal of a private college situated on the outskirts of the capital. Ayushi, a student of his college, commuted regularly from Cuttack to Bhubaneswar in a particular bus. Yesterday, she too was commuting by the same bus. Taking advantage of the bus being so jam-packed that even mustard seeds wouldn't reach the ground when dropped, the conductor misbehaved with some girls. He tried to derive the pleasure of a pervert by touching their sensitive organs. Ayushi noticed all this but tolerated everything initially, but when he displayed the same behaviour towards the girl standing in front of her under the pretext of pushing the passengers forward, Ayushi couldn't control her anger any more. Gathering all her strength, she slapped the middle-aged conductor and shouted, "Are you a human being or an animal?"

Soon after, events took a different turn. The passengers stopped the bus, hurled abuse at the conductor, and threw him off the bus midway.

While handing over a bouquet to Ayushi during the felicitation ceremony, Sidharth said proudly, "It is great to light a lamp instead of cursing the darkness a thousand times. I hope the courage displayed by Ayushi will spur the students of our college to raise a voice of protest against injustice." Sidharth marked that Ayushi looked like Rani Sukadei while coming out of the hall, the bouquet in hand. He instructed his colleagues, "Let the news be published in the newspaper. Other girls will surely be inspired, reading it."

That evening, discussions centred around that event. Sidharth went to bed late. The telephone in the house started ringing at about 12:30am. Sidharth got up, rushed towards the telephone, and heard Ayushi's worried voice from the other side, "Sir, please don't misunderstand me. My parents are annoyed with me. They don't want to drag the matter any further. Please ring up to the newspaper office and ask them neither to publish my photo nor the news."

Sidharth found it hard to believe his ears. Was it really Ayushi or someone else? He was left with no time to ponder over that. For him, it was most important to ring up to the newspaper office and ask them not to publish the news: "Please do not publish the news under the heading "Felicitation to Girl Student". A storm raged within him – whether he should ask them to publish the news or not. Many a time on earlier occasions, he had rung up the newspaper office just to request them to give prominence to a piece of news and print them. Today, for the first time, he was going to request them not to carry the news.

The next day, Ayushi didn't come to the college. The professors and students had hoped that the news related to their college would be flashed in newspapers, but when they discovered that no such news was published, they gossipped for sometime, and then remained silent. Sidharth felt uncomfortable. He felt angry with the parents of Ayushi: "How would life go on if someone got so scared? Oh, what cowards!"

Today, Arundhati showed Sidharth a piece of news while handing him over the morning newspaper. At Saradhabali in Puri, amidst a huge crowd of thousands of pilgrims, a security personnel who had been deployed there to provide security, misbehaved with a medical student. The highly educated girl, instead of going for a *darshan* of the deities, went in search of the S.P. and complained to him. The S.P. told her carelessly, "Register your complaint in writing. I'll see." The girl was very brave. She not only slapped the police personnel but also posted everything on the Facebook. The Director General of Police had instructed his officials to conduct an enquiry. The culprit might have been caught and punished, but suddenly the parents of the girl said, "We don't want to proceed any further. If our daughter is disgraced, it'll be a great shame for the family. Those who praised their daughter today would leave no stones unturned to defame her. Even, political pressure was being exerted on them."

Sidharth sighed after reading the news. He could now understand the problems of the parents of Ayushi. Their daughter commuted from Cuttack to Bhubaneswar every day. The conductor of all the private buses might target her unitedly; their daughter might be in trouble or might be defamed; this fear had scared them.

Arundhati said, " You may condemn the cowardice of the parents of Ayushi; you may brand the parents of the girl associated with the Saradhabali incident timid; but just think for a moment, what you would have done had your own daughter come to such a pass."

Sidharth suddenly felt as if someone struck him on the chest with a hammer. He sat down with a thud.

Arundhati continued, "Have you marked a girl passing by a market alone in the evening? How she walks … scared like a defeated animal, with her head lowered… as if she is not a citizen of this country… as if the country is not hers … as if she is a refugee here. The girls who come from distant villages in search of jobs, and even the ladies, spend their time counting the days. Raising a voice of protest might bring them acclaim for a day or two, but then things would change for the worse."

A student of sociology, Sidharth wanted to say, "These days more and more highly educated girls are coming in search of jobs. Where knowledge and intellect are concerned, they far exceed the boys. This has created resentment in the male-dominated society. A man feels as if his food bowl is being snatched away by a woman. Besides, lack of reform in the family, lack of jobs, misuse of social media, alcohol and drug abuse are responsible for such things. But, such incidents must be protested against."

Arundhati listened to him silently. She said, "You are finding an easy escape route by blaming the small fry for the state of the country. What can the parents of this country, who live with their small families and small dreams, do when the SPs, ministers, Chief Minister, judges and parliamentarians remain indifferent to it?"

Sidharth answered, "Despite all this, I am very hopeful, Arundhati". Ten years ago a girl in Odisha could never raise a voice of protest against such incidents. She has started protesting. The day that girl turns a mother, you will see, the situation will certainly change.

Cock-fight

The sight of the way Bubun's mother dragged him from the bed reminded Sidharth of a chicken seller at Priyadarshini market. That evening he had seen a similar sight at Sohanchacha's shop. The sight of Sohanchacha dragging the chicken that was lying squeezed up by its wings had caused much pain in Sidharth. However, that was the relationship between the consumer and the consumed. In all crossroads of life and all its lanes and bylanes, one did not search the meaning of emotions and passions.

The sight of Bubun's mother dragging him by his shoulders on that rain-infested cold morning upset Sidharth much. Last night, Bubun was insistent on sleeping late. It was only six o' clock in the morning. Everything outside looked blurred as the sky was overcast. The child might have slept for some more time! Sidharth could not advise anything of that sort. Bubun was being dragged to the bathroom with sleepy eyes and a crying face; from there he was taken to the dining table and thereafter, to the outside verandah. Sidharth marked how the three and a half year old Bubun was being dragged from place to place like a puppy of the circus party (Bubun's lock of hair hanging forward gave him the appearance of a circus puppy). He didn't wish to eat anything so early in the morning but was fed forcibly. He also didn't wish to carry the heavy school bag but he would have to carry it. Desire or the lack of it didn't mean anything. He had to submit himself to discipline.

"It's all right. All children submit to these disciplined ways. Sidharth should not be unnecessarily worried about these small problems for the sake of his love for children. If they grow up amidst discipline, they will become worthy men in future. Parents won't have to face problems to ensure a secure life in future." Sidharth preferred to remain silent showing sympathy for Bubun's subservient childhood.

Bubun crossed the school gate and started moving towards the class room taking long steps. In the school playground, one could find hundreds of small children in similar uniform. Sidharth's paternal love was extended towards all of Bubun's classmates. How these small children had to shoulder the burden of routine, heavy bags, water bottles, tiffin boxes etc. at such a tender age! Someone was calling Sidharth from behind. Sidharth had made friends with five or more fathers as he went regularly to drop and pick up Bubun. Mrutyunjay said, his wife had given a slap to his daughter that morning. He could not protest then but he was not feeling well since then. "Small child, what does she know about the ways of the world?"

"What was the mistake of the child?"

"Her mistake was that she had not stood first in the class."

Sidharth shuddered. He remembered that Bubun also at times received scolding from his mother for similar lapses. Bubun should stand first in all unit tests in his section; he should stand first in the class; he should stand first in the entire school. Bubun's mother wanted that he should stand first; he should stay ahead... always... followed by all the rest. Sidharth, for his part, also harboured such hopes at times.

Mrutyunjay said the same thing; his daughter should stand first in the class. But, how can this be possible? No...no. Mrutyunjay's daughter should lag behind; only in that case Bubun could stand at the front of the line.

Sidharth once again looked at the school playground, the grass growing in the field, the trees, and the innocent small faces of boys and girls who had left their school bags at the foot of trees and were busy at play. There was no sign of any competition or enmity.

Then who experienced the desire— this desire to march forward; or the passion for sprinting ahead, by pushing someone else behind or by dragging one's legs; or the illegitimate desire to forcibly transform a dream-filled childhood into an artificial machine? Was it the desire of Sidharth or Bubun's mother or Mrutyunjay's wife? Sidharth fails to comprehend why all the forty parents of a section expect only their son or daughter to come out top of the class? Why do they expect their child to stand first in the exams, sporting activities, drawing, plays and in everything else? Why does it so happen? Why don't they understand that it is impossible for everyone to stand first in the class? Does Sidharth himself understand? No. He only expects Mrutyunjay to understand the thing, not he, himself.

When he was putting the scooter key into the hole, he discovered Baijayant with a smiling face. He was a successful man; he could do wonders. He had registered the date of birth of his son after lessening it by one year. During the admission time Sidharth asked, "What is the need of this?" without answering anything, Baijayant had flashed a cunning smile. Will the child live with a falsehood from the very beginning? Sidharth didn't like all these things. If the child grew into a man of worth in future, astrologers would get confused by a false date of birth. Patting Sidharth on his back Baijayant said, "This time my Tuku has stood first in the unit test. After all, whose son is he?"

His was another contender in the cock-fight. Small children like Bubun, Tuku and Mithu were getting transformed into chickens, and their parents into blood-thirsty competitors. The chickens fought among themselves until they drew each other's blood. Seeds of jealousy and enmity were being sown in children like Bubun, Tuku and Mithu. The chickens were getting themselves hurt. Their owners were shouting, "More aggressive... more aggressive... kill him... kill him." Sidharth's wife, who never stood first in any class in her entire life, would say, "Bubun, you have to stand first...or else I will not send you out to play." Mrutyunjay's wife, who worked as a clerk in the secretariat, would slap the younger daughter and say, "Get out... don't show your face to me. If you don't stand first, I will not serve you any food." Baijayant, on the other hand, had won the war. Taking the chick into his lap, he had started shouting, "I have won...I have won. My son has stood first... stood first." His clothes were soaked in blood but he ran with his hands raised upwards.

Sidharth felt shocked but soon returned to his natural state. He felt sorry for his son. No... his son must live like a human being. He will live with all qualifications and disqualifications; with successes and failures but not like a chicken.

He was running with his back towards that school and men like Mrutyunjay and Baijayant. He felt much relieved now.

Coffee with Cats

Neither Sidharth nor his friends had imagined it would rain so heavily. Sidharth's wife reminded him about the request of 'Thomas Cook,' the tour operator company which was in charge of their tour through Japan, to carry umbrellas. Sidharth immediately alluded to a line from a popular writer in his language and said, "One who carries an umbrella despite the faintest possibility of rain, is old. On the other hand, despite continuing heavy rain one who believes 'it will subside soon' and goes out without one, is a young man."

His wife replied, "You… and a young man? That which fades away before being fully realized, is youth, and that which persists without any trace of disappearing, is your old age."

Tour Manager Rohit said, "Dinner will be served at the place where we stay tomorrow. Tonight, you have to have a meal at the nearby restaurant."

Sidharth asked, "Nilima is not to be seen anywhere. Has she been left in her room?"

Within two days, Nilima, the Delhi girl had become the favourite of Sidharth and his wife. She sang most beautifully; her ability to sing Hindi *bhajans* was impressive.

Rohit replied, "No. I rang up to her room; she might have gone somewhere."

He had spoken the truth. When they were returning from the restaurant after dinner, they found Nilima reaching the hotel and unfurling her umbrella. Her face reflected loads of self-satisfaction.

Sidharth asked, "Hey, Nilima. Where have you been without informing us?"

"Coffee with a cat…," Nilima answered with a smile on her face.

"Coffee with a cat! Do cats drink coffee in Tokyo?" asked the surprised Sidharth.

"By interpreting my experience of the evening like this, you are trivializing its gravity. Really, I will fondly cherish the experience for days."

Sidharth's curiosity to hear more about her experience increased.

Nilima went on, "Sir, you can book a table in "Cat Cafe" in advance by ringing them up. For that, you have to cough up something between twelve hundred to sixteen hundred yens, equivalent to six to seven hundred rupees in Indian currency. Besides, you have to pay for coffee and snacks."

"What about Cats?"

"Oh! Sorry, I forgot. The Japanese have built the Tokyo city, keeping Nature and modernity in sync with each other. These Cat Cafes are nothing but small forest dwellings strewn throughout the city. Inside those cafes, there are small houses of different shapes for the cats. For the citizens of Tokyo, keeping cats is easier said than done because they are very expensive, and rearing them is toilsome and time-consuming.

"Yes, yes. On the way, I saw a cat shop. The kittens there were really living comfortably."

"Here, you won't find cats and stray dogs roaming on the street. So, they are scarce here. In the cafes, one can find cats of good breed. Each one excels the other, both in appearance and in intelligence. A look at them fills the heart with pleasure. I spent two memorable hours of my time with one of them."

"Bah, excellent. When you reach there, do the cats come to you?" Sidharth could experience the stirring of child-like innocence within himself. In his mind, he was transported to his childhood days. He had a kitten and a puppy as pets. One had been driven away by his mother and the other by his father. First, the kitten was shown the door. Mother believed, "Cats are extremely selfish. They always wish that the landlady should not have children at home; no guests should arrive, so that they can sleep in her lap. Extremely selfish of them." But the dog has opposite characteristics. He thinks, "Guests should visit the master's house often; feasts must go on, so that he will get plenty of bones to eat." Father drove the dog away saying that if the dog bit someone a number of injections would be required. He felt overjoyed, in Tokyo today, on this rain-laden evening, hearing that the elite were drinking tea and coffee in the company of cats.

Nilima added, "The pictures of cats were flashed in the website of the café as well as in its menu cards. You will spend the evening with the cat of your choice. In the courtyard of that cat's house, your table would be placed. You will sit there and drink coffee. However, how the cat will behave with you depends much on your personality. Yes, the café has certain conditions. You can't pull the cat to your lap nor offer it outside food. Don't use flash cameras to take its photo because that will make the cat angry. The most important thing is that you must not offer food to the cat with a collar because it might have taken its dinner or it might be on a diet plan for being excessively fat. Entry into the café is prohibited for children below ten years of age.

"How was your cat?"

"Who… Mopu? He was extremely intelligent. You won't believe it; he listened to me silently for two hours. What strange patience he had!"

"What did you talk to him for two long hours?"

"I will talk about myself later. In the room next to mine sat a young man and a lady. The lady had laid down one condition- if her boyfriend impressed the cat, she would marry him. She believed that animals could read the inner thoughts of men quite well."

"Why did you decide to go there so suddenly?" asked Sidharth in a serious voice.

Nilima said, "These days, one's own people don't have the time to partake in one's sorrow. I wished to share some disheartening experiences. I divulged all those before Mofu. He listened to me attentively. That was it; coffee was only a plea."

"But you could have shared your grief with some human friend of yours."

"Yes, I could have. I was doing so. I was sharing all my problems with my most intimate friend. One day, I found him disclosing my secrets to others and deriving pleasure from those. I had never imagined that a misery of one could become a source of great pleasure and fun for others."

Nilima's voice sounded heavy. What a load of grief Nilima, the girl who had appeared most cheerful till that afternoon, concealed in her heart?

"I wish to go to that café after listening to you."

"What makes you sad?"

"Who isn't sad in this world, Nilima?" Sidharth said.

Nilima changed the topic and said, "I have conveyed the best wishes and love of all Indians to Mopu."

"How did Mopu respond?" asked the seventy-year old Sidharth like a kid.

"Mopu wished us all the best for our Japan tour," answered Nilima giving a naughty smile.

Conflict

Sanatan's face looked devastated like a broken drumstick tree. At the sight of his withered face that replaced his usual smiling one, Sidharth became worried. It's only then that Annapurna, Sanatan's wife, appeared and said, "Please sit down a while with your friend. Let me prepare tea for you."

"Why has his face gone sour? Is he not well?"

"His mother called up some time ago. Since the time he received the phone call, he has been sitting like that."

Annapurna entered the kitchen. Sidharth enquired, "What happened?"

Sanatan replied, "Duing the Ganesh Puja this time, instead of waiting for the brahmin, I performed the *puja* myself. Besides, I conducted my father's *shraddh* as per the christian calendar instead of the lunar calendar. Some money has been deposited with the Jagannath temple at Baramunda for *annadan*, the ceremonial donation of food to Gods on anniversaries, as per the lunar calendar. My mother was very harsh with me in regard to these two things".

Annapurna brought in the tea.

Sidharth asked her, "I had heard you were staying out of town; when did you come back?"

I arrived this morning, in fact moments before your arrival. I'll leave when my daughter sends her car to pick me up."

Sanatan said, "Listen Sidharth, since the birth of my grand-daughter, Annapurna has been living at Patia. I have been living here alone for the last four months. When we first started living here, some thirty years ago, there were no houses in the vicinity. My daughter's school was situated far away. So, we organized Ganesh Puja and Saraswati Puja here, at home. Initially, we would bring clay-images, but we had to face a great deal of trouble for their immersion. For the immersion of the Ganesh image, we often got a pond or canal filled with water; but during the month of *Magha*, we would not get a water source for immersion of the Saraswati image. One year, I felt repentant after I had to dispose of the image in the dirty drain water. So, we have procured two stone images of Lord Ganesh and Goddess Saraswati, to which we offer worship. My mother has complaints regarding that puja, too. I had started organizing the *puja* for the sake of my daughter. In the meantime, she has been married off; owing to my mother's insistence, I cannot even do away with the *puja*. Besides, the brahmin never arrives before one o' clock for the *puja*. He even forgot about us for three or four years.

"Arey, how irresponsible he is!"

"No, he is but profit-conscious. During the Ganesh or Saraswati puja we offer him two or three hundred rupees; but if he attends a house-warming ceremony he earns two or three thousand rupees. So, he intentionally forgets us."

"Is he the only brahmin in the city? Why didn't you search for another one?"

"We undertook a thorough search," said Annapurna. While picking up the tea cups, she continued, "We have conducted many experiments regarding that. Once we got hold of such a brahmin, who, after offering flowers recited mantras that should have been read during the installation of the *kalash*. Later we learnt, he wasn't a brahmin at all."

Sidharth could not help laughing loudly.

Sanatan further added, "I am living here alone. Where from would I get the five things required for making *panchamrit*; where from would I collect *barakoli* leaves, *doob* grass and mango leaves? There was a time when there was not a single house in the vicinity, but it's next to impossible, to find a patch of soil in Jagamara.

"How long will *bhauja* stay there?asked Sidharth"

"Who knows? Our daughter works at Cuttack. She commutes there every day. Our son-in-law leaves early in the morning only to return at eight o' clock in the evening. My *samuduni*, my daughter's mother-in-law, is ill. Can my *samudi*, my daughter's father-in-law, take care of the new-born baby?" asked Annapurna.

Sanatan said, "A man, assailed by grief, calls for the intervention of God. The way he can convey his troubles to god, can a brahmin in a hurry do that? The same with the *shraddh* for my father. According to my mother, it is customary to organize the *shraddh* and offer food to the brahmins as per the lunar calendar. After the *shraddh* is over, some food should be offered to animals like crows and dogs. They enjoy direct access to Lord *Yamaraj*. One should invite learned brahmins to perform the *shraddh*. A greedy, or limbless brahmin in a hurry is of no use. Tell me, how would I find out one who is not too busy? I can't read the lunar calendar myself. That's why I manage the show by offering food to some poor children as per the Christian calendar.

Sidharth now fully understood why Sanatan's face bore a sour expression. He said, "I wonder when the blind beliefs born of tradition will be done away with in our country. They might cease to exist soon, but the newspapers and television channels would never allow it to happen. In most channels, one finds the cinestars or *babas* discussing horoscopes, and promoting the sale of stone-rings, *rudraksh* and many more items. Throughout the evening one can watch many serials and films dealing with ghosts and witches, incantations and charms, rebirth or human sacrifice. Most people know that the world that has been constructed around worship and offering, gods and goddesses, *mathas* and *mahantas* are based on fantasy and false stories. The basis of all this is man's lack of confidence. The mass media is rife with the stories of a convicted *baba* from Haryana. But, does anyone ask why most of his disciples and supporters belong to the lower strata of the society. Where would such men go if we don't allow their devotees to rise up the social or administrative ladder?

Sanatan sat silently.

Annapurna said, "My mother-in-law believed whatever good happened to the family was because of the worship of gods; and if something went wrong it was because of her son's bad deeds."

Sidharth understood Sanatan's problems. This was not a problem concerning one Sanatan but the problem concerning lakhs of Sanatans. He said, "The conflict between the old and the new was a well-known chapter in human history. It is immaterial to explain that today's man has reached his current state wading through many obstacles and devastations. Man, who once led a nomadic life and roamed here and there in search of food and shelter among the mountainous valleys and riverside pastures, must remain indebted to Nature for his growth and development. I strongly believe, man would surely get past the blind beliefs that engulf him because he is the child of God. Defeat is not the last episode of history. Please listen to me. Please spare some time and meet your mother. She might be listening to others, but believe me, every mother keeps a special place reserved in her heart for her child. Forget about outsiders, she doesn't even allow her husband to occupy that spot. Go and tell your mother all those problems that you talked to me about today; you will surely find her telling, 'There is no need of my son getting into so much trouble for these *pujas*'. There is no use in remaining silent. Tell others openly what you believe."

The withered looking Sanatan began getting back some confidence.

A Dak Bungalow

The young man had returned from the gate four or five times since morning. Perhaps his moped had run out of fuel or some mechanical problem had cropped up; he was busy repairing that moped. The engine worked and then stopped.

When the young man came to the dak-bungalow for the first time, its gate had not been opened. Fog had surrounded the two-storeyed dak-bungalow situated adjacent to a mountain. Perhaps he had received the message from some source that a very powerful minister of the State cabinet had come here the previous night. He waited to get some help from him. Perhaps the young man needed a job or a small contract or a supply order.

The news of the minister's visit to the town must have spread everywhere in the meantime. Sidharth failed to understand how news about ministers' visits spread faster than floods or incidents of fire.

The number of people coming to the dak-bungalow had started increasing. Two or three more motorcycles had arrived. Sidharth had reached here the previous day. Banamali uncle of his village was the gardener there.

Sidharth had thought he would be able to arrange a comfortable stay for the night without asking for payment. But forget about a comfortable stay, he was not even able to sleep throughout the night. Sidharth had slept comfortably near the stairs with hands and legs stretched. The poor fellow had no idea that the minister would reach in the middle of the night. The moment the minister's car crossed the gate, Banamali uncle dragged him from beneath the blanket like one dragged a chicken from the coop. He thought that the minister might not approve of someone sleeping near the staircase in that posture.

The bright light of the minister's white ambassador car brightened up the dak- bungalow. Sidharth's sleepy, pale and sad appearance now looked very pathetic.

In the meantime, a crowd had assembled. It was ten o' clock. The minister hadn't got up. In the courtyard, all kinds of people gathered. This included old men and women, young men and women, and two widows. Everybody carried applications; everybody had problems. Life without problems is unheard of.

They were getting anxious. They frequently addressed impatient queries to the peon of the dak-bungalow and the minister's driver. The young men walked about anxiously. The condition of the young man who had reached first was the most pathetic. He reached here early thinking he would be able to talk about his problems to the minister in private. Now, a huge crowd gathered there. The minister hadn't got up. He would not be able to convey his difficulties and helplessness amid such a large crowd. His condition was similar to the condition of the mother who was compelled to be delivered of her baby in a crowded train.

"The minister had not got up. He was very tired. He

returned very late at night," were the answers of the peon. "It is already eleven o' clock. We reached at six. Kindly inform the minister," were some of the complaints of the people waiting there. In the middle of all these spread the huge dak-bungalow, its gorgeous flower garden, tall domes, soft and colourful carpet, teak-wood table and comfortable sofas.

The minister had not got up. Those who arrived in the morning, came by rickshaws, cycles, mopeds and scooters. Those who were reaching now were coming by ambassador cars, maruti cars, contessas and other expensive vehicles. They didn't have to wait on the verandah. The peon called them inside and made them sit. They had appointments. "Please come, the minister will get up very soon," the peon would say smilingly.

The crowd suddenly became active; as if waves lashed the shore. With the help of support-staff, the old men got up; the old women stood up with their heads raised up from their knees; young men rushed forward. The safari or coat clad people were found smiling unnecessarily and extending their hands. The minister appeared on the verandah. This anxiety and restlessness was only to meet him.

Distributing smile equitably among the public and conveying *namaskar* equitably to the public, the minister climbed down the stairs. He collected applications expressing grief from some; bouquets of welcome from some others; garlands of praise from some; and handed them over to his assistants. The attention of the crowd was now centered on the back seat of the minister's car. The minister had already got seated there.

Sidharth looked as the car disappeared from view. The crowd started thinning out. Near the portico, leaning against the wall behind the croton bushes, stood that young man who had reached the dak-bungalow before anyone else. He could not meet the minister to convey his grievances. Neither did he see the minister nor did the minister see him.

Suddenly, Sidharth grew sad. The unknown young man had not asked Sidharth to share his sorrow. Let him not ask for anything; does anybody need permission to show sympathy? He felt as if he himself stood in the place of that unknown young man.

What an attractive and beautiful pose with which the guests of the dak-bungalow turn their backs on the miserable widows, poor destitute old men, and jobless young men! Last night the dak-bungalow that had appeared a reliable refuge as well as a humble, dependable rest house seemed as a den of vulgarity where days became excessively short and nights turned excessively long for celebration with chicken, fried rice, beer bottles and green lights.

Dazzling Example

Sidharth was waiting for the bus that usually left the Badambadi bus-stand at 4:10 pm. The smell of burnt mobil, diesel and petrol, and the dust that followed the wheels of buses almost stuffed his nostrils and ears. Such moments of waiting were extremely painful. It was really very difficult to wait, whether for the bus or the train or the arriving guests.

On the other side of the bus-stand there existed some second-hand book shops. During the college days, Sidharth would spend a lot of time in front of these book-shops. There was no restriction on going through the books by turning their pages. It was never a problem whether one bought any books or not. Sidharth would find the attraction of going through books of different languages, varieties, and styles irresistible. It was immaterial whether they catered to one's choice, language or requirement. The book-shop had a rich collection of literature books starting from Rabindranath to Rabi Singh, Thomas Hardy to Kanhucharan, Gurky to Gopinath; old text-books; the eleventh chapter of the Bhagavad; guides required for those in search of jobs as well as popular novels. No one knew where these books came from. Some of them were deprived of the kind glances of high-ranking-officials; some others were displaced from the book shelves of the affluent. They had reached the paper-packet-making shops before finally reaching the footpath. The memory of the old days lingered on the pages through stamps and signatures.

A large crowd gathered in front of the bookshop. Sidharth looked at his watch once, and then at the bus-stand. No... the bus had not reached till now. It was four-thirty already. He grew irritated. He cursed the bus-conductor and the driver along with the entire transport department. He concluded that India is a hell because of the irresponsibility of such officials. He glanced through the books once again.

Suddenly, he noticed a leper in a wheeled-box, some ten to fifteen hands away. He rolled the wheels himself and moved by the side of the road. Sidharth had marked this infirm human being but he had not paid him much attention; just as he had not given importance to the signboards on the walls and cinema posters of the past. Sidharth felt somewhat amazed because that leper was coming close to the second-hand bookshop.

The man would be around forty years of age. He appeared ten or fifteen years older because of this affliction. On his cheek grew an uncared for and coarse beard. The man had put on an extremely filthy t-shirt and a pair of colorless trousers. Inside the box, in front of him, was placed an aluminium bowl. The bowl contained some coins- the contribution of kind donors. The man came slowly and stopped in front of the bookshop. Sidharth moved to one side, avoiding him. Three or four probable customers fled the spot as the leper came in sight. What can a leper need in a bookshop? Sidharth watched the leper, keeping his curiosity in check.

The leper glanced through the books on the book shelf. After some time, his glum face turned bright. Perhaps he got the book he had been looking for! He asked for the price of the book. The shopkeeper answered, "Two rupees and seventy five paise." The man picked up the five and ten paise coins from the aluminum bowl and counted them. He could gather two rupees and sixty five paise. It was ten paise less than the price of the book. His face reflected his helplessness and feeling of distress. Worried, he looked to the right and left of the box, thinking he might get a ten paise coin somewhere but in vain.

He handed over all the coins to the shopkeeper and said, "There is a shortage of ten paise."

The shopkeeper counted the coins. Among the coins, he found a ten paise coin which was worthless; both sides of it were worn out.

At one point of time, Sidharth thought of handing him over a twenty paise coin. This would supply his want. But the next moment, he restrained himself. At that moment, both of them were customers; no one was a beggar or a donor. He didn't want to offend the beggar by being unnecessarily kind to him.

The shopkeeper was a charitable human being. He handed over the book to the man without making any more demands. What book had he bought? Sidharth became inquisitive. The next moment, he became astounded and elated to find a copy of Upendra Bhanja's *Koti Brahmanda Sundari* in the hands of the leper.

Soon after, the man was found riding away in his box, pushing the hard surface of the road with his hands. Sidharth looked at him, transfixed.

Most of the intellectuals, affluent high-class people, as well as those who call themselves controllers of the fate of

Odisha, do not purchase Odia books. They sneer at Odia language as they consider it a language devoid of merit, and a language spoken by poor people. They derive much delight by openly announcing that they lack the ability to write a letter in Odia. Their drawing-room centre tables are adorned with English magazines; in their office and reading rooms, they watch English films and sports. There is a lack of appreciation for the dance forms, songs and literature of Odisha. Sidharth wondered how Odia language and literature had survived, assaulted by such revulsion and disrespect. Sidharth got his answer today when he saw the infirm poor leper buying Upendra Bhanja's *Koti Brahmanda Sundari* with great love and emotion from a second-hand bookshop, paying two rupees and sixty five paise.

A Dead City

Who was banging on the door so loudly at this hour of the night? When the door was opened with such an element of surprise in mind, Sidharth found his neighbour Pattanayakbabu and two or three members of his family. At the first sight of them, any one would comprehend their worry. The almost breathless neighbour said, "My daughter is serious. Will you please phone for an ambulance?"

"Phone… Where is the phone?"

Sidharth understood what Pattanayakbabu was hinting at. About three months ago, two employees of the telephone department had fixed a wire from the telephone pole to his house. "We will bring the phone and fix it tomorrow," was what they had said and gone away with the tip. Three months had elapsed in the meantime; no one else from the department had visited him. The existence of the wire made Pattanayakbabu think he had a telephone connection.

However, Sidharth didn't consider it appropriate to say so many things in such a situation. Another friend of his stayed at the other end of the colony. He had a telephone.

"Don't worry so much. I will go there and call for an ambulance," said he.

Pattanayakbabu felt a little relieved, just as a drowning man clutching at a straw feels.

"Hello, is it Red Cross ambulance? A girl of our colony has suddenly become serious. Doctor has forbidden carrying her to the hospital in a scooter or a motorcycle. Would you please send the ambulance?"

'Sorry, sir, all our ambulances are out of order." This followed the clicking noise of the receiver being put down. Sidharth, who considered himself a messenger of God a moment ago, felt helpless."

He picked up the receiver once again.

"Is it Unit Six hospital?"

"Wrong number."

This time Sidharth dialled each number carefully. He could hear the voice of a woman that said, "This number does not exist." "Surprising! What is happening to everybody today?"

Sidharth felt dizzy. The worried members of Pattanayakbabu's family running helter- skelter; the faith that the family placed in him; and the apathy of the careless Red Cross people made him feel helpless.

"What can be done at twelve at night? What can he do to transport the patient over a distance of four kilometers?"

Sidharth carried the patient to the hospital with the help of a kind neighbour at one o' clock at night. When he reached there, he witnessed another rare sight. That sight was so much more pathetic than his own problem that he forgot his own grief for some time. Two brothers of Nayapalli area had carried a pregnant woman for delivery on a moped. The husband of the woman had put her on the moped. The woman in pain leaned on the shoulder of her husband. The younger brother had pushed that moped so far in that cold night.

"We rang up many times, sir but no one listened. What else would we have done at twelve o' clock at night?"

"Did you ring up Red Cross?'

"Leave it, sir. Red Cross, hospital, ambulance; all these facilities are for the rich. Their shedding crocodile tears does not mean anything other than cheating the poor."

When two families were thus reeling under helplessness in the Unit Six hospital campus in an intensely cold night of December, Sidharth was reminded of a piece of news that he had read a few days ago. That news was published in a reputed newspaper. While addressing a rally at Bhawanipatna, the nose of the Chief Minister bled as a stone struck it. A very senior minister of the state, on hearing news of the Chief Minister's bleeding nose, flew to Kalahandi in a special flight, accompanied by a specialist doctor. Sidharth was thinking of two things while reading the news. "Are there no doctors in Kalahandi who can treat a case of mere bleeding, which forced the specialist to be flown in a special flight? Children must have been taking birth in Kalahandi; travellers must be getting hurt in road accidents; the common man must be getting afflicted with incurable diseases. Then, who treats these patients? Secondly, if a common man had suffered miserably, would the honourable minister have thought of sending a specialist? How nice it would be if the Chief Minister's suffering was weighed in the same scale as that of a common man's suffering?"

But forget about Kalahandi, even the residents of the state capital were deprived of basic healthcare services. Sidharth had no doubts about that. Those, who have money, are provided with all types of government and private healthcare facilities. What does the city symbolize for those who depend upon elected representatives, popular government or the so-called kind social service organizations? "Nothing but a dead city," Sidharth answered his own question.

■

Deceit

Just as an animal, accustomed to moving here and there freely and without restraint, feels uncomfortable when it is leashed, similarly a workaholic human leading a routine life every moment feels equally uncomfortable when he is suddenly allowed a day's holiday.

Sidharth Mohapatra was feeling uncomfortable. Sidharth, who had spent a considerable part of his career outside the state, worked as the General Manager of a newspaper published from the capital. When he worked under the central government, this day was not included in the list of holidays.

Sidharth, a widower, felt distraught the moment he got up as he thought of the holiday. How would he spend such a holiday? Government offices, banks and other offices didn't have any holidays of that sort. Had it been a common holiday like Sunday, he could have gone to Mohapatrababu or Patnaikbabu's house and spent some time there. However, there was no such possibility as they would have left for their offices. What will he do then?

Someone had opined once that at times being subjugated was more acceptable than being free. When one is subjugated, he has to follow a system, where one task follows another. A man does not have to strain his intelligence much, or be in a quandary thinking which task he has to accomplish first and which one is to be done later. Sidharth remembered the words.

Even though the office was closed, as a matter of habit he shaved, took bath and put on clothes at the appointed hour. After that he should have left for office but unfortunately there was none that day. He opened the door of the car, entered it and drove aimlessly. The car stopped in front of a petrol pump; he wished to fill up the tank with fuel before he went further on his aimless journey.

Had it been some other day, Sidharth would have left after refuelling the car but it was different today. Today, he was not busy but rather free. Even though it was not needed, he drove the car to the service station to check the tyre-pressure.

As usual, the small child with a smile on his face ran up to him. In one hand, he carried the meter to gauge pressure and in the other, he had the tip of the pressure tube. Sidharth usually felt very happy to see the child. His face had a sort of flamboyance, and he was the picture of great possibilities. The child's father must be poor, otherwise the child would not be working so hard at such a tender age of eleven or twelve. Earlier, at times, Sidharth had noticed that the child took out the tube from inside a car or truck tyre with great difficulty. His sweat-drenched chest would be covered with black grease and dust. On these occasions, Sidharth would be hard pressed for time; so, he would leave immediately after getting his work done.

However, today he had time enough for a talk with the child; but what would he talk about with so small a kid?

Sidharth asked, "Don't you have any holiday today?"

"Holiday! Why holiday?" the child asked, surprise writ large on his face.

Sidharth asked, "Don't you know today is May Day?"

"What is that, *baboo*?" the child said in surprise.

Sidharth heaved a sigh. No, there was nothing more to ask. While getting back into the car he asked, "What is your name?"

"My name?" he asked, as if shocked at the fact that a *baboo* driving a car was asking his name for the first time.

"Ramulu."

"Only Ramulu? What's your full name?"

Ramulu could not control his laughter. 'I have a full name, *baboo*. It is G.C.Ramulu but, everybody calls me Ramulu.'

Sidharth was already inside his car. Rajbhawan stood in front of that service station. If one headed towards the city, one found the bungalows of ministers, the Chief Minister and the secretaries. Each of them stood for a rung in the bureaucratic and constitutional ladder. However, did any one of them care for the unfortunate G.C. Ramulu, who lived only a few meters away from them?

Sidharth had a lot of free time on his hands but he did not want to prolong the conversation. He knew that the 'May Day' holiday was only meant for Mr. Ramachandras; people like Rama, Ramia or Ramulu did not have anything to do with that. They would be sweating as they laboured, like on other days. For them, May Day meant nothing at all.

A Deceitful Abhimanyu

Though Chandrakant hardly ever came to office on time, he never came to office this late. Sidharth got busy doing the job at hand thinking that he might have gone on leave or some important work might have detained him. At about two o' clock, Chandrakant rushed in gasping for breath. It was evident from his appearance that he had returned accomplishing a very difficult feat. Sidharth asked him why he was late. "My son's school admission was to be done. That's why I got a little late. What a heavy rush!" Looking in the direction of the chamber of the boss he asked, "Was he searching for me?" "No," whispered Sidharth.

Chandrakant's father and brother lived with him. His younger brother studied in a college. "He could have taken care of the admission work. Was it necessary for you to go there? Today, there is a meeting. If the boss had searched for you, then..." Bringing his face close to Sidharth's ear Chandrakant said, "The old lady (School Principal) wasn't ready to accept the proposal till the end. I had a hard time convincing her. After much effort, my son's date of birth was brought forward, decreasing his age by one year. From next year, municipal certificates will be mandatory."

Sidharth felt like tumbling from the heaven. Even Chandrakant did the same thing that he had heard other opportunistic parents were doing. Why did Chandrakant shatter the beautiful image that he had created?

Sidharth's son was also admitted in a public school of the same town. That he was younger than most of the students of his class, was clearly visible. Once, he asked a friend the secret behind this. He revealed that the parents of other children must have hidden their real date of birth. Otherwise, why should a child, who was five years of age look like one who was six and a half years old.

However, Sidharth could not do anything of that sort. His wife Sumitra would blame and abuse him for his inability to do that. "All parents recorded the date of birth of their children bringing it forward by a year, but only you could not do it. What would my child do amidst elder children? He would lag behind both in academics as well as sports."

Sumitra wasn't altogether wrong. A five-year-old child would surely understand things better and run faster than a four year old child. There will be difference in their abilities and levels of maturity. The kind of competition between two such children was competition between two unequal persons.

But by the time those children pass the matriculation examination, they would not have crossed thirteen years of age. Would not they stop there for a year? Sidharth had asked such a pertinent question that day. However, only last week, he read in the newspapers a strange policy announced by the government. That was another striking example of cunning. Students who had not attained fourteen years of age were given admit cards to appear at the examination.

What's the use in altering the date of birth of a child? It's true that he would get the benefit of another year in attending the interviews and for securing jobs. He would earn more and enjoy more power by staying in the job for another year. In what other ways would be benefit?

Sumitra argued, "When a candidate is prevented from attending the interview just by being overage by a day or a month, a year shouldn't be dismissed as insignificant, Sidharth. You should have learnt this from your own experience." Sidharth felt as if someone branded him with hot iron. His father was not educated. His education had commenced in the thatched village primary school. The day his father took him to Kapil Pandit of the village school with a tray laden with rice, betel nuts, coconut, and a pair of dhotis, Sidharth had not even completed five years of age. Kapil Pandit was a man of principle. He refused to allow anyone into the school unless he was five years of age. Sidharth had left home at the auspicious hour. Even though he was four and a half years old, his father was compelled to increase the age by advancing his date of birth. In a moment, Sidharth turned five.

Truly, if he had six more months at his disposal, he could have appeared at the civil services examination once more. At least, he could have sat for the P.O. examination a second time. At times he felt like complaining bitterly against father. He would show the insect-infested palm-leaf horoscope to the selection committee and say, "I am not overage. There is still some time, six months to be exact."

But, who would listen to him? He lived in a world where official stamp, signatures and seals could easily convert falsehood into truth. Did Budha Nahak's brittle palm-leaf have the same authority?

Sidharth argued, "One day, my son might become a great man. Many astrologers would do research into his horoscope and date of birth. They may prove that a person born on a certain date in a certain year becomes a great intellectual. The parents of Gandhi and Nehru would never have recorded a wrong date of birth."

Let Chandrakant advertise the intelligence of his son by decreasing his age. There was no pride in being a deceitful Abhimanyu.

Chandrakant bent over a file and scribbled something in it. The hair near the ear had turned grey. He would retire three or four years after Sidharth's retirement. Who knew whether his recorded date of birth was true or false?

Sidharth let out a heavy sigh. He wondered where the question of values, truth and morality were, when an innocent child's date of birth was changed, without his own knowledge, just for an extra year's slavery or opportunity to search for a job. His son's face flashed before his eyes. He might be defeated in an unfair competition; he might lose the benefit of an extra year; but he would never live his life wallowing in deceit.

Patriots at Wagah

The *Asadha* afternoon at Amritsar that day seemed more ruthless and fierce than the usual *Baisakh* noon at Bhubaneswar. The taxi driver had dropped Sidharth at the Golden Jubilee Gate saying that the Beating Retreat ceremony would be held at four o' clock. However, the people who had gathered there on the gallery were heard saying that the ceremony was scheduled for six-thirty in the evening.

Sidharth was waiting to witness the Beating Retreat ceremony held every evening at the Wagah border to lower the national flags of India and Pakistan. Since 1959, it has been a daily chore for both Indian and Pakistani soldiers to lower their respective national flags every evening before sunset. On every occasion, the Border Security Force personnel of both the countries posted there participate in a brief but spectacular ceremony. A senior officer receives the salute. A platoon of the Border Security Force performs parade. The security officials reach the flagpost after opening the iron-gates on their side of the border, with decorum and etiquette. They bring the flag of their own country down slowly, but in perfect sync with each other.

"However, what's worth watching is the way the parade is conducted and the way the border-guards display their bravery and valour by raising their legs high and puffing up their chests," Amarpreet, the cab driver, who accompanied him from Chandigarh, had informed him earlier.

The eagerly anticipated moment was approaching. Hindi film songs were blared from the speakers. From the microphones on the other side, Pakistani songs were heard. Wagah stood at a distance of thirty-two kilometers from Amritsar in India whereas it was only twenty-four kilometers away from Lahore in Pakistan. Sidharth turned his head to look at India once and then at Pakistan. A tree with its roots on the Indian side bent towards the Pakistani side. The dry leaves on its branches were blown away towards the Pakistani fields nearby. He glanced at the galleries meant for Indians. More than five thousand Indians waited with bated breath for the ceremony to begin.

A soldier of the Border Security Force, donning a white dress, came running to the road. The way he entered the Amritsar-Lahore highway-pandal, a cordless microphone in his hand put one in the mind of the anchor of a cultural programme. He lustily raised the slogan "Bharat Mataki ..." to which the eagerly waiting spectators responded shouting "Jay". Forgetting his own exhaustion and discomfort, Sidharth joined the slogan-shouting crowd. The soldier continued raising slogans one after another and the spectators responded, shouting "Jay…jay…jay". The entire place reverberated with the sound of jubilation.

However, the young soldier didn't seem much animated. He fell silent for a moment. He cast a glance towards the gallery and asked with gestures, "Don't you have courage in your heart? Haven't you had your lunch?

Shout so loudly that the noise will silence the spectators in the Pakistani galleries."

What he was hinting at was not at all difficult to guess. Sidharth knew that he had to drown the cries of the Pakistanis in an attempt to prove his patriotism.

The enthusiastic spectators didn't disappoint the BSF soldier. The place soon resonated with slogans like "Bharat Mataki Jay, Bande Mataram, India… Jindabad" etc.

Sidharth raised his head. The scenes on the Pakistani side were no different. However, the preparations on the Pakistani side weren't at all remarkable in comparison with the tall galleries, spacious surroundings, and the large gathering on the Indian side. The gallery on the Indian side resembled the affluent and crowded gallery during an international cricket match, whereas on the Pakistani side, it was nothing better than an ordinary gallery during a district level football tournament. In the absence of adequate number of spectators, the level of noise, that reached the Indian side, was rather low. To compensate for this, they had hired two drummers that day. In any case, the sound of screams and the thundering noise was to be carried to the other side. Sidharth felt as if this was not an army parade near the Indo-Pak border but an international cricket match played between the two countries. Here a thousand black cobras of hate, violence, enmity and jealousy hissed under the façade of patriotism.

The parade went on. The trained feet of the army men sporting suitably long and broad moustaches, would touch their turbans. The soldiers of both the countries were found gazing at each other with wide eyes, bloated chests, and clenched fists, which meant, " Watch out or be ready for the consequences". The parade and the antics of the soldiers went on for about twenty minutes, after which they shook hands with each other, briefly, and disappeared into each other's territory. The Beating Retreat ceremony came to a close.

Sidharth found himself completely soaked in sweat. He bought a bottle of water from the peddler who sold soft drinks, chips, and water and drank the water in great gulps. Before arriving at Wagah he had heard, "This parade is a manifestation of envy as well as brotherhood." However, there wasn't even an iota of brotherhood in whatever he had witnessed today. Of course, he didn't expect a sense of brotherhood to prevail at the Indo-Pak border. What he wondered at was whether it was necessary for thousands of countrymen of both the countries to gather at a place, to incite each other, and to abuse each other. He failed to understand why people felt the need to sprinkle salt on old wounds, open them up, and make them bleed profusely. This can be done without any noise and hullabaloo and without the aid of any speakers, showing perfect self-restraint and respect for each other. The spectators can watch silently. He feared a recurrence of the 2014 incident when sixty spectators on the Pakistani side perished in a suicide bomb explosion.

Whenever thoughts of the patriotism of Indians crossed Sidharth's mind, headlines from the pages of newspapers taunted him. Does an Indian love another Indian who is unknown to him? How much does a doctor love his unknown patient? With how much affection and fellow-feeling does the officer in an Indian office help a poor fellow human being? How does a young man in India treat an unknown girl in the darkness of night? Does the sky, at which the Indian farmer looks after consuming poison in his agricultural land, look noble and generous, as the sky of independent India should be? When one had thousands of opportunities every day to prove his patriotism, where is the need for organizing a ceremony at Wagah border, to display spurious love for one's mother land?

Before returning to his car, Sidharth looked back. An unknown bird that sat on the tree that had its root on the Indian side and branches on the Pakistani side, flew to the Pakistani gallery before returning to the Indian side. Then it soared high into the sky, where the boundary between the two countries disappeared. Sidharth didn't know whether the bird belonged to India or Pakistan but he realized the bird never felt the need to proclaim its love for the sky.

Dream of the Grass

Sidharth didn't look at Sanatan or smile or say anything as he usually did every day. Sanatan waited for some time silently. Since Sidharth didn't open his mouth, he asked, "Which one, whether the body or the mind, has gone sour?" Sidharth answered 'both' and remained silent.

In the row in front of them, sat Chaitanyababu and Bishnubabu. Both of them were senior clerks. Chaitanyababu had dragged his chair towards his friend Bishnubabu and was deep in conversation. Both of them had grown oblivious of the files and papers heaped on their tables. Sanatan saw that Sidharth was eavesdropping on them. Chaitanyababu was saying, "I was buying arum from Sahidnagar market. I met my neighbour. From him I came to know that the price of arum was forty paise less at the Unit-1 market. F-O-R-T-Y! Do you understand, Bishnubabu?" Bishnubabu answered, as if he had discovered a great truth hidden from the world, "Really?" Chaitanyababu felt inspired and went on. He said, "I dumped the arum into the shopkeeper's basket and sped towards Unit-1 market. Yes, the price of arum was less there but..."

"Why this if and but? Is forty paise a small sum?" Bishnubabu spoke in the manner of a patron.

"The mouth is itching. Perhaps the quality was not so good."

Sanatan was going to laugh. He controlled himself. The reason was that he felt Sidharth did not like what they said. He had turned his face away in disgust and was busy working.

Sanatan said, "I am sure something has happened. Tell me what it is."

Sanatan could not contain his laughter after listening to what Sidharth had to say. Sidharth was a strange person. Some preacher had told him once not to waste time purchasing vegetables or raising a family. The preacher was not a sage but a noble-minded friend whom he addressed as 'guru'. His wife was very angry with him today. He had gone to the market with her. He had purchased a big packet of bread and kept it in the basket of his scooter. He was buying vegetables when a cow came and ran away with the bread packet. Sidharth ran after it a couple of metres but what he retrieved from the mouth of the cow was not the bread but the polythene wrapper. Sidharth found people around him looking at him, bemused. Pieces of bread lay here and there; he was unable to do anything. The most uncomfortable thing was that his wife was watching him from a distance.

Sidharth had really gone crazy.

Sanatan knew Sidharth was not like his other colleagues. He sang well; he played the guitar well. He once wanted to become a great musician. While in college, he was a good player and talented writer. Finally, he thought he had no time for all these distractions. He had to make a living as a clerk at this office.

Sanatan, to change the topic said, "Never mind. You know so many things; what's the harm if you don't know how to buy good vegetables."

While Sidharth ran his fingers through his hair, a grey hair was uprooted. Displaying that in the manner of a philosopher, he said, "Look at this. I have already been served notice. The time for the return journey is approaching. What account of my life shall I give to the Master?"

"Master?" said Sanatan.

Sidharth pointed his finger upwards and said, "Is there a Master over there or not? When he asks, "Others have done so many things; what have you done?" what answer shall I give?"

Suddenly, Sanatan was reminded of what a great man had stated a few days ago. He said, "The Master has placed you here, He will take care of you as He understands you better. Who, other than a gardener, understands the condition of a tree? One seed got fertile soil, water, air, and light; it grew fast and bore fruits and flowers. But another seed got none of these. By the time it sprouted leaves, the conditions had become unfavourable. The soil had stones; the surroundings were dark and wild. Neither a drop of water nor a ray of light reached it. There was no soil beneath to hold the roots nor any open sky above. If the plant veers around the obstacles in search of space and light, and spreads a branch and if a small flower blooms ever on that small branch, should the plant not display it proudly?"

A grim-looking Sidharth flashed a smile. He got up from the chair and stood near Sanatan, with his hand on the latter's shoulder. Like an innocent child, he asked, "Will the Master take all these into account?"

Sanatan, unconsciously, had been transformed into

another being. His voice appeared unfamiliar even to himself. From a distance, he answered, "Yes, yes. He will take all these into account."

Sidharth was no more able to remember the disappointing experience at the vegetable market; he also did not regret his failure to achieve the higher goals of life. He raised his head and looked at the sky out of the window. It looked blue as ever; the air was cool as ever. The description of the experience of buying arum by Chaitanyababu and Bishnubabu did not seem distasteful anymore. He hummed a song and got busy with his work.

Dreaming of Siuli Flowers

Sidharth met Narendra Mohapatra after a long time. In the meantime, floods had come in as well as receded from river Mantei many times. Mango blossoms had danced on the branches of the nearby mango tree many times before disappearing. Everything had changed while negotiating the curves of time. But Sidharth encountered no difficulty at all in recognizing Narendra Mohapatra. Mohapatra was crossing the alley beside the bookshop near Balubazar, walking alongside his cycle. Sidharth shouted from behind, "Namaskar."

Mohapatra turned around and gave a look of surprise. It was clearly evident that he had failed to recognize Sidharth. Sidharth, in a vain attempt to make time move backwards by a few years, asked "Don't you recognize me, Narendrababu?"

During the last twenty years, time had done strange things to Narendra Mohapatra. His dress had lost its luster. The eyes had dimmed and the power of his legs had dwindled. Looking at Sidharth through the thick lenses of his spectacles he had been trying to place him but he stumbled as his memory played tricks with him.

Sidharth had to introduce himself—"I am Sidharth. Don't you remember the printing of the Ravenshaw College magazine in your press? I was once its editor."

From the corners of Mohapatra's mouth emerged a laugh that resembled a bunch of *siuli* flowers. How enticing were that smile and his manner of talking! He was always like that. He would come out of home on some errand, but if he happened to meet some writer or reader on the way, he would stop there. From the handle of his bicycle would be hanging an empty bag or a bag full of vegetables. Mr. Mohapatra would completely forget about the vegetables and his family. A simple-natured person with a tinge of anxiety and deep emotion was he.

"Is 'Manimala' not getting published these days?"

'Ma-ni-ma-la'? When these words were uttered, a sigh issued from the nostrils of Mr. Mohapatra and disappeared into the dark sky of Balubazar. 'Manimala', that was like a personal dream, lay beyond the memory of some bygone era. It had created a sensation as the most popular magazine in the state. 'Manimala' had inspired many new writers. It had opened up new possibilities for novellas in Odia. Despite all kinds of difficulties- lack of patrons, government advertisements, and inadequate supportive customers, 'Manimala' was published for a period of more than ten years. Narendra Mohapatra was its printer, editor and publisher. He had named his press 'Manimala Printers' after the magazine.

Sidharth asked once again, "Won't 'Manimala' be published again?"

Mr. Mohapatra gave a smile, but that smile was a pathetic one. "Who remembers whom in this world? Many magazines have taken birth here, only to die a premature death. In front of our own eyes 'Nabarabi' ceased publication; the same was the case with 'Manimala'. The other day he heard the news of 'Asantakali'. It was very difficult for magazines being born on the Odia soil to thrive. Never mind, where are you studying now?"

"Studying? No…no… I'm not studying anymore. I have been doing a job for the last fifteen years. I am now working as a manager in a company in Rourkella."

Mohapatra looked a little excited. Just as a traveller, lost amid darkness, feels delighted at the sight of a little light glimmering at a distant village, Mr. Mohapatra seemed animated. He held Sidharth by the right hand, dragged him towards the other side of the road and said, "Sidharthbabu, can't you arrange a job for me –either in Bhubaneswar or in Rourkella?"

Sidharth couldn't believe his ears. What did he hear? The editor of 'Manimala'; the owner of 'Manimala Printers' was asking him for help at this advanced age! How helpless that voice sounded! Perhaps the words had issued from his mouth unwillingly, and under compulsion. That voice did not match his personality. Just as the utterances of a rich man, seeking someone's sympathy under adverse circumstances, sound unconvincing, Mohapatra's voice reflected the same helplessness.

Once, when this man sat by the small table at Manimala Printers and read the manuscripts or corrected proofs, Sidharth would be jealous of his good luck and popularity. He would wonder if he would ever get such a job, where he would engage himself doing something he liked; where he would find himself lost in literature; where he would promote new writers and show a great deal of respect to the elders in the field. However, that person who had aroused his envy once, stood today in front of Sidharth and was begging, arms stretched, for a petty job…

"Why do you want a job? Is your press not working anymore?"

"Certain things can never be told. But believe me, I would never have told you anything of this sort unless I was in difficulties. I have made the same request to a few others also. I will manage with something like one thousand or fifteen hundred rupees. Please, seriously look for a job."

Sidharth winced at the harsh truth. Narendra Mohapatra, the headman of a poor family, turned around and moved away.

What sort of job would Sidharth search for Narendra Mohapatra? What sort of job he would search for a former editor of a magazine; or, for the aged owner of a small printing press?

A dreamy youth bubbled inside Sidharth. Overcome with resentment and helplessness, that youth was busy hurling word-bombs at an unknown enemy. He would like to break this system. He would establish another system where honour and respect would be bestowed on people like Narendra Mohapatra but not any third-rate cunning individual; where dreams and emotions would get enough promise and a hard ground beneath their feet to prosper; where poets, artists and editors would get enough opportunities for survival.

Things never happen that way. Where talented people like Biswanath Kar, Gopinath Nandasharma and Nilamani Bidyaratna lie forgotten beneath heaps of worm-infested paper, who cares for a poor editor of a popular magazine like 'Manimala'? Let them be lost amid the silence of oblivion like bubbles; who cares for that? Neither any government falls nor does the progress of the nation come to a halt if magazine-editors like Narendra Mohapatra fall on bad days. ■

A Tall Man Turns
into a Dwarf

Last evening, Sidharth felt reassured to find that tree in front of Ashoka Jatree Niwas at New Delhi. He felt that the tree would help him locate his hotel as he was unacquainted with the geography and roads of this city. The tree was very dense and tall; so, a brown kite had made a nest in its branches.

Sidharth felt miserable when he got up in the morning and did not find the tree. Did the tree disappear overnight? He found a brown kite descending to sit on the branches of a tree. Now, Sidharth had no difficulty at all in searching for the tree. Initially, he wondered how the tree suddenly turned dwarfish? But, then he remembered that the tree had not turned dwarfish, but rather, he was living on the fourteenth floor of the hotel.

In the afternoon, he met Mr. Mohapatra. He was well-known as a powerful political leader of Sidharth's state. Even he and his supporters did not hesitate to consider him its future Chief Minister. Sidharth had great respect for Mr. Mohapatra since childhood as he belonged to his area. Every morning and evening one would find seven or eight bicycles or motor cycles parked in front of the house of Mr. Mohapatra. At times, a few four wheelers would also pull up there. Wherever Mr. Mohapatra went, people would follow him. Even the birds of his area, it was said, did not visit the paddy fields without his permission.

Mr. Mohapatra appeared very grim on Janapath of New Delhi. His so-called own people were not seen in the vicinity. True, it was not possible to bring so many people to Delhi paying for their train-fare or air-fare every time. The lonely state of Mr. Mohapatra in Delhi's crowd appeared a little odd. Mr. Mohapatra was standing alone, some distance away from the crowd. All others stood surrounding another leader. They looked as if ants surrounded a pot of jaggery. Some of them carried garlands, and some others had bouquets in their hands. From among the sea of humanity, the cap-covered head of the leader looked much like the moon of *pratipada,* the first day of lunar fortnight. Despite his best efforts, Mr. Mohapatra was not even able to reach the leader.

Suddenly, the sea of humanity stirred a little. The big leader had got into his car. When the car moved, the party workers surrounded it, just to have a glimpse of the great man. When the vehicle passed by Mr. Mohapatra, he also stirred. He ran after the vehicle for some time. But, no… the leader's vehicle disappeared. He moved away, throwing 'namaskars' into the wind.

Sidharth felt distressed to think how the powerful leaders of the state suddenly turned helpless when they reached the Janapath. Just as the tall tree appeared dwarfish from the fourteenth floor of Ashokaniwas, Mr. Mohapatra, running after the vehicle of the big-leader, appeared pitiable like a midget.

End of Illusions

Even Umacharan himself didn't know for how long he had felt a strong fascination for airplanes. It was not easy to say why, for a man like him, who was born and brought up in a village on the bank of a river and who had spent sixty long years working in the fields, developed a strong fascination for an object that loved the sky and not the earth. However, Umacharan's young friend, Sidharth, the science teacher of the village primary school, knew pretty well that this weakness of Umacharan's had persisted since his childhood. Since the day he had grown familiar with the airplane, or the picture of an aeroplane to be precise, this air-borne machine had secured a place in the aerodrome of his heart. Since then, Umacharan had fallen in love with the airplane.

Whenever the grown-up Umacharan saw the picture of an airplane on the page of a magazine, he would immediately cut it out and paste it on another piece of paper. At times, they appeared to him like swans flying across the blue sky; or like fish swimming in the river; or like the kites flying on the top of a tree. Most of the time, he was found explaining his idea to some listeners, no matter whether they were interested or indifferent. He would wait for hours near his crop-field or on the bank of the pond to watch the aeroplane that flew above the village, once during the day and once during the night. The airplane flying at a great height would appear small like a sparrow. And yet, Umacharan would wait with great interest and eagerness. He would never turn his eyes away from the sky until the airplane completely disappeared or the 'broom…broom' sound completely faded away. He would be airplane-minded, absolutely unmindful of whether the tilling of the field was disrupted or he would be late coming home.

Who could have entertained the doubt that the good relationship he shared with the science teacher, Sidharth, was a result of this fascination for airplanes? Sidharth had once held the pages of the science book wide open before Umacharan and explained many things about this mysterious machine. From that day, Sidharth had become Umacharan's most intimate friend.

In fairy stories, we all have heard about water seven fathom-deep; below that lies seven fathom-deep mud; again, below that lies a golden box with a lid; the golden box contains a lock of tangled hair; hidden beneath the lock of hair, a red insect. Like this, in some deep corner of Umacharan's heart lurked the sweetest and most secret desire – won't he be able to fly in an airplane even once? But, the distance between the desire for and the possibility of flying in any plane was equal to the distance between Umacharan in his field and the airplane flying up in the sky.

Perhaps, the wish of Umacharan would have been left lurking in his heart had an interesting mishap not taken place. Umacharan's only son, who worked as a senior official of a bank in the capital, arrived at the village suddenly one day and insisted on taking his sick father to Kolkata for a medical check-up. It is unnecessary to mention here that for Umacharan and his friends this 'check-up' was an incomprehensible business His son took it upon himself to convince Umacharan. This was precisely because, if he would not take his father to Kolkata, everyone would condemn him later in life. The criticism that a son, who earned so much, didn't even care to take his father to a good hospital, would be an insult difficult to digest. Despite his wife's advice against spending so much money, the son was determined to take his father to Kolkata.

Two to four days after arriving in the city, one evening the son delivered the news that was as unexpected as it was exciting. For Umacharan's journey, he had purchased an air ticket. Sleep eluded Umacharan that night. It pained him to think that neither his fellow villagers nor the science teacher, Sidharth, was going to witness the historic feat of his boarding an airplane. Had he got a whiff of it earlier, he would have asked at least Sidharth to accompany him. Poor fellow!

While the airplane-obsessed Umacharan was discoursing with his dreams, a lot of argument went on between his son and daughter-in-law. The daughter-in-law argued, "The old man could have travelled by train; what was the need of spending so much on purchasing a plane ticket." His son answered, "You don't know anything about his desire to board a plane. I am his only son. God knows whether father will return from there alive or not. Can't we fulfill this small wish of his?"

Fifteen days later, Umacharan returned to his village. By that time, the word of his boarding an aeroplane had spread through the village and its nearby areas. Of course, it would have been decent for the newspaper correspondents to mention that in their area, Umacharan was the first among the people of his age to board an aircraft. After reaching home, Umacharan went off to take rest. After the elders, and then the children, had departed taking the sweets and fruits that he had brought from the capital city, Umacharan asked his science teacher friend to meet him.

Sidharth came and sat down beside him. A small child shouted from the street outside—aeroplane... aeroplane. Every day, at this hour an aeroplane flew above the village. Umacharan would eagerly wait, throughout the afternoon, for this moment to arrive. Today, Umacharan did not come out of his house. He no longer felt the desire that had consumed him in the days gone by.

"Won't you go out to watch the plane?"

"No, Sidharth. Today, I don't feel like going out to watch the aeroplane. Earlier, I used to wait for hours especially for this hour of the evening and for the airplane, didn't I?" Umacharan asked.

Sidharth realized that the airplane was no longer an object of fascination for him. Dreams appear attractive and colourful till they are fulfilled. If the moon descended from the sky onto the palm of an innocent child, would it call him *'Janhamamu'* or *'Saradasashi'* anymore?

He asked, "You have not told me anything about your experience of boarding a plane."

Umacharan laughed loudly. "No. no, Sidharth... It's not as exciting a thing as I had imagined it would be. Just add two wings to a bus or a train; an airplane would be something like that. I wonder how madly I had behaved earlier even at the thought of it!"

Now the question is: What dream would help Umacharan live through the rest of his life? ■

An Expensive Dream

The boy wore a navy-blue dress, a black cap; a rexin belt was wound tightly around his waist. The name of the agency for which he worked was written in three letters of brass, just as the ones policemen had on their shoulders. When Sidharth entered the office, the boy stood to attention and saluted him. He was recently posted at the office. Since Sidharth was not at all ready for such a reception, he shrank a little, and then looked into the face of the boy. He would be hardly fourteen or fifteen years of age. He looked like a school-going child wearing an N.C.C. uniform.

After the crowd at the office thinned out, Sidharth called him and asked him his name and the name of the village he came from. His village was some distance away from Dhenkanal. One had to cover the distance on foot. He worked for a security service organization here. He told him the name of the organization. Sidharth further asked, "How much salary do you get from the organization?" In reply, he smiled a smile that reflected sadness. He paused a little and said, "The office gives me three hundred rupees." Sidharth was not surprised; he was used to such answers.

Pramod would come to office exactly at twelve noon. He would stand at the gate and salute the *baboos* entering the office by clicking his boot. After the *baboos* passed through the gate, he would close the door and stand there till eight o' clock in that position. Whenever Sidharth saw him striking that pose, he would feel as if a class ten or eleven student was playing the role of a security guard.

Pramod, for his part, felt he was not playing any role; he was simply doing his 'duty'. He stood there for eight hours a day and got three hundred rupees as his salary at the end of the month.

One day, Pramod came to Sidharth at an odd hour and saluted him. Sidharth was taken by surprise by this. Before he could say anything, Pramod said, "Sir, from tomorrow, my duty here will come to an end. Another person will be posted in my place. I have been transferred to another site."

He came to Sidharth just to deliver the news. He was going to salute him once again; Sidharth stopped him. He explained to him that he was not worthy of such respect.

Fear of uncertainty was writ large on Pramod's face. He would have to go to a new place from tomorrow.

Sidharth considered this quick and energetic salute silently for a long time. He felt as if a small calf was hopping about in front of him, a calf whose feet had not grown strong. Just as a small school child ran to his mother's lap soon after the school bell rang, Pramod went away in the same manner. However, his return-path didn't lead to his own house but towards a safety-less uncertainty. No one explained it to him but it was clearly understood.

Sidharth didn't know Pramod's parents. But from a distance, he could visualize their faces and comprehend their helplessness. Had it not been for helplessness, no one would have allowed such a young boy to leave home and work elsewhere.

"Do you save anything from the three hundred rupees you get here?" asked Sidharth.

Pramod shook his head. Over the last four months, he had been able to save only twenty-five rupees. If he could arrange the bus fare, he would return home and see his parents. In the village field, on the bank of the river, he will play a game of *bagudi* with his friends for three or four days before returning to the town again.

How expensive Pramod's dream was! A deep sigh escaped Sidharth.

A Lost Childhood

About four months ago, I had met this boy in a second-class compartment while travelling from Howarah to Bolpur. That dark and dwarfish child entered the compartment near the Bardhaman station. He would be seven or eight years of age. With the broken broom that he carried, he swept the cigarette stubs, groundnut and banana peels, biscuit wrappers, and pieces of paper thrown on the floor. He would get under the lower berths, hold the shoes of gentlemen and ladies, and clean all the dirt. After the work was over, he would stretch his hand asking for his reward. His eyes didn't reflect any feeling of distress but sheer self-confidence. Some people dropped ten or twenty-five paise coins into his hand. He would thank them and get off the train.

That day, the child had become an example of self-confidence for Sidharth. Through his movements, perhaps the child wanted to tell people that when he grew up, he would never be a dependent, certificate-centred individual or one who lived at another's expense. He would also never become crippled by politics of reservation. Under any circumstance, he would stand on his own legs firmly planted on the ground.

However, that day, Sidharth had not at all realized that children like him were also caught in the octopus-like tentacles of exploitation and their innocent childhood was mortgaged from early dawn.

A few days ago, Sidharth met two other children like him while travelling to Delhi. He does not remember the name of the station. The moment the train stopped, two boys, about ten or eleven years of age, entered the compartment, brooms in hand. Sidharth, who had kept an eye on his luggage, grew suspicious thinking they might be thieves. But, he soon realized that his suspicion was baseless. Not even once, did they look here and there but soon got busy doing their work. Their dedication to sweeping the floor was beyond doubt. Sidharth handed over a fifty paise coin to the younger of the two and asked, "How much do you earn in a day?" The child answered in his own language, "Fifteen to Sixteen rupees". Sidharth felt very happy thinking that the child must be comfortably off. But, that feeling did not last long. The boy added, "We don't take the entire amount." The sweeper of the station, who is a paid employee of the railways, takes a major portion of it. Why does it so happen? He gets his salary without doing his duty; why does he, then, take money from the boys? The child cleverly answered Sidharth's foolish question, saying, "This is his area. He has given us permission to work here. Would not he take a commission for that?"

Sidharth was perplexed to hear the word 'commission' used by the boy. It was as if the entire country had grown accustomed to that word. Starting from buying a bus ticket to the purchase of Bofors tanks, everywhere commission ruled the roost. Commission had become a synonym for

India. He didn't ask any more questions. The two boys left after completing their task.

A fellow traveller said, "The sweeper, donning clean dresses, must be whiling away his time on the platform near his house. These children are doing the work for him. The day some railway official would go this way, he would attend to his work wearing his uniform. The other days are holidays for him. He gets his salary; in addition to that, there is the commission."

Kharagpur was only a few metres away. Two aged transgenders entered the compartment. The torture they inflicted on the passengers was difficult to digest. They also practice a form of exploitation. Sidharth closed his eyes and acted as if he had gone to sleep. From Delhi upto the border of Bihar, one never found a beggar; but from Tata to Bhubaneswar, the number of beggars would never be fewer than one hundred and fifty. In the midst of the odour and unhygienic atmosphere of the second-class compartment, the begging of the beggars made the passengers exasperated.

Amidst the crowd, the faces of the two sweeper boys were visible. They were moving from one compartment to the other. They moved from one place to another, holding the untidy pants with one hand, and the broom in the other, just to earn a little money. Whatever was left after paying the commission to the railway sweeper, was theirs. Nobody knew where they slept after eating a few slices of bread and drinking water from the station tap. Perhaps their tired eyelids closed on their own. The broken handles of the brooms were their certificates. To Sidharth, the list of their miseries was pitilessly long.

The First Encounter with the City

Probably, they had been living in the decrepit house since yesterday evening. Their clamour floated in the *Chaitra* air like the chirping of unknown birds. Sidharth went up to the terrace to find out what was going on. Yes, some students had arrived from a distant high school to appear at the matriculation examination at the high school of the colony. About twenty-five to thirty students lived in the dilapidated house of Mohanty babu.

Sidharth was reminded of the experience he himself had undergone twenty-five years back. One *Chaitra* morning, his mother, after her morning bath, put the sacred *kalas* on the verandah; his younger brother, an obedient child, broke a small mango twig with leaves, which was to be set on the *kalas*. Sidharth left for the examination centre after paying obeisance to his parents, his uncle and aunt, the Brahmin priest who worshipped the village deity, and the village astrologer. Ahead of them ran a bullock-cart loaded with their bags and trunks, like one carrying the articles of a village drama troupe. It was followed by

Sidharth and his classmates, like trained soldiers marching forwards to an uncertain war. The memory of this journey made Sidharth feel exhilarated even today. Just to have a look at the children who were going to appear at the matriculation examination, the children and elders of the entire village had assembled. The village high school had an undeclared holiday to see the children off. The walls were adorned with signatures of Sidharth and his friends as well as slogans and emotional appeals like "Goodbye, friend,' 'forget me not, friend,' 'forgive me, don't forget me' etc. These had been written on the school boundary wall, walls, black boards, tables and desks since the previous evening. Sidharth had shed copious tears the day he finally left his school.

That was Sidharth's first encounter with the city; sweet as the first love of one's youth. The surrounding roads, vehicles, tile-roofed houses, and the indistinct figure of young girls behind the windows of some, would make Sidharth absentminded. During the late afternoons, while sitting on the bed of *karanj* flowers, on the bank of the pond, legs outstretched, Sidharth would frequently feel absent-minded; his own reflection in the rippling water of the pond would remind him of the beautiful memories he had left behind within the four walls of the school.

Did the Tihidi Bazzar of Bhadrak district deserve being called a city? When Khaga sir announced a day before the end of the examination that he was going to take us to Bhadrak the next day, Sidharth jumped two feet in the air and his head hit the low door-frame. Irrespective of what happened in the examination, the seven-day stay at Tihidi promised a novel experience. In place of the traditional *pakhala* and boiled potatoes, there were *puri* and *aludam* for breakfast; in the afternoon, fish and rice were ordered from the hotel; and for dinner, they had roti and mutton. During the examination, *luchi* and rasogollas were served. How Sidharth wished the matriculation examination had been held much earlier.

Khaga sir had already announced the three attractions related to the Bhadrak tour. He could never keep anything a secret. The first of the attractions was watching a movie at the Draupadi cinema; the second was having a group photo at Charampa; and the third was watching a train at the railway station.

Sidharth, of course, had seen a train earlier but, for most of his friends, seeing a train was limited to the experience described by Gopabandu in his poem 'Reladarsan'. However, watching a movie and having a group photo – these two were excitingly new for even Sidharth.

Even today, Sidharth remembers the uncomfortable moments that he and his classmates had at Draupadi Cinema. From the back, amidst darkness, came a collective and harsh order, "Sit down… sit down" followed by an acid remark, "God knows where these bloody village lads come from". Sidharth failed to realize where their mistake lay. However, after the show was over, while answering the question of Prafulla who had failed to understand anything of the film, Khaga sir said, "We were late in coming to the hall. Really, we reached after the half time." Only then did Sidharth understand why they had been the butt of the sarcastic remarks.

The next thing to be done was to have the group photo taken. At first, everybody combed their hair at least two or three times. This was followed by the desperate attempt to look charming by rubbing their faces with talcum powder. Sidharth failed to notice when the photo was taken by the photographer amidst the shouting of 'smile please'. That day, Sidharth had heard from his friends that he was looking absolutely smart but even after the passage of twenty-five years, he had not got the opportunity to see that first photo of his life. After almost a decade, Sidharth heard from Dhruba that the studio owner did not hand over the photo as some of his friends were unable to pay their share of the cost.

Sidharth was not interested in watching a train pass by. At about nine o' clock in the night, Khaga sir shouted, pointing at a freight train, "Hey, look". Brundaban was not able to understand, for a long time how passengers travelled in closed wagons. Of course, Brundaban is now working as a station master somewhere.

The hot sun compelled Sidharth to come back to the real world. He wished to see the examinees once again from the terrace. No, these students had not come from a real, unspoilt village, like Sidharth had. Everybody had put on full trousers. Sidharth was able to wear one six long months after enrolling himself at a college. That day he had asked his neighbour, Mohanty babu, where the examinees had come from and the latter informed him, "They are from a school near Khorda. They are all town boys."

"How backward we were during our days! At that age, we were utter strangers to betel cones, cigarettes, and trousers. These boys are smart and therefore, fortunate."

Sidharth's opinion was not in consonance with that of Mohantybabu. Mohantybabu was perhaps aware of what these boys had got, but did not realize what these boys had lost. The boys did not have young Sidharth's curiosity about the town and his expectations from it.

Good Men Bad Men

Sidharth shrank a little at the sight of him. Chintamani Roy Mohapatra suddenly flew into a rage. Chintamani Roy Mohapatra was Sanjay's father. Sanjay was Sidharth's most intimate classmate. The angry father was certain that if he expressed his angry displeasure at his son to the son's most intimate friend, the words would be directly transmitted to the latter. This was why he used all those objectionable and unparliamentary words while talking to Sidharth but keeping Sanjay in mind.

In the opinion of Chintamani Roy Mohapatra, Sanjay was a worthless, foolish black sheep. He himself had committed an unpardonable sin for being the father of a worthless shirker of duties.

However, what sin had Sanjay committed?

Chintamani Roy Mohapatra worked in the supply department. He made a handsome extra income. Had it not been the case, he would not have been able to purchase a piece of land measuring one and a half *gunths* in a place like Cuttack and constructed a house on it. Despite all this, the shadow of poverty had not been completely dispelled from the household. This fact was confirmed the moment one entered his house. The lack of affluence was manifest in everything starting from the maxi of the unmarried sister to his mother's faded cotton *saree*.

Chintamani had four daughters. In his attempt to father a son, he had fathered four daughters. He had never imagined that the son, who was born after so much sorrow, would turn out to be such a worthless fellow.

Sanjay was just the opposite of his father. Throughout the day, he would be found reading books, writing poems or painting. At times he would utter nonsense like philosophers. But he was unable to do the most vital thing — earn money.

Sanjay was thirty-five years old. Chintamani complained that young men at his age engaged in various activities and earned money. They were working as contractors by the grace of ministers; they were supplying orders and making money. But, Sanjay, for his part, was not able to do anything worthwhile. He went out in the morning, only to come back in the evening, with a grave face. Can something worthwhile be ever done by such a useless fellow?

Out of the four daughters, Mr. Mohapatra had got three married off, with much difficulty. The youngest daughter had attained marriageable age two years ago. He was going to retire soon. Even at this stage, Sanjay was not trying to earn some money. Once he retired and got a pension, how would the ship of life sail?

It was not true that Sanjay wasn't able to understand things; but how and to whom would he explain that a job did not come one's way that easily these days!

That day Sanjay was found saying, almost all the jobs of this state were sold in the chambers of ministers. Dealership of all branded products went to the relations of

MPs or MLAs. Without any recommendation letter, banks or finance corporations didn't give loans. However, if he got a little help, he would start a new type of industry. He would lend a new design to Odishan handicraft starting from appliqué to door mats. He found art in everything starting from the pebbles to the rivers and mountains of Odisha; he would take art to everybody. But, who would listen to Sanjay? No rich would be in-laws would like to invest in such projects.

Chintamani, in his poor English, was found repeating his one-line philosophy. He was saying, "What you achieve is important, how you achieve it is not important. You have to earn money by hook or crook. Morality, value, humanity are nothing but adornments of a middle class mindset. They merely turn people into sentimental fools."

Sidharth was unable to wait any longer. He could visualize the dream-laden face of Sanjay. The university champion Sanjay had surely failed to meet the demands of the time he lived in. On the other hand, Sidharth and some of his friends who were academically inferior to him had gone so far that Sanjay would never be able to catch up with them.

Sidharth was in a hurry. He had to reach the dak-bungalow bringing with him an expensive wine bottle. His officer was staying there. His new building was being built. For that, he had to arrange iron rods and cement. Otherwise, he would have to say goodbye to the contract worth ten lakhs.

"I take leave of you, uncle. If I meet Sanjay, I will surely convey your feelings to him."

Someone was sitting on the culvert with his head lowered and his back towards the electric pole. Sidharth slowed his motorcycle. Sanjay! Yes, Sanjay sat there like a philosopher. He would be mulling over a new way of reforming society. Could not Sidharth sit a while with Sanjay, ignoring for a while this noise and this mad rush? Could not he discuss the weal and woe of five others, except him?

No, Sidharth didn't have the time for any such work. If he sat down beside Sanjay, others would get ahead of him. He could never bear being left behind.

Before finally disappearing round the bend of the lane, Sidharth once again looked at the electric pole. Sanjay was still sitting there, like the protagonist of a tragedy. This time, his face appeared surprisingly bright to Sidharth. "It's very difficult to be someone like Sanjay," said Sidharth to himself.

A Guest

In this part of the town, night descended quickly. The colony looked like dozing at eight o' clock; and at nine o' clock, it would be fast asleep. Load-shedding had made life in the city annoying and short. Life in the colony had become pathetic as man had grown attuned to a mechanical life.

Under such circumstances, it was a rare incident to arrange for food and lodging for a stranger at ten o' clock at night. One should not blame Barsha, the mistress of the house. She was a working lady. She left home after completing all the chores in the morning, and after the office was over, she would return by the town bus. Therefore, by the time she returned she would become very tired. She thought of taking rest after cooking a meal in the evening. The next day, the same routine would be followed.

The stranger was an old man; he had come to the city on some work in the court. He said that he was the uncle of Sidharth's classmate. His problem was that he didn't have any acquaintances in the city. He didn't prefer to spend thirty to forty rupees in a hotel or a lodging house and that too, when he had to spend only one night.

From the way the old man talked, Barsha figured out quite clearly that he was very cunning. She called Sidharth inside and told him, "Tell him clearly to go to the lodging nearby. He is having some work in the court. He would have to attend it at least once or twice on the scheduled date every month. Now that we are not known to each other, it would not feel bad to ask him to stay in the lodging. Once familiarity grows, he would come again and again. We have only two rooms. Can we allow him to stay here every time?"

Barsha was absolutely right. Rent in this city was sky high. We had only two rooms, small as match-boxes. One was designated as drawing-dining-reading room; the other was the bedroom. Both the rooms were filled to the brim with wooden chairs, benches, almirahs, and other belongings. Still, half of the things were packed in Amulspray-packets and were lying untouched like the 'Ahalya turned into stone' under the bed. In such a condition, where would the guest stay? Had he been an acquaintance, the matter would have been different. He was an old man, not even a child.

Sidharth was going to tell the guest what Barsha had in mind, but in his own language. Suddenly, he was reminded of a small incident that had happened to him twelve years ago.

Sidharth was moving from place to place in Cuttack city to make a living. With much difficulty, he had admitted himself in the I.A. class of a night college. His evenings were spent at the *mudhi* shop at the College Square and the water tap at the back of the library, whereas in the mornings he survived on a few slices of 'Raja" brand bread. The little money he made giving private tuition helped him to pay for a meal at "Bisudha Hindu Bhojanalaya" during the day.

The resting place at night was the verandah of Lower Primary School in the Labour Colony.

It was one evening during April. School examinations were over. This being the case, tuition teachers got a break of two months. Children would spend their time playing; why would parents spend fifty or sixty rupees on their education? Poor Sidharth! Children could manage without education but how would he manage without money?

Throughout the evening Sidharth was found standing near the Ranihat square. Looking at the gun shop, stationery shop, the traffic post on the right and its red and blue lights, he was wondering where he would go. If he could arrange some money, he could go home. He could return after the schools and colleges opened. The I.A examination was a few days away but he had no money. He cursed himself. The *mudhi* from the sack and the fried groundnuts made him absentminded. Why did not the government hold the school and college examinations at the same time?

Suddenly, he found a cycle going past him and then returning to where he stood. The rider applied brakes in front of him. Sidharth recognized him; he was a classmate, Pratap. The number of students enrolled at Ravenshaw College was so large that it was not possible to recognize everybody, but, however, he could recognize his face. Once or twice, they had sat close to each other in the class.

Pratap said, "Why are you standing here for such a long time? Half an hour ago, I went by this way to Mangalabag. Are you waiting for someone?"

Someone had said, "Poverty is the greatest curse of mankind. Poverty during one's youth is distressing, intensely painful." Sidharth could not open his mouth. His eyes turned moist.

Pratap, in a manner of giving orders said, "Sit on my

cycle. Let's go to my house." Sidharth sat on his cycle. He had neither the energy nor the ability to say 'no'.

Pratap's brother was a municipal tax collector. His job was a small but regular one. He stayed in a small rented house behind the Medical College. The family consisted of husband, wife, a small child and Pratap. A Small house. Two sixty watt bulbs lighted it. The moment one entered the house, one would know that a poor family lived in it.

It was more than eight o' clock at that time. Pratap's brother and sister-in-law waited for him. Pratap made Sidharth stand on the verandah and went inside.

Pratap's brother, sister-in-law, and Pratap himself were busy arranging a meal for Sidharth. Pratap's elder brother said he was not feeling well and he would not eat anything that night. Pratap's sister-in-law told him it was not right to sleep on an empty stomach; he should rather eat one roti. She further said that since she had eaten at the odd hour herself, she was not feeling hungry. Pratap himself was found saying that he had eaten a *dosha* at Mangalabag. He would rather not eat anything.

Sidharth was served seven of the thirteen rotis made that day along with more than half of the curry. Sidharth could clearly understand that the discussions about 'ill health', 'odd time', and '*dosha*' were nothing but false stories cooked up by the family members so that they could leave their portion to Sidharth.

That night, sleep didn't come to Sidharth's eyes, but tears did. He was thinking about the deep humanity displayed by that poor family. His heart overflowed with respect for them. He told them a lie the next morning, He said he had some urgent work to do and left the house, once again adrift in a world of uncertainty.

This had happened twelve years ago but Sidharth

hadn't forgotten the experience of that night. In addition to the memories of suffering caused by poverty, he also had some pleasant memories to cherish.

Barsha asked, "Why are you standing? Go and send away the man."

Sidharth said, "No… Barsha… he will stay here tonight."

"What will he eat at this odd hour? Where will he sleep?" complained Barsha.

Sidharth said, "Barsha, guests don't arrive on fixed dates and days. I will tell him whatever I want to in the morning, but for now, he will stay here. Give me ten rupees and the tiffin box. I will be back from the market soon."

Gurudakshina

Harekrushna Mohanty was famous as an ideal teacher in our locality. Few other teachers were famed for being disciplined and student-friendly like him. So, Sidharth remembered him clearly even though he had left primary school years ago. He remembered how he read out news about our own country and abroad in the prayer class. He would take children to the nearest market, police station and post office on Sundays and inform them how they functioned. School was a man-making factory for him. His close association with that factory was something to be seen to be believed.

However, all memories of Sidharth associated with Harekrushna Sir were not pleasant. Even today, whenever the lines on a sheet of paper were askew, he would shudder at the thought of the blow on the fingers. Whenever he reached office late, he would remember the angry face of Harekrushna sir and his hand would automatically reach the cheeks to caress them.

Once, Sidharth had indulged in a childhood prank with another classmate. During the afternoon break, both of them got hold of a *biri* from somewhere, lit it, smoked it and released the smoke into the sky. This had remained a secret from other classmates but Harekrushna Sir had got a whiff of it. After punishment was meted out to them, welts appeared on their backs.

Harekrushna sir's anger took some time to subside. After it did, he felt extremely sorry to see what had happened to the two. He promptly administered first aid to them. Even after becoming an adult, whenever the smell of *biris* and cigarettes reached his nostrils, Harekrushna Sir's face would float into his mind.

Why did the same Harekrushna sir become prone to despair? Sidharth, after welcoming Harekrushna sir, asked about his health. He felt as if sir had some secret to divulge but he was not able to do so. Finally, when Sidharth almost forced him to disclose what ailed him, he opened up.

The incident had happened a few days ago. Sir had punished an errant fourth-grader with two slaps on the cheek. This was nothing new. He had never imagined that the matter would take such an ugly turn. The child's father brought the boy to the school the next day and abused sir heartily in front of others. He even didn't forget to remind that poor teachers like Harekrushna sir got salary that was less than what his driver was paid. He asked, how dare he raise his hand on his son?

Sidharth was shocked to hear this. He found it hard to believe that the incident had taken place in his own village. He was reminded of his own childhood. Every time his father met the teachers he would repeat the same thing, "Sir, you can beat every part of his body except the eyes and the ears. The child needs to be disciplined. Please leave the eyes so that he does not become blind, and consequently, worthless." A feeling of revolt would rise in the child Sidhu, the moment he heard his father speaking something of this sort. His mind would be filled with confusing thoughts—whether it was his father who was speaking or an enemy? But he was helpless. All complaints against sir returned as graver sins and the gravity of punishment rose in proportion. A headmaster of the school was insulted for punishing a student!

Harekrushna sir got up to take leave. He had grown old and was going to retire in a few days. He had moulded many students in his life. They had all occupied important positions. They had become doctors, engineers, and professors. The pride he experienced because of this was not in any way inferior to the pride a father experiences at the success of his own children. He would frequently say that he was a matriculate but his students had all occupied great positions in life. However, such a teacher…

Sir was unwilling to reveal the name of that guardian. When Sidharth persisted, he disclosed the name. Had Sidharth not persisted, it would have been better. The reason was that the guardian was Sidharth's cousin, Nilamadhav who was a lecturer himself.

Harekrushna sir got up to go. He had become old. His hair had turned grey but the glitter of his personality hadn't diminished. Throughout his life he had turned his back on social appreciation and a well to do lifestyle; he had never compromised with his dignity. Did he ever imagine that he would get insulted as *gurudakshina* for the dignified life he had lived?

Sidharth wished to run to him and beg apology, holding his feet. He would request him to forgive Nilamadhav, people like whom had lost their morality and dignity in their hunger for money and power. But, Harekrushna sir had gone far away.

Helpless Bridegroom's Companions

Casting one glance at the sleepy-eyed stars in the dark sky and another at the serpentine red-gravel road, Sidharth helplessly asked someone, "How far more do we have to travel?"

An elderly companion, who seemed to be a know-all, replied, "I am also new to this area. I don't know how far we have to go. Still then, we may have to cover a distance of about four miles more."

"F-O-U-R miles! Then, it may be dawn by the time we reach there."

"Why do you think that dawn might break? Dawn will break. Should the bridegroom reach during the night? The custom here is to reach in the morning."

Drained out, Sidharth sat down on a ridge with a thud. He was perhaps wondering about the sin for which he was being punished like that.

Sidharth lived in afar-off town. During childhood, he went to the school near his village. He was reminded of a day during his school days. For some reason, the most punctual geography teacher had failed to turn up in time for the class. Taking advantage of his absence, his friends wished to spend time talking about their marriages that would happen in the future. Chandramani asked, "Sidharth, will you come to my marriage? After schooling, you will perhaps leave the village and go to town. Once you leave the village, we may not meet at all." Sidharth was well versed with Chandramani's anger and grief. Besides, Chandramani's marriage was not going to be held in the next few days. Discussions about marriage at a tender age are not only useless but also safe. Sidharth answered in a dramatic style, "Don't talk like that. If I am alive when you get married, no matter where I live, I will surely come to your wedding."

Sidharth had undertaken a bus journey lasting six hours since morning. This was followed by a terrible trekker journey from Bhadrak. (Sidharth fails to understand why trekkers are used to carry human beings on the Bhadrak-Chandabali route whereas they are normally used to carry goods. Perhaps, the transportation authorities don't distinguish between human beings travelling along the Bhadrak-Chandabali route and gunny bags containing goods.) Finally, he had to walk eight kilometers to reach Chandramani's village at five in the afternoon yesterday. The bridegroom was to leave for the bride's village by ten o' clock. But it was around midnight when they got ready. Chandramani, seated in a palanquin had already left some time ago. He was forced to take the help of a palanquin as vehicles could not reach his village. Sidharth made fun of his being carried on the shoulders of human beings as a vulgar display of the aristocratic mindset. The band and light party was acquainted with the road. It was not possible to know where they had disappeared amid the darkness.

Sidharth, along with three or four others, was lost midway. He felt worn-out walking on the ridges in the dark, and by the fatigue of the long journey. He was completely shattered to learn that he might have to spend a sleepless night.

Finally, they reached a village. In the middle of that village, a video show was on. Sunil Dutt and a young heroine were found singing and dancing on the screen. After they crossed it, they reached the Mangala field. Chandramani had reached there safe, being carried in the palanquin. Some other companions of the groom had gone to sleep in that open field, spreading their towels on the ground. Some others slept on the bare ground.

The drum beaters woke up. Lights were switched on and crackers were burst. It was about two in the morning. The bride's house was only a few meters from there. But the procession was not moving even an inch. Sidharth asked once again, "What's the harm if we proceed to the bride's place directly instead of waiting here so long? Was it really necessary to suffer the bites of mosquitoes and fleas? He met with the same reply. The groom was not expected to reach the bride's place before sunrise. The reason wasn't clearly understood. Sidharth looked around, confused. By that time, some interested villagers had gathered around the procession. Some sleepy-eyed maidens were lazily inspecting the groom Chandramani through the windows. Dawn was three hours away. Worried, Sidharth was not able to do anything other than looking at his wrist watch frequently.

This is exactly why Sidharth didn't want to accompany any marriage procession. It was a great nuisance. Last week he had joined a marriage party in the town. Sidharth never understood what charm was there in starting the procession at two in the morning, accompanied by bursting crackers, high-sounding sound-boxes and a band party. But there he saw a strange sight. From among a group of young men dancing in break-dance poses to the tune of the band party, someone started throwing notes. They were one rupee and two rupee notes. Sidharth didn't appreciate the display of extravagance in a poor country like India, where people worked tirelessly for some rice or wheat flour. By the time the groom's companions reached the bride's residence after the procession was over, it was three o' clock. The food which was cooked at three in the afternoon was served at three in the morning. It was immaterial whether such food was worthy of being consumed. This was exactly why Sidharth preferred not to accompany a marriage party. Wherever one went, one found the same dishes served—it all started with *kanika* or fried rice and ended with *khir* or rasogollas. They had the same taste and smell. In view of this, the invitation to Chandramani's marriage was certainly different. Here, there was no dearth of love and affection.

The procession didn't advance an inch. In the middle of the village road, spreading a mat, the drama troupe performed Ramlila. They were followed by a group of musicians playing *telingibaja* that included dhols, cymbals, and bugle. Far ahead, two young men displayed their skills, staffs in hands. Everybody waited for the dawn to break.

Sidharth once again looked at the sky overhead. Visibility was increasing. He saw a huge pond on his left. It was surrounded by coconut and betel-nut trees. The Mangala Mandir stood at the back. The village resembled a portrait that he had seen on the cinema screen or theatre screen. Sidharth dozed off for awhile, soothed by the cool breeze of the dawn. Someone called him, "Let's go. The groom has advanced." Sidharth drank a palmful of water from the pond and steadied himself. He said, "Is it worth getting stuck to this place throughout the night?" his voice reflected disgust and dissatisfaction.

"*Arey baboo*! The bride's family is making arrangements for breakfast. Unless the cooking is completed, how will the groom's party go there? You may go without food on the way, but you can't be allowed to remain hungry once you reach the bride's residence. That's the reason for the sleepless journey." Someone from the bride's family rushed in carrying some twig tooth brushes and a lump of *gudakhu*. Sidharth refused saying 'No" with folded hands and went ahead asking, "Where is Chandramani?" Chandramani flashed a divine smile and asked, "Did you reach here without any problem?"

Hungry, sleep-deprived, and worn-out Sidharth responded, "I had promised you once that if I was alive, I would certainly join your marriage party. But who knows whether I would return to the city alive?" Chandramani said, "Don't worry so much; it is only a matter of a day or two." Sidharth questioned himself, "Aren't the groom's companions considered human beings either by the bride's side or by the groom's?"

The Helpless Divine Child

For the last few days, a seven year old girl of a non-descript village named Parbatipur had become the centre of attraction for lakhs of people. Without verifying the veracity of the claims, lakhs of people poured into the village in the morning and in the evening, like ants, and congregated in the village fair-field, either to get cures for their diseases or for the fulfillment of their wishes. The seven-year-old girl, Savita Swain of that village was giving *hokum* as an incarnation of some goddess. It was heard that the very sight of the goddess-incarnate was capable of curing people of complicated and incurable diseases.

I had never got an opportunity to examine the veracity of the claim; nor was I interested to do so. I had heard that the village near Satasankha had already been converted into a place of pilgrimage. The narrow road leading to the village was filled by hundreds of buses, scooters and rickshaws. From miles around, people arrived here with ailing children, sick old men and women either by vehicles or even, on foot. Taking advantage of the swirling crowd, a regular bazzar had cropped up, which contained many tea and tiffin shops. The devotees stood watching the goddess at a distance of a mile or two. Owing to the heavy rush, they were not able to proceed any further.

I also heard that the goddess-incarnate, no more went to the village school. Even some of her friends who read with her, were found selling garlands, incense sticks, earthen lamps and *bhog* to be offered to the deity in the fair-field. It was also heard that a sum of rupees three lakh had already been deposited in the name of Sabita in a nearby bank during the last two months. The amount was enough to support her for the rest of her life. I don't say whatever is being said about Parbatipur is untrue but, I have my own doubts.

Amidst the crowd, the rush of vehicles, and the gathering of people, I could visualize the lean and thin figure of a seven-year-old child. The figure was that of Sabita Swain, who, until a few months ago, was reading in class three of the village school. She used to play a game of *bohubohuka* in the tender sun with her friends, who ate *pakhala* before leaving for school; and who chased dragon-flies during the recess. She used to swim in the pond and roamed with her friends. With the fickleness and innocence of a bird and soft-winged butterfly, her childhood was spent happily in the village lanes. Her childhood was like that of a princess, complete with a game of *puchi* on the occasion of Kumarpurnami, plucking of water-lilies from Tubigadia and the singing of '*Akal makal takal tian*' in the faraway fields.

Later, the picture of a transformed childhood sprang before me. The figure of the divine-child was so complex, mysterious, and blurred that I grew scared, and took pity on the figure. The girl sat with a garland hanging from her neck. On her entire body were drawn designs that were usually found on a *kaleshi*. On her head, a hibiscus garland was found tied to the spot where, usually, a flower made of ribbons appeared. She had been transformed into a machine dispensing things from morning till night; and a reluctant traveller treading a specially-carved path. Her innocent pet name was lost amidst adjectives such as *Thakurani, Maa Mangala, Parbati, Mahamaya* etc. Her hands and feet were tied by invisible shackles and she remained hanging in the middle. She was neither a human being nor a deity; she was a helpless divine-child found suspended between heaven and earth. I suspected that henceforth Sabita Swain would never be allowed to lead the life of an ordinary girl. She would frequently appear on the pages of newspapers and magazines; she would be popularized and maligned frequently. She would lose the freedom to escape these. From morning till evening, she would be surrounded by devotees and followers. She would be unable to avoid them. Enveloped by uncertainty, an innocent childhood would be transformed into the suffocating life of a divine-child. She would not be allowed to lead a normal life.

I don't know whether something strange and mysterious is happening on the pandal set up for the deity at the fair-field of Parbatipur, but I have no doubt that an innocent and sinless childhood is meeting a premature death.

A Hunger for Affluence

We all called Udhav a miser during our school days, but we never stopped being friends with him. The reason was that only he helped us in bad times. In view of this, despite his miserliness and narrowness of mind, we all were tied to him in bonds of friendship.

At times, it would really become impossible for us to tolerate his miserliness. Once, Udhav invited Ghanashyam to breakfast. On getting the invitation, Ghanashyam wondered in which direction the sun had risen that day; he could not take a decision in this regard as he himself got up from bed quite late every day. Vanivihar square was not as much crowded those days as it is today. Udhav placed orders for four *samosas*. Ghanashyam was going to eat the *samosas* when Udhav asked the hotel boy, "What is the price of each *samosa*?" The child answered, "Twenty-five paise." Udhav immediately got up and asked Ghanashyam to come out. Ghanashyam felt shocked. By the time he asked, "Why should we go away?" Udhav had already stepped out of that low-thatched hotel and come to the main road. He said, "The price of one *samosa* is twenty paise and how dare this man demand twenty five paise per piece?"

Udhav of course purchased *samosas* for Ghanashyam but the interest to eat these had dissipated while they walked from Vanivihar to Master Canteen.

On another day in the economics tutorial class in the college, Chandramani sir asked, "Which flower is the most beautiful and essential?" Someone answered it was rose while another one said it was sunflower. For someone else it was *kadamba*. But, in Udhav's opinion, it was cauliflower. Everybody including sir laughed loudly. Was cauliflower a flower?

Udhav said, "Sir, Please keep the cauliflower on the table. The cauliflower surrounded by leaves will look very attractive. After two days, you can cook this. That's why cauliflower is the most attractive and essential vegetable."

Sidharth had not met Udhav for the last many years. The latter's father was a prosperous farmer. He earned a handsome income; but there was hardly any expenditure to make. Throughout the twelve months, he could manage with one shirt, two dhotis, and two five-hand-long Khurda-gamchhas. In the mofussil, where he lived there arose no occasion to spend money. Udhav was just like his father. He always carried five hundred or one thousand rupee notes in his pocket. Now he worked in a bank. He was so thrifty that he must have deposited thirty or forty thousand rupees in his account.

On the other hand, I was perpetually poor. My poverty was made worse by the demands of my wife for new things every three months. In this scenario, the sudden demand of my father for five thousand rupees to meet the expenses of my sister's marriage came as a bolt from the blue. If Udhav wanted, he could give me a loan of five thousand rupees.

The drawing room of Udhav's house was richly decorated. A colour television, a V.C.P., and a two-in-one music player were placed at their appointed places. The sofa had excellent soft cushions. The carpet matched perfectly with the colour on the wall. The symbols of affluence could be marked on the other side, through the gap in the curtain: an expensive dining table, a washing machine, and a mechanical broom to sweep the floor lay there. I was extremely happy. This was a dream house, and it had things most suitable for it. Udhav was always a miser. With the effort of his wife, a lot of changes have been introduced in his life.

Udhav arrived. He wore tidy trousers and a *punjabi*. He was happy to see me, and ordered tea to be brought, looking inside.

I did not wait to broach the topic of the loan. I said, "Udhav, I need five thousand rupees for the marriage of my sister. It will take at least two months to withdraw money from the provident fund account."

Udhav's face turned pale. As a childhood friend, I was well acquainted with this expression on his face. Without giving any importance to it, I repeated the request. Udhav held me by the hand and took me outside. I was surprised. Why was he taking me outside? What was it that he could not say inside his house?

Udhav said, "I know you think I am telling a lie. But I swear in the name of Lord Jagannath, my condition is pitiable. You know the nature of my father. He never gives me any money."

"Let him not give anything. You are getting a salary of eight thousand rupees. Besides, your in-laws ..."

"The problem lies there. My wife is accustomed to an affluent life-style. The moment she reached here, she asked for a Colour TV, a fridge, jewellery, a mechanized broom, a washing machine etc. There are as many advantages in our job as there are disadvantages. Everything can be paid for through installments. If you want to procure some item, you have to pay one hundred rupees and for some others, you have to pay two hundred. When you bring home something new, you feel as if it is available for free. The thing may be priced eight thousand but you can take it home for two hundred rupees. Would not it feel like an item obtained for free?"

"This is how we are spending our life. There are regular expenses; besides, there are the installments. The installments come to four thousand rupees every month. This morning, the person who has provided cable connection came. I did not have money. I asked him to come on the first day of the next month."

I still did not believe what Udhav was saying.

Udhav showed me his salary bill. Last month, he received two thousand eight hundred rupees after all the deductions.

I sighed deeply. My wife told me yesterday that colour TVs were available on installment. One had to deposit three hundred rupees every month. Everybody was going for that...

On hearing what Udhav said, I immediately took a decision. These things were not required. Consumerism had been trying to engulf us with all its hundred arms outstretched. Pervasive advertisements; unavoidable enticements. They looked so attractive from outside that middle-class people die to acquire those. Once a person fell into the trap of consumerism, there was no way of getting out of its claws.

I was reminded of my childhood days. How easily this Udhav was evading the attraction of *rasogollas, gulabjamuns,* and hot *jalebis* on display at Sahu Sweets

Store. When we helplessly devoured ground nuts and lozenzes, Udhav would walk straight like an ascetic, without even casting a glance at those delicacies. But, if any of the friends was in trouble, he would immediately take out a fifty or hundred rupee note to help him out. Why then the same Udhav suddenly grew so poor?

Udhav said, "These objects have given the house its identity. However, we can't buy a kilo of prawns or a little curd for our children. What is the use of having so much wealth? Are they like gold or silver that would come to our rescue at our hour of need?"

I thought of the difference between Udhav's father and Udhav's wife. The hunger for consumerism had encircled man like an all-consuming dread. It was as if the entire human race would be wiped out because of it. The tea in expensive tea-cups on Udhav's sophisticated centre table of his drawing room was getting cold but I didn't feel like going inside to drink it.

Udhav was sorry for not being able to help me. I patted him on his back and returned after asking him not to worry about my problem anymore.

A Hungry God

Sidharth didn't understand why the bus had stopped at such a deserted place. Initially he thought perhaps the vehicle had developed some mechanical snag. He felt slightly irritated as the bus stopped so early in the journey. But the reason was not exactly that. The moment the bus stopped on a small bridge, the cleaner got down and placed four bananas and three half-burnt incense sticks on the cement-parapet of the bridge. Sidharth looked in the direction from which the fragrance was coming. The vast blue sky spread above; all around there was a belt of coconut trees. In the absence of the moon owing to the dark fortnight, the importance of the stars had suddenly increased. The cleaner planted the incense sticks in the bananas and paid his obeisance. Sidharth looked around. No... no images of gods and goddesses were visible anywhere. The prayer was for a happy, trouble-free journey. Perhaps this was an accepted custom here.

Sidharth felt reassured that the bus had not developed any mechanical snag. Things would have made sense if he had discovered the image of a god or goddess under some tree. The place lay in between Panaji in Goa and Mapusa.

The entire area looked so forlorn that if the bus had not stopped there, there would have been doubts about whether there was any human settlement in the vicinity. The next stop was Mapusa. After twelve hours of bus journey from Mapusa, they would reach Bombay. On the way there were dangerous mountain passes. In the darkness of the night, if something happened, there would be no trace of either the vehicle or the passengers. They were thousands of kilometers from home; if by chance something happened…. Thoughts like this would make Sidharth shudder.

This is the reason why a mere stone lying by the side of the road was revered in the form of 'shalagram'; and trunks of trees became gods and goddesses – strong protecting walls of faith. No insurance company of the world could guarantee such protection of life and property at a mere fee of two bananas or a coconut. Sidharth had come across such gods and goddesses hundreds of times. Whenever the bus stopped in front of a tree-trunk smeared with vermillion or a stone-image or the entrance to a temple, he would bow his head, not as a matter of faith but as a matter of habit.

The cleaner blew the whistle. The bus started moving. Through the window of the bus, Sidharth saw a strange sight. An eight or nine year old child suddenly arrived from somewhere, picked up the bananas like a kite would pick up a fish, threw away the remnants of the incense sticks that the cleaner had in the bananas, and disappeared into the darkness.

The bus ran at a high speed. In order to entertain the passengers, the stereos blared popular Hindi film songs that were played during elections in Pakistan. In the place of bright lights burnt the blue dim lights. Leaning against the soft seats, the passengers sat in a relaxed mood.

Sleep eluded Sidharth. He was not able to discuss with others what he had seen a moment ago. He was reminded of a similar incident that had happened years ago.

He was a student of seventh class then. He had gone to the 'Badapokhari' with his friends to participate in the immersion of the image of goddess Saraswati. The moment the image was thrown into the water, some naughty boys would jump into water and pluck out the idol's head, hands, fingers or crown, ridiculing, as it were, the artistic skills of Bana Moharana that had gone into the making of it. It was impossible on the part of any student to bear witness to the misery of their beloved deity. Consequently, Sidharth and some of his friends decided that they would provide protection to the deity for some time after immersion by remaining present on the bank. Among them was Kulamani sir, the teacher who would not differentiate between a human being and an animal, when punishment was to be meted out.

The image of goddess Saraswati would be taken around the pond three times; after this, it would be immersed. Kulamani sir was a Brahmin but he was not accorded much respect in the Brahman village. He would not be invited on the *puja* day. The immersion was different in the sense that one marked a clear decrease in jubilation in comparison to that shown on the *puja* day. The Head Master would advise students to complete the immersion process with the aid of Kulamani sir.

It was a morning in the month of Magha. On the bank of the pond, at the foot of a wood-apple tree, sat two small children. They weren't school children. They collected cow-dung, gathered twigs, and for most of the day wandered here and there aimlessly. The moment they saw the immersion party, they started running after it. No... they were not interested in the jewellery worn by the goddess but in the green coconut on the sacred pitcher. The elder boy was moving around them with the coconut in mind.

Sidharth, who was in charge of protecting the image and the items of *puja*, felt angry. He ran towards the boy, with a stone in hand, thinking perhaps he was not a human being but a puppy that had entered a feast without permission. However, Kulamani sir shattered all his plans. Sir had to throw the coconut into the pond after emptying the pitcher and throwing the mango-leaves. He handed over the coconut to the younger of the two boys. The small child vanished from the spot even before Sidharth and his friends got a hint of what had happened.

Sidharth could understand what Kulamani sir had done, after witnessing a similar incident after so many days. He understood why a small child waited for four bananas in the darkness of night; and why a small child waited eagerly on a cold *Magha* morning for an almost dried up coconut or green coconut. However, man disregarded these living gods to smear the images of stone or wood with vermilion, drape those with red cloth, and unnecessarily bathe those in milk and cream.

Hymn of the Soil

Intelligent people don't value their relationship with their close relations, but they never shun influential people. If one wants to remain safe, one has to spread one's roots and aerial roots into strong places. One has to maintain amicable relationship with the higher-ups of the department; besides, one has to keep the influential people of one's locality, small and big, happy and satisfied. Sarbeswar was posted in this backward district as he did not follow the above unwritten laws; if he does not want to follow those, he must be ready to be sent to a remoter place.

Sidharth has grown close to Adhikaribabu because, a doctor by profession, his hand effortlessly reaches the corridors of power in the nine-storied building and the secretariat.

Adhikaribabu was constructing a building in Cuttack; he had decided to spend the last part of his life there. He would open a clinic and 'serve' people. He had got wind of the fact that Sarbeswar and the local forest department officer were classmates. Both of them were close to each other. If Sarbeswar tried, he could easily arrange good quality teak and sal wood for the windows and doors of his nine-roomed house. The moment the proposal was made, Sarbeswar raised objections. But Adhikari explained to him, "Look, Sarbeswar… government has already formulated rules to prevent use of wood. Government organizations like BDA, CDA, Housing Board etc. are using iron door frames in place of wood frames. But, during the summer, those frames are heating up. Has anyone thought of the danger they are posing? Whether the houses of the *baboos*, who are instrumental in prohibiting the use of wood, at Cuttack, Bhubaneswar, and Rourkella have been fitted with wood frames or not? Forget about door frames, they have even constructed staircases inside their houses with wood. Rules move in one direction whereas people go in another. I can get wood at Cuttack but it will be a little expensive. Your friend is a forest officer; if he wants…"

"Will he honour my request? He is a very honest officer."

Adikaribabu gave a smile. From the smile, it was evident that he had more experience than Sarbeswar in this regard. In the manner of expounding a great truth, he said, "Everybody has a price. Please go and ask him what his is."

"Perhaps you had gone to him." Sidharth cut in.

Sarbeswar said, "Yes… but…"

"What does this 'but' mean?"

On the advice of Adhikari, Sarbeswar met his forester friend. That was Sri Panchami day. Winter had just receded. The sky looked clear. Trees had come into leaf.

The forester friend was happy to see Sarbeswar. Both the friends had tea and biscuits. Sarbeswar waited for an opportunity to discuss 'the thing' at the right moment. At that moment, something like this happened.

"What happened?" asked Sidharth.

The forest officer Ramprasan's daughter had organized Saraswati Puja. The semi-insane old man who worked in their house, had gone in search of a mango twig that was to be put on the sacred pitcher. The old man had been working in Ramprasan's house for the last three or four years. The old man returned empty-handed after half an hour. Ramprasan was short-tempered. The Brahman priest had already arrived. However, the sacred pitcher was not ready. He asked the old man, "Where have you been for such a long time? Where is the mango twig?"

The old man looked at Sarbeswar once and then at Ramprasan and then bowed his head. He said, "I moved around the house. Every twig is laden with mango blossoms. Which branch should I have broken? If you ask me to bring leaves, I can bring them immediately. But... say whatever you will... this time plenty of mango blossoms have appeared...only if they can survive."

Ramprasan flew into a rage. "Here comes the greatest tree-lover!" He asked Sarbeswar to wait a little and went out himself to arrange a mango twig.

After Ramprasan disappeared, Sarbeswar asked the old man, "Why did you not search a little longer? Your master turned angry."

The old man answered without emotion, "I searched for it, *baboo*, but I didn't find one anywhere. If someone asks me to pick one up from the ground, I will immediately do so. My master has gone out himself. Let him come back. How will we break the branch when it is full of bloosoms? Do the blossoms have fewer enemies? Dew, wind... in addition there is man..."

Sarbeswar fell silent. From whom was he hearing such things? From a poor old man who worked in someone else's house for a paltry sum of fifty or hundred rupees! However, those who were educated to save the forests of this country, those who received training, and those who received salary to save the forest thoughtlessly felled trees each day and each night and supplied these to others outside. Sarbeswar was eager to leave before Ramprasan returned. He realized that he could never ever make the proposal in the presence of this tree-loving old man.

Sarbeswar met Ramprasan on the way, near the elevated road. Ramprasan was returning with a big mango twig in his hand. The old man had told the truth. Among the leaves, he found hundreds of mango blossoms, pressed against each other. Ramprasan had callously broken the branch which the old man had found impossible to break.

Sidharth felt sad listening to Sarbeswar. He said, "Sarbeswar, there is no need of reading a lot or receiving much training if you want to love someone. The hymn that the soil of the country teaches is not available in any English book."

In Memory of the Toilers of the Earth

About two years ago, a huge market complex was being constructed exactly in the middle of the city. A renowned contractor was given the contract of this enormous project involving crores of rupees. Every day, more than two hundred workers slogged there.

At times, I would keep looking at the figures of these hard-working coolies. When I had nothing else to do, I would look at them vacantly out of the window. In my mind, I developed a relationship with those unknown people.

Throughout the day, they would work with great pleasure and interest. They would move from one end to the other of that half-finished building carrying cement, sand, bricks and iron-rods till darkness descended. Using the bamboo scaffolding built around the structure, they would climb up swiftly, carrying cement or brick-filled containers. The building was very tall. Besides, one could not always trust the bamboo-scaffolding. If one's foot slipped, one would sustain grave injuries. However, while handing over container filled with sand or cement to each other on the swaying bamboo scaffolding, they would exchange jokes with each other. The mason would say something now and then. The female coolie would turn around flashing a quick smile while the male-coolie would laugh loudly while climbing down.

I would watch for hours the house rising from the ground through the window, from the safe confines of my house. The male coolies and female coolies would be standing on the bamboo scaffolding in tiers. The coolie on the ground would pass the container containing the sand-cement mixture to the coolie on the first tier; the coolie on the first tier would pass it on to the coolie on the next tier; finally, the coolie on the last tier would pass it on to the mason. While working, they would sing a few lines of a song just to cope with the fatigue.

In the evening, a complete change would come over their dejected, sweaty, and hardworking appearance. On one side of that half-constructed building, lived the masons and coolies. They would wash themselves clean first. Then, they would light their own fire. Rice or curry would be cooked on the *chullah*; the men would be lost in a friendly talk. During certain evenings, some young coolie would display his virtuosity by playing the *dholak* whereas some other coolie would play the flute challenging him. They would place bets. The one who won would be honoured and become the cynosure of all eyes. Everybody would praise him. The honour and respect was sufficient for the one who won the bet. Were the secret smiles of the female coolies less attractive than money or medals?

The construction of the building continued for many days; in fact, for more than a year. Some of the two hundred workers and masons working there grew acquainted with me. Even I knew those who sold vegetables, betels and *biris* in the vicinity. Especially, one of them had become a little closer to me. His name was Karuni, a pathetic derivative of his full name, Karunakar Samantray. Karuni's history was also a very pathetic one. However, he cared two hoots for the past. He never reminisced about the time when he had owned a house and landed property. At present, he had only one identity; he was a coolie. His job was to carry sand and cement mixture and obey the orders of the mason.

The construction of that huge building came to an end one day after more than a year. Once it looked like a dome of iron rods, bricks and cement; it looked attractive after the white washing was done. The building was inaugurated in the presence of engineers, contractors, high-level officials, state minister and cabinet ministers. Red ribbon was cut; *sandeshes* were distributed; and photos were clicked. Everybody danced in joy.

I was on my way to the bazzar along that road. When I watched the inauguration ceremony, I thought Karuni and his friends might not be there anymore. They had occupied the building till the construction was over, but now the construction work was completed. Now, it would be inhabited by bureaucrats.

The next day, I chanced upon Karuni in the market. He had gone there to pay what he owed to the shopkeeper. I asked him, "Arey, Karuni. The building was inaugurated yesterday, but why were you not present during the ceremony?"

Karuni only laughed, displaying some of his betel-stained teeth. He wanted to inform me, through that smile, "We have already completed our job. What do we have to do with the inauguration?"

'Where will you go now? Will you stay here?"

Karuni answered, "We feel a sense of belonging to the place as we had been staying here for the last one year. We know that we will never stay at one place. We will go to different places to construct buildings and build bridges. If we stay at one place, who will build other houses?"

I could quite comprehend the uncommon philosophy hidden behind his matter-of-fact answer. I suddenly remembered Karuni's most intimate friend, Raimani. Raimani was a female coolie who had joined them recently. Jokingly I asked, "Where will Raimani go?"

Karuni looked solemn. Then he replied, "How will I know where she is? She will go with her mason wherever she wants to."

'What about you?"

"I am going outside the state this time. There, we will be given better wages. Besides, I have no parents, not even a wife or children."

I could feel the desire for love stirring in Karuni.

But, where will Karuni go?

"I will go to Punjab, *baboo*. I have heard that the Yamuna-Sutlej canal is being dug. A rich contractor will take us there. The work will continue for many days."

Many days had gone by in the meantime. I had forgotten both Karuni and Raimani. I had no idea where they would be and what they would be doing. But, the newspaper report brought back their memory to me. Thirty Odia workers were shot dead by militants – this news alarmed me. What a great distance separated Odisha and Dhara Kamjat village of Punjab. They had embraced death while working on the Sutlej-Yamuna canal.

Was Karuni among them? Maybe or maybe not. No matter who they all were, they were like Karuni. They all sought love; they were innocent like children. They had migrated to another part of the country, putting their lives at risk, just to earn more money.

I had been thinking about only one thing since reading the news. What promise did the world hold out for people like Karuni? Hard-working men like Karuni work for years together constructing buildings and *bunds*, putting their lives at risk. The foundation stone carries the names of some minister or some engineer. Maybe, the name of the contractor and his firm and their address are written down below. However, no one remembers people like Karuni. No one cares whether they die or remain alive after the work. Throughout their life, they move from one place to another. They move from town to town, constructing buildings for others; but these unfortunate people can't even build a hut with a thatched roof for them. They build the *bunds* of rivers and canals, but they can't own even an inch of land.

Intimate Grief

Minu, unlike on other days, didn't come out today. Throughout the day, she had been looking at the road out of the upper-storey window. At times, she would fix her gaze on the house opposite hers. Nobody lived there now; the people who had occupied it, had left in the morning.

The song of a koel came floating in from a nearby mango tree. Such a small black bird; how intoxicating and enticing her song was! Had it been some other day, Minu would have jumped, even without fully making out the meaning of the song. But today, she wasn't interested in anything. What had happened to her?

Minu shifted to this house of the colony about six months ago. For the last six months, in this unfamiliar colony, Kunmun was her only friend. While shifting a house, elderly people worry about the rent of the house, water and electricity, and the distance of the new place from the office and the bus-stand. But they hardly care for the needs of small people like Minu. Elderly people hardly find any time to find out if there is a playground for children or if the child would find friends to play with.

Minu was fortunate because she found Kunmun as soon as she reached there. Kunmun's father didn't have a big job; he didn't own a car. But why should Minu care! They had grown close over the last six months. When the clock struck four, Minu would call Kunmun from the upper floor window; Kunmun would yell from the other side. Both of them would play together till evening, after which they would return to each other's homes.

Kunmun would not now come back; this morning her father took her away in a rickshaw. The household articles were carried in a matador. Kunmun was sitting in the middle, with her parents sitting on either side of her. When Kunmun waved her hand to say bye-bye, nobody knew what happened; Minu suddenly rushed inside.

Father came to Minu's study. He asked, "Why have you grown so absentminded these days? In the morning you forgot to carry your water bottle to school; while returning from there, you forgot your eraser and pencil. You are only interested in games and sports; you aren't at all interested in your studies."

Minu could hear nothing. She asked, "Papa, do you know Kunmun's new address?"

Father was startled. Mohapatrababu had lived here for only six months; he had invited Minu's father many times to come to his house. But, he intentionally avoided him as he lay several steps down the social ladder. This was exactly why he had not cared to collect his new address.

Minu said she had got two toffees for Kunmun. "Will you please take me to her house? I don't have any friends here. Kunmun was saying they had many small children at the new place. With whom will I play here?"

Father lifted the child to his lap. He pressed the child's palms, which were as soft as flowers, on his bearded cheeks.

For the first time in his life, he was feeling miserable for his inability to fulfill the child's demand. What could cause more grief to a child like Minu than losing her friend?

After many years, the memory of a grief he had experienced in his childhood got reflected in Minu's. Most children in the city faced the same problem. If a sapling is uprooted again and again while it was spreading its roots, it can call no soil its own. Similarly, a child loses all his friends and a sense of belonging to the area if he is shifted from one place to another in quick succession. . This type of shock sucks away the child's emotions and sensitivity, rendering him emotionless. In this respect, the children living in the villages have more freedom. There is a dearth of colourful dresses no doubt, but there exists a close circle of friends. Those friends, those *gohiris* and jamun trees, the temples and mathas always give company. They hold the child's hands and help him move past his childhood.

To get rid of Minu's trouble, her father was trying to listen to the song of the koel, but the koel had disappeared. Father looked once at the mango tree and once at the deserted house and appeared forlorn. While pulling Minu towards his lap, he was found saying, "Man's life is beset with problems; you will understand these only when you grow up."

Invitation

Raicharan frequently looked at his wrist watch. He had spent three hours in the meantime; there was no sign of the crowd dispersing. Old as he was, it was not possible for him to push his way through the crowd, upto the dining table. Once again he craned his neck to look at his destination and sat leaning against his chair.

Raicharan had never come to any reception in Bhubaneswar. Such feasts were not good for his health. He had already grown old; his body could not stand food eaten at unscheduled hours. In addition, one had to cope with the crowd. Raicharan usually preferred to send a letter or money order. But, he had to come here. Mukund Prasad was a former colleague of his. Both of them worked in the same office for ten years. Later, Mukund Prasad joined an All-India service, outstripping fifty or sixty of his colleagues. Had he not come to the marriage of his son, it would have looked odd. Mukund Prasad's children were like his own children. There might be inconveniences but who cared.

The crowd was a little denser here. When a feast is organized at the residence of such *baboos*, a crowd gathers for various reasons. All the acquaintances unfailingly arrive;

there is no escape from them. The distant relations also don't forget to come. A different set of people is found in Bhubaneswar. When children of ministers, engineers, commissioners, secretaries and other such people get married, they arrive uninvited and extend all possible co-operation.

Raicharan had been observing the arrival and departure of such guests since six o' clock. Gradually, the swelling crowd had taken the shape of the Maghasaptami crowd that came for a holy dip. All kinds of people came—single or in pairs. Many men arrived accompanied by their beautiful wives. Ladies who looked like fashion queens arrived with their children, spreading the beauty of *Phalguna* with their lipstick-covered lips. College-going young men and women, moved about the lawn saying 'hello-hey' to each other. The peons of the office where Mukund Prasad worked before retirement, were found discussing the result of the just-concluded election for the state legislature, chewing betel cones. On one side, a group of English-medium students was found praising Kapil Dev, while denouncing the self-righteous ways of Bishen Singh Bedi. A fat lady, laden with at least one and a half kilo of imitation jewellery, was lavishing praise on her parents at every opportunity. Some other guests were enjoying 'Chitragiti,' on the screen of the colour television. Some others felt elated to hear the Hindi song 'Hawa…hawa' that the cassette recorder was blaring.

The rest of the guests were like Raicharan. They frequently looked at their watches and waited. Three hours had passed in the meantime; but Raicharan had not met either Mukund Prasad or his children. Perhaps Mukund Prasad's children were present somewhere there, but he was not able to recognize them. However, Mukund Prasad himself should have moved around the place. Perhaps that was not possible owing to the crowd. Raicharan had grown weary answering his own questions.

Raicharan also noticed that the guests carried big packets with them. They would proceed towards the room where the bride sat, carrying the packets wrapped in red paper. Two or three young ladies welcomed the packets there. Raicharan moved his fingers on his breast-pocket to make sure that the packet was there. Yes, the fifty rupee note lay safe inside the envelope.

A loud sound emanated from the dining room. Perhaps another batch had just finished taking their dinner. The guests around Raicharan stirred. Raicharan also proceeded towards the dining hall.

Someone gave him a hard push. A group of people wanted to go through the narrow passage leading to the dining hall. The people from the dining hall also moved towards the narrow passage, with their unwashed hands raised higher. Perhaps someone lost his balance and fell on Raicharan. His hand soiled Raicharan's shirt.

This time, too, Raicharan failed to occupy a seat. Raicharan had faced the same situation three times already that evening. Once again, he had to return to the 'Chitragiti,' discussion of politics, repetition of songs like 'hawa-hawa' or 'eik-do-tin'.

Raicharan managed to secure a seat in the dining hall at ten thirty, after a long and wearisome wait. The leftover food lying on the table had been hardly cleaned, when the next batch of people sat to take their dinner. The plate was placed on leftover fish bones. The glasses carrying water had become oily. Raicharan felt annoyed. "Fie! Fie! The man has no manners; it matters little how affluent he is." The shoving and jostling forced Raicharan to think perhaps hungry dogs, and not human beings, sat on the chairs, donning trousers and shirts. Those who served them were no less savage; perhaps they were averse to bending. They almost threw to the plate some *kanika*, a few pieces of potato, and a little *sag*. They were unconcerned whether the potato fell on someone's face or if the sauce used in the fish curry stained someone's glasses. Some distance away sat some so-called *baboos*. Their children sat on the front benches. There, the situation was a little better.

The child who sat on Raicharan's left side was asking for some water. The glasses were there but they didn't contain any water. The boy who was serving said, "The tanker has run out of water; drink some after you reach home." What a brilliant suggestion! By the time they had finished eating, another group was found rushing in from the lawn. To escape from the stampede, Raicharan got up and went away from the spot. If someone had watched him, he would have reminded him of a dog running away, its tail between its legs, just to protect itself from an impending calamity.

The time to return home arrived but he had not met Mukund Prasad yet. He must be busy somewhere. Otherwise, would not he have met him even once since evening? He thought of sending the gift of fifty rupees through someone else. There was no way to find out who was an acquaintance and who was not. He put the thought out of his mind and came out to the road. The exhaustion from waiting since evening, the uncomfortable feeling of having dined at an odd hour, and the cold reception accorded to him had completely worn him out. Besides, he had to return to the village the very next morning.

Raicharan was reminded that the previous year Pari Behera had invited him to the marriage of his daughter.

On the morning of the marriage, he had sent his elder son to invite him. Towards the evening, he himself came to invite him to the dinner. He frequently requested him not to cook anything that evening. Finally, in the evening, he almost dragged Raicharan to his house. While the food was being served, Pari Behera's sons stood nearby. The elder daughter of Pari served fried yam and banana. He didn't have enough money; how would he cook chicken or mutton? He had caught some fish from his pond. He managed with those. Fine rice, dal, fried yam and banana, and a little fish curry; that was enough for his daughter's marriage. By the time Raicharan got up from his seat to wash his hand, Paria himself stood there with a towel in his hand; he led him to the water tank. While he handed the towel, his grandson stood there with betel cones. Raicharan felt touched by the way Paria had looked after him.

Raicharan wondered if he should meet Mukund Prasad and tell him about Pari Behera's feast. That poor Pari Behera had perhaps mixed something with that fine rice and fish curry, so that the food tasted like ambrosia. Would he disclose the secret? Would he tell Mukund Prasad why despite his display of wealth and grand arrangements, his guests appeared nothing better than a group of dogs licking plates?

No. Mukund Prasad would never understand this. Raicharan departed through the gate decorated with red and blue lights, just as unnoticed as when he had arrived.

■

Is the Minister Homeless?

Felu stayed with his parents in his village and read in class two of the village primary school. He was seven years of age. There were no pucca roads leading to his village. There was no electricity. From the market to the outskirts of the village ran the river embankment. That embankment prevented flood water from entering the village and was used as a road. This year the flood came four times and ripped through the embankment at seven places. Felu was sad thinking that he would not be able to wear the pair of red shoes his father had purchased for him after repeated requests.

Sidharth met Felu all of a sudden. Felu's uncle was Sidharth's neighbour. Felu was on a visit to Puri with his parents. They came to Bhubaneswar from there. Felu's father had collected many things in the meantime. Those included a grinding stone, an aluminum vessel, and a biscuit tin-container. Felu's father was a little heavy. When the couple sat in the rickshaw with their belongings, the rickshaw-puller looked apprehensive. Where was the space for Felu to sit? When Felu's uncle Brahmanand noticed that Sidharth was ready to leave for office, he requested him to drop Felu at the bus-stop.

It was not a problem for him to give Felu a ride; the problem was the lack of time. No matter how slowly he moved, his two-wheeler was surely going to reach faster than the tricycle. Can he wait for such a long time at the bus stand? Sidharth was going to explain his problem. But, Felu had already started climbing on to the seat. Within the last two days, he had grown close to Felu. An inquisitive child, he was keen on knowing everything. He asked thousands of questions like why the sky was blue, why that building was tall, why school children here wore dresses having similar colours, why trains and buses cannot run on the same road. Sidharth liked to hear Felu's questions. He was going to go back to his village. He may not meet him again; it would be better if he dropped him at the bus-stand.

Felu sat on the pillion. Sidharth said, "Hold on to my tummy. We will go slowly, but you may fall at the humps."

Felu immediately asked, "What are humps?" Sidharth smiled. Sidharth answered his question. On the way, they came across 'Raj Bhavan'. When Felu saw the huge gates, he asked, "Whose is this huge house?"

"The Governor's."

When Felu saw the sentries posted near the gates, he asked, "What are they doing here?" "They are guarding the house." Felu proposed, "Let's go and meet the governor."

Sidharth was taken aback. He had never entered the Governor's residence. What did clerks like him have to do there? In order to evade the proposal he said, "The Governor isn't there today. He has gone on tour."

The cunning Felu immediately shot back, "Who are the police guarding then? Why aren't they going home?"

Sidharth didn't answer this question. After the traffic roundabout, there were government quarters on both sides of the road. These were residences of government officers and ministers. Felu once again asked, "Whose are these houses?"

Sidharth answered, "These are government bungalows."

Felu again asked, "Who lives here?"

Sidharth absentmindedly answered, "Ministers live here."

Felu was taken by surprise. He was so surprised that he took his hands away from Sidharth's tummy. Sidharth, while applying the brakes, asked, "What happened? Why did you take your hands away?"

Felu's eyes were still filled with surprise. He asked, "Are the ministers homeless?"

For a long time, a truck was running ahead of Sidharth's scooter. He increased the speed of the scooter in anger and overtook the truck.

Felu was not a child who was going to remain silent. He repeated his question, "Government gives homes to those who don't have homes. Doesn't the minister have a home?"

Sidharth was unsure as to what answer he would give. Felu's innocent mind might not have understood the answer to his question. He could never have told Felu, "The written law says that houses should be provided to those who don't have houses. In spirit, that law is not followed. Those who have one or two or three or even four houses, are allotted government quarters. Well-to-do people like officers, doctors, engineers, and professors take loan from the government, build houses with this money, and rent out the house to different organizations but live in houses allotted by the government.

Felu pinched Sidharth on his back and asked, "Why don't you answer my question? Don't the ministers have houses?"

Sidharth was now thinking about himself. He had spent almost six years in Bhubaneswar. He couldn't arrange any quarters for himself. Many days ago, he had submitted an application requesting allotment of quarters in his favour. The application was misplaced three times; so, he decided to forget about it. For the last five years, he had been living in a rented two-roomed house at Gandamunda, at a monthly rent of nine hundred rupees. After nine hundred rupees went towards rent from a clerk's salary, it was very difficult to manage household expenses with the remaining amount. Who will he request? The condition of Felu's uncle was even worse. He was an O.F.S. officer; however, he was not able to arrange any quarters for himself.

Felu perhaps wanted to ask his question once again. By chance, a brand new car with a red beacon on top passed by. Felu forgot his old question and asked a new one, "Whose is this vehicle?"

Sidharth was going to say 'minister's' but he stopped abruptly. He knew that the moment he gave this answer, Felu would remember his earlier question and pester him with, "Does not a minister have a house of his own?" Since Sidharth didn't know whether the minister had any houses or not; or why the officers or ministers occupied houses despite having their own houses, he preferred to remain silent.

Felu's unanswered question ran ahead of Sidharth and blocked his path. Sidharth thought, if the rickshaw carrying Felu's parents arrived a little early, he would get respite from such questions.

Modern Kalapahads

If Sidharth had known that the guide of the tourist bus would be so punctual, he would rather have gone on the journey at his own convenience. Sidharth feels uncomfortable at this type of inflexible discipline while meeting friends, going on a journey, and watching a song and dance programme. However, it was not known where the punctual guide had suddenly vanished. If he had allowed them more time at Agra, they would have felt happy; what were they going to see here? Sitting for an hour looking at the Taj Mahal was a dream he had cherished for years. But, the guide had passed a strict order. "You have to return to the bus within fifty minutes (not even an hour); otherwise the bus will leave. You will have to make your own arrangements to return home."

Sidharth had felt angry with the guide even before reaching the Taj Mahal. The history of Agra Fort that he had narrated in poor English and rustic Hindi, even the history professor would not have any knowledge of it. The imaginative flights of the person deserved appreciation. When he directed everybody to return within thirty minutes after going through the Agra Fort, Sidharth lost his patience. Three-fourths of the Fort was under the control of the army, and hence, it had been closed to the general public. A minimum of two hours was needed to tour the remaining one-fourth of it. Was it like to going through an album, where one turned the pages quickly? Consequently, all one did was enter the fort and come out of it.

However, that punctual guide suddenly vanished somewhere after reaching Brindavan. When they reached the Balgopal temple, another group of tourists was sitting in front of the image. In obedience to a rule in Brindavan, no tourist keeps standing while paying obeisance to the lord. The devotees have to sit on the ground while having a *darshan* of the lord, lest his shadow should fall on the lord. Since the earlier group of tourists had not come out of the temple by the time Sidharth's group reached there, the guide immediately thought of a plan to keep them busy and asked them to sing *bhajans*. What else could be done? For twenty minutes, Sidharth repeated "*Govind Jay Jay, Gopal Jay Jay*" in tune with the guide.

They had been sitting in front of the image of Balgopal for more than half an hour now. It was eight o' clock. By the time they reached Delhi, it would never be earlier than eleven pm. But, where was the guide? Since the time of singing the *bhajans*, he was nowhere to be seen.

Sidharth only waited for time to pass. He was tired, annoyed and angry. Whatever the guide had told them about the glory of this place, both the priests of the temple were repeating. However, they were frequently stressing one thing—they should make a donation to the temple. If the devotees wanted, they could inscribe the names of their parents on slabs of marble, making a donation of one hundred and fifty rupees. They also frequently said that one could donate anything in excess of five hundred rupees to feed the widows. Some of the interested people made some donations; others sat silently as they were not prepared to make a donation. But, the priests would not let them go. It was announced earlier that no devotee would leave the premises without receiving *'prasad'*; it would be against the tradition of the place. The religious as well as the god-fearing people sat there waiting for *'prasad'* to be distributed.

Incensed by the attitude of the two priests, a woman from West Bengal started protesting. She told the priests, "You have already talked about giving contributions about seven or eight times. We have heard everything. Those who had money with them have already made their contributions. Others will do whatever is possible on their part after returning home. Kindly allow us to go home."

Quite unpredictably, the two priests became angry even before the lady had finished talking. Remarks like, "How dare you talk like this despite being a lady?" reminded Sidharth of the behavior of the *pandas* at Puri in his own state. Within a few minutes, the soft emotions arising in him evaporated. Some tourists supported the woman and registered their protest. But, this protest was very faint in comparison with the aggression displayed by the two priests.

Brundavan is considered the best place of pilgrimage in Vaishnabite literature and Hindu culture. The exquisite images of the temple remind us of the concept of ideal family consisting of father-mother and brother-sister. Sidharth felt distressed at the way a female tourist was treated in the premises of such a glorious temple. Kalapahad, the iconoclast, had destroyed the Hindu temples and images, ironically increasing the importance of these monuments. But who would get rid of the base and mean fellows who now infest the places sacred to Hindus?

The Key to Happiness

Sidharth was busy gazing at the *kadamba* trees growing on the other side of the road when Nilalohit appeared on the scene. His face resembled the overcast sky of *Shravan*; it was as if a small question would open the floodgate of tears.

Sidharth was in no mood to listen to the complaints of Nilalohit so early in the morning. The dew drops still lay on the leaves of the *kadamba* tree like drops of perfume. He just wanted to relish this *Margasira* morning to his heart's content.

Nilalohit could not keep his impatience in check. Without being asked, he started on his own, "It's not possible on my part to compromise any longer. I don't like the bickering and arguments every day. She is progressing rapidly in her career, but I'm not able to concentrate because of the lack of peace."

Sidharth knew pretty well that Nilalohit's complaints were directed at his professor wife, Chaitali. As both husband and wife worked, they were financially secure. Theirs was a love marriage. Both of them were contemporaries; they were intelligent, too. They shifted to the colony when the construction of their house was completed about a year ago. Everything had passed off quite well, until a year ago, when some rift cropped up. The chasm had grown so wide that Nilalohit didn't hesitate to complain about the impossibility of living together any longer.

Had Sidharth not known Chaitali at all, he could have blamed her; but he knew her quite well. Her father was a former colleague of him. He somehow felt that the problem lay with Nilalohit. A dominating person by nature, Nilalohit's expectations were unlimited. He craved to attain a lot within a short span of time. Of course, there was no dearth of hard work and sincere effort on his part. However, at times, the desired goal eluded him. Another problem with him was that he judged everything keeping himself at the centre. He wished to be opposed by none.

Sidharth was reminded of a speech of the Dalai Lama. Without being worked up, he said, "Nilalohit, you think that the solution to your problems lies outside your home. That's why you are searching for it outside. But the truth is that, it is lying very well inside your house, not outside. Yesterday someone asked the Dalailama, 'What is the biggest trouble the world is facing now?' In reply he said, 'There is a famine of emotions and a drought of compassion.' 'What is the remedy for this?' In answer to the second question he said, 'Every human being who wishes peace to prevail in the world should love his family; adore his children; treat his wife or husband with an abundance of love and affection; and treat his parents with respect. This is how peace will surely be established in this world."

Sidharth felt as if Nilalohit was a little shaken.

Sidharth added, "I had read it somewhere that delusion gives rise to jealousy. This delusion, that grips us at some point or another, tells us that the person we are jealous of is quite happy; his life is extremely successful; and his family experiences an abundance of bliss. I know you for a very long time. You are extremely intelligent, no doubt, but you are argumentative. But, can arguments solve all problems? You yourself have confessed many times that Chaitali, on losing arguments, would apologize without any inhibitions. I guess, she must be accepting defeat at times without really being vanquished. This is ample proof that she gives more importance to her relationship with you than to her ego. During the sixty long years of my life, I have realized that no new relationship can compensate for the lost one. A newfound relationship with the richest person can't compensate for the relationship with the poor childhood friend. You must have met many notable people lost in the equations of such relationships in hotels, clubs and coffee-houses."

Nilalohit responded, "If Chaitali opened her mind and heart to me, I would understand what went on there; but if she kept everything a secret, how would I understand her feelings."

Sidharth said, "If you don't accuse me of speaking in favour of Chaitali, I will tell you something. The truth is that a woman, who is not telling anything, or not making unreasonable demands, deserves everything, and deserves more than what you can give. To find access to her feelings, you have to remain silent at times. I am reminded of the Dalai Lama once again. He says, 'If we continuously keep talking, we'll repeat only those things that we already know. Instead, if we keep mum and listen to another, maybe we'll get to know something better.' What is true for our social life is also true for our family."

"But by nature, I have been very restless since childhood. I prefer to say things to people to their face," said Nilalohit.

Sidharth returned his gaze to the *kadamba* tree once again. In the meantime, two birds had descended on the middle branches. One of them seemed to be telling something to the other; and the latter was listening intently, just as a disciple listens to a Guru's words of wisdom, with a pleasing countenance.

Sidharth said, "You told me once that a human child took only two years to learn the art of speaking, but the entire life was insufficient to learn what sort of talk was appropriate for which occasion."

Nilalohit was going to say something, when Annapurna came out and said, "Arey! Nilalohit. When did you come? Shall I make tea for you?"

Nilalohit wasn't interested in having tea. He appeared crestfallen as he didn't derive the satisfaction that he had expected from his discussion with Sidharth.

Nilalohit said, "Aunty, I'm getting late. Maybe next time I'll have tea."

"Next time when you come, bring Chaitali with you. You two always discuss things; wouldn't we spend some time together?"

"Do I refuse her anything? She is always reluctant to go anywhere except home and office," Nilalohit said complainingly.

"Don't talk like that. When you came to the colony for the first time, she gave you a pillion ride on her scooty. You might have forgotten but I haven't," said Annapurna smiling.

Nilalohit was going to say something but he was distracted by the mobile ringing. He found Chaitali's name on the screen. Before answering the phone, he looked at Sidharth and said, "I am barely away for half an hour. She phones and tries to find out where I am."

Sidharth patted Nilalohit on the shoulder and said, "You are fortunate, Nilalohit. I know hundreds of people who wait for a phone call from home but it doesn't come at all."

Nilalohit gave a startled look to Sidharth. Sidharth was now looking at the tree. The discussion of the two birds sitting on the *kadamba* tree was still not over.

Known Man, Unknown Voice

Some "poor men" had been listening intently to the 'brown sahib' who had forgotten his mother tongue, either intentionally or unintentionally, owing to his long stay in a foreign country. During his discussions, he expressed a deep sense of reverence for the life style maintained in the 'States,' the vision of its people, and their values while expressing a deep sense of regret and revulsion at the system of Indian administration, education, and the vision of the people. The conclusion he drove at was that no civilized human being could ever prosper in this country.

About twenty or twenty-five years ago, the gentleman left for a foreign country for higher studies after completing his medical education in Odisha. He was able to arrange the required amount through generous contributions of some charitable people and organizations of Odisha. Before leaving for America, he had sought their good wishes and blessings and promised to come back to Odisha to serve its poor people. Many people did not remind themselves of the fact that not only the political leaders of the country but also the worthy, intelligent and highly educated masses of this country had mastered the art of forgetting their promises.

The gentleman had accepted the citizenship of that country. His children were the students of posh schools in America. The gentleman had long forgotten Odisha, his riverside village in Odisha, the angry look of the headmaster of his village primary school, the greenery of the fields of rice, the colour of *kainchakoli*, the taste of *pakhala* and *badichura*, and all those fond memories associated with village life. Before his eyes danced the dazzling sights of New York City, and the gorgeous things associated with the smart society there. The gentleman seemed to have no emotions but only motion.

He was talking about the work culture at the schools, colleges, banks and hospitals, the wealth of the people, as well as their punctuality, sense of responsibility and discipline. Odisha presented to him a pathetic picture of poverty and exploitation, exemplified through Kalahandi. The gentleman was expressing sympathy, unasked. He was expressing surprise saying, "Can human beings live here in these conditions?"

Sidharth felt as if someone slapped him very hard on his face. Who was he hearing all these from? Who was saying all these? Sidharth would not have reacted if some American or British person had said such things. What hurt him was the fact that the gentleman who was shedding crocodile tears for Odisha and its three crore people was also an Odia, a son of the soil.

Sidharth remembered that government servants who lived in Bhubaneswar or Cuttack expressed similar sympathy, from a safe distance, for the simple and poor people who lived in villages. There is no English Medium school there, no electricity, no piped water, and no latrines.

There are no roads; no buses ply on those roads; the buses don't have any proper seats. There are no sophisticated markets selling expensive commodities; the schools do not have teachers; the hospitals have no doctors, no cotton, no gauge cotton, no medicines. It is a never never land." Doctors on getting transferred don't go there; the lecturers don't go there; neither the ministers nor the engineers nor the administrators go there. All of them reside either at Bhubaneswar or Cuttack or Puri or Rourkella and distribute favours from there, and even shed crocodile tears in the newspapers, just as this 'brown sahib' was doing after staying for a few years in America.

Sidharth wanted to say, "Sir, who had made you worthy of higher education in America? Did the affluence of New York and London make you worthy? Was not the amount of more than one lakh that was spent in making you a medical graduate, spent from the ever-empty treasury of this poor Odisha? Who had paid you the money that was required to send you to the States? Some loving individuals and charitable organizations. You promised to them that you would return after receiving higher education. Did not you promise to serve those who are dying, those who are afflicted with incurable diseases, and those who suffer in the absence of qualified doctors? However, you don't remember all those today. Why are you, then, displaying sympathy for us by pointing at our poverty, when you have come on a two-day vacation?"

Sidharth wondered why such things ever happened. Why all worthy young men from villages lived in the city and all worthy Indians left for foreign countries? Why do they return once every year or every two years or every five or ten years as if on a picnic and show their sympathy for the village that had helped them grow up? Why do they hate the same Odisha which made them engineers or doctors by spending money that could have been spent on a more meaningful project?

Kuber's Store-house of Treasure

After sitting down in the chair, the man looked here and there for a while and then, rested his weary limbs. He hesitated to sit on a soft, cushioned chair in a room lit up by bright lights and fans rotating overhead. The scorching sunbeams of *Bhadrab* and the salty breeze had turned his dark skin rough. His face was covered with stubble; only a wisp of hair decorated his forehead. Grit drenched in tear stuck to the corners of his eyes. Just to give him an opportunity to settle down, Sidharth turned his eyes away from him and started scribbling something on a piece of paper lying on the table.

"Tell me," Sidharth comforted him, "I am not that busy today. There's plenty of time at hand."

The man belonged to Astarang. His son worked in a motor company as a driver. His village was vulnerable to floods. He owned two acres of land. The data gave more satisfaction than real benefits. The entire family depended on his son. The son was married. He had four children. Three years back, the son died in an accident. As the only earning member died, the family was in great distress. The words emerging from old man's throats were smothered in sobs.

"No, no. Don't cry. Tell me how we can help you." Sidharth felt pity for the old man who had lost his child.

From inside a grubby cloth-bag, the old man took out a bundle of papers. The papers were copies of applications. The daughter-in-law should have got some money from Life Insurance Company after the death of the son. Although more than two and a half years had passed, they had received no money. His son was working in a motor company. If the company people didn't get the papers ready, the life insurance people would not pay any money. The old man asked, "Will you please publish this in your newspaper? If the government turns its face away, who would take care of poor people like us? The government owns the motor company; the life insurance company also belongs to the government. They should settle the matter between them. I am an unlettered person; tell me, how many times I will run from pillar to post with the daughter-in-law."

Sidharth took the papers from the old man and went through them. The life insurance people were not able to settle the claim due to the lackadaisical attitude of the O.R.T company. He wanted to tell the old man that the motor company belonged to the state government whereas the life insurance company belonged to the central government. Both of them were different organizations. But, he didn't say anything. The idea that the old man had harboured in his heart was not such a foolish one. In his opinion, government was an alternative to God. Certain things in this world belonged to God; and the rest belonged to the government.

Sidharth took another look at the papers. He kept a copy of the paper so that he could publish a news item in his newspaper. He assured the old man, "We shall surely publish the news. Something will certainly be done. You may leave now."

The old man kept looking at Sidharth's face. Perhaps, he thought of saying something more. Sidharth asked, "Do you want to say anything more?" The old man had fallen silent; he was not getting up from the chair.

After some time he said, "Son, I am an old man. I don't know anything about the newspapers. How much money will be required for the purpose?"

"Money? What money?" Sidharth was so shocked at the innocence of the old man that he could not control his laughter.

Notwithstanding Sidharth's objections, the old man was trying to take out a few crumpled notes from inside the pocket of his frequently-mended shirt. Sidharth got up and held his hand. He tried to explain to him that he was not doing him any favour. His was not asking him to publish an advertisement; it was news. No one has to pay money for this. The old man was insistent. He thought that, if he left without paying any money, the news might not see the light of day. Would his visit to the newspaper office be a fruitless one?

Sidharth didn't blame the old man. How would he know the difference between advertisement and a news item? How would he know for what he would have to pay, and which was a matter of right? For years, he had bribed everybody starting from the government or non-government officer to the peon of the peoples' representative. Everybody gnawed at the torn pocket of his frequently mended shirt or the knot of his shabby *dhoti*.

Innocent people like him form the majority of the population. No one had ever tried to explain to them their rights. They pay rent to till the land but everybody starting from the settlement officials to the R.I. collects money from them. They have to pay bribes to stand in a queue to buy kerosene or sugar. No one even writes an application for them without being paid bribes. Without bribes, the minister's peon doesn't allow the innocent villager to cross the gate; the lawyer stupefies his client with laws that go above his head; and the doctor disappears after cutting open the patient's stomach. Except sunlight and wind you will get here nothing if you don't pay bribes. This man has bribed everybody; the Kuber's storehouse of treasure has become completely drained, but the number of the greedy has not decreased.

The old man had left long ago. Till the end, he could not trust Sidharth. "Without money, nothing could be done in this world," was his lesson distilled from long experience. Some newspaper people might have accepted bribes from him in the past.

While sending the news item for that day's edition, Sidharth was thinking that the helpless old man symbolized Odisha.

Kulamani's Patriotism

Kulamani had a sense of humor and everyone found him entertaining. It's precisely for this, he not only kept his saloon neat and tidy but also brought new cassettes and played them on his tape recorder to entertain his customers. Besides, he ordered a weekly colour film magazine for his saloon. Kulamani did not know English; this was for the benefit of the customers. Just above the mirror, he placed huge posters of heroes and heroines of films so that the eyes of the customers waiting for a haircut would fall on them. Walls on three sides were already covered with their posters, just as the walls of Sri Ramachandra Bhawan were covered with the photos of littérateurs and famous persons.

Once Sidharth asked him, "You are spending so much on all this; how much would you be spending on watching films?"

Moving his fingers through his hair, Kulamani answered, "This is the only passion I have; what else could I do? Can people like me go on a tour or have meals in expensive restaurants, like the rich? All we can do to indulge ourselves is to spend rupees five or ten." After a pause he continued, "The pleasure that one derives from watching the first show of the film, can one derive the same pleasure from the second day's show? At times I can't leave work and make it to the first show. A few days ago, an excellent film was released but…"

Sidharth did not know when the saloon of Kulamani came up in the colony, which was situated on the outskirts of the city. The saloon was famous all around the colony as "Kula Saloon". It was so famous that a new resident of the colony would be compelled to think perhaps the saloon came up first, and then the colony did.

Kulamani's behavior exuded intimacy. Whenever he met a customer who had trimmed his hair somewhere else, he would shout, "Where did you spoil your hair?" Of course, nothing of this sort had happened; something could be done about the length of the hair or the parting. Such minute details never escaped Kulamani's eyes. He would ask someone else, "Did you pay a visit to your village? Why were not you seen for a long time?" For the young men, he always had a topic for discussion — films or cricket. He would be working with his scissors and razor but he would be continuously chattering. His prattle would come to an end only when the work was over and done with. The customer would have no knowledge of the passage of time. However, there was one topic which he never discussed—politics.

Sidharth had surrendered himself completely before Kulamani's scissors and razor. He was sitting with his head bent downwards. Kulamani had finished trimming the hair and was giving final touches with his razor. This was not the right time for a conversation. Sidharth was late in getting up that morning. If he did not reach office before ten thirty, the gates would be closed. So, he was not interested in talking much with Kulamani that day.

Kulamani, however, went on chattering while giving him a haircut. He went on talking on topics like how the mosquitoes of Bhubaneswar had proved more lethal than the mosquitoes of Cuttack; how the life of a man was ruined the moment he got married. Sidharth was responding to him with only 'hmm' at times.

When Sidharth raised his head, his eyes fell on a vacant spot on a wall. On both sides of it were posters; this would have been easily led the onlooker to guess that someone had taken away a poster from that place.

Sidharth asked, "Why has this space been kept vacant? Did the poster get torn?" Kulamani, with a faint smile, solemnly answered, "It did not get torn. I tore it up."

Sidharth fell silent seeing the expression of Kulamani's face. The day Kulamani was pasting the photograph of the cinestar on the wall of the saloon, by chance Sidharth was present there. That cinestar was a superstar and his popularity among young men and women was unsurpassable. Because he was associated with a scandal, his name had travelled from the pages of film magazines to the first pages of newspapers. But what might be the reason of such a great personality losing his hold over an uneducated barber like Kulamani? Sidharth asked, "Why did you remove that photo?"

This time, Kulamani's voice sounded strange. For a moment, Sidharth thought this was not Kulamani's voice; it was as if someone else was speaking.

Kulamani said, "Should I hang the photo of a person who is the enemy of the country?" Sidharth was awe-struck. No, Kulamani did not have anything more to say; he had said whatever he wanted to say. Sidharth argued, "Why did the idea come to your mind that he was a traitor? The case is still under trial."

"Let it be settled. If he turns out to be innocent, I will have two photos of him. I will hang one on this side and another on the other. But, not now."

Sidharth returned home after paying him. He had known this man for a long time but he felt as if he was getting to understand him for the first time.

Much noise is heard these days, about cinestars and pop singers, in the drawing rooms of the rich and the educated. Their popularity has dimmed the popularity of even national leaders. The day this cinestar was arrested under provisions of TADA, even Sidharth's college going younger brother had not desisted from abusing the government. However, what a deep sense of love the illiterate Kulamani had for the country; and what deep faith he had in the administrative system of the country!

Kulamani is never found among people who draw benefits when the country prospers. They are pushed to the corner, miles away from fame and brilliance. Such people protect the invisible soul of the country calling it 'my country'. Sidharth had not seen such intimacy in the cotton-Punjabi-clad and Gandhi-cap wearing obese leaders and political party workers.

Kulamani suddenly grew taller in the eyes of Sidharth.

Land Beyond Maps

Raicharan, completely drenched in sweat, was on his way back from Ghanteswar. He had to reach Kaduanasi soon. The sandy footpaths of Ghanteswar sizzled in the *Baisakh* sun. It was so hot that paddy, if thrown on the ground, would immediately turn into puffed rice. The shade of wayside trees provided some shelter to the pedestrians. Raicharan almost ran on the hot sand, hopping like a crane. From forehead to heels, he was completely covered with sweat. He carried a red towel on his shoulder. When he felt uncomfortable, he would wipe himself with it. He had left Kaduanasi far behind. Mantei ran in the middle. He had to climb into the boat wading through knee-deep mud. The boatman, Pagal Nayak, was truly insane. If he dozed off, after lunch, in the hut on the other bank of the river, the matter would end then and there. Even if the Governor came there, he would not care to respond. He would get up only after having slept to his heart's content. However, one would get respite from unnecessary trouble if the boat was moored to the bank on this side.

Raicharan quickened his steps. He owned a temporary book-stall in the Kacheribazzar of Bhadrak. Raicharan carried it and took it everywhere. The entire book-stall could be accommodated in two bags. The stall consisted of both big-sized and pocket editions of almanacs by Kohinoor, Radharaman and Biraja presses; books entitled *Khulana Sundari, Trinath Mela, Sanischara Mela, Bataosha, Khudurukuni Osha, Sabitri Brata, Gopalila* of Jagannath Das's *The Bhagavad, Jagannath Janan, Mrugunee Stutee, Dardhyata Bhakti*; books dealing with the effect of Zodiac signs; books dealing with sex; picture books for adults wrapped in yellow wrappers; and Odia calendars. Raicharan was both a whole-saler and retailer. His area of operation spread over most of Bhadrak town, starting from Charampa to Bhadrak. A Vaishnabite, he lived alone. He would often drape himself with a cloth with the hymns to Lord Ram written all over. A tattoo of Radha-Krishna was etched on his left hand. A simple look at him made one gauge his character. He was a poor but compassionate human being.

Raicharan belonged to Kaduanasi. At home, stayed his widowed mother. She was seventy-seven; just like a ripe palm fruit, only Lord Akhandalamani knew when she would drop. Raicharan found it hard to meet her frequently owing to his business commitments. He had no family. Since the day he was initiated into a *matha*, he had developed a sense of indifference to the world. Of course, he had not been able to give up his habit of consuming opium in the evening. He was a very noble human being. If people of his area wanted to travel to Cuttack, Bhubaneswar, Baleswar, or Kolkata, he would come out to help them. He would gladly arrange for them a seat in the bus, a stamp-vendor in the court, or a shopkeeper to supply necessities for a wedding. Almost everybody in that area knew Raicharan quite well.

Noticing his scamper and dishevelled appearance,

Mukund asked, "Uncle, why are you in such a great hurry? Is anybody seriously ill?"

Mukund alias Mukund Charan Mohanty was a ninth standard student of Aparti Charan High School. He had made acquaintance with Raicharan when he visited Draupadi cinema once or twice.

Raicharan answered, "What should I say, my son? In the morning, Nakhia Mahakud visited mother to supply cheese. It's from him that I learnt mother had become bed-ridden. It is as if thunder struck me! I got up immediately, and am going to meet her."

Mukund looked serious. Raicharan, usually, was very lively and humorous. Mukund was alarmed to see his sombre face and teary eyes. Raicharan was an old man. He had already travelled a long distance carrying a heavy bag. The distance between his residence and Rajgurupur was around five miles. It was so hot that walking even a few steps was getting difficult.

"Uncle, why don't you hand me the bag? I'll carry it for you for some distance…" Mukund stretched his hand to take the bag.

Raicharan objected, "No, no. You are a child. Walk comfortably. I'll get late."

Mukund was carrying two or three books. He was returning to Sandhagada after the morning school was over. He insisted, "Uncle, I can also walk fast like you. Give me the bag."

While handing the bag to Mukund, Raicharan said, "Please be careful, son. There are some sweets for mother in it. Old lady… She had been craving for sweets for long. I have brought some sweets for her. I have covered the mouth of the glass container securely. Be careful… the syrup might overflow."

"What else are you carrying home?" asked Mukund for the sake of keeping the conversation going.

"No, what else could I carry? What's my worth? I am carrying a bunch of grapes and some apples for mother. The old lady always longed to taste these fruits. Who knows in which state shall I find her?" Raicharan was found paying obeisance to invisible gods... praying for good health for his ill, bed-ridden mother, no doubt.

When they reached the Sandhagada pond, Mukund handed back the bag to Raicharan. Raicharan blessed him, "May you live long! May God grant you a long life!"

Raicharan ran towards Kaduanasi. Raicharan,a fifty year old man, was running like an eighteen year old boy, to meet his mother.

Standing beside the Sandhagada pond, Mukund stared in the direction in which Raicharan had disappeared. He was feeling thirsty. While he bent down to take a little water from the pond in his cupped palms, he saw that some syrup from the rasogallas had stained his pants. He rubbed it clean with water. The beardless tender youth, Mukund felt as if pent-up emotions choked his heart. He was reminded of Raicharan and his old mother; more than anything else, his mother's wishes and regrets. She wanted neither gold nor silver; neither bungalows nor delicious dishes; but only two *rasogollas*, a bunch of grapes, and a couple of apples. Mukund knew such fruits were not grown here. Raicharan ran home with a bunch of sour grapes and a couple of rasogollas that came from far off Madras or Kolkatta for sale in Bhadrak, just to be tasted by his mother before she died. This last wish of his mother was going to be fulfilled by her son, Raicharan. What else could be more important than this?

Didn't thousands of villages like Kaduanasi exist? Didn't

lakhs of helpless sons like Raicharan inhabit them? Didn't crores of helpless and old mothers like Raicharan's mother hanker for a few *rasogollas* and a bunch of grapes in India? Yes, they did and they belonged very much to India.

The geography book fell from the hands of the absentminded Mukund. Its pages fluttered in the *Baisakh* wind.

A Letter Without an Address

All letters don't reach their destinations. Some letters disappear midway whereas some others are imprisoned. What about the letters without addresses written on them? They are the ones whose fate hangs in balance.

Such was the condition of a letter found without address. The letter bore no information about who had written it or where it was meant to go. The sender and writer of the letter might exist among you. Entertaining such a hope, an exact copy of the letter is being reproduced here.

Dear Tukubabu,

Now the month of *Magha* is in progress. Cold in the village is crueller than cold in the city. The sun had disappeared for the last two days. Turning my back at the morning sun, which reappeared today, I am writing this letter to you.

You were asking my father about "*Rupa sagada re suna kania,*" weren't you? Do you not remember the excitement of children sitting on the bullock carts laden with bundles of hay? Blue are the hills that are far away from us. If you had a closer look, you would realize how the lands of our village had been devastated in the rain that lasted a whole year and the storm that blew during *Kartik Purnima*. Where is the paddy that can be carried in bullock carts? Hiring a labourer was not required; my father and brother carried the bundles home on their heads. How long will the paddy last? Maybe, we will manage till the end of *Chaitra*. After that, we will be left at the mercy of the heaven overhead and the earth down below.

You have asked about the person who prepared *'muan'*—sweets balls of roasted paddy and jaggery. What a sharp memory you have! You have not forgotten the experience of catching fish with your fishing tackle near the screwpine groves. You must be reading the newspapers. The fish were afflicted by diseases. It's a dream these days to find a flower, not to speak of oil and sugar. After the government changed, did the control dealers change? The government got comparatively fewer votes from our village. Only for that, smaller amount of rice and sugar are being supplied to our village. Does it ever happen in an independent nation? The village folk are unaware of the developments taking place in the world; why don't you talk about our village to the minister?

The old woman who sold *'muan'* died a few days ago. Her son was going to Chandabali in a truck to attend a meeting. You must have heard about the death of twelve people there; the poor old lady's son was among the dead. The lady died bemoaning her loss. When she was well, she would often ask about you. The city conveniently forgets the village; but the village keeps the city in its heart, cherished like a wall calendar.

Why have you enquired about the village school? The school building was demolished some seven or eight years ago. People carried away the chairs and benches to use them as firewood. The teacher was coming at his convenience but the students refrained from going there. The children of our village won't be able to read anymore. So many things happen in this world; only a primary school could not be repaired. The Behera family and Dash family have employed private teachers for the education of their children; who would listen to wretched, poor people like us?

Leave it; I won't burden you with my worries. You were talking about the feast during the Saraswati puja. Really, you remember a lot. The tomato *khata* prepared by Chagalanana was really tasty. The price of tomato has gone up to rupees ten this year. The price of a piece of cauliflower is eight rupees. Hence, there will be no feast, nor will any play be staged. Chagalanana felt very bad. He is not getting an opportunity to showcase his talent. Why are prices going up like this? Villagers talk about some war being fought. Can you ever understand how we are managing ourselves? Perhaps not…

You have mentioned electrification of our village. You can't imagine the difficulties we have hurled ourselves into by depending on the mechanized rice crusher in place of the wooden husking paddle. The lights at the market burn like kerosene lamps, that too, only seven days a month. During the rest of the period, darkness pervades everywhere.

Maguni Mohanty says he will contest the elections for the post of Sarapanch. He is talking about some temple; perhaps the locals in the market understand him. He is making people take the oath of allegiance by making them touch the picture of Lord Akhandalamani. I refused to accede to his demands. Is this how votes should be cast? Have I done the right thing? Since that day, he is angry with me.

You must have read about Runa in the newspapers. Her in-laws didn't care to send even a message about her. She was three months pregnant; they killed her by pouring kerosene over her. Let their wealth go to hell. We hear that they did all this for the sake of a T.V. set. You must have heard about Runa. She was very innocent. Didn't you make her cry for the sake of a dried mango, once? Did she tell you anything then? I can never erase her memory from my mind. Even *Yamaraj* would not have wished to burn such a beautiful girl.

What would I write about our village? Almost every day, something terrible takes place. The shutters of houses had to be downed on account of this on the first day of Raja. A lot of fighting went on, on account of Bada Pokhari. Jagudadi's skull was fractured. Police from the police outpost came and arrested the people of the other village. The month of *Asadha* has given way to *Magha* but people of both the villages still harbour ill-feelings towards each other.

We all have been spending our time, leaving everything to fate. Why do you need to come to the village? Who are us, for you? But, you must be reminiscing about the game of *bagudi* that we played on the bank of river Mantei, and how we caught fish from Arjun Babaji's pond.

The Magha Purnami, when we make a bonfire, is only a few days' away. If you visit us, we will have much fun. It's true that those days can't be brought back but we can relive the fun we had those days. On the dew-drenched ridges of distant fields we will light a fire, roast brinjals and nuts in it.

Yes, I have not shared with you the most important information till now. Why don't you inform some important persons about the state of the Ghatswar hospital. The health minister lives in your city. We have only voted for him but we have never seen his face. Every month, one or two people die due to lack of treatment. Besides the red tincture and the white tincture, there is hardly any medicine worth mentioning. We live here relying on fate. The youth of the area organized a strike; they met the minister in the city. You know many great and noble people. Should not they raise voices of concern for these destitutes?

What shall I tell about myself? I feel like committing suicide whenever someone comes to 'see' me. How many times shall I appear, with tea or sherbet tray in hand and a bent head, before them? My father is thinking of sending me to my maternal uncle's house at Chandabali. He experiences great shame and pain when so many candidates return, rejecting me. Don't you know about our villagers? It's better to be visited by a prospective candidate in a temple or market. The truth is that everybody needs a lot of dowry. Does my father have the capacity to accede to the demands? I have already crossed thirty two winters; how long will I survive?

Father reported that your son had started going to school. Why don't you bring him to the village once? Through him, you could visualize the Mantei of your childhood. The village might be having a school whose roof has been blown away, ever bickering villagers, and barren rice fields, but it still has enough love and affection for all. Won't you take your son around the village?

I'm not writing this hoping to get a reply. I have already told you that the city never remembers the address of the village. What else other than hope is left for us to bank on?

Lovingly,

Mina

The letters were illegible at many places; even at places they were wet with water or dew or may be tears. However, it can be understood that it was written to a close childhood friend by another who lived in the village. Through her, the helpless village expressed itself. It is not possible to decipher, from the letter, which village the lady belongs to but in this letter one would discover the geography of many villages.

Life

Looking at Anirudh's distressed face in place of the one that every day sparkled like a white tecoma flower, Sidharth Mohanty realized that some serious problem had beset him. Otherwise, the innocent, 'youthful' seventy-year-old Anirudh would not be looking at the overcast morning sky striking such a pose.

Sidharth Mohanty went and sat down on the cement bench beside Anirudh. He was late in reaching the park that day. Other friends had already gone back after the morning walk. He gently put his hand on Anirudh's shoulder. Anirudh said, "Yesterday, Rohit said the same thing. He wasn't feeling well."

Sidharth said, "You don't have any important business to attend to here for the time being. I advise you to go and spend fifteen days or a month with Rohit."

Anirudh looked at Sidharth. He paused for a while and then said, "Perhaps you are right. But, why did you come up with such a proposal so suddenly?"

Without uttering another word, Sidharth handed him the morning newspaper. A young IAS officer of the Bihar cadre, barely twenty nine years of age, had committed suicide by jumping off the terrace of a five star hotel in Delhi. In the suicide note that he had left, he wrote, "I feel there is no meaning in remaining alive anymore".

Anirudh was startled. He was reminded of one such incident that had taken place a year ago. In a luxurious hotel at Panaji in Goa, a young couple, who worked in a reputed software company with an attractive salary had written such a letter before committing suicide. The husband was thirty-nine whereas the wife was only thirty-six. The South Indian couple wrote in the suicide note, "We have already accomplished whatever we should have. We have visited all those places in the world that people dream of visiting, and enjoyed all the privileges that money can buy. We don't see any purpose in remaining alive any more. Hence, we are committing suicide."

Anirudh took a deep, long sigh.

Sidharth added, "Times are changing. There was a time when we laboured very hard just to buy a cycle or a scooter or to build a house. Half of the life was spent trying to meet the small requirements of life. Then would start the treatment of old parents. By the time one got over that, the troubles related to children stared into one's face. Just take me as an example. At this old age whenever I think of going on a pilgrimage for ten or fifteen days, the little fingers on the palm of my granddaughter hold me back like a trap. It is easy to escape from an iron trap, but to escape from the trap of a six month old's soft fingers is extremely difficult. I don't understand how these middle-aged young men of today say that they have accomplished everything; so, they found no meaning in remaining alive any more. In reality, their self-centredness has shrunk their world."

Anirudh was thinking about his grandson till then. He added softly, "Yes, you are right. Rohit's parents go out at eight o' clock in the morning only to come back after eight p.m. The child has hardly anybody to talk to, after returning from school. These days, in most families, one finds only one child –alone and companionless. There is no playground near the house. How long will they play with the machines? If they demand some 'time', parents, as compensation, procure for them expensive things.

Sidharth added, "Last month, I visited my daughter. Pointing at the luxurious childhood of her daughter— my granddaughter, she remarked, "Her childhood is much better than the childhood we had. Even before birth, they get everything starting from vehicles to expensive toys to soft beds." I protested. I said, "You spent your childhood in the company of the village paddy fields, touch-me-nots, squirrels and cranes. You floated paper boats, drenched in the rain. Having been enticed by the fragrance of *kia* flowers along the river bed, you looked at the sky during Kumar Purnima. If you think your daughter is more fortunate because she has expensive toys, a television and a computer, I'll not argue with you." She understood the folly of her view at once. No matter whatever machines we gift them, the most important thing for them is the company and friendship of man. Children grow tired and worn out without these.

Anirudh returned the newspaper. He said, "To commit suicide and die is the last step, but what is more damaging is the growing disinterest in life, while remaining alive. It is the duty of parents and family to worry about this. Today, we make our children proficient in all other arts, but not in the art of how to live one's life."

Sidharth was about to say something in reply. His eyes fell on Mayadhar sitting some distance away. After having completed the everyday task of feeding the pigeons, the aged artist Mayadhar was busy drawing a picture with his brush and colours. Mayadhar, irrespective of rain or shine, would feed the pigeons at a fixed place of the park every morning. Even the pigeons would wait for him every day.

When the pigeons flew away after being fed, Mayadhar would complete the half-finished canvas. Today also, he was busy completing his unfinished picture.

Both Sidharth and Anirudh approached him. Mayadhar said, "Please come. I couldn't read the time properly today as it was overcast. I have many things to do, but I don't understand what to start with."

"What sort of picture are you making?" Sidharth asked.

"Just watch. I saw the scene here only two days ago. Anticipating rain, the ants were walking in a line after collecting food grains. So small were these insects, but how intense was their struggle for survival! I'm painting just that. I can now understand why art is called the best embodiment of all positive emotions of life. We were wasting our time discussing suicide – summation of all negative emotions, and the worst complaint against existence."

Mayadhar smiled and turned to the task at hand.

While returning from the park, Sidharth said, "Even today, all the roads of Kolkatta haven't been concreted, and all the soil isn't bereft of grass. You should take Rohit to a playground. Let him get drenched in rain; walk barefoot on the grass soaked in dew drops. Let him raise his head from books and notebooks, mobiles and computers. Let him look at the moon and the stars. Only then, he will feel blessed."

Anirudh, as if suddenly remembering something, said, "Arey, your newspaper is left on the bench."

Sidharth replied, "Don't worry. Do we need something that advises us to run away turning our back on life? Yes, please teach Rohit to love life. He should love life so deeply that he should never feel the need to complain about it."

Anirudh nodded his head in agreement.

Memories and Dreams

Even though the rain had subsided, patches of cloud still hung around in the sky seen through the window, just like an obstinate child who refuses to return to school after the summer vacation. Casting a glance at these, Managovind contemplated what he would do. When he thought he would have to settle in Bhubaneswar leaving the village home far behind, many incidents relating to the house flashed in his memory. Whenever he decided in favour of spending the rest of his life in the village, the thoughts of the comforts of city life and the company of his children appeared to be more attractive. In order to resolve this mental dilemma, he shut the door and tossed the coin twice but the dilemma of his mind was soon transmitted to the coin – once it showed 'Head', the other time, it showed 'Tails'.

Managovind never thought he would come to such a pass in his life. Many of his contemporaries had already left the village to stay with their children. Most of those had settled in foreign countries. Managovind often wondered how those people, who had spent their entire life immersed in the culture of Odisha, adjusted themselves to life in alien lands at a ripe old age.

"Am I going to get some *raja-pithas*, the cakes especially prepared during Raja celebration, or not?" yelled Sidharth as he rushed in. The jasmine hedge on Managaovind's gate stooped a little after the previous day's rain. Sidharth, while pushing the creeper up onto its iron-trellis, said, "Perhaps *Bhauja* is not at home."

Managovind came out of the drawing room. Flashing a smile on his lips, he said, "Come, Sidharth, come. Your inference is absolutely correct. *Bhauja* has been staying at Bhubaneswar for the last fifteen days, with our daughter."

"Oh! Deserting another person's son, a mother has gone to spend time with her own daughter then," Sidharth made fun of Managovind.

"What will you take – tea or coffee?"

"Who'll make it? You?"

"You just give the order. When I was a student in a college at Cuttack, I used to cook for a family of ten. Ever since your *bhauja* has gone, I have been managing quite well cooking rice and *dalma*. There has been no problem. I'm also keeping well."

Sidharth said, "Your words bring to mind the words of someone else. Every word of solace is a kind of self-explanation. When did I say you would face any trouble in her absence?"

Managovind replied, "Barsa is going to deliver her child next week. My Samuduni, Barsa's mother-in-law, lies bedridden. Barsa's father-in-law, lives elsewhere. My son-in-law serves in the army. How would Barsa manage herself under these circumstances? She is also a working woman. She is on three month's leave now but she has to join the office after that. Who'll take care of her child? All these had been the topic of discussion at our home for the last five years but I could never take a decision on the matter. Her mother angrily decided to leave for Bhubaneswar on her own."

"Couldn't they have come here?" asked Sidharth.

"That's out of the question. Electricity supply to this village, which is only thirty kilometers away from Bhubaneswar, is disrupted many times a day. The roads become muddy in the rainy season. It's better not to talk of the hospital. Can she live comfortably here? My daughter and her husband have purchased a flat next to our apartment. My daughter tells me, "It will hurt your pride if you stay with me in my apartment. Why don't you come and stay in the adjacent one? What is left in that house in the village? So much emotional attachment for a huge house like an elephant-shed, four or five cart loads of books and a few trees is not worthwhile. People are ready to leave for America or England for the sake of their children, but you can't even come to Bhubaneswar for our sake. Who'll take care of the house after you? It's better if you sell it off now."

"She is right". Sidharth supported what Managovind babu's daughter had said.

"Where'll I go leaving behind this house, these books, and this orchard? I and your *bhauja* built this house brick by brick. We would often get scorched by sun, sprinkling water on the half-built walls. We have planted champak and *siuli* trees in the backyard. When we lounged on the terrace, the moon would look enchanting when looked through the fronds of the coconut tree planted in the corner. The champak and *siuli* trees would constantly compete with each other to spread their fragrance. This jasmine hedge, when I go out, seems to say, "Come back soon"; and asks me when I return, "Why are you so late?" How can I tear myself away from them?"

Sidharth placed the tea cup on the teapoy and said, "Whatever you say is correct but think of Barsha's problems. When she was young, the two of you never allowed her to go out of your sight. The wheels have turned. She has grown up and you have become old. She doesn't want to allow you two to go out of her sight. You should be happy with this."

Managovind said, "Where shall I keep my books, and my other belongings? The three-roomed apartment doesn't have enough space for all these. I asked your *bhauja* once but she replied like a philosopher: "One day or the other, man has to leave everything behind and go away. Why don't you select a few and discard the rest?" Tell me Sidharth, does man leave everything behind at the time of death at his sweet will? He leaves everything behind simply because he can't take anything with him."

Sidharth knew Managovind quite well. He was an old, emotional professor. He couldn't decide what to tell him to solve the dilemma facing him. After a while he said, "A wise man once said, "Man always tries to avoid change. He thinks that going to the new place may invite problems. This fear prevents him from moving elsewhere."

Managovind brightened up as if he had found the answer. He told Sidharth, "I have found the answer. I'll visit my children at times and spend a few days with them but I'll never leave this house."

"But, but this is not what I meant," protested Sidharth.

"No, the crux of what you said is this: You said there was no harm in going away from here, didn't you? Tell me, what is the meaning of life? Memory. Memory, for a man like me, is life. A man without memories is as good as dead.

When I look at this house, its walls, its compound walls, the trees, the appliqué work of Pipili adorning the walls, the palm-leaf hat from Assam, the memories associated with these flash before my eyes. This is the place where my daughter was born; this is where she grew up; this is where she received her education; this is the place where we used to install the sacred *kalasa* on her examination days; this is where her mother would light the inextinguishable lamp. This is the place from where we bade her goodbye as a bride. How can I leave these memories behind?

"But Barsa and her husband live in a new apartment."

"Siddharth, this is the difference between old age and youth. In old age life means memories but for the youth, it means dreams. Our life is the thread that keeps memories and dreams strung together. Barsa has just started setting up a home. This is the time for her to dream. She will love the world that gives her opportunities to dream. One day, those dreams will turn into memories."

Siddharth got up to go. Managovind said, "Come here when you feel like. I'll ring up Barsa and tell her to rent out her new apartment, otherwise the new house might have a pest attack."

The Song of Life

Sidharth had never thought he would meet Gobardhan so unexpectedly in front of Indira Park. Gobardhan had a family. Whether it was Sunday or some other holiday, mattered little to him. He would say, "The sahibs were different types of people. They came here to rule. India prostrated itself at their feet. If they ordered someone to do something, the work was done. They went to church on Sundays. In the afternoon, they would visit the parks or fields; in the evenings, they would go to clubs or have a party. What's our worth? How many of us go to such places? Sunday or Monday makes no difference for us. We are not concerned about how many three, four, or five star hotels are there in Bhubaneswar. Rather, on Sundays, I find myself surrounded by more work. In the morning, one has to collect wood from the timber merchant, then collect ration from the control shop, then buy vegetables from the market. In the afternoon, one had to remove cobwebs from the entire house starting from the bathroom to the bedroom, give a bath to the child, and clean the plug of the moped. In the late afternoon, he had to run to the laundry with clothes to be ironed and finally, sit down to plan a budget for the rest of the days, negotiating with an ever-emptying purse. Where was the time for rest amidst all this? Where was the question of enjoyment? Gobardhan hardly told lies. The day-to-day lifestyle of most of the low-paid employees was like that. Sidharth was no different from them.

"Gobardhan! Did we not have fantasies about life in the city when we were students?"

"Sidharth! It was the biggest dream those days to land a job carrying a salary of one thousand rupees and spend one's life in luxury. Having ten one hundred rupee notes in those days seemed impossible, like winning a lottery. Look at it now; my child has been demanding to eat fish for the last three weeks; I'm not able to buy him any. Is hilsa available in the market?"

Sidharth was startled at first; then he flashed a pale smile. That morning, his experience of purchasing hilsa had been a painful one… that's why. He had gone to Unit Four fish market that morning. Since Sidharth's family came from the coastal areas, they obviously had a weakness for non-veg food. When Sidharth was a college student, hilsa was available in plenty at the price of only one rupee for one. Sidharth liked hilsa fish cooked in mustard paste, with two green chillies floating in the sauce. Ah! With Lilabati variety of rice, hilsa in mustard paste was a mouth-watering delicacy in the rainy season. When Sidharth asked for the price of hilsa in Unit Four market this morning, he got the shock of his life. The price of one kilo of hilsa was a staggering seventy rupees! While Sidharth was busy bargaining with the shopkeeper, someone came from behind and snatched the fish away. It was as if the betel-stained teeth of the fish-seller were making fun of Sidharth. The other person bought the whole fish without even enquiring about its price. When Sidharth looked up, the fish-seller was there, but no fish.

Gobardhan said, "Sidharth, during this season a few years ago, in your village, quintals of prawns would be left to dry on reed mats, wouldn't they? Where from did you people collect so much fish? Do the villagers catch so much fish even today?"

Sidharth was reminded of his village street. Gobardhan was not lying. When it rained incessantly, it was difficult to dry prawns. The sellers would sell them for any price. With simple bamboo fishtraps like *khainchi* or *khalei*, one would collect a basketful of prawn. However, whenever Sidharth, earning two thousand rupees a month, came to the Unit Four market, he would turn away from the prawn shops, as if they sold gold ornaments. Even casting a glance at them was an unaffordable luxury for him.

Gobardhan was getting ready to take leave of him. Sidharth remembered that he had forgotten to ask him the real question. Gobardhan was a family-man; so, he was never found near parks or hotels or cinema halls. Sidharth was a little surprised to find him sitting alone in the park. What might be the secret of Gobardhan's delayed romantic escapades?

In reply to Sidharth's question, Gobardhan smiled a little. He said, "Arey, no…no. I had not come to the park. I was going to the market to buy three or four *rakhis* for children and vegetables for home. The rear tyre of the moped went flat. I have already asked the mechanic at the P.M.G square to get the tyre repaired. It will take at least half an hour. Just to pass time, I entered the park. Many days ago, I had heard that the park was a beautiful place. Thank god, I got an opportunity to move around a little. If the tyre had not got punctured, I would not have come here."

Gobardhan walked away, with his back turned towards Indira Park, Sidharth, the crowd inside the park, the groundnut and balloon sellers. Gobardhan was not like that always. He was very emotional when he was young. Others would become jealous of him for his singing skills and his talent as an actor. He had devised a plan to become a cinema director or a cassette company owner. What a pathetic chasm separated the moped-rider Gobardhan of today, and the dreamer Gobardhan of the past.

After Gobardhan had left, Sidharth was lost in thoughts about him. In the race of life, Gobardhan had turned into a machine to fulfill the demands and needs of his family. Places like parks and the cinema had become irrelevant for him. Of course, what was there to be surprised about? With devils such as uncontrolled rise in prices on one hand and devaluation of currency on the other, Sidharth wondered how long he would be able to have the pleasure of visiting the park regularly. He felt as if the sweet, beautiful, and pleasant world would disappear from sight like the hilsa fish selling for seventy rupees a kilo. He would be left in the middle of the street, an empty bag in hand, surrounded by other helpless people like him.

A Lottery Ticket

Shyamalakanti said once again, "Look, Sidharth, this is a friendly lottery. Nobody harbours any business motives. Whatever extra money is generated, will be spent on some developmental project." Sidharth had made up his mind; he didn't want to buy any lottery tickets. His daughter insisted, "Why don't you buy a ticket? The first prize is a colour television. If we win it, we would get a colour television. We watched Ramayan on that black and white TV; the telecast of Mahabharat is about to be over. By the time you purchase a colour TV, telecast of the Bible serial would be over."

Sidharth caressed the child's head and said, "No, dear. We will buy a TV with our own money. Don't ask me to buy the lottery ticket."

Shyamalakanti returned empty-handed.

It was an afternoon of *Baisakh*. Sidharth stood on the verandah of his house and noticed that the gulmohur tree had put out bunches of flowers. How beautiful the red flowers amidst the green leaves looked! His daughter Luna was not wrong. Pictures do look beautiful on a colour TV.

Sidharth was reminded of the peon of his office,

Mukund. Almost every day of the week Mukund would buy some lottery ticket or the other. He would be searching for his own number from among the almost illegible numbers printed in the newspapers. He dreamt if by chance he hit the jackpot, he would get all his money back. But poor Mukund's dream never came true.

Sidharth would take pity on Mukund. What other ways were left for a low-paid employee like him and Mukund to rise higher up in life? Higher-level officials; even low-level officials posted in important departments; ministers or political leaders had the opportunity to make money from different sources. Where was the opportunity for hard-working men like Mukund to make an extra income?

The wants of Sidharth knew no limits. His income was not sufficient to meet all his small and big demands. Children's demands, wife's strong warnings, and his own situation often combined to make Sidharth feel utterly helpless. On the way to office, he would find lottery ticket sellers sitting in a row selling Rajasthan lottery, Uttar Pradesh lottery, Dhanalaxmi, Dhanabarsha etc. Some of these carried the first prize of one lakh rupees whereas some others carried the first prize of one crore. Some others offered even larger sums of money.

What would Sidharth do if he won so much money at one go? Just the thought of this would keep him occupied for hours and hours.

But, why didn't Sidharth buy any lottery ticket?

Many years ago, Sidharth had once come to Cuttack from his village. A cousin of the village worked as an officer at Cuttack. He had planned to stay with him in his house and visit Dussehra pandals.

One afternoon, the gentleman's wife gave Sidharth five rupees and sent him to the market at Buxibazar to fetch flour and sugar. Sidharth, a bag hanging from his hand, went out to the market.

The enormous market complex of the Cuttack Development Authority that stands today was not constructed in the seventies. Gopabandhu Park was used as a free open air defecation centre. Some chicken shops dotted its boundary. Finally, at one corner, sat a dark-complexioned man with thick moustaches. He was the lottery seller. He carried on his business with a few playing-cards, one box and a few dices inside. He shouted to announce his challenge, "Come, come. If you invest rupees five, you would get rupees ten; if you invest rupees ten, you would get rupees twenty." Sidharth didn't realize when he had strayed from his path and stood in front of this man. After standing there for some time he realized it was very easy to win some money from that fat man. He took out the five rupee note from his pocket and placed a bet for rupees two.

Within the twinkling of an eye, Sidharth's two rupees got converted into rupees six. He had never imagined such a large amount of money would come his way so easily. He continued there for half an hour, and it was no surprise that after half an hour he had become penniless.

The bag that hung on his left hand now seemed very heavy to Sidharth. The wife of the gentleman, in whose house he had taken shelter, was a hard-hearted woman. Sidharth shuddered in sadness, grief and helplessness at the thought of the physical and mental torture that he would be subjected to.

Ten to fifteen customers had already surrounded the lottery seller. He was instructing Sidharth to move away from the spot and give way to others, "Run, run. Allow other customers to come."

A moment ago, Sidharth was a respected 'customer' but the moment he became penniless the lottery seller was driving him away like one shoos away wasps. The realization of this simple but hidden fact of life made him experience the pain caused by a thousand scorpion stings.

How would he escape from such a situation? If he went away without taking the money, he would not be able to buy flour and sugar. On one hand, the landlady's angry look and on the other, the expressionless face of the fat lottery seller danced before his eyes.

Finally, the young child Sidharth cried with tears rolling down his cheeks. His words of distress amused all those who were present there that day.

It was then that something unexpected took place. The lottery seller took out the five rupee note from his tin box and handed it to Sidharth saying, "Go… run away from here. Don't ever participate in gambling again. All this is not your cup of tea. Go."

Many years had passed since then. The child Sidharth had grown into a young man. However, he had not forgotten the immortal words of the lottery seller.

His daughter Luna was going to mention the lottery tickets again; she stopped short for she found tears in her father's eyes.

Sidharth made Luna lean on his chest and ran his fingers through her hair. He continued, "My dear. Once in the past, a teary-eyed small child had promised never to participate in lotteries. I was just reminded of his promise. Make a promise today. Don't ever nurture the hope of earning twenty five rupees investing only five. Don't ever participate in gambling or buy lottery tickets."

Man

From the premises of the Dhabalaswar temple, the sea looked like a placid lake. The patch of sky beyond the belt of casuarinas hung on the bosom of the sea just like the untied hair of a maiden taking bath in the pond. The ambassador car carried nine people.

No… this was not the Dhabaleswar temple on river Mahanadi in Cuttack district. This Dhabaleswar temple was situated on the sea beach at Gopalpur. Perhaps the visitors didn't know that there existed a temple with the same name. Therefore, they were found challenging each other's knowledge of geography and culture. Sidharth was listening to them from a distance.

All of them hailed from Bhubaneswar. They worked for a newspaper agency. The agency didn't give them many days off. This was why the owner arranged the meetings of the managers at a distant place like this. The meeting would be held in the usual way; but the employees would get an opportunity to refresh themselves. This is like killing two birds with one shot.

The sea shore would do away with all self-imposed restraints. Minds would fly unsteadily like a timid butterfly.

The grown-up manager of the company felt liberated, reaching the sea shore. Usually, he would feel breathless under the weight of files, but today, he did not have to worry about them. By chance, the name of a young female colleague slipped out of his mouth; other colleagues present there took advantage of the situation and were busy making fun of him.

There was no specific reason for Sidharth to come here. He had visited Berhampur two times earlier. Of course, the pressures of work didn't allow him to visit Gopalpur. That morning the idea of visiting the presiding deity of the place had crossed his mind. When he was a child, his father had told him, "No matter whether you visit a friend or an acquaintance, don't forget to visit the head man of the place. Besides, you must pay a visit to the presiding deity of the area."

Dhabaleswar Mahadev was so unlucky that he wasn't offered even a few bel-leaves. The beach at Gopalpur was full of sand. The priest informed him that bel trees did not grow up here. Sidharth felt like saying, "Wouldn't it help if you dug a deep hole, filled it with soil, and then planted a bel tree?" Perhaps the priest had not given much thought to the bel tree, thinking that the God who had taken the trouble of appearing in that remote place would make all provisions for his worship himself. Sidharth, instead of getting into an argument with the priest, turned his attention to the *baboos* from Bhubaneswar.

The young manager was heard telling his friend, "Gopalpur beach is not like the one at Puri. If a steel plant came up here, the place would be transformed completely." Others were listening to him with rapt attention.

"Why didn't you pay a visit to the temple, Bibhuprasad? We all went there."

"The priest there was asking your name and *gotra*. I don't believe in that. If God were omniscient, what was the need of telling your name and *gotra* just like showing your visiting card to gain an entry? Would not he know it on his own?" the young man named Bibhuprasad was asking the one who had put the question to him a moment ago.

At that moment, another of the young men, pointing at the huts of the *nolias*, asked, "Look there; what are those?"

The young man perhaps saw the *nolias* for the first time. His voice and face reflected his sense of surprise.

The elderly co-traveller answered, "They are all *nolias*. They stay here on the beach. They are not worried about the sun or the rain, cold or fog. The men enter the deep sea during the day to catch fish, and return in the evening. Don't you know this much?"

"They live in such a pathetic condition! Fie… fie. Don't they have any civic sense? They dine here on the beach and answer the call of nature here, too. How disgusting! …" the young man could not complete his sentence. Perhaps he was not able to accept his discovery of human beings in such a state.

Their tour of the sea-shore was over. Smoke rose from the *nolia*-huts — the smoke from their fire places. The bold answers to the questions of the highly-educated and affluent young men from the capital city mingled with that smoke and turned it into the fragrance of incense sticks. Sidharth felt like running to the young man and giving answer to his questions. The pathetic state of man, which the young man interpreted as his helplessness or weakness, was actually the source of man's real strength; the self-righteous dignity of having survived in the midst of adverse conditions. The circumstances owing to which many animals including dinosaurs had already become extinct, and many others were on the verge of extinction, had actually been converted by man into opportunities; he has not only survived, his progeny has also multiplied. The struggle of man in the face of a hostile nature may not be called worship or *sadhana*, but should never be dismissed derisively.

They piled into that white car. Sidharth looked at the cloud of dust that chased their vehicle for some time, before returning to the sea.

Maternal Uncle's House

The worth of a thing that is out of one's reach or not in one's possession constantly keeps increasing in one's mind. Sidharth keenly felt the absence of one thing in his life: He didn't have a maternal uncle and therefore, never had the opportunity to visit his maternal uncle's house. His mother was the only daughter of her parents. When mother was alive she would point at a village surrounded by tall palm trees and short babul trees across the river and tell him, "That's your grandfather's village." Sidharth would feel delighted at the prospect of calling another place his own. But when he was still very young, one day his grandfather passed away, and consequently, all his relationships with that village snapped.

Of course, Sidharth had a few uncles, though none of them was his own. However, Sidharth neither felt any attachment for them, nor did he expect any love and affection from them. This was why Sidharth was jealous of a few of his friends, especially Baguli, who would frequently refer to his uncle and aunt. When Sidharth reached Baguli's house with a marble or a fishing tackle in the morning, the latter's mother would inform him that he had already left for his maternal uncle's the day before. Sidharth would return disheartened. He would be angry with Baguli and at the same time pity himself.

If he had a maternal uncle, he would also visit his house. There, he would not be required to submit himself to his parents' control. He would climb trees at will, swim in ponds, hurl sticks, or play a game of *kitkit* without going to bed during the day. If his aunt tried to impose restrictions, she would be told bluntly, "I shall return to my village tomorrow." Uncle would get angry with aunt and say, "Why are you trying to control the child? If his mother comes to learn about it, it would unnecessarily create trouble." Sidharth would laugh a hearty laugh like one who had returned home after conquering the universe. Winning a war without having to participate in it brings a different kind of pleasure. Wearing new dresses and being carried by uncle on his shoulders, he would visit the pandals where the deities were being worshipped. He would purchase balloons, sugarcane and trumpets. He would roam happily all over the festival grounds. After his return, aunt would make him sit in her lap and feed him with fried fish and *pakhala*. Uncle's children would grow jealous of Sidharth's good fortune. After spending ten or twelve days like a king, he would return home. The thorny fruits of the *guguchia* plant would stick to his trousers and socks.

The song that began with, "*Mamughar Chaunri, chakachaka bhaunri*" remained confined to the text book *Mo Chhabi Bahi*. Sidharth grew disheartened whenever he read it. He felt as if everything related to maternal uncle, uncle's house and the songs and stories related to the two, were meant to make fun of him. These should be removed from his books.

At times, Sidharth felt like asking his mother, "Everybody has maternal uncles, uncle's house; why don't I have any?" He could not bring himself to ask such a question. When he insistently asked question like this in his childhood, his father would take him to the market or towards the ferry *ghat*. He would point at the sky and address the moon as '*Jahnamamu*'. He would explain to Sidharth, "Hey, look at *jahnamamu*. Is he not your uncle?" Sidharth failed to see this connection. His father would point at the moon and call it frequently in his hoarse voice. He would sing songs entreating the moon to descend from the sky and fall into Sidharth's palms. But the moon never showed any inclination to do that. Sidharth, who had much faith in his father, would stand with open palms in a place surrounded by paddy fields. His body would shiver in the cold breeze; his eyelids would droop. While being carried homewards by father on his shoulder, he would tell himself sleepily, "*Janhamamu* is not like my own maternal uncle. I wish I had an uncle like Baguli's uncle. ." Uncle would pick Sidharth up and run on the boundary ridge placing Sidharth on his shoulders. He would teach him how to blow whistles; teach him the tricks of catching *dhanduri* fish; and teach him how to imitate the voices of different birds. With these thoughts in his mind, the song "*Aa Janhamamu Saragasashi*" would appear ridiculous. '*Janhamamu*' or 'Moon" could never be equated with a maternal uncle.

Sidharth wondered why the thought of 'maternal uncle' appeared so suddenly in his mind. Faced by the problem of increasing population, the government slogan 'we two... our two' had already been replaced with 'we two... our one'. A clerk serving the health department, Sidharth understood the enormity of the population problem. He would cite the example of his grandfather at times, among his friends. How farsighted his grandfather was! Even in those times, he was satisfied with being the father of one child, that too a girl. His friends would express gratitude to his grandfather, on behalf of the nation.

Despite the awareness and consolation, at times, the image of the soft palms of a small child singing "*Aa janhamamu Saradasashi*" would rise from the red and yellow posters, as well as, the lifeless yellowing files, and float before him. He would hear the sounds of a male voice singing that song, just to divert the attention of a child from the pain of not having a 'maternal uncle'. The aged clerk would grow emotional — sandwiched between the tearful red eyes of the child and the fruitless efforts of a helpless father.

A Model Teacher

I distinctly remember, when I was a student of class four or five, and when I read the magazine '*Manapawan*,' I would give preference to the stories and poems of those writers under whose name or in whose introduction the words "Governor's Awardee (Teacher)" appeared. Regarding the word 'Governor', I had a rather muddled idea. However, for the governor's awardee teachers, I felt a strange sense of reverence. I had no doubt that in such a big state the teachers who could attract the attention of the governor himself must not be ordinary teachers. The sorrowful experience of not having met such a decorated teacher, till I was twelve years of age, only strengthened my earlier assumption. When I left the primary school and came to the minor school, I was compelled to read the books penned by these teachers. While reading their books, I would consider myself inferior; I would also curse myself for having not got the opportunity to be directly taught by them.

Had I ever imagined that the idea nurtured since childhood would collapse like a castle made of sand one day?

The incident took place when I paid a visit to the office of an editor of a newspaper on some work. When I was sitting inside his office, a slip was sent inside; someone wanted to meet him. The editor called the gentleman inside. A dhoti-punjabi clad person came in, with folded hands, saying 'namaskar'.

Before the gentleman started the conversation, he looked at me. I understood that he was not feeling comfortable in my presence. I felt obliged to leave the chamber.

Later I came to learn that the gentleman was the teacher of a high school. His name was included, at the block level, in the list that was sent for the governor's award that year. He had but one deficiency — lack of literary publications. The gentleman had not produced any literary works during his lifetime. On the other hand, a few stories, poems, or criticisms of his competitors had been published in different magazines and journals. He was worried that his name might be excluded at the last moment.

If the editor could issue a certificate mentioning that some of the articles, which were published in the newspaper at different times earlier without mentioning the names of the writers, were actually written by him, then he would be successful in bagging the award.

I don't know if the editor helped him or if the gentleman was awarded by the governor that year. I was no more interested to know what happened. Once I learnt how one of those people, whom I had considered models of exemplary character and noble conduct since childhood, could try to collect a proof of fake qualifications without any regret, I lost all interest in the matter.

After many days, I asked an officer of the education department, what was the secret behind the award. Why was there so much eagerness to get it? He smiled and said, "Perhaps you don't know. The service period of the governor's awardees is increased by two years. That's the reason for the greed for it. Besides, there is the added attraction of the awardee's photo being published in the newspaper and consequently, the publicity."

Mummy and Maa

It was well past evening when I reached my friend's house. In towns, one really felt guilty about visiting someone at odd hours. This was not a village; here relationships were as fragile as a glass bangle; the slightest carelessness would make it break into pieces.

My friend was not at home. Therefore, I wanted to come away. My friend's wife said, "He is away only for a while. Please wait for some time, he will come back soon."

Allowing me to sit in the exquisitely arranged drawing room, my friend's wife went inside, perhaps to make tea or coffee. Bubu, my friend's elder son, was reading with his head bent over the nearby table. He had started going to school for the last few days.

In the meanwhile, my friend's wife re-appeared with two cups of tea laid on a beautiful tray. Looking at Bubu, she blurted out, "Bubu, go to the other room."

Bubu, like a trained circus dog, left the table, silently picked up his books, and left.

Then, the friend's wife started talking about Bubu's studies – how he got up at six o' clock; went to the washroom at six thirty; got dressed for school at six forty-five; and reached school at seven. She also talked about how he obeyed his mother; sat down when he was ordered and got up when he was asked to. The lady didn't forget to mention how she would fly into a rage if she marked the slightest deviation in his manner of talking or behaviour.

I didn't like her method of rearing him up or the strict discipline she imposed on him; still I listened to her silently.

During the course of this one-sided conversation, the friend's wife called, "Bubu, come in here." Bubu came running. I handed him the chocolate I had kept in my pocket for such a long time. Like a trained circus dog, he accepted the chocolate politely, nodded his head and said in English, "Thank you, uncle."

I noticed from Bubu's behaviour that he had already been trained to walk on the trodden path. Bubu was being brought up like a soldier under the strict supervision of his English-educated mother, but I could detect signs of muted resistance in the innocent, tender face of the child. My village-shaped mind could not accept such strictness.

My friend arrived. Placing me in his care, my friend's wife went to the adjacent room to help Bubu with his homework. I was reminded of the evenings of my own childhood days. We would hardly notice when evening fell or deepen into the night as we would be lost hearing the stories of '*Budhi Asuruni*' or '*Kalureibenta*'. While the stories were still being presented to us, our sleepy eyelids closed. Home tasks never troubled us at such a tender age. We had only two things to do –either swim in the ponds or throw stones at the small frogs or do both.

If one killed a frog, one would grow deaf. Who told us this? Who else, other than mother? Unlike Bubu's mummy, she would never finish giving advice in a few words. She would take at least half an hour to complete something. She didn't know how to talk, 'properly'.

Since I was reminded of 'Bou', I was also reminded of an incident related to school. I reminded my friend of that incident.

Bou was not at all concerned about our education. She was worried about only one thing: whether we children had eaten or not. She would not feel satisfied until we ate three or four complete meals every day. Every day, she would put in the bag rotis, *santula* or *chakuli* or *gaintha*. I may mention here that I had to take the help of a few friends to polish off the food that she packed for me only.

One day, after reaching school, I found that the mathematics and English books were missing from my bag. That morning, before going to take bath, I had packed all the books according to the routine. I had put the two books in the bag. The books were needed during the first two periods but, surprisingly, they were not to be found. I was made to stand on the bench for my negligence. When I returned home in the evening I found the books lying upside down on the bed. I knew Bou was the culprit. I asked her why she had done this. She explained, "You had taken eight or ten books to school, so what if I took out only two? There was no space for the tiffin box in the bag; so, I took out these two books."

I had not forgotten the pain of the insult and helplessness that I had experienced in the class that day. I spoke angrily to her for her thoughtlessness. She listened silently and went away without saying anything.

My friend laughed loudly. He said, "Quite true. Our mothers were not machines like these T.V. mothers. They were not keeping a watch on every movement of ours. If they had any worries, it was but one – whether their children had eaten. Then, children were allowed enough freedom to take care of themselves."

After some time I suddenly thought that children living in the city like Bubu might appear very handsome and smart, but someone had cruelly snatched away from them the innocence and freedom of childhood. They were being made to grow up like the pruned flowering plants of the parks or gardens; they lacked the beauty and freedom of growing up wild in the forest.

Mutation

Sidharth didn't want to remind himself of the troubles he had faced at the Tehsil office. Had he not met Ramakrishna Parida, his work wouldn't have been completed even today. In comparison to that place the Unit IV fish market looked better organized. Those heaps of old, foul-smelling files lying on both sides of the verandah, made him feel as if he had entered some tunnel dug into the pre-historic era. At those moments, Ramakrishna was like a candle for him. There was no option but to meekly follow the man, who appeared in a white *punjabi*.

His brother's constant pleas rang in his ears: if their father's name was not replaced with theirs in the land records, he would not be able to obtain a loan from the bank. Sidharth told him, "If the mutation is so badly needed, you should come and get the job done. What would I do if you remind me at regular intervals of the need to do the job like a money-lender." Even though younger than him, in terms of knowledge of the world his younger brother stood far ahead of him. If Sidharth got angry, he would suddenly become subdued. He would place before his brother a list of difficulties that he would face unless he got the bank loan sanctioned – his half-built house would remain unfinished; he didn't have enough money for the treatment of his ailing wife; he needed to arrange quite a sum for the admission of his daughter etc. Sidharth also realized there was some truth in what his younger brother had said. Besides, one day or the other, the old records had to be replaced with new records.

Sidharth grew emotional at the tehsil office the moment he was reminded of his father. During his childhood, when he went to school holding his father's hand, he had never thought even once that his father would desert him and he would be left all alone. Then he considered that his family, which consisted of his parents and his younger brother, was as timeless as the portrait that hung on the wall. He felt disturbed for a moment when he applied for the replacement of his father's name with his own.

His father, towards the fag end of his life, moved from Rourkella to live with him. He had a few books at home. Besides, there was a park nearby. His father was fascinated by books and trees. In addition, there was Sidharth's young son, Sonu. Park, books, the company of Sonu – these kept his father occupied.

By the time his work at the tehsil office was over, it was two o' clock. Ramakrishna had grown tired of running from the typist to the tahesildar's office, and from there to the clerks. Sidharth offered him green coconut water to drink. Ramakrishna finally said, "I will be coming to the office regularly. I will ring you up once the job is done."

Sidharth replied, "The work could have waited. I am giving you all this trouble only because my younger brother wants it urgently done."

Sidharth started his scooter and returned from the tehsil office. If he didn't show up at his office, the head clerk would rebuke him tomorrow. He went there even though he didn't want to go in that sweat-drenched state. Oh! What troubles he had to face getting the paperwork done. The time of his father's death flashed before him once again. What troubles he had to go through to obtain the death certificate! He had to obtain a copy of the paper from the hospital first; then he had to apply at the Registrar's office behind Keshari Talkies; he had to go the treasury office to deposit two rupees along with the application form; he had to stand in long queues to obtain the counterfoil of the challan form as a proof of the deposit. If in the meantime, the clerk concerned left his seat, the day was completely wasted; one had to run there once again the next day.

Sidharth did the right thing in visiting his office again. The office had received communications from higher officials to provide replies to some assembly question; and the head clerk was looking for him in that connection. Sidharth apologized for his absence, gave out a smile and remained busy in office work.

It was eight o' clock when he returned home. His seven-year-old son was a great friend of his at home. He had only one complaint against Sonu – he displaced his things. That a belonging should be placed at its proper place, was something that Sonu didn't approve of. Only for that, Sidharth never found his scooter keys, or his spectacles, or his mobile phone at the time of need. These days, Sonu even spent his time disarranging Sidharth's books in his almirah. The key to the almirah was lost. Thinking that Sonu would leave the books in a mess, he had explained to him, "One day or the other, these books would belong to you. So, don't ever spoil them." An experience from childhood led him to say so. His father had kept some books in an almirah in his village and had warned them not to touch those saying, "These are mine, don't dare touch them." But prevention augmented their attractiveness. One day, when father opened the almirah, he found only two books – the Khadiratna almanac and the eleventh book of *The Bhagavad*. He grew distressed when he discovered that his son Sidharth had taken away all those books and distributed them among those who needed them.

Sidharth opened the gate and parked the scooter on the verandah. The entire compound was filled with the fragrance of jasmine flowers. The lights were on in the outer room. Sidharth raised his head and found Sonu sitting on the ground with his legs spread apart and scribbling something with a pen. He inched closer. What did he discover? Sonu had taken out four or five books from Sidharth's almirah and was writing something on the first page of each. Sidharth was shocked. He asked Sonu, "What are you doing? Why are you scribbling on my books?"

Sonu looked up at him. Sidharth picked up the fat English book from the ground. He suddenly felt as if Sonu had reached the tehsil office and had written his own name in place of his in the substitution form.

Annapurna rushed out from the kitchen and asked, "What happened? Why are you so alarmed?"

Sidharth didn't say anything but handed the book to her. Sonu had brutally crossed out what Sidharth had written on the first page. In place of Sidharth Das, Third Year Arts (Honours), Ravenshaw University Sonu had written Sanat Das, Standard Three, D.A.V. Public School Unit-VIII, Bhubaneswar. Sidharth bent down and picked up two more books. He found the same thing there, too. Sonu had crossed out Sidharth's name and written his own name.

Annapurna asked Sonu, "What are you doing? Why are you crossing out father's name and writing yours?"

Unperturbed, Sonu answered, "Father himself had told me that these would belong to me after him. That's why I am crossing out his name and writing my own. One day or the other, I have to make the corrections; where is the harm if I do it today?"

Sidharth was speechless. He felt that Sonu had given him an opportunity to foresee the mutation that was inevitably going to take place in twenty-five or thirty years.

■

A New Incarnation

The intensity of this particular incident surpassed all the devastating and shattering experiences that he had come across in books or films. The untimely death of his friend Ramahari shattered his family completely. His house appeared wretched like a bird's nest thrown out of the branch of a tree by an untimely storm and smashed on the ground. The members of his family cried inconsolably.

Sidharth didn't have the courage to console Ramahari's parents. He could imagine the grief that had engulfed his old parents at the untimely death of their only bread-earning son. Sidharth had never ever found his words so ineffectual nor had he found himself so helpless ever. The two-year-old daughter of Ramahari, unable to realize the gravity of the situation, looked here and there, utterly confused. Sidharth's heart was filled with intense grief the moment his eyes fell on her. Poor girl! She was deprived of a father's love even before fully realizing its value. Henceforth, she would identify her father from his photos. Ramahari's widow appeared the most disconsolate. Only three years ago, she had come to the family as a bride. She was painting rosy pictures of her future with her husband. That family now looked completely devastated and wretched. She rolled on the ground and cried bitterly. Her hair lay dishevelled. Like a bird with broken wings, she gave out a heart-rending cry at times and scratched the earth.

The corpse of thirty-two year old Ramahari lay on the courtyard. His bier lay amidst the sand and bricks that he had procured last week for constructing the house. A new cloth covered his dead body and a bouquet was placed on it. Nothing including the groans, the tears, the sobs, the sighs, and the grieving words reached him. He lay motionless like a man lost in deep slumber.

Sidharth found it impossible to control even his own tears. The moral lessons prescribed by scriptures, mythologies, literature or philosophy didn't now come to his aid. He stood silently, gauging the extent of man's powerlessness and the depth of his helplessness. He had read about the brittleness and meaninglessness of life from books like *Tika Govindachandra* and *Manabodha Chautisa*, but the reality was far harsher than what he had expected.

Sidharth knew Ramahari closely. Sidharth understood the meanings of words like 'life' and the 'struggle for existence' only when he saw him. How much pain one had to withstand and what struggle one had to engage in to survive: Sidharth would learn about these from Ramahari's life. However, Ramahari left for his heavenly abode, leaving his dreams unrealised. He didn't even wait till the construction of the boundary wall and repair of the courtyard were finished.

Ramahari belonged to a poor family. He had established a small press, braving much difficulty. He got married. To meet the demands of his household, he worked hard from morning till night. He also helped his neighbours. He would be at the forefront of all arrangements during *pujas* and functions in the colony. On the way back home after the day's work, last evening, his path was suddenly veered towards the hospital, and from there, it further swerved towards death.

In cities like Rourkella, there is always a dense crowd, and a great deal of noise; but where was humanity? Even the officials issued preventive warnings— "Don't offer rides to unknown people". A lack of faith in people defined life here. Even people were afraid of rendering help to victims of accidents lying on the roadside in a pathetic state. Why should one enter mud and then wash his feet clean afterwards? Under such circumstances, where was the unusualness that Ramahari's blood soaked body lay on the roadside for hours?

Ramahari's bier was carried to the van. Another wave of wailing rose in the inner corners of his house. His younger brother carried the bier along with others. Someone started throwing coins and *khai*. Others in the funeral procession started singing *"Ramanam Satya Hei,"* *"Harinam Satya Hei"*. It was time the dead body was carried to the cremation ground.

The sand on the bed of river Brahmi was burning hot in the heat of *Baisakh*. The garlands and bouquets were removed from the bier of Ramahari. His younger brother cleaned Ramahari's face. He put a grain of rice in the mouth of the corpse. Four people carried the dead body. They moved around the pyre seven times and placed it on the pyre. His younger brother lighted it. The dry logs of wood started burning brightly. The physical form of Ramahari was reduced to ashes in no time.

For some reason, Sidharth could not control his emotions. The tear drops in his eyes made the sand on the bed of the Brahmani appear blurred. He felt as if one vital organ inside him had been rendered dysfunctional. Sidharth was not able to reconcile himself to the brute fact that he would not be able to meet Ramahari or have a chat with him. He was looking at the pyre again and again. He spoke as if Ramahari was listening to him, "Go, friend, go. You were fortunate to have gone away ahead of others. Those who go away do not feel any pain; those who stay back feel it."

Tears in the eyes of Ramahari's brother didn't dry for a long time. The elderly people present there were trying desperately to soothe him.

Sleep eluded Sidharth's eyes. The sights and scenes of the crematorium kept dancing before his eyes. He could visualize the pots and pans, the pyre, and the old belongings quite clearly. The banyan tree of detachment was spreading its branches within him. Was it the life one dreamt of? Were friends, children, family, and dreams part of it?

While roaming purposelessly, after a week, Ramahari reached Vedavyas. He reached the place of the pyre where the dead body of Ramahari had been cremated last week. He found someone had made a small heap of ash. At the top of a stick, a piece of red cloth was tied. Sidharth took a piece of stick and spread the ash. The sight of something green surprised him.

On the day of '*Rai Sitala*,' that is a day after the dead body was cremated, while collecting the bones, Ramahari's younger brother had scattered some mustard seeds as per the custom. He had also sprinkled some water on these. Ten or twelve of the seeds had sprouted after a spell of unseasonal rain. Despite the unfavorable surroundings and the scorching heat of *Jyestha*, the sprouting of the seeds claimed the victory of life over death.

Ramahari's widow sat in a dejected and hopeless state,

like the heap of ash, in the courtyard of her house, her hair dishevelled by the wind. Sidharth turned his face away from her and looked at the little girl sitting on her lap. Surprising! Like the sprouted mustard seeds at the cremation ground, the little girl was staring at the neighbours' hens and when they came near, she was driving them away, clapping her hands.

Sidharth heaved a deep sigh. Despite God's conspiracy and lack of support man deserves to live afresh. He felt that, somewhere or the other, like the seed beneath the heap of ash, the spirit of life lay hidden in man. That 'spirit' urged man to continue to exist in the wake of all calamities; it provided one with the courage to look ahead disregarding the drops of tear.

Nityanand Sir

For a long time, they had been swimming in *Bada Pokhari*. It was a day in the month of *Jyestha*, notorious for its sultry heat. The water on the surface had already turned warm; what to speak of roads? No one wished to come out of water. It was now about two o' clock, although they had started at twelve. The eyes of Aparti and Nakul had already turned red like a hibiscus flower; it was as if moss had grown on their lips and chins. However, no one refrained from displaying their swimming skills. They held demonstrations of all kinds of swimming styles they knew including backstrokes and swimming underwater in the muddy water.

Nakul, at first, reported that someone was watching them from the back of the school for a very long time. He had noticed a red towel shaking in the wind. Who could this gentleman be? Might he be the Headmaster or the Superintendent? 'No,' Nakul discounted all such possibilities. Had the person been any one of the above two, he might not have waited with patience for such a long time. Abhaya proposed that one of them should go and find out who it was. He ordered that Sidharth must carry out this task.

Sent as a special emissary by the friends, Sidharth proceeded towards the spot, feeling cowardly and apprehensive, from where someone had been watching their unruly swimming for a very long time. But, after discovering the gentleman who had kept himself concealed, he felt alarmed and amazed. Even the sight of a snake would not have terrified him so much. The gentleman who was standing in front of Sidharth was none other than Nityanand Sir. Sidharth wished to retreat from there and pass the message to his friends. But Sir advised him, by pressing his finger on his lips, to keep quiet.

The fog of curiosity was still not dispelled from Sidharth's mind. 'How long will you wait here, Sir? They don't feel like coming out of water today."

Nityanand Sir replied, "They will come out on their own, after some time. Small children; they are feeling delighted to swim. If they find me, they will come out of water without delay."

Nityanand Sir was the most qualified teacher of the school. He was the only child of his parents. After passing his M.A. examination, he didn't look for a job, but decided to work as a teacher in the village school. No one knew whether his decision pleased his parents, but this news made the school children extremely happy. Sidharth remembered how, when Nityanand Sir reached school on the first day, he wanted to take a look at the school library. Library those days meant a broken almirah that contained thirty to forty text-books, two dictionaries—one English, another Odia - and a few old magazines. Nityanand Sir announced the decision he had taken; he would not take any salary from school. The amount which he might have received as salary would be spent on purchasing books for the school library. That was exactly what was done. Within a span of two years, the library came to be well stocked.

So, it was not at all surprising if the same Nityanand Sir had decided to postpone his time of taking bath for the sake of naughty children who wanted to have a little fun.

However, one day he gave Sidharth a surprise. Sidharth was then a student of class ten. He had a very good handwriting and wrote both English and Odia impeccably. Once, Nityanand Sir gave Sidharth the task of copying his manuscript. Needless to say, for Sidharth, it was not a responsibility but a great privilege. Even when he talked to his friends or went shopping, he would carry Nityanand Sir's manuscript with him. His intention was to prove that he was not an ordinary student like others; that he was held in high esteem; and that was why Nityanand Sir had given such a responsible job to him. He completed the task in seven to eight days and returned the notebook to him.

A week elapsed. One afternoon, Nityanand Sir suddenly appeared in the hostel. The boarders were busy gossiping. They all got up when they saw him. Sidharth advanced towards him. He had pronounced himself the most favourite student of Sir. Nityanand Sir handed him over a packet wrapped in red paper. Sidharth's joys knew no bounds. He opened the packet after Sir's departure and found two story books, one exercise book and an elegant pen. This was the remuneration for the job he had done.

After a few days, they all had to leave school. The memories associated with the high school days are unforgettable. These memories are deeply entrenched in one's heart and, therefore, very intimate. After a few days of leaving school, Sidharth was informed that Nityanand Sir had died of cancer. On receiving the news, Sidharth felt completely devastated.

Nityanand Sir was no more; but most of the time he would stand out of the crowded memories. In this city life where everyone was bent upon dealing with others professionally, Sidharth fondly remembered Nityanand Sir.

These days, one finds the sahibs and the rich as well as the renowned so fond of beating their own drums that they behave as if they are accompanied by a storm whenever they appear somewhere. Their followers shout, "Here we come," "move aside," "make some space". You common folk; make way for *'baboo'* to go or, 'sahib' to come. The moment they reach, calling bells spring into action; the noise of orderlies' shoes can be heard; telephones start ringing; the sound of motor cars deafens everyone. The more noise, the more buzz surrounds one, the more respect and importance he gets. One who is lonely and silent is considered backward, weak and worthless.

Sidharth was reminded of Nityanand Sir the moment he found the strong trampling upon the emotions and sentiments of the poor. A slightly dark person of an unknown village was he. Sidharth would remember how he had waited on that sultry summer afternoon, tolerating the mischief of undisciplined boys. He felt as if the bracing *Chaitra* breeze was blowing, pushing away the sultry heat and the hot breeze of *Jaistha*. The fragrance of fresh *siuli* flowers suddenly pervaded Sidharth's entire being.

Obeissance to Lost Childhood

I don't know why, but for some reason, all villages, whether small or big, look like my own village from a distance. A strange weakness crops up in the mind for the calm, serene and peaceful atmosphere of the village. I have spent the memorable days of my childhood and youth nurtured by the soil, water and air of the village. Consequently, a great weakness for my village has automatically struck deep roots.

I had not visited my dear village for long. In spite of myself, I had turned into a city dweller in quest for a few square feet of land beneath my feet and an identity of my own to display before others. If I had not visited my village, the fakeness of my new identity would never have been revealed.

The pitted road that runs from Gaddi to Ghanteswar leads to my village. Ten years back, when I was a student of the village school, I and my friends, after school was out, would walk home along this road. We would reach home only when we grew tired after a game of *dalamankudi* played on the branches of the banyan and peepul trees on the way. We never ever felt tired walking home. We felt as if we flew in the air.

This time when I reached Gaddi bazzar, I clearly perceived that the place was not the one to which I had grown accustomed ten years ago. The winds of change had swept through and transformed the Gaddi Bazzar as well as the surrounding areas of my village. Those days, there wasn't even a good road leading to Ghanteswar. The wheels of cars and buses had never rolled along those roads. The milkman carried pots of milk on their shoulders for sale at Pirhat. The fishermen of the area would sell their fish in the Ghanteswar Bazzar. Their goods didn't and couldn't reach the bazzar at Gaddi. Consequently, there was no dearth of fish, milk, and milk products at Ghanteswar.

Once Nabakrushna Chaudhury, the former Chief Minister of Odisha, expressing his opinion about Ghanteswar had said, "The three strongest economic pillars of this area are paddy, milk and fish. So the area would never encounter any problem in future." His remarks rang very true those days, but today it would be hard to credit them.

I have vivid memories of my school days. Whenever we crossed Gaddi on our way to Bhadrak or Chandabali, father would feed me with cheese or *mudhi* at the Ghanteswar Bazzar. In addition, I would be treated to a few *ladoos* at times. They tasted like nectar. For us, Ghanteswar resembled affluent cities like Delhi or Kolkata. Its cheese *mudki* and rasogollas were irresistible. Even when we grew up, while paying a visit to the village, we would pause for a moment at Ghanteswar bazzar, perhaps as a matter of habit, and would treat us to cheese *mudki*. The confectioner would flash a faint smile of recognition. He would hand the cheese bowls without even caring to weigh the cheese.

During a recent visit, I didn't get an opportunity to taste those delicacies. One of my classmates informed me that these had grown out of fashion. When I reached there this time, the familiar confectioner invited me inside the shop but the food and drinks served were completely different. He served me two *sandeshes* and a bottle of limca. I was not eager to consume those. Those items belonged to Cuttack or Bhubaneswar. My friend also hinted that the shopkeeper would promptly serve me a drink, foreign or Indian depending on my order. These were available in plenty in the Bazzar. Even country liquor worth five thousand rupees was being sold every day.

I had no patience for all this. I realized quite well that just as I would never be able to get back my childhood and youth, no matter how hard I tried, I would never get back to the scenes and situations that prevailed at Ghanteswar Bazzar some ten years ago.

Indian and foreign liquor are being traded in broad daylight in a rural market like Ghanteswar. Sale of intoxicants like ganja, and opium has increased manifold. In the darkness of the evenings, the sons of the farmers watch pornographic films, with money made by selling paddy or rice. I also heard from my childhood friend that the children of rich families of the area had grown addicted to 'campose tablets'.

In the past, whenever I thought of visiting my village, my feet would get ready to fly. But these days, I have shackled them. The geographical entity that I called my village; the houses I grew up in and the trees that grew around them still exist, but the soul of the village of my childhood and youth had died an untimely death.

Our Village

That it would rain in the month of *Phalguna*, and that it would pour incessantly for four or five days, was something Sidharth had never expected. Otherwise, he would have paid a visit to his village in his office jeep; he would never have brought his brand new Maruti car.

"Fie! Fie! Does a road like this lead to your village? You are concerned about the vehicle but if I had heard about the condition of the road beforehand, I would never have accompanied you. Now, do what you wish. Both the front wheels have completely sunk into the mud. Can we lift these on our own?" remarked Lalita.

Sidharth was a senior officer placed at Bhubanewar. Usually, he was very busy. He hardly found the time to visit his village. He would make time to visit his old and sick mother once every five or six years. Many a time, he had tried to convince his mother to come and live in Bhubaneswar. His mother, however, insisted on staying on in the village. The reasons against visiting Bhubaneswar were not only many but also quite complex. There would be neither the sacred tulsi plant nor any ponds nearby. She could never use tap water to worship gods. Chicken, mutton, eggs and crabs were cooked in the kitchen. She would feel suffocated in such a place. Sidharth would return disappointed every time. However, another story was heard in the village about the old lady not visiting Bhubaneswar. The reason was, obviously, Sidharth's wife, Lalita.

Lalita, the only daughter of a retired Executive Engineer, had never visited Sidharth's village even though ten years had passed since their marriage. The marriage took place in Bhubaneswar. She was visiting the village for the first time. Two motives guided such a visit. The first one was to pay a visit to the perennially sick mother-in-law. The second reason, more significant than the first: she had to find out about how to bring the landed property and homestead land under her control after the death of the mother-in-law.

The problem now was, the wheels had sunk into the soft earth of Nalabandha. No one could be seen for miles around.

Sidharth was paying a visit to the village after some seven years. He expected that the condition of the road to his village would have become black-topped as the local M.L.A.'s village was only a mile away from his. The village would have become electrified. The children of the village would be watching 'The Mahabharat" serial on T.V. There may not be piped water connection, but three or four tube-wells must have been dug. A primary health center must have been opened near the market. Passenger buses must be plying from the market to Bhubaneswar regularly.

While wiping the sweat from her forehead with a perfume-laced handkerchief, Lalita said, "While leaving home I was asking you to bring one or two peons or drivers. You refused. Wouldn't they have been useful now?"

"Oh! What's the point in talking about all this now? I am worried about the car; it has scratches all over now. We don't even find a single person nearby. How would the car come out of the mud? It would have been better to bring the jeep. Oh! My new car. What bad luck!" Then he commented on the village road, saying, "Do human beings live in such a place?"

A few cowherd boys who were grazing cows near Nalabandha gathered there to witness the wretched condition of the brand new car. One of them, while clutching at the buttonless loose pants so that it did not fall off, ran towards the village to present a first-hand account of such a rare but astonishing incident. On hearing the news, four or five people rushed to the spot.

Sidharth recognized the eldest person who walked ahead of others; it was his uncle. On seeing him, Sidharth had already felt better. It was natural that the same Kartik uncle, who appeared insignificant on other occasions, now seemed extremely important.

Kartik Swain, on seeing Sidharth, said, "Arey! This is our Sidhu. Perhaps he is accompanied by our daughter-in-law. Yes, yes. Brothers, run… run… let's push the car out of the mud. Run…" Needless to mention that the call given out by Kartik uncle left the others no option but to set to work.

Sidharth and the five other people, with much difficulty, pushed the car out of the mud onto the road. The cowherd boys got busy pushing the car even though their help was not sought. They were performing their duty quite sincerely, thinking that such an opportunity might never befall them.

Kartik Swain said, "You were not at home that day when I came to your quarters to enquire about the address of Lakshman. My daughter-in-law gave me a glass of water."

Lalita faintly remembered the incident. About thirteen or fourteen days ago, this man clad in a torn shirt had come to their residence. Before he met her, he was found talking to the cook, Nabina. That day, Lalita had not paid him any attention as she was very busy. She had to attend the wedding of the Executive Engineer's daughter. The man was asking about someone's address. Lalita, while going out, had remarked, 'We don't keep the address of such people." Then the man asked for a drink of water. She had asked Nabina to give him water in an aluminium mug, before leaving the house." Was he referring to that incident?"

While walking into the village, Kartik uncle was heard saying, "You people got educated, became officers, and lived away from us. You wish to visit the village once in six months or a year in a car. You can't travel like us in a bus or bullock cart. If you use your contacts at higher levels, the road can be black-topped in a year. We don't have any problem; we walk. A good road is needed for your vehicles. The local M.L.A. got a red gravel road constructed up to his house. Who will bother about our village?"

Sidharth was speechless. He had come to the village riding his car to exhibit his wealth and importance, but how cruelly the village cut him to size! Truly, he had never done a thing for his village.

His face turned red from shame and regret. Lalita had absolutely no idea about villages since she was born and brought up in the city. Enticed by the sweet fragrance of the wet earth as well as the sight of the narrow lanes and natural drains, and enchanted by the sincerity of the village people, Lalita told Sidharth, "Yes, you were right. Only the soil and people of one's village give away everything, asking for nothing in return."

Sidharth had forgotten completely about his car and was deeply engrossed in thinking about his village.

■

Pearl and Oyster

She glanced around her in such a way that it seemed as if she did not feel safe in that place. She clung to her mother. In one cloth bag, she carried an extra dress to change into. She was wearing the other one; the dress was mended at five or six places. Her head looked like a hornet's nest. She had grown tired from travelling forty kilometers in a passenger bus. She was sobbing.

Varsa comforted her, saying, "You will stay in this house from today; this is like your own home. Go, wash yourself clean and eat something first."

The child was staring at things she had never set her eyes on ever before. From the television, the fridge, the sofa set, the table and chairs her eyes turned to the ceiling and got fixed there. Then her eyes fell on the shell of the tortoise on the mosaic verandah. Novelty enveloped everything.

Just as the seven or eight-year-old child gazed at everything in surprise, the people of the house gazed at her consumed with curiosity. They watched her as if she was a strange animal.

The landlady felt happy. Thank God, finally they had found someone to do the house work. Was cleaning of utensils an easy task? She had been on the lookout for a suitable girl.

In the afternoon, the child's mother as well as Nimain Mohanty, the person who had persuaded the child to serve this family departed.

On finding that her mother was going away, the child let out a sudden cry. The landlady gave her a chocolate and took her in. Her words seemed very soft and sweet.

The child lived in that house since that time.

In the beginning, her name was Malati, the same as the name of the mistress of the house. Everybody objected. "How could the mistress of the house and the servant have the same name?" The mistress was not supposed to change her name and therefore, the child was made to change hers. There was no need of asking Malati. From the next day, her name was changed into Sebati; after a few days, it was shortened into Seba. Thereafter, she was known as only 'Seba'. Time came when she forgot her original name completely.

Gradually, Seba was needed by everybody. She did the dishes, washed clothes, swept the floor, wiped the table clean, and carried out the orders of the masters. When she had nothing else to do, she would keep standing in one corner of the dining room.

No one knew when Seba ate; no one knew when she took her bath. By the time they got up, Seba would be ready to help. No one ever saw her eating just as no one ever witnessed the blossoming of the fig flowers. Surprisingly, she never fell ill.

On some days, Seba would sit alone, her face wearing a sad expression. While she was sitting like this one day, Sidharth called her and asked, "Are you not happy here?" Seba gave only a smile in reply. Only she knew whether she wanted to say 'yes' or 'no'. Sidharth further asked her about her parents. Seba made bold to answer this question. Their village was on the other side of Tangi-Chandpur. There was a mountain near the village; at the foot of the mountain, stood trees of a forest. She would go to the forest with her friends in the morning to fetch wood. She would pluck tendu fruits and *kaicha* nuts with friends like Malli, Mina and Tukuna. She would play hide and seek and *puchi* in the forest. She would return, carrying the bundle of wood, by noon. The afternoon would be spent near the village pond. While returning from the forest, she would collect wild white tulips and pebbles. She would play a game of basket or *bohubohuka* with her friends.

"Do you remember your friends?" When this question is asked, two drops of tear, like pearls, rolled down her white cheeks. Sidharth changed the topic.

"Do you have any brothers?"

"Yes, two brothers—Inder and Chandar."

"What do you mean by Inder and Chandar? Does anybody say the names of one's brothers like this?" Sidharth would ask her.

She bit her tongue. "Indramani Gouda and Chandramani Gouda. Besides, there is an elder sister, who is already married."

Her words made Sidharth feel helpless. The sister, who has two brothers like Indra and Chandra, has to work in someone else's house to earn a living!

One day, Sidharth offered ten rupees to Seba. He said, "I will take you to the bus-stand and put you in a bus. You can go from Tangi. If you want to go home, you can. Nobody will say no."

Her smiling face brightened up for a moment. But the next moment, it fell. If she goes home, her father will be angry with her. Her mother will drag her by the hair and send her to someone else. She is quite happy here. Here, there is a TV; she watches films; she watches the Mahabharat. Although she has to sleep on the floor, she sleeps under a fan. She will not go anywhere. She is mortally scared of her father. He will throw hot water on her.

Before coming to this house, Seba was working in someone else's house. The mistress of the house used to throw hot water on her on some pretext or another.

Seba said, "I am leaving now. It is time for my mistress to return. I will mop the floor. I will go to the village for two or three days during Raja. But, I will return."

Sidharth agreed to her proposal.

While Sidharth thought of Seba's thin body and the demands of her family, he felt that every oyster did not turn into a pearl. Very rarely, only a few fortunate oysters who got the opportunity to drink rain drops under the star Arcturus, turn into pearls. Most others remain as useless shells forever, like Seba.

Selling Mirrors in the Country of the Blind

Karababu was always concerned about matters related to the education of his children. He would flare up if his son or daughter committed the slightest mistake. He would react instantaneously. For the last few days, he was busy with matters concerning the Sanskrit tuition of his daughter. Tuition…that too in a subject like Sanskrit! The day Sidharth heard of it, he was shocked. During the time he was at school, nobody gave any importance to either Sanskrit or the Sanskrit teacher. He found it hard to imagine that the English medium students of the capital schools would read Sanskrit, and that too, would require the help of tutors in the subject. Karababu explained the matter carefully: "If one opts for Sanskrit as the third language, one can score very good marks in the examination." Sidharth said, "It's okay but what is the need for tuition? Can't you teach her yourself?" Karababu smiled and said, "You see, Sidharth, Sanskrit is not my cup of tea. Did we ever give any importance to the subject when we were students? How could we teach others? Now, one tutor has agreed to provide her coaching. He lives in Chandrasekharpur. He will teach for three days a week, forty-five minutes each day. It takes forty minutes to go from Unit Eight to Chandrasekharpur and come back. I don't return after dropping my daughter at the teacher's house; I roam around the market there. I return only after her classes are over."

Sidharth was impressed with Karababu. How deeply was the poor gentleman concerned about the education of his children!

However, Sidharth was not able to get used to the idea that Sanskrit teachers were a rarity. He was reminded of the ever-ignored Sanskrit pundit of his village school.

Sidharth studied in a mofussil school, far away from the capital. The Headmaster of the high school was a citified young man. The Sanskrit pundit was an adult, a contemporary of Sidharth's father. Whatever happened elsewhere in the world, also happened in their school. The students were excessively scared of the headmaster and the English teacher whereas they treated the poor Sanskrit teacher with contempt. That the Sanskrit pundit didn't know anything about the children's lack of respect for him was inconceivable; the fact was that he didn't take anything to heart.

When someone compared him with the young headmaster, he responded by alluding to a hymn from *Kumara Sambhavam*: When Parvati was lost in deep penance wishing to get married to Lord Shiva, numerous attempts were made to dissuade her from doing so. Some said, "Lord Shiva doesn't own any landed property; he lives in a cremation ground. If she gets married to him, she will ruin her life. It is hundred times better to get married to Lord Indra than to Lord Shiva." Without being perturbed at all, the strong-headed Parvati retorted, "Lord Indra may be the Lord of Gods but if he comes across Lord Shiva, while going on a tour on his elephant, Airabat, he would immediately get down and prostrate himself at the feet of Lord Shiva. He would not get up until the pollen grains from the divine flower *parijat*, which adorned his head, turned the feet of Lord Shiva red." When alluding to the fable he would compare himself to Lord Shiva and the young headmaster to Lord Indra, the children would fail to make sense of the comparison. They would listen to the story and smile. The bald-headed Pundit would leave the classroom, umbrella and attendance register in hand.

Sidharth had met his former Sanskrit teacher about eighteen years ago. He had been waiting at the bus-stop. He wore shabby clothes; his face looked withered. The lively personality who could elevate himself to the seat of Lord Shiva, and who could counter every insulting situation by reciting Sanskrit *slokas*, appeared utterly defeated. Sidharth went and bowed before him. Pundit looked crestfallen. Despite the best of his efforts, he could not hide the sadness lurking within. The school managing committee had dispensed with his services. The current secretary, who was once his student, didn't heed his earnest request for a year's extension. "The elder son is going to appear at the matriculation examination; daughter, already marriageable, is sitting at home. Your *guruma*- my wife is sick…" "The man who lived amidst the heroes and heroines of great epics like *Raghubansam, KumarSambhamam, Meghadutam* etc. had so many troubles surrounding him," Sidharth wondered.

He said, "Sir, you taught us so well. If you provide tuition to children, you will not have any trouble."

Sir smiled a pathetic smile. "You know very well how

subjects like Hindi and Sanskrit are regarded in mofussil villages like ours. Here my fate is like that of a person who goes out to peddle mirrors in a country of the blind. Let's see..."

The bus arrived. Sidharth got an opportunity to escape from the uncomfortable situation.

Karababu was heard saying, "Sidharth, the Sanskrit teacher that we have arranged is very knowledgeable. He has learnt all the *slokas* by heart. There is a beeline of children at his house."

Sidharth didn't want to hear anything more. He knew, in the capital city, demand from the parents and not talent was what mattered most. Everything was dictated by fate. Somewhere *salagram* was treated like pebble whereas somewhere else, a pebble got the respect due to a *salagram*.

Planning and Kashinana

Sidharth would not have believed it if he had not seen and heard it himself: the anti-establishment revolutionary Nabakishore had turned into an ideal pro-establishment employee. A few years back, on the Jyotivihar campus, Nabakishore was a staunch revolutionary and anarchist. He had absolutely no faith in India's democracy, judiciary, administration and system of education. Against all these, he would wage a unilateral war. His fiery speech in the cold evenings; his allusion to celebrated world leaders would fill the otherwise dull life of Sidharth and his classmates with excitement. We all had tremendous faith in Nabakishore; we believed that revolution would surely take place today or tomorrow or the day after tomorrow. People like Nabakishore would lead that revolution. They will remove the mask of deceit, treachery and cunning; they will bring about revolutionary changes in the lives of common people.

Within the last ten years, many changes have surely taken place. However, perceptible changes have taken place in Nabakishore's mind. In the place of a revolution, an anti-revolution feeling has clouded his consciousness. Otherwise, that revolutionary and fiery youth of Jyotivihar would not be singing the names of his superiors like a professional eulogizer.

Nabakishore is a block-level official now. He is a responsible patron of the just- concluded literacy movement of the district. "On the fifteenth of the last month, our block became completely literate. Everyone, old and young, man and woman has become literate." He has stressed this fact. He spouted facts and statistical figures to highlight the revolutionary importance of the scheme, its necessity, and hundred percent utilization of both labour and resources. His arguments appeared to Sidharth not only irrefutable but also sweet to hear.

After listening to Nabakishore for a long time Sidharth asked, "Do you remember Kashinana of our village, who died two years ago?"

Nabakishore was wondering what the relationship between Kashinana and a government programme might be. Without leaving him in a state of prolonged doubt, Sidharth told him about Kashinana.

For a very long time, Kashinana was the only Brahmin *purohit* of Sidharth's village. After the demise of his father, Chandrasekhar Mohapatra he performed priestly duties on all festive occasions. At times, it would become extremely difficult on his part to perform *pujas* in twenty to twenty-five houses. On auspicious days like *Ekadasi* and *Sankranti*, Kashinana would move breathlessly from house to house.

It was the day of *Bataosha*. Sidharth and Nabakishore were school-going boys. Their mothers and aunts were waiting for Kashinana without going to sleep. When Nana came he would read the *Bataosha* book. Then there would be worship of the deity and offerings would be made to her. Only then the ladies would return home. Some worshippers were yawning in disgust as Nana was late. Nabakishore had lost his patience hours ago. His mother was sending him out frequently with the words, "Go and see if Nana has completed the *puja* at Das family's house." Nana had to visit the Parida family after this, which would be followed by a visit to the Mohanty family. The worshippers, who sought the blessings of Yamaraj and who loved their children dearly, had no other option but to wait patiently for Nana to arrive.

At last Kashinana arrived. His arrival was such a cheerful event that all female worshippers became active immediately. They paid obeisance to him with the ends of their *sarees* tied around their necks. Sidharth, however, had an old axe to grind with Kashinana. It was caused by jealousy. Sidharth sang well. At school, he would sing the prayer and others would follow. If someone fell ill or was on death-bed, his father would immediately send him there to recite the eleventh book of *The Bhagavad*. Sidharth would go there and start reading the verses. But he would not enjoy reading the text as he would be reciting it to a desperate person hoping to earn merit. However, on festive occasions like *Manabasa* and *Bataosha*, no one required his help. On those he would feel unwanted. On these, singing the verses would fill one with an unexpected excitement. The simple reason for this is that on such occasions, not only Sidharth's mother, aunts or sister-in-laws would be present but also Sidharth's classmates and their friends would be present as apprentices to learn the nitty-gritty of this *puja*. Sidharth would curse Kasinana as he prevented him from displaying the sweetness of his voice and his ability to sing lines from the scriptures. He would lie in wait to point out Kasinana's defects.

Kasinana would be pressed for time. Since evening,

he would have completed reading the *Purana* in seven houses, with thirteen more houses to be visited. He would immediately start reading the *Purana* standing. He would not have the patience to read all the twenty-four pages of the *Bataosha* book. The sleepy worshippers, after the long wait, would also not be in a mood to wait so long. What would follow was mutually agreed upon. Kasinana would shout, *"Anandekbar haribol"* (take the name of God once in pleasure), and in response to it the female-worshippers would fill the place with loud ululation. Kasinana would take the opportunity to turn four or five pages of the book at a time. During the course of the singing of the *Purana*, Kasinana would persuade the audience to take the name of god three to four times, and complete turning the pages in fifteen to twenty minutes. Then he would start the process of offering bhog to God. All would take leave soon after, fully satisfied.

Once Sidharth asked Kasinana boldly, "Why are you cheating the female-worshippers by turning the pages so fast?" Before the short-tempered Kasinana could answer the question, Sidharth's grandfather took him away, dragging him by his ears and saved him from the curse of the Brahmin. Sidharth found it hard to forget the insult and grief he had endured that day.

Nabakishore was feeling a little uncomfortable to remember things associated with Kasinana. Sidharth, of course, didn't want to make his friend feel sad. While returning, he just wanted to say that his government machinery had the ability to read the *Purana* like Kasinana. Nabakishore would surely think deeply about the goal of making everyone literate in a year, just like Kasinana read the *Purana* in twenty-five houses in one evening. There was a qualitative difference between construction of buildings and bridges on the one hand, and spread of literacy on the other.

It was time for Nabakishore to go back. Sidharth somehow felt that his words had not been received favourably. Sidharth was prone to making such mistakes. During childhood, he was scolded by his grandfather for pointing out the mistakes of Kasinana, and today he was going to lose Nabakishore as a friend by giving him unwanted advice. It's true that Sidharth had not gone far in life but his friends like Nabakishore had mastered Kasinana's skills quite well.

A Picture of Arrogance

The presence of a large number of rustic old men and women at the literary meeting despite the inclement weather in that cold evening, made Sidharth think that perhaps the people of the area felt great love for literature and culture.

The meeting started two hours late. But the presence of the minister overwhelmed the organizers and the common people to such an extent that they endured the two-hour wait without resentment. Microphones continuously blared out slogans like "Honourable Minister... welcome...welcome," "Honourable Minister...long live... long live," Kalika club... Long live...long live". Just as hymns are continuously chanted on the marriage pandal, slogans were continuously raised. Curious people from the market followed the minister up to the pandal; they returned only after the minister ascended the dais. Some people were already present on the dais to take the programme forward. They kept placing one garland after another till they touched the tip of the nose of the minister. Thereafter, the minister would touch the other garlands with both his hands and lay them on the table.

Several chairs of different heights and shapes were placed on the dais. Two out of those appeared huge and exquisite like the thrones used by kings in films and plays. The minister who frequently repeated 'all are equal in a democracy and we are only your representatives' sat on one of those to display his grandeur. On the other impressive chair sat the president of the meeting, who was a former minister. The entire thing appeared repulsive to Sidharth.

The report of the secretary was read out and was followed by a welcome speech, introduction of the guests and reading of citations. This was to be followed by speech of the Chief Guest, Guests of Honour, Chief Speaker, other honourable speakers, and finally, the vote of thanks. The thanks-giving could not be completed within the stipulated time. In a meeting Sidharth was once surpised to find that the thanks-giving speech was much longer than the speech of the Chief Guest. Later, he was informed that the chief dish of the dinner had not been prepared by then, and the long speech was a calculated ploy of the organizers to keep the guests confined to the dais.

Small children in the audience had started dozing. Their mothers were growing absent-minded, unsure of what they should attend to— the familial duty of taking care of their children or the social duty of listening to the speakers. The statistics presented by the speakers flew over the heads of the audience, just like empty clouds flying above the withered fields. Despite this, the inspired Chief Speaker didn't see the need of abridging his speech.

After addressing the audience for about an hour, the honourable minister sat down and drank the water kept on the table in great gulps. In the meantime, a handsome man came to the microphone and announced that it was time for old age pensions to be distributed among the old men and women. Sidharth felt shocked by this strange item on the agenda of a literary meeting. He now realized that the old men and women adorning the seats on the front row were not really interested in literature; they were poor citizens waiting for the distribution of old age pensions.

The cameramen got ready to click photos. The Block Development Officer, president of the meeting, and the Minister also got ready. The beneficiaries were called to the dais one by one. Five of them got up and received one month's pension of one hundred rupees from the honourable minister. The act of distribution of pensions was stopped midway. The handsome man came to the microphone again and announced, "The Honourable Minister has to leave soon to attend another programme. So, he would not be able to distribute pension to others. Others have to go to the Block office where the BDO will distribute the pension."

People now rushed out of the site of the meeting like they run towards safe shelters on being informed of an imminent flood or storm. The helpless old men and women, defying the bitter cold of winter and darkness of the night, ran towards the Block office. After a long time, they were able to visualise golden days ahead as there was the prospect of earning one hundred rupees every month. They didn't want to give up such an opportunity. If they were late, the BDO might close the office!

The next morning, Sidharth saw the photo of the minister distributing pensions from the dais of the literary meeting in a newspaper published from the capital. The photo clearly showed the smile on his lips. It also showed the old lady's fatigue. Sidharth felt as if the camera had also vividly captured the minister's conceit and arrogance.

■

Protest

That a tiny bird will build a nest in the brightly lit drawing room; that it will gather everything from dry twigs to withered grass; was something the master of the house could not tolerate. Last year, exactly at this time, the two birds had made a mess of the house. They built a nest; they laid eggs; they forcibly occupied that place till the hatchlings came out of the eggs and learnt to fly. The egg shells, the remnants of insects they had eaten, and the twigs falling from their large nest left the room dirty. Besides, the birds had to be protected from the blades of the rotating fan. The uncommon eagerness of the youngest child of the family to save the hatchlings from the cat had surprised him.

This year also the two birds had already started building their nest. No, he had made a great mistake by allowing the birds to do what they wanted. Before anyone else got up, Sidharth had left the bed that morning. He brought a long broom and swept away the nest under construction. He felt comfortable after throwing the twigs and blades of grass some distance away. He thought to himself that, if the birds had a little self-respect, they would never come back.

The moment he returned in the evening, his eyes were immediately directed towards the spot near the skylight. Surprising! The birds were back! Even more weeds and twigs had been collected. He laid the tea-cup on the teapoy and was going to fetch the broom when suddenly his eyes fell on his younger daughter. She was a staunch ally of the bird-couple. "Let it be; it will be dealt with later." The next morning, Sidharth had left this bed before any other member had. He went out quietly and brought the broom from a corner of the house. He held the broom like a raised sword and climbed up the table as if he was climbing a horse. "Hum, what a farce going on here! Wait, I will show you what I can do," said Sidharth to himself.

Sidharth's surprise knew no bounds the moment he climbed up the table and looked into the nest. Both the parents looked at him silently in the manner of 'satyagrahis'. Perhaps they wanted to say, "You have the power; you may displace us from here. But, where will we go in this helpless condition? For human beings like you, there are hospitals and nursing homes; intensive care units and ambulances. We don't have access to these. This is precisely why we have taken shelter here. Where will we go?"

Sidharth remembered his own pregnant wife writhing in pain. Her painful cries from the delivery room had terribly shaken him that day.

He took the broom close to the two birds. Had they gone mad? They were not showing any sign of budging from there.

Sidharth finally climbed off the table ridden by a sense of defeat, sadness, and sin. He had seen or read in newspapers about many mass protests, strikes, *dharnas* and *satyagrahas* organized on the highway to protest against displacement from one's own land or to exercise one's right. However, he had never witnessed anything like the peaceful and meek protest of the two birds.

When he tried to jump off the table, he found his younger daughter standing there; she had come some time ago and been watching him silently. When Sidharth got down the table, she asked, "What were you doing, father?"

Feeling awkward, Sidharth replied, "No…no… I was just watching if the two birds had any problems. Anyway, they are our guests."

His daughter looked cheerful.

The broom which resembled a raised sword some time ago, now lay abandoned on the ground.

Relationship

Drops of tear rolling down from Amrita's eyes had dried up.

Sidharth felt guilty. Malati looked at him once and turned her face away. Every husband understood the meaning of such a glance. This glance was certainly devoid of love or affection.

Dragging the blanket up to his lips, Sidharth shut his eyes. Perhaps, under the circumstances, there was no alternative other than shutting the eyes. The room was calm; it was the calm before a storm. It was as if a bomb would go off somewhere or a mountain would be blown up to pieces. At least, breaking of a couple of glasses, or a mirror, or plates of clay could not be ruled out.

Sidharth mustered courage and asked, "What would have gone wrong if you had sent the child to Luna's house?"

Perhaps, Malati was waiting for a question like this. "People like you don't have any sense of shame. You can go anywhere you want to without being invited or without taking gifts. My daughter is not shameless like you. Let me hear what arrangements you had made for her? For the last two days she had been constantly reminding you that

Amrita's birthday was going to be celebrated today. They read in the same class; they meet each other every day. But, despite living close to Amrita's house, she could not attend her birthday; rather, she was thrashed and put to sleep."

Sidharth felt sad to learn that his daughter had been beaten and had to go to bed on an empty stomach. This pained him more than the fact that she could not visit her friend on her birthday. To tell the truth, Sidharth had not at all forgotten that it was Amrita's birthday. However, he was unable to arrange fifty or hundred rupees to buy something as a present. He didn't want to tell Malati of this. Malati would either disbelieve him; or, if she believed him, she would mock at his poverty.

During the last two months, he had to attend ten marriages of either friends or the children of his friends. With a clerk's job, it was not possible to set aside forty one or fifty one rupees to buy gifts on every occasion. Still, he should have bought a gift for his daughter's friend.

Malati, making an effort to sleep, turned over and faced the wall; let her do so. Sidharth brushed aside the hair falling on the eyes of his daughter. He wiped the tear marks with his palm. He sighed deeply.

Sidharth was reminded of his childhood days. He didn't have proper school uniforms, text books, expensive shoes or good quality dresses. But what was important was they lived in a world full of freedom. They roamed freely. Wherever evening set in, there they ate the evening meal, irrespective of whether it was Baguli's house or Sridhar's house. Fresh *pakhala* with the aroma of new mango and fried dried-fish would be served. There would also be *badichura* in a bowl. There existed no feeling of deprivation or embarrassment. There was no distinction between of my house and their house. The marriage of Gelhi dei was a festive occasion for the children of the entire village. The *kirtan* at Nakul's house was a three-day function for the children of Mohantysahi. On the holidays, they would eat cakes and *mudhi* at someone's house; in the evening they were treated to delicacies like *endury* or *podapitha*. Only when one felt sleepy did one return home.

There was poverty in the village, but side by side existed a feeling of independence. There was no need of exhibiting closeness in relationships through presenting a pen or two or three tea-cups or steel utensils wrapped in blue or red paper. Relationships were not governed by conditions. Even though Amrita stayed only a few metres away from Luna's house, she did not go to attend her birthday party and no one cared to send for Amrita; this might never have happened in the village.

Sidharth said, "It was better that Amrita had not gone there. She should not be accustomed to giving presents from such a tender age. You should give something only when you have the ability to give it; what would happen if you don't have something? What sort of relationship is this which depends on the ability to give something?"

Malati hissed like a cobra. While turning the pillow over three or four times to make her anger subside, she said, "Is there any difference between people like you and bullocks wandering in the streets? You don't have any sense of shame. Can I show my face to Luna's mother again?"

Sidharth didn't argue. He knew he would not be able to pacify Malati. He also knew he would never be able to explain that love, affection, and fellow-feeling couldn't be tied into a packet wrapped in blue and red paper.

Relief

First, he came out of the gate and looked here and there, before hiding near the boundary wall. Usually, the gate of this house would not be opened so early. New guests had come; they opened the gate as the bus-time neared. His master and mistress were not even aware of his escape through the gate.

The national highway ran some five hundred feet away from the house. A red gravel road led to it. On no occasion in the past had he come this far. He lacked the courage to do so. On this road, two or three mangy and bad-tempered dogs would often roam about. The moment their eyes fell on him, they would start barking and rush towards him. He felt safe on the other side of the gate. From there he would look through the gate and answer the mangy and the bad-tempered dogs back.

Both his master and mistress were good human beings. They never allowed him to go outside. Earlier, they would keep him tied throughout day and night. These days, they unleashed him during the night. He would twist and turn; he would resist being subjugated. He would not eat at times. If he found some young bitch on the other side of the gate, he would feel tormented. He would lose his calm in the moonlight of *Sarad*. However, he would find it impossible to leave, breaking the iron-leash. He would vent his anger and frustration by barking furiously at people passing by. He would grow jealous of the cats, bullocks and goats moving in the street.

When he was six months old, he had fallen ill. He endured the injections given to him at the hospital calmly. No one thought he would survive, but he did. During his illness which had lasted for two weeks, he made the place where he was tied very dirty both by urinating and passing stool. The entire family felt disgusted and said that he should die. But surprisingly he survived. He not only survived but within a span of six months, he turned himself into an animal that any owner would be proud of.

He didn't know what his name was but the members of the house called him 'Bunty'. They gave him biscuits, rice and mutton to eat. But he craved for a little freedom. He could not accept the iron leash and the leather belt as his fate.

Now he had hit the gravel road. The guests were going to the bus-stand in a rickshaw. He ran after them. He ran wagging his tail. He would hop at times and, at others, he would jump. A sweet breeze and bright light caressed him. The national highway stretched in front of him. Vehicles passed by. He didn't know they were called trucks, buses, cars, and jeeps. He felt scared. A man from the master's house ran after him to catch him. He had found relief from slavery and restraint; the moment of freedom had arrived. He would not allow himself to be caught. He jumped forward, to the national highway.

Squashed under the tyres of trucks and buses, the blood-stained lump of flesh of the small dog soon vanished.

A leather belt hung around his neck. It was nothing but a careless master's symbol of ownership, which the small dog always defied.

That night, the terrible death of Bunty became the main topic of conversation in the family. His mistress picked up his chain, plate, mug, and mat from his kennel and threw them outside. These would have painfully reminded her of him. In order to calm his wife, the master turned the talk to topics like 'transience of life,' and 'the inevitability of death'. Others in the family tried to console her, saying, 'Anyway, one day he would have died,' 'what is our fault?' 'he died because he ran away,' 'we will bring another dog of good breed'.

As decided earlier, the members of that family cooked rice and fish curry. In the morning, the master went to his office; the mistress went to the market, and from there to her friend's house. Everything passed off quite peacefully. At least, Sidharth, who stayed in the neighbourhood, could not notice any change in the lifestyle of the family. Only the youngest member of the family and the rival of Bunty while he was alive; the six year old small girl looked sad for many days. Whenever she approached the kennel while playing or whenever she crossed the spot where Bunty was crushed to death, her eyes would grow moist.

A Strange Counterstroke

The crowd had grown thicker. It was quite natural for a rare incident like that in the city to draw a crowd. A woman was wiping her tears with the end of her torn *saree* and crying inconsolably. She continued narrating her distressing story in a tear-soaked broken voice. Beside her stood a strong and stout man sporting a moustache. He was the husband of the woman. His wife had left home for some reason. The husband followed her and stopped her here.

Some onlookers looked sad and anxious. Such dramatic scenes were not frequently seen on the streets.

The woman emphatically said that she would rather commit suicide than go back with her husband. For six days and six nights her husband had confined her to a room and beaten her mercilessly. The woman's back and arms bore distinct marks of beating. Her hair was blown by the wind. Drops of tear had rolled down to the chin before drying up. From the clothes she wore, it was clear that the poor woman had been subjected to unspeakable torture.

Stories of discord between husband and wife are nothing new. Sidharth had heard that at times such discord would reach dangerous levels. He had never imagined that a sweet conjugal life could be subjected to such ruthless horrible tyranny.

What sin had the poor woman committed?

The husband worked as a peon or driver in a government organization. A drunkard, he would beat his wife mercilessly on reaching home every day. It was as if she was responsible for all of his worries and failures. The poor lady would never object. But one day, when the torture inflicted on her crossed all tolerable limits, she raised a voice of protest. The ruthless husband dragged the woman and locked her in a room for six days and six nights. He also beat her mercilessly. This morning, the woman somehow escaped from her jail. She had sworn that she would rather go to her parents' house or commit suicide than return to the husband's house. It was more painful to receive beatings every day than to lay down one's life.

Someone asked, "Can you go to your parents' house alone?"

The woman answered, "Yes".

"Do you have money to pay the fare?"

"Yes, I have twenty rupees with me. That should be sufficient for me to reach there."

Sidharth felt as if a patch of dark cloud descended on him. It was the day of Saraswati puja. At various places of the city, one could find pandals and images. Children were busy making merry. However, on the highway, stood a helpless woman. Where would she go? What could she do when the very solution was a problem for her?

A police sub-inspector now reached the spot. The woman once again narrated her story to the policemen, to the bystanders, and to her husband standing some distance away. The policeman said, "Both of you sit in the jeep. I will listen to you in the police station. Why have you held up the traffic here?"

The husband was moving towards the police jeep as reluctantly as a goat which is dragged towards the altar of sacrifice.

Someone from among the bystanders said, "Go, now. If it is proved that you are beating your wife, you will lose your government job. Only then, will you learn a lesson."

The words reached the ears of the woman, who was shaking with tears and sobs. Suddenly, she took a few steps backwards and said in a normal tone, "Who says he will lose his job? What has he done? He has done absolutely nothing."

The bystanders stood awestruck. The policeman got down the jeep. The husband stood gaping, with his eyes wide open. Why had the woman suddenly changed her mind?

Then she spoke addressing her husband, "I am walking ahead. Reach home soon. We will talk to each other there." she headed towards her home. The husband meekly followed her.

How could Sidharth have guessed that the matter would take such a turn? How could the woman grant pardon to her husband despite being subjected to so much torture? If she went to the police station, he might lose his job—this fear dispelled all her sadness and grief.

In the eyes of Sidharth, respect for that poor woman grew manifold. The cruel husband had been beating her for the last six days and six nights; it would have bruised her badly. But the way she returned the blow by granting her husband pardon, it must have directly hurt his soul. Which husband had the ability to tolerate such a counterstroke?

Rootless

They were two of them. One was giving more importance to drinking than to eating food, and the other was spending much time displaying his knowledge of culture. He expressed his regret at how Odias were becoming rootless.

Sidharth was sitting at one corner of the same motel and listening to both of them. Both the friends were middle-aged. But, there were marked differences in their appearance. The gentleman, who had emptied three bottles in two hours, was bald-headed, short, and obese; but his friend was tall, fair, and thin. Both of them earned handsomely from comfortable jobs— this was evident from the expensive vehicle parked at the entrance of the motel.

The culture and tradition-conscious friend was giving such a look at his bald-headed friend at the end of each sentence that it seemed as if the latter was responsible for all the miseries of Odisha, including the damage that Konark temple had suffered. The friend who had gulped three bottles of beer, and consequently was feeling sleepy, was accepting all allegations levelled at him. Sidharth failed to understand whether he remained silent owing to his inability to speak fluently or being under the influence of the liquor.

Their lunch was over. From their discussion near the reception counter, Sidharth learnt that the fat man was named Sundaray and the thin man was Dasbabu. By the time they came out of the motel, the sunlight of the afternoon had grown mellow. The place was deserted as it was situated on the outskirts of the city. Sundaray, while coming down the staircase towards his vehicle, suddenly stopped on the way. Sidharth turned towards him. Sundaray stopped near a flowering plant and asked his friend, "Dasbabu, can you tell me the name of the plant?"

Dasbabu who had been portraying himself as a connoisseur of Odia culture and tradition, fumbled. It was obvious that Dasbabu didn't know the name of the plant. He heard him speak in a defensive voice, "Let's go. It is some flower! How does it matter if one does not know its name? You always behave in a childish manner."

Sundaray was not satisfied. He took a few steps and stopped. This time he was standing in front of a dense tree. In a child-like, curious voice, he was found asking, "What tree is this?"

Dasbabu who looked angrier than before said, "This is the problem with Odias like you. They stopped at trees and plants; they missed the woods."

Sundaray said, "But both these two belong to Odisha. I know them although I can't remember their names. I should not have drunk so much."

"It's OK. Let's go. You don't feel good unless you drink; but the moment you drink, you forget everything."

Sundaray was not ready to take another step forward. "Without knowing the names of these two, I am not leaving this place. Despite being Odias, how could we not recognize plants and trees of Odisha?"

Dasbabu's face had grown pale and looked as if it was not the face of a human being but a withered mushroom. He had given long speeches about the culture of Odisha a moment ago; he had expressed much pride in giving those; it was as if someone was snatching all his claims to superiority from him. He dragged Sundaray just as an angry guardian would drag his disobedient child away.

Sundaray called the gate-keeper of the motel and asked him, "Can you tell me the name of these plants?" The gate-keeper shook his head. He did not know their names. The restless Sundaray looked for the manager next. The South Indian manager of the motel became very worried as if he had failed to serve them a dish on the menu. His knowledge of the Odia flowering plants was much more limited than that of the gate-keeper. Dasbabu was not ready to wait for another minute. He very angrily said, "Are you coming or not, Sundaray? Otherwise, I will go away alone. I can't understand why you are so much worried about the names of these useless plants?"

"I am not worried about the plants; I am worried about our lack of knowledge, Das babu." He then turned towards the manager and said, "Where is the gardener? He must know the names of the two plants." Sidharth was a little surprised by the tenacity of the man. A very strange man!

The gardener came running to the spot. He had never thought that he would receive summons from the manager at such an odd hour. Sundaray repeated his old question, "Can you tell me the names of the two plants?"

The gardener felt a little relieved. He answered with a smile, "This flower is called periwinkle and the name of that tree is *kadamba*. You must have read about *kadamba* flowers, the favourite of Lord Krishna. These two are famous plants of our state. Did you summon me for this only? I thought there was some other problem."

"Thank you very much… thank you very much," saying this Sundaray hugged the gardener. Sidharth saw him thrusting a twenty rupee note into the gardener's pocket.

The car with both the friends drove off. Sidharth's mind reverberated with Dasbabu's speech and the child-like curiosity of Sundaray. He wondered who of the two had a deeper concern about Odishan culture and traditions. Who was better: Dasbabu who repeated a hundred times that he was an Odia or Mr. Sundaray who acknowledged his ignorance before others unhesitatingly so that he could arrive at the truth?

Sanatan Sir

Baguli had sent a letter from village. Now that the Panchayat election dates had been announced, Baguli wanted to organize cultural functions and thereby increase his popularity among the voters. Sidharth quickly realized that his being invited to stage a play on *Magha Purnami* in the village was a political stunt.

For him, the past had lost its charm. Old friends had settled at different places to make a living. Sidharth didn't feel like smearing his face with coloured-powder and stage mythical or social plays like "*Karnarjun Yudha*" or "*Lal Chabuk*". Besides, Sanatan Sir now lay bed-ridden.

Baguli's letter stirred Sidharth's emotions. How the days of his youth had disappeared, borne on the battered wings of kites whose strings had been cut! Whenever he stood in front of the school gate of his children, he felt like shedding tears. If it were possible for man to get one of his impossible wishes fulfilled, Sidharth would wish to retrieve the days of his lost youth.

That year, Bhabagrahi, the secretary of the amateur drama troupe 'Chandrasekhar Opera', who was thirty five and a father of three children, insisted on playing the role of Uttara in the play "*Abhimanyu Baddha*", Sidharth and his young friends snapped all their ties with the troupe. What a shame! The hollow of Bhabagrahi's cheeks could hold a handful of rice. His hands and legs were so full of hair no amount of powder would hide. Such vulgar impudence was never to be tolerated.

Of course, Baguli convinced his mother and converted their cowshed into a rehearsal room. He put a torn mat on a mound of ash and hung a curtain at the doorless entrance. But when they started the rehearsals, they felt the need of a musician, who would play the *dhol* and the harmonium for the young actors. The wealthy drama party owners had money, influence and power but Sidharth and his company had nothing of that sort. The concert party was to be hired on the day of the performance, but where from they would get a music master for the rehearsals. Sanatan Sir took everybody by surprise by arriving at the rehearsal the next day. He was an expert in playing the *dhol*, tabla, kettle drum, and harmonium. His very presence infused a sense of pride in Sidharth and his friends.

Sanatan Sir was a real professional. Forget about betel or *biris*, he would not even demand tobacco leaves from the trainees. He was very fond of *chilam*- a pipe for smoking tobacco. He would arrange for this at his own expense. Rehearsals went on. The number of interested spectators increased on the other side of the window. Sanatan Sir, with great enthusiasm, would play the *dholki*, kettle drum and harmonium. The palms of his rough hands would turn red; and veins would bulge out. But, he never grew tired.

That year, during the *Magha Purnami*, despite the influence of rich people, their wealth as well as the presence of the honourable M.L.A. near their pandal, the spectators ran towards the field adjacent to the Mahadev temple. There, Sidharth and his team presented a new play entitled "*Biplabi*". Whether others accepted it or not, Sidharth knew it pretty well that Sanatan Sir's zeal and dedication and perseverance had brought them pride and glory. How much Sanatan Sir cried that day, embracing Sidharth and Baguli, on the wintry dawn after the play was over! How humble a man becomes when he is filled with a sense of glory!

Despite all this, one of the desires of Sanatan Sir remained unrealized. He didn't get an opportunity to fulfill the desire of playing the *mridanga*, a musical instrument, during the "*Bhagavad Saptah*," the week during which the glory of the Bhagavad is celebrated. The reason was Sanatan Sir was a *harijan*, a low-caste. Despite his utter lack of knowledge of time and measure, Jadumani Mohanty had the unique privilege of playing the *mridanga* at the Bhagavad House. Sanatan Sir would listen intently from a spot not too far away from there; if Jadumani made a mistake in playing the *mridanga*, he would shout madly. He would throw stones at the Bhagavad House in fruitless indignation. Ah! If someone gave him an opportunity to have a *mridanga*-playing-contest with Jadumani! He would teach him what beats and measures really were. But that never happened. Sidharth had noticed another cause of grief in Sanatan Sir when he himself was a child. That day, Sidharth had failed to gauge the depth of a young Sanatan's sufferings and the pain that the wound caused him.

Early on the *Kumar Purnami* morning, Sanatan would enter the pond overgrown with water-lilies. Sidharth had heard from his friends that cobras lived in such ponds; so, nobody dared venture into them. However,in autumn, the pond was filled with white and red water-lilies, just like the sky filled with stars. The young Sanatan would enter the pond, anointing himself with a few drops of oil. By the time he would return to the bank after two hours of hard work, he would have collected a few loads of lilies. Sidharth's sisters would dance happily—and their *chauras*- platforms with the basil plant- would be the best in the entire village. The afternoon would give way to evening. Girls would gather to worship the full moon of *Kumar-Purnima*. While taking bites of the special cake prepared during the occasion and moving towards the pond to feed the snails, Sidharth would search for Sanatan uncle. The person, whose hard work was responsible for so much happiness and celebration, would not be seen anywhere. Once he had asked his elder sister about this. Gelhadei, pointing at Sanatan uncle sitting some distance away from the basil platform, had said that he was but a *harijan*; he was not expected to come near the platform.

Why did the person whose unpaid hard work made the moon descend from the sky to the clay platform; whose hard work resulted in bringing victory to the inexperienced and young drama troupe stayed away from limelight and from the celebration of victory? Young Sidharth didn't understand this for a very long time.

Baguli's letter lay like a lifeless object. Baguli had written that, if Sidharth visited the village for four or five days, the young men would feel inspired to work under his leadership. In that case, victory would certainly be theirs.

A pen in hand, Sidharth searched for a post card. He would write, "Baguli, whatever you have written about leadership or inspiration does not apply to me. Of course, some of us had played the role of Arjun in the Mahabharat, but Lord Krishna is lying, old and ailing, among the *harijans*. Go to him. If he leads us, the dead plants would bear flowers and fruits."

Planned Accidents

The seriously wounded man raised his right hand seeking someone's help in that pervading darkness. He wished someone should come and save him from the danger. He would give him a drop of water to drink and wipe blood from his wounds. He was in deep distress. He felt as if he would lose his life in another moment.

A dim light was visible from a distance. Someone must surely be coming. The rays of light were becoming brighter. The wounded man felt hopeful. The sign of a man approaching lessened his pain.

The man arrived. He looked here and there. All around him, he could hear the shouts of injured passengers. Their luggage lay scattered. The accident-ravaged bus lay some distance away. Perhaps the man was a little unhappy in the beginning. But, now his eyes glistened with pleasure. He could hear the sound of other people approaching the spot. They also carried torches and lanterns. The man hurried up. Whatever he could collect, he stuffed into a sack. He rolled the dead bodies over to loot their belongings. That wounded man, on the verge of death, was not able to see his movements. He waited with anxiety inside. Why was the man not coming to him?

The man finally approached him. In the darkness, he could see a gold chain glittering on the chest of the seriously wounded person. He clutched at it and pulled it. The seriously wounded man shouted loudly, "Save me… save me… otherwise I will die." The plunderer became cautious. A thief becomes nervous and cruel when he is caught red-handed. He kicked the wounded man very hard on the chest. The man who had been struggling till that time, became still.

Somnath woke up from the dream. He left the bed. Sidharth, lying on the adjacent bed, also got up. Somnath was terribly afraid. Sidharth left his bed, came and sat by his side. In the dim light, his face looked like that of the plunderer he had seen in his dream. He got up suddenly and edged away from Sidharth.

This morning a truck had met with an accident near their mess. The truck carried the goods of a transport company. It was loaded with everything from TV to radio to books in packets. The villages were situated some distance away from the mess. However, the news of the accident reached the villagers in no time. Old men, young men and women, even children rushed in. They picked up whatever they could lay their hands on and escaped. The wounded man lay there for an hour and a half, till the police arrived. Sidharth, despite Somnath's protests, picked up a small book packet from the truck.

Sidharth looked into Somnath's face. His eyes reflected hate, fear, and disbelief. He realized that Somnath had not forgiven him for his sin.

To the account of every accident involving a bus, a train, or a truck, the story of the second accident could be

added. In rare cases human beings arrive as god's
messengers. Otherwise those who come to the spot descend
like vultures, foxes, wolves or dogs, only to snatch away
gold chains, money purses, or wrist watches. The second
accident, unlike the first, is not accidental but planned.

The Rain of Shravan

Rain danced on the Ghutur hills like a naked adulterous woman. The invitation of the rain was difficult to resist. The drops of rain were blown away by the West Wind, just like the end border of the *saree* of a completely drenched female pedestrian. The rain of *Shravan* catches men unawares.

Whenever Sidharth came to Keonjhar, he remembered two places – Ghutur hills and San Ghagra. These two places seemed like close relations, even though he lived far away from them. His friends and acquaintances had all gone away. His friends, who had now grown old, had gone to different places to take care of the affairs of their grandchildren. The friends and acquaintances had all been separated, except Ghuturu and Ghagara, which exist even today. Human beings were hopelessly transient in comparison with hills and waterfalls.

Sidharth had decided the previous evening to pay a visit to the temple in the morning. He found the naming of all rivers, hills, waterfalls, and streams of Keonjhar, the playfield of his youth, extremely evocative. He found poetry in the sky, in the *sal* forests, and in the serpentine course of

Machhakandana river of this land. He would have rested for an hour in the shade of a tree on the premises of the Baladev temple. But when he got up in the morning, the first thing that he saw was the rain. That rain dragged him, holding him by his hand, to the lap of Ghutur hills and from there, to San Ghagra.

Sidharth was always like that. He respected the temples equally; but the respect concealed a deep-rooted fear. Hills and waterfalls are naughty friends of adolescence and they symbolize close, sweet friendships of youth. Can anyone ever resist their enchantment?

It was as if someone threw two palmfuls of water on Sidharth's face. It was *Shravan*. Since the wind had changed its direction, the rain of *Shravan* was splashing water onto the face now. In the world above the moist eyelids, someone's picture flashed before it split into pieces and disappeared. Who was he? Who was it who, while moving along the banks of Mantei, would slyly move away and throw water onto Sidharth's face? Ah! the poor creature didn't live beyond fifteen winters. Sidharth found it extremely hard to believe that Kirtan, who crossed Mantei river so frequently, could drown near Bhanrabanka. Sidharth, now on old man, felt like crying as he remembered his departed friend. How many tales did *Shravan* bring back to one's mind!

The scooter slowed down as it negotiated the elevated hilly area. A truck coming from the opposite direction had stopped near the bend. Rain danced in ecstasy and presented the '*tandav*'. Sidharth parked the scooter and tried to net the rain in his palms, stretching both his hands. The blows of *Shravan* striking the palm excited him.

San Ghagra lay ahead of him. The grass lawn was submerged in a sheet of water. The roar of the waterfall deafened everyone. The muddy waters of Machhakandana rushed towards the plain areas of the nearby town. San Ghagra didn't appear so fearful in summer; one could go and touch it. But now it looked fierce and wrathful like *Bhairabi*. It no longer appeared enticing as it did in summer.

The strong raincoat was now not able to shelter one from the rain. The clothes under it had got soaked. It had become a little cold but he never felt like turning away from the banks of Ghagra. Suddenly, Sidharth remembered Maguni Majhi. When he was a student at Bhadrak, Maguni would carry a variety of berries for Sidharth every holiday. There were not many berry bushes in Sidharth's village. Maguni Majhi would carry, besides amla, black berries, and jujubes, a great variety of other berries such as *khirkoli, pichkoli, dudhkoli, narakoli, bhainchkoli, sagadabatuakoli,* and *kanteikoli*. Now Maguni Majhi of Keonjhar lived with his son in Bhubaneswar.

Patches of cloud floating across the sky made it difficult to guess the time correctly. Sidharth came to his scooter. He had to watch the anger and grief of San Ghagra. The scooter would slip on that sloppy road if he didn't ride it carefully. How sharp were the bends on that mountain road! A Juang couple walked along the edge of the road wearing bamboo hats. Sidharth's nostrils were assailed by tobacco smoke from the husband's *bidi*. Sidharth now realized that, if he continued getting drenched in the rain, he would certainly go down with flu. He had already spent a long time although he had borrowed the scooter from Basanta Mohanty for only two hours.

That night, Sidharth's loud snoring interrupted Sarmistha's sleep. Throughout the day, she had locked herself up in the Dak Bungalow, waiting indefinitely for her absentminded husband to come back and take her to her daughter's would be in-laws' family. Sharmistha asked him, irritated, "What urgent work detained you until evening, and made you come back completely drenched? I would never have come with you if I knew that you had so much office work to do. Tell me where you had been. You have already grown old but you never understood the value of punctuality. Humph! How can this man get his daughter married..."

The Shravan-engrossed Sidharth, while feigning sleep in order to avoid the reproach of his wife, thought that he would never be able to tell her of his fascination for Ghutur and Ghagra. He didn't wish to descend from the heaven of dreams to the shabby geography of reality; similarly, he didn't wish to be called 'irresponsible' and 'old' once again by Sarmistha.

How would he explain to Sarmistha that advancing years never made one old?

A Silent Query

Within ten years of raising a family, this child that Chita had arranged to work at his house was the forty third to have been hired. Even this child had left for his village some three days ago, when no one was at home. Thank God, he had not decamped with any valuables. Sidharth decided not to bother about having a servant ever again. Was his house a training centre? A servant would arrive; new dresses, shoes, toothbrush etc. would be purchased for him; he would be given lessons in housekeeping while cups, plates and jars of sweets and pickle would keep disappearing. But one fine morning the fellow would leave for his village, taking the return fare, of course, but would never return.

Both Sidharth and his wife were employed. They had no problems on the days their daughter went to school; it's only when she had holidays that, they had to worry a lot. Who could they ask to take care of the child? Everybody was busy. It felt really bad when they had to drop the child with someone without prior intimation. The problem became acute during the puja, summer and x-mas holidays.

Sidharth's wife was in a state of shock since the servant

boy had left three days ago. She was not expressing her feelings openly but the contempt that lurked within her for Sidharth for his inability to find a servant hardly remained a secret. Even Sidharth deliberately avoided any discussion on the topic. This problem was not confined only to his family; hundreds of families living in the city faced it. The boys and girls who wished to be employed as domestic helps wanted the assurance of being given government jobs. Sidharth could never arrange one for them. Besides, there was the question of salary. In addition to food and accommodation, if someone was given six or seven hundred rupees, perhaps they would be interested to stay but he could never afford to pay so much money.

Sidharth's wife was working in the kitchen. She shouted intentionally, "You father and daughter, do your own work yourself." This was an indication of the tempest that was going to rage. Sidharth responded to his wife calmly, "It's better if we don't hire any servants. The kind of news that gets published in newspapers these days makes me worried. At one place, the servant boy killed his mistress by choking her; somewhere else, another one decamped with the master's money. No one keeps servants even in rich countries like America."

His wife moved menacingly towards him. "Oh! It is as if the servants who were hired were working only for me and I was relaxing on a swing." Then she fixed her gaze on her daughter and said, "Only for this child we are suffering like this, both mentally and physically. How much worries one has to cope with!"

Not only his wife, Sidharth also said things like this at times to his daughter. He would make her sit in front of him and explain to her how as parents they were working as well as making sacrifices with her welfare in mind. In return, she should work hard and study well so that her parents are satisfied.

All these had happened yesterday. Sidharth had secretly left his office and collected his daughter from her school. He and his daughter usually dined at four o' clock together. Today, one of Sidharth's friends had invited him to lunch. Hence, he did not have to eat anything. Sidharth waited for his daughter to finish eating so that he could take her and drop her at a neighbour's house before leaving for office again. When his wife returned from office at six o' clock, she would collect the child from the neighbour's house.

The child said, "Papa, if you are not interested in eating, then why are you waiting for me? You can go. I can keep the used utensils at their proper place."

Sidharth hung his head as he felt like an old sinner. He said, "No… no. You please finish eating… I will go out after you do." The child was busy eating. Sidharth sat on a nearby chair, a newspaper in hand and furtively looked at his daughter. Unknown to him, he was transported to the days of his childhood. How enjoyable those days were! Those days, no daughter ever went to bed on an empty stomach, waiting for her mother to return from her office; she was under no compulsion to make new friends and play new games every day for the sake of her parents. He was looking at the small child mixing dal to the rice with her tiny fingers. He was worried that in this busy life, parents were not even finding the time to look at the face of their children lovingly. From morning till evening, they had only to run after money and focus on files.

Sidharth noticed his daughter doing something strange. She gobbled up the food thinking that her father was getting late for his office. She was not even seggregating bones from the fish. She took only ten minutes to eat the food that she usually ate in forty-five minutes in the presence of her mother. Besides, she was getting ready to pick up the plates herself after she had finished eating.

Sidharth experienced deep agony. Aha, how sensible she was! How worried she was thinking that her father was getting late! How hurriedly she finished her eating and how she was getting ready to pick up the used utensils! The scenes of his childhood flashed before him once again. His mother would serve rice and curry and sit beside him. She would never remain busy elsewhere until Sidharth finished eating his food.

Sidharth got up from the chair, his eyes brimming with unshed tears. He snatched away the utensils from her hand and said, "I don't have anything else to do, my dear. Why are you so worried? I don't have to go anywhere. I will sit here. Why did you eat so hurriedly? Bones could have stuck to your throat."

His daughter did not say anything. It seemed as if her eloquent eyes told him, "Papa, only elders do not sacrifice everything for the young; the young also sacrifice a lot for the elders. But they do not use the high-sounding words that the elders mouth."

Social Service

Tilottama Devi's name found mention in the pages of newspapers many times as a social worker. Since the newspapers gave publicity to her speeches and advice Sidharth felt a lot of respect for her. She was a Professor at a reputed college. Most of her writings had been translated into different regional languages. In brief, she was a social activist, educationist, writer and social worker. Her husband was an influential businessman; but he was identified more as the husband of his wife.

The other day Sidharth met Tilottama Devi in Kolkatta. Sidharth had gone there to participate in a seminar. He thought Tilottama Devi must have also come to take part in the seminar; so he decided to talk to her.

But no, Tilottama Devi had not come to participate in any seminar. "I was invited. But, I am on medical leave now. It would be wrong if I participate in the seminar. So, I am not taking part in it," she said.

"But you have come to Kolkatta."

"My husband has also come. An editor is publishing a compilation of my speeches, which I had made in support of the *adivasis, harijans* and the poor. I want that the book should be published in four languages— Hindi, English, Bengali and Gujarati simultaneously. I am staying in a hotel nearby. I will stay here for two weeks. Quite a big hotel; centrally air conditioned."

The application of artificial beauty products had made her look more charming and healthier. Sidharth failed to understand why she was on medical leave. Suddenly the question arising in his mind escaped his lips.

The two beautiful eyes now turned vicious. "What are you saying? Should I have joined Dhenkanal College? So many unworthy people have been posted in Bhubaneswar; why should I go somewhere else? I am on medical leave. Let a few days pass. "

Sidharth was getting late. Tilottama Devi's words stung him like the tail of the scorpion. He went away from there, throwing a 'namaskar' in her direction. She was absolutely right: influential Professors like Tilottama Devi were fit only to serve in Bhubaneswar. Why should she go to Dhenkanal?

A few days after returning from Kolkata, he read from the newspapers that Tilottama Devi's famous book entitled *"Odishara Daaridrya"* (Poverty in Odisha) had received rave reviews from critics. The proposals of the writer to dispel regional imbalances and her sympathy for the poor have been praised by the newspapers.

Sidharth threw away the supplement of that newspaper. He grew worried at the thought of the vicious demon that lay hidden behind the golden deer that Tilottama Devi looked like. The professor, who conveniently forgot her responsibilities towards her students and who had unilaterally decided never to leave Bhubaneswar had no right to write a book highlighting the poverty of Odisha. He knew pretty well that if Tilottama Devi gave up her job, her family would in no way suffer. The money made by her husband was enough to manage the expenses of the next seven generations; but people like Tilottama Devi clung to their jobs tightly.

The gap between what people like Tilottama Devi professed and practiced bewildered Sidharth.

A Social Worker

Since childhood, Sidharth had developed a sense of respect and reverence for Rudramadhab Mohapatra. Rudramadhab's fine figure, noble manners, and dignified conversation had led Sidharth to form such an idea about him. Such a dedicated Congress worker and social worker like him, despite his social status remained confined to local politics, or in other words, could not climb higher politically. Sidharth was sure that there could be no other reason for this than party's indifference to leaders in rural areas.

When Sidharth read the letter written by Rudramadhab, he felt a tremor inside him. He went through the letter two or three times. The letter was not fake; Rudramadhab himself had written it. The envelope bore the stamp of the Pritipur post office.

Rudramadhab's youngest son, Swapnakant, had written the Board examination this year. He had not done well in his mathematics compulsory and extra-optional papers. Rudramadhab was worried if his third son passed in the second division, he would feel sad as the two other sons of him had passed their examinations in the first. This was why he had written a letter to Sidharth, an employee in the Education Department, and 'a man from his own village,' requesting him to render necessary help. In the *nota bene* of the letter appeared the words, "Don't worry at all about the money required for the purpose."

A very old but exquisite vase fell on the floor, scattering the pieces all around. While he was busy collecting the scattered pieces, two drops of blood appeared on his fingers.

Before his mind's eye rose, battered, the image of Rudramadhab.

What a high opinion he had formed of this man! He had never imagined that behind the elegant façade, there lurked such a hideous reality.

He crumpled the letter and threw it in shame, humiliation, and disgust. Sidharth had nothing to lose if such a child failed or passed. It was good that another source of ignorance was removed and truth was revealed.

A few months passed.

Sidharth visited his village during the puja vacation.

He met Rudramadhab. This time it was not clear whether Sidharth's eyes or Rudramadhab's face had lost its luster, but the former warmth was missing. Rudramadhab smiled and said, "I had written you a letter but because I heard nothing from you, I had to go to Cuttack myself. Although I had to spend four thousand rupees, Babula got a first division."

Sidharth could not decide whether he should distrust his ears. In front of his eyes danced an answer script, where, in the twinkle of an eye, twenty-eight or thirty-eight marks conveniently turned into eighty-two or eighty-three. It was believed that morally upright people checked answer scripts and awarded marks, correctly evaluating them. There was no question of doing anyone any favour or acceding to anyone's unfair request.

Sidharth was reminded of his own high-school days. The high-school examination centre was not situated nearby. They had to go to a school some thirty kilometers away. There they had to reside and write the examination for no fewer than ten days. Back at home, mother had put the sacred *kalas*, father had offered *bhog* at the Shiv temple. The matriculation examination was a great hurdle. One had to overcome it anyhow. His teachers had told them at school, "There is no place for any favour or ill-will in the board examination. You will be rewarded marks that you deserve. Go on reading things, working out sums, and memorising answers."

Sidharth had to spend many sleepless nights. From under a blanket, he would work out sums, mug up Sanskrit, before finally writing answers in the examination. He firmly believed that he would get whatever he deserved; not a mark more or not a mark less.

Not only Sidharth, lakhs of other students of the state do that. They eat *pakhala* and tamarind paste and study in the thatchless schools. Books are supplied to students six months after the session begins. The problems of a year are postponed to the next, but they are never solved. Students read thinking that if they anyhow pass the matriculation examination, they would grow wings. But they don't realize that a student passing the examination in third division can easily secure a certificate for a sum of four to five thousand rupees stating that he has passed in the first division.

Rudramadhab stood in front of him, the incarnation of resourcefulness. But, what was his fault? Perhaps someone had said, "Here, every dog has a price; some are cheap, some are pricey. But everybody is saleable like a commodity."

To Sidharth, Rudramadhab looked like a businessman,

who had a corrupt teacher in his clutches. Surprisingly, the price of the teacher was written on the collar of his shirt—four thousand rupees only."

Sidharth shut his eyes.

A Solar Eclipse

By the time we reached the Bhagat beach, the February sun was beginning to set. Sidharth had heard many times about this beach in Goa. This morning, they were touring Northern Goa. Tomorrow, they plan to visit parts of South Goa. At first, their tourist bus dropped them near Mulgaon temple. While the other tourists got down to pay a visit to God, Sidharth was trying to locate where the temple was. One who has visited Lingaraj, Puri or Konark temples of Odisha would never accept a plain *pucca* house as a temple. Of course, a few dome-like structures had been erected to give the building the appearance of a temple. The tourist guide was a young man. He had mugged up some information about Goa. Perhaps, that's the reason why he didn't talk much. The knowledge that he dispensed was equivalent to donations made by a miser; it didn't seek to satisfy our curiosity.

During the Portugese invasion, the gods and goddesses of Goa were devastated. In fact, this is the first chapter in the history of any colonial invasion. Those who arrive with the intention to attack or loot a country try to shake the very foundation of its culture. They damage the temples and images. The Goans had to hide their deities in remote villages to prevent them from being desecrated.

The bus very soon reached the Bhagat beach. This place is immensely attractive. It was as if someone sprayed gusts of cool air on Sidharth's parched face. The coconut trees on the beach appeared like children who stood in front of the mirror to comb their dishevelled hair. The sight was a magnificent one. God has gifted Goa with long beaches. Man has added to these many temples and churches. This is now a heaven for tourists.

The friend was inviting everybody to pay a visit to Anjuna beach. But Sidharth wanted to spend some more time on the Bhagat beach. Crowds were conspicuously absent here. The number of shops was also small. The beach looked charming as well as spotlessly clean. The seashore was uneven and stony; one's legs never became covered with mud. It was lit up by bright lights. On small hillocks stood lines and lines of cement benches. If one sat there, one could watch the sea meeting the sky in the far distance.

Sidharth might have sat there for some more time. His friend had been trying to capture the sea at Goa, the sky, the coconut trees and the tourists in his camera. A small girl was passing by. She would be ten to twelve years of age. She was carrying a basket. Sidharth's friend looked at her in amusement. The small girl's eyes brightened up at the prospect of having found a customer. She came closer and spoke something in her language which meant, "Will you take beer?... Beer?" Sidharth felt shocked. The word 'beer' was not unknown to him. But what shocked him was the sight of a little girl carrying beer bottles on her head to sell. Sidharth refused, "No...no... We don't need beer." The small girl continued saying, "*Baboo*, take a beer bottle... take one."

Sidharth walked towards the bus. When they had got down, they had selected a road between the Anjuna beach and the Bhagat beach. They returned from the opposite direction. The place had been smothered in marijuana and ganja smoke. Groups of foreigners sat in restaurants surrounded by bamboo matting, and sang the praise of Goa amid the smoke of ganja and the tinkle of drinking bowls. The time allowed by the guide was over long ago. Their next destination was Aguda fort.

The little girl's helpless face appeared before Sidharth while he was returning to the bus. If Sidharth had purchased a beer, that poor girl would have earned two rupees. Sidharth's daughter was calling out from inside the bus., "Father, come quickly, the bus is ready to leave." Sidharth wanted to cast a departing glance at the sun setting over the Bhagat beach, the enchanting beauty of the place, and the coconut trees bending on the beach from the bosom of the hills. He found it extremely difficult to erase the memory of the helpless girl, who appeared just like a stain on the glistening wrapper of a brand new book, emerging from the gold-hued Bhagat beach.

Faith

Patches of clouds carrying unseasonal rain hung over the mango grove just as a little girl hangs on the back of her father. It may rain once again. It had been raining for the last two days. Just as water never dries up in the bowl of a magician, the palms of the cloud never dried up. The foggy lines of rain hung like aerial roots of a banyan tree. It was better to leave home before it started raining again.

Sidharth had come to Bhadrak on some official work. After the work was over, he paid a courtesy visit to his friend, Sarbeswar. Sarbeswar was his childhood friend. During the school days, if any one of them stayed away, they would feel restless. There existed a strong bond of friendship between the two till the end of their matriculation examination. After that, Sidharth had to leave for Bhubaneswar and Sarbeswar remained in Bhadrak. Soon their meetings became infrequent as their places of work were far apart. There came a time when meeting even once or twice a year became difficult.

Both Sarbeswar and his wife had jobs. The financial condition of the family in which both the husband and wife have jobs is comparatively better. But one has to pay a price for such financial benefits. The expectations of parents, relatives or even distant relatives rise. Jealousy, intolerance create family disturbances. Sarbeswar told him of this last night. He explained how he had become a victim of misunderstandings. He expected consolation from Sidharth.

Sarbeswar's wife was of the same opinion. They faced a lot of trouble because they were not able to find a good servant. Both of them slogged from morning till night. Sarbeswar's wife felt very unhappy because they were not able to take proper care of their child. Six or seven servants had left in the meantime. Someone stayed for four months and someone else stayed for two months. "When a new servant comes, it takes around a month to teach him different things. If he decides to go away on his own way after only a month, what can someone do?" Anger and helplessness filled the voice of Sarbeswar's wife when she talked about this.

Sarbeswar had only one son- Sonu. He was about seven years old. That day he could not go to school owing to the heavy rain. Most of the time, the child lived alone. The child would not meet his mother as she would be away during the day. Whenever he would ask for something, his mother would be busy cutting up vegetables or cooking. He would not get any answers to his questions but would be scolded by his mother. Sidharth could well guess Sonu's predicament.

Sidharth felt sad for Sonu. He himself was born in a joint family. One did not have to go out in search of a friend as there were brothers, sisters, uncles and aunts in the family. It was difficult to know how time passed. At times, they were visited by guests. The days were spent in playing games and eating.

Sidharth put on his trousers and shirt and got ready to go. Sarbeswar said, "It felt so good to see him after so many days." Sarbeswar's wife remarked acidly, "He came only because he had some official work here, otherwise, would he ever have come?" Of course, she was not completely wrong. Who visits a place these days just to meet friends?

When Sidharth came to the courtyard, he saw that his shoes were missing. Where had they disappeared? He had put them there. The question of dogs or thieves taking those away did not arise.

Sarbeswar also became worried. He searched for the shoes everywhere. Even Sarbeswar's wife grew worried. Sonu was busy riding his tri-cycle. There was nobody else at home. Who took away the pair of shoes?

Sidharth felt impatient not because his new pair of shoes was gone but because the time for the bus to leave was approaching. He sat on the chair and thought hard. Where had he kept his shoes? Sarbeswar's office time was approaching; his wife was also to go to her school. Examinations were going on there; she had to reach there on time. Both of them had planned to lock the house and leave Sonu with a neighbour. Sonu had to stay with him till four o' clock.

Sarbeswar went inside for some time to say something to his wife. Sonu got off his cycle and said, "Uncle, why don't you stay in our house for one more day? You will go away tomorrow; today, we shall play."

"Ok…ok… I will stay but where are my shoes?"

Sonu smiled. It was a mischievous smile. He stretched his right hand and said, "Promise!" Sidharth touched his hand and did as he said. Sonu once again stretched his hand and said, "God promise!" Sidharth did the same. Sonu immediately ran away and brought the pair of shoes from somewhere. Sidharth, Sarbeswar and Sonu's mother—all were taken by surprise.

Sidharth was reminded of his childhood days. Whenever college-going Udaya Uncle or Rabi Uncle returned home for the vacation, they would become extremely active. Fish would be caught and tasty curry would be prepared for Uncle. New games would be devised. So long as one sat with either of the two, mother would not ask him to read the lessons or father would not warn him to take bath quickly. Those three or four days they considered themselves free from all constraints. But, very soon it would be time for the guests to leave. They would get ready to leave for the town. Sidhu and his friends would feel extremely sad. Just to make the guests stay back a few days more, they would hide their shoes or dresses or their wrist watch.

Sidharth looked at Sonu. Sonu was neglected as both his parents worked. Besides, he was not living in a joint family where the presence of grandfathers, grandmothers, uncles and aunts would have helped him to dispel his loneliness. This was why he felt so happy whenever a guest was around.

Sidharth felt, with the passage of time, changes had taken place everywhere including villages, towns and cities. Only one thing had remained unchanged: childhood had not lost its innocence. Childhood still had a lot of faith in the elders.

Sarbeswar's wife was getting restless to lock the front door. Sarbeswar was bringing the scooter out from the courtyard. For them, the guest Sidharth had as good as gone. There was no need of stopping him from going away.

Sidharth once again cast a glance on Sonu. The

childhood in Sonu looked at him expectantly. His firmly believed that Sidharth would never break his 'promise' and 'god-promise'. Sidharth felt as if something choked him somewhere. He did not know what he would tell Sonu to express his helplessness. The world of faith was falling to pieces in front of his eyes.

Sweet Lies

Sidharth didn't wish to waste a *Chaitra* evening that spread its fragrance like the sweet-smelling jasmine, listening to those oft-repeated things. But the sheer delight and intense emotion with which an old father had started listing the qualities of his son, forbade him from raising a voice of protest. Mandhata Mohapatra, taking Sidharth's silence for consent, started repeating old tales about his only son, Chitaranjan.

Mandhata Mohapatra went on, "When Bulu (Chitaranjan's pet name) was a student of class three, he spotted his natural talent. He would easily solve the sums set for students who were reading in higher classes. Even before the examination, his father and teachers knew that Bulu would be selected for a scholarship in class three, securing the highest marks in the entire block. Bulu also won the National Scholarship in class seven before getting enrolled in high school.

Mandhata Mohapatra would go on and on. After talking about his son's education in school, he would come to his M.B.B.S studies. Then, he would take almost two hours to explain that his son's talent as a doctor could be compared with that of 'Dhanvantari'. Then, Mr. Mohapatra would talk about Chitaranjan's humility and his devotion to his father. Mandhata Mohapatra would describe, quite excitedly, how his son and daughter-in-law exulted at the sight of him; how they would always entreat him to stay with them; how they never wanted to let him leave them; and how the attraction for the ancestral land made him stick to the property of his forefathers.

He would however forget, on these occasions, when the long list of the qualities of his son and daughter-in-law sounded exaggerated. Sidharth didn't really have the time to listen to these. He had to do everything that needed to be done in the village before returning to the town the next morning.

Mandhata Mohapatra would take out from his shirt pocket an old pocket diary. From inside its crumpled pages, he would take out a paper cutting, which bore news of Chitaranjan's success. The paper-cutting, published some twenty-two years ago, had become tattered, as it was frequently exhibited before unwilling guests and reluctant strangers. However, Mandhata Mohapatra was never tired of cataloguing the qualities of Chitaranjan, whose blurred photo appeared in that yellowing paper.

Sidharth said, "I beg your leave now. I'll come once again when I have enough spare time at hand. We will have a longer talk."

Mandhata Mohapatra would smile. When he smiled, spittle dripped from the corners of his toothless mouth. He would say, "Who has control over time? It's great that, despite living in the town, you still remember me."

After the departure of Mandhata Mohapatra, Sidharth didn't feel as cheerful as he had expected. A sense of apathy enveloped him. He developed sympathy for this seventy-year-old, as a small stream of respect and compassion ran from an unknown corner of his heart. No matter what Mandhata Mohapatra had said, Sidharth knew everything about Chitaranjan; and this was precisely why he felt sad.

Mandhata Mohapatra had retired as the headmaster of a lower primary school. Chitaranjan was his elder son. The old man had to encounter many years of hardship, just to ensure that his son grew up to be a doctor. The land under his possession had to be sold off after being mortgaged. The black cow from their cowshed, and all the silver and bronze utensils that the old couple possessed were sold to the money-lender one after another. The old man became a widower very early as there was no money for the treatment of his wife. Throughout his life, he lived with one dream, one mission – his son should become a doctor.

Despite having gone through so much hardship, Mandhata Mohapatra's dreams seemed like arid deserts, and pricked him like cactus thorns. No matter how much he tried to hide his bitter feelings behind the broken glass of his spectacles, he failed bitterly. Not being able to reconcile with old age, a man's desperate attempts to conceal his grey hair miserably fails. Similarly, despite the careful attempts of Mr. Mohapatra to paint a glowing picture of his son's success, Chitaranjan's real character could never be concealed.

Chitaranjan never acknowledged the poverty of his childhood; he disowned his past and disregarded the helplessness of old Mandhata Mohapatra. Mr. Mohapatra would visit his son with much hope. But, neglected and offended by the daughter-in-law, he would return to the lonesome hut of mud and wattle. Like the shivering old man in a cold *Magha* night he solaced himself with the memories of a *Chaitra* evening.

Sidharth failed to make sense of Chitaranjan's mental state. That's why, willingly or unwillingly, irrespective of his busy schedule and personal problems, he would pay a visit to Mr. Mohapatra whenever he visited his village once every two months. How much the old man craved for the warmth of human contact in this remote village!

Mandhata Mohapatra had left long ago. The warmth of the place where he had sat, was gone. He would now be sitting on the hospital verandah or on the platform of the temple, describing to someone else the great qualities of his doctor son. Disapproving of the cold truths of the present he would be transporting himself to the colourful world of dreams, hopes of the past. There, Mandhata Mohapatra would be searching for his happy family like searching for coins in a street enveloped in darkness. For some reason, Sidharth failed to blow the lid off the ugly truth in front of Mr. Mohapatra. He could not bring himself to say, "I know how miserable you are. Throughout your life, you have been wallowing in a sweet lie."

No, let Mandhata Mohapatra spend a few more years comforted by a sweet lie. Never ever would he have the bad luck of learning that another person, besides him, knew the terrible truth.

Talabandha

The child was sitting. It was raining outside. Sidharth sat inside but felt as if he was completely drenched.

Sidharth would be reminded of Talabandha when the water-hen cooed during the summer afternoons from the other side of bamboo clumps. He would be reminded of the rainy days in that village, when he got thrilled at the fragrance of the bunches of *kia* flowers hanging from the bushy nut-bearing-plants. Perhaps the child didn't know. How would he? Sidharth had spent a few years of his youth in Talabandha about twenty years ago; perhaps the child wasn't even born then.

Talabandha village occupies an inconsequential spot on the map of Baleswar. Sana Talabandha had twenty to twenty-five houses, and the other village had a few more. People of the village depended on agriculture for a living. Youths of some families eked out a living by making gunny sacks or working in soap factories of Kolkata. The new-born calves and small children play a game of *bagudi* in the open space in front of the houses.

The child said that the village now had electricity. Barring one or two families, no other family had taken electricity connection for lack of funds. Now, as on earlier occasions, they didn't have to cope with half a dozen floods. The road that led from Kharagpur had disappeared among the fields of corn. Government hadn't constructed any new roads. It had constructed a mound, it was said. If someone got washed away in flood, he would reach this mound.

Sidharth remembered the festival of Ganesh Chaturthi celebrated when he was in the class eight. That year, in the month of *Bhadrab*, came flood-waters as high as the berry trees standing around the Ghatapur school. There was no limit to the students' sadness. Only the previous evening they had returned home after decorating the room where the Lord would be worshipped, arranging the croton plants, and putting the festoons over the threshold. By morning, the entire village and the connecting roads were submerged. That year, children couldn't reach Lord Ganesh; rather Lord Ganesh came to the children in a boat. The image of the Lord was placed in a boat with a Brahmin and four or five class representatives accompanying him. The image of Lord Ganesh was taken around the villages. Students had to clamber into the boat to offer *puspanjali*. Then, the boat was rowed to other places. Sidharth could never forget that year's Ganesh Chaturthi.

The moment Sidharth recalled matters related to Talabandha, the old lady of Mahapatra family flashed in his memory. Once, out of youthful innocence and inquisitiveness, he had asked this woman, a mother of seven children, "You have such a huge family consisting of so many children and grandchildren. How do you keep a watch on them?" The old lady laughed a hearty laugh. Along with the laugh, dripped betel-leaf-juice and bashful affection. "You talk of only seven? A mother can keep a tab on hundred children. Even the queen of Dhritarashtra kept a close watch on her hundred children. I have given birth to them; shouldn't I be able to find out who has eaten what? I recognize my grandchildren when they shout 'grandmother' even in the dark. Even though she was close to sixty, the old lady shone like an image made of marble. Hearing her, Sidharth fell silent. He wished to say, "Dhritarashtra's wife didn't have to ask her children such trivial things as whether they had taken their meals, for she would be surrounded by many female attendants.

The old lady of Mahapatra's family was a very loving person. Two of her sons worked somewhere in Kolkata. The old lady would take care of the guests, when they came to her village, as her own children worked far away. Sidharth had himself seen the old lady, lovingly, forcing the guests to have some more food, like a mother. She would put into their bowls an extra piece of fish or a little more curry. "My children are working outside; if I don't take care of others, why would someone else take care of my children?" The old lady's eyes would grow moist when she remembered her children. Sidharth, on those occasions, would fondly remember his own mother.

Sidharth's mind was crowded with many such memories. He didn't understand why the memory of Talabandha remained fresh in his mind even though he had travelled to many villages, many towns, bazaars as well as lanes and by lanes. Around the village ran a small canal, just like the coiled snake in the snake charmer's basket. The farmers irrigated their fields, with its water to grow wheat or marsh rice. During summer months, Sidharth, with his friends, would catch prawn there. During the rainy season, he would remain awake throughout the night with friends who set their fish-traps and catch fish. During the floods, he would float in rafts made of banana-trunks. He loved the mornings and evenings, the young boys and girls, the labourers and servants of that village. He also fondly remembered his experience of singing, "*Mangale Aila Usha*," with his fingers on the 'sa-pa' reed of the harmonium with Nilanana during Goddess Lakshmi's immersion ceremony.

"The bus would arrive any time soon, Sir. The rain has subsided. May I take leave?"

"Um…stop…stop. I would like to talk a little more. Your village is not far; you will surely reach by nightfall. Is the old lady of Mahapatra's family well?"

"Who are you talking about, Sir?"

"Govindabhai's mother…"

"She left for her heavenly abode two years ago."

"Oh my God!" Sidharth felt as if something had broken into pieces. The old lady of Mahapatra's family passed away but Sidharth was not even informed!

"Are others in your village well?"

"You must have heard about the murder that took place two years ago. From that day, people of the other village aren't paying any visit to this village. The Mahapatra family visits Kherang through their backyard. On the other hand, the Hota family and the Behera family take a circuitous route near the school to reach the tube-well. The village has lost its earlier charm, Sir. Politics has poisoned everything."

What was this that Sidharth heard? A village of twenty-five families was divided into four groups!

How could Talabandha, the village of his youth, which stood like a mole on the chin of a young maiden and that lay amidst paddy fields by the roadside between Bhadrak and Chandabali, suffer such a terrible fate? A sob rose from within Sidharth.

Turning his back on time, he wished to hide his face in the lap of the old lady of Mahapatra's family. But the old lady had departed from this world two years ago. Where would Sidharth go today? Who would now recognize the guest who had visited the village some twenty years ago?

"You can go now, friend. The rain has completely subsided. It's good that we met each other. Had we not met, it would have been better."

Thank You, Kerala

When Sidharth departed from Bhubaneswar, he was accompanied by unseasonal rain and a cold breeze, but he was woken up by the cooing of the *koel* and the sweet breeze of *Phalguna* at Thiruvananthpuram. Winter had not receded from Bhubaneswar even though it was the second week of February but at Thiruvananthpuram, it felt very hot even at ten in the morning. The shawl and sweater he had brought with him lay like obsolete currency notes; their presence mocked at his ignorance about the weather of Kerala.

That Thiruvananthpuram was the same as Trivendrum, Sidharth knew it quite well before reaching there. However, he took some time to realize that the capital of Kerala was not the cultural, administrative and political hub of the state as it was in the case of Odisha. The Sahitya Akademi of Kerala was situated at Trichur, at a distance of about six hours journey by train from Trivendrum. The most renowned writer of Kerala and 1995 Gyanapith awardee M.T. Vasudevan Nair lived at Calicut whereas Kamala Das lived at Cochin. Thiruvananthpuram housed the Secretariat and some government offices like the A.G.

office whereas other organizations were scattered over places like Cochin, Ernakulam, Trichur or Calicut. "Our Bhubaneswar is much better in that respect. You can shoot two birds with one arrow," said Sidharth. But his views changed after he met Mrs. Pranati Mohanty, the Press Information Bureau official placed at Cochin. She argued, "Simply because everything significant happens at either Cuttack or Bhubaneswar, the people of north, south and western regions feel resentful in Odisha. There was no such feeling of being marginalized in Kerala because things are scattered all over Kerala." Mrs. Mohanty was an Odia; her husband was an Odia I.A.S officer of the Kerala cadre. Both of them were intimately connected with the social and cultural life of the place.

Sidharth had no first-hand experience of the lushness of Kerala. The place was much greener than he had expected. Each house was like a farm house. In the middle of it stood a not-so-tall building. Coconut trees surrounded it and a pond lay at the back. Long dikes ran into rivers; branches of coconut trees bent over the heart of the lakes. At places one would find rows of rubber or banana plants surrounded by green fields.

The only thing that made Sidharth feel uncomfortable amidst so much beauty and greenery was the food of Kerala. Every dish starting from *dosas* and omelettes to dal and curries was cooked in coconut oil. Forget about eating, Sidharth found it difficult even to put them in the mouth. At home, dishes were cooked either in mustard oil or refined oil. He could make do with groundnut oil, with some difficulty though. But coconut oil! Never. The home of the Mohantys came to his rescue. Cochin was on the way between Trivendrum and Trichur. Their hospitality, both during the onward journey and return journey, saved him.

Apart from coconut oil, Kerala presented him another difficulty; it was the language. He could not understand a word of it. He marked a great aversion for Hindi in the south. The cobblers on the footpath or betel shop owners didn't understand English. The language problem presented a bigger crisis than the problem with the food. However, difficulty made man invent new things. Sidharth put some Hindi, Odia, English and Malayalam words together and tried to communicate with the help of this potpourri.

The purpose of the Kerala tour undertaken by Sidharth and a few of his friends was to acquire knowledge about the literature of the state and to meet its renowned writers. Mrs. Mohanty had advised him: "Go to Trichur. You can meet M.T. (M.T. Vasudevan Nair) there. Mohan Verma is also a renowned writer. You can see the portrait hall and library of the Sahitya Akademi there." Following her advice, they went there and lived in the Sahitya Akademi guest house a day before Shivratri. "Caretaker David understands Hindi well and will take good care of you," the Secretary of the Akademi told them. From him they learnt that Vasudevan Nair was scheduled to visit Tirur the next day; however, he had no plans of visiting Trichur. If Sidharth wanted, he could go to Tirur and meet him. After that, they had to depend on David to find out how to travel from Trichur to Tirur. David said, "I was in the army for fourteen years. So I know a little Hindi." His pronunciation of Hindi made Sidharth and his friend laugh. They realized it was not possible for them to comprehend David fully.

The next day, when they reached the bus-stop, they learnt that there were not one but two Tirurs near Trichur. The Tirur they wanted to go to had no direct bus service. They had to go to Kuttipuram first, and from there to Tirur.

They felt disappointed. They didn't have much time to spare. They had to reach Tirur by noon. All the place names in the buses and on the shops were written in Malayalam. Besides, the buses travelled at a speed of seventy or eighty kilometers an hour. Who would tell them where they would get down? They grew extremely nervous. His companion was both scared and shy. He was not ready to ask anybody anything. Sidharth tried to explain his problem to a gentleman roaming nearby. He expected that the gentleman would tell him the number of the bus and go away on his errand. Surprising! The gentleman kept his own work aside, took them to the appropriate bus, and explained everything in great detail to the driver and conductor before leaving. They did not have to face any problems thereafter. The conductor asked a Kuttipuram-bound traveller, to look after them. He, in turn, requested a Tirur-bound passenger to take care of them. It was as if he was looking after members of his own family, and not outsiders. They had the same experience while returning from Tirur to Cochin later that day. Otherwise, they could not have returned to Cochin that night. Sidharth and his friend were amazed at the Keralites' loving concern for strangers and willingness to help them. They wondered silently if they would have received the same affectionate care in their own state.

Sidharth stayed for a week in Kerala. Everywhere he experienced the same generous hospitality and the willingness to help. The day he left Kerala, unknown to himself, he felt emotional. The question that frequently came to his mind was, shouldn't the people of Bubaneswar become courteous and helpful like the Keralites? At the same time, he was reminded of a shameful news that he had read a few days earlier: the local people turned their faces away from a poor woman beggar who lay on the footpath on the Nandankanan road; a foreigner took her to a hospital.

Sidharth felt immensely grateful to the coconut trees, the rippling water of the lakes, the mountains and the trees of Kerala and he wanted to thank them all. But how would he do so? He was reminded of something that he had heard long ago from someone. An Indian professor once visited Japan. One day, the poor professor forgot his way to the hotel. When he consulted the guide book, he learnt that he had travelled in the opposite direction. He explained his problems to a Japanese student. The Japanese student not only listened intently to his problem but also stayed with him throughout the day without attending his classes, and dropped him in his hotel by evening. The Indian made an offer of some money as a token of his gratitude. But the Japanese student rejected it. He said, smiling, "If you are really grateful to me, please do me a favour. After you return to India, whenever you talk to your friends, please narrate your experiences in Japan. At the end, please inform them that the Japanese are good people."

Sidharth didn't know whether the Indian professor kept his promise; but he didn't forget his own experiences in Kerala after his return to Odisha. Whenever he said something about Kerala, he couldn't help saying that the Keralites were very good people.

An Auspicious Beginning

The gentleman was describing the experience of his Goa tour. At times, he was getting so absentminded while describing the things that he was forgetting to throw the card.

When one goes on a long tour, new relationships are formed. Otherwise, Sidharth would never have known Narayan of Visakhapatanam and Dr. Ali of Sikanderabad. He was sitting some distance away, near the window. On the one hand, he had the desire to make an acquaintance with the unknown by starting a game of cards; on the other, there was the desire to see the unknown world glimpsed through the window. Because of this attitude of placing one's feet in two boats at the same time, he was not able to sail to any destination. It is a common problem with all those who, like him, want to buy everything, see everything, and know everything.

The gentleman said, "Have you seen the Kamal Hassan film "*Ek Duje ke Liye*? Oh! What a wonderful film! And the songs… how wonderful!" He sang two lines from that love-themed film. That was shot on the Dona Paula beach. A beautiful place! Good quality vests were sold there at a cheap price. I bought three or four of those. Would you like to see? O.K… later on. The beach has been named after a girl. That Portugese girl was in love with a fisherman boy of Goa. She committed suicide, just as it happens in many love stories. Poor girl! Then we visited the Miramar beach and the James of Basilica church. The dead body of St. Francis Xavier is preserved here. For the last five hundred years, the dead body has been looking fresh. He is dead, but alive. Can't you understand?" By then, the gentleman's turn had come. He threw a card and resumed narrating his experiences. "Then we visited the Kolaba beach. Where can you find such a splendid beach? Cement benches have been installed in the shade of coconut trees. The beach is as splendid as the Madras beach. The next day, we went to the Mangueshi temple and Durga temple. Four days were spent happily, weren't they?" It seemed as if the gentleman was expecting his friend to give evidence in favour of his statement.

His companion said, "You are talking about the good things only. Why don't you tell what happened in the Mayem Lake?"

The gentleman's face fell. The changed color of his face could not escape the absent-minded Sidharth. Darkness had descended around the train. The lights in the compartment were still not on. Gusts of cold air blew into the compartment.

Sidharth turned his gaze into the compartment. He was not interested in the Goa experience of the gentleman. Darkness had blotted out the world outside. He could only guess the existence of greenery along the railway tracks. When one goes out of one's state, one constantly remembers his home. One remembers the railway tracks in Odisha, along which no vegetation grows. The area along the tracks looks barren, like a desert. We may not grow grapes there, but can't we grow chilly or banana throughout the year?

The gentleman talked about his experience at Mayem Lake. After the boat ride, they dined at a restaurant on the other side of the lake. He had spent three days by then in Goa. The gentleman did not like the food there. Every item was cooked in coconut oil. The gentleman could not live without mustard oil. He could have managed with refined oil though. The moment the hotel boy brought the menu card, the non-vegetarian gentleman's eyes fell on the words 'fish'. Immediately, he placed an order for the item. After a long wait, the boy brought, in a medium- sized bowl, a soup. The sight of the soup filled the gentleman with a sense of revulsion. The effort to trace the almost invisible fish slices in that deep bowl filled with watery soup was as difficult as the attempt to trace a live pomfret fish in an ocean. What was most disheartening was the fact that the pomfret fish of the restaurant was also cooked in coconut oil. The pleasure of boating in the lake; the joy of feeding the small fish swimming in the lake; and the delight of taking photos of the gliding swans had all been forgotten. He somehow swallowed the rice. The gentleman's problems were far from over. It was no less of a shock to look at the bill which waited at the counter for him. The price of the pomfret curry was seventy-five rupees!

Sidharth laughed; others present there joined him. The gentleman now looked crestfallen. What made him sad was the fact that instead of treating him with sympathy, his friends were making fun of him. That his lack of farsightedness had become a subject of ridicule made him feel deeply hurt.

The card game did not interest anybody any more. Everybody went back to their own berths. Sidharth climbed to the upper berth and slept there. The express train was converted into a passenger train after entering Andhra Pradesh. Who knew whether it would reach Bhubaneswar by the next day or not?

The call of the tea boys disturbed Sidharth's sleep. The gentleman returning from Goa looked up at Sidharth from the lower berth. Sidharth wished him good morning. The train had stopped at the Palasa station. Somehow, when one reached the Palasa station, one felt as if one had reached Odisha. Today, one can find many Odia villages and Odia people in Andhra Pradesh or Bihar or Bengal.

A small child had entered the compartment to sell cucumber. The price of a piece of cucumber was one rupee. Most of the passengers had not got up till then. Who would eat cucumbers so early? The child's eyes reflected hope and faith. The gentlemen were returning from Bombay. They must have spent much money, as in Juhu the price of a few peanuts was rupees two and the price of a green coconut was rupees eight. Would they not buy cucumbers, which were priced at only one rupee per piece?

Sidharth called the boy and said, "*Do kakudi.*" His Hindi pronunciation, made the child reply in Odia, "Should I give two cucumbers, babu?" Sidharth felt ashamed.

The child peeled the cucumber, sliced it into four pieces, spread salt and red chili powder on them before handing them to Sidharth. Before Sidharth could hand the child a two rupee note, the friend returning from Goa took out a neatly folded two rupee note from his pocket and gave it to the boy. Sidharth was in the middle of passing a two-rupee note from the upper berth. He took the currency note back and thanked the gentleman.

The two-rupee note was the first income of the day for the boy, and therefore auspicious. Sidharth felt overwhelmed to watch the love and affection with which the boy kissed the note and touched his chest and head with it, before putting it in his pocket. On earlier occasions, Sidharth had seen shopkeepers receiving their first income and treating it with reverence. But he had never seen the way this fourteen-year-old thin and dark boy kissed the note with such love. So much eagerness, so much love for the hard earned two rupees!

The boy got down the train. The speed of the train increased. The gentleman returning from Goa was munching the cucumber. Still, Sidharth was lost in thoughts of the way the boy had kissed the note.

Then the shock came. The Goa-returning gentleman looked at Sidharth and spoke as if he was revealing a deep secret, "You know, sir. I am quite clever. You saw the way I used the useless two-rupee note"

Sidharth could not understand anything at first. He stopped munching the cucumber and looked at the gentleman. The gentleman continued, "That two-rupee note was completely torn. It was full of holes. But I had folded it so neatly that even the boy's father would not have found anything wrong with it. It would take him at least ten minutes to open the fold."

Before Sidharth's eyes, danced the face of the small child selling cucumber, his way of kissing the note, and the tearful eyes of the child back at home on realizing how he had been deceived. The gentleman who had been cheated at the Mayem Lake restaurant for his own foolishness, was feeling delighted after cheating a boy of his own state. Sidharth could not bear to look at him. He was praying to God that the child should not open the note any time during the day. Otherwise, his day would go waste.

The Lac-house of Pretence

Sidharth Biswal would never have accepted the matter as true, if his younger daughter Nandini had not opened the Facebook account on her laptop and shown it to him. The twenty-two or twenty-three year old Sumitra, who was working as domestic help in the house of his elder daughter a few months ago, had opened a facebook account with a fictitious name. She had put her name as Shruti Bhujabal. Sidharth would not have been worried so much if she had limited the changes in her identity to this. The dusky, slim, semi-literate girl had mentioned that she was now a student of KIIT University after completing her education from Unit-8 DAV school of Bhubaneswar. Sidharth was amazed at the false information provided by Sumitra. Her audacity stunned him, too.

The drain that had been left uncovered for repairing the road prevented the summer wind from wafting in the fragrance of jasmine flowers. The capital city, Bhubaneswar has been declared by the government as 'smart city". However, the odour from drains pervaded the air. Sidharth's dissatisfaction with his surroundings often made his wife angry. She would say, "This is a bad habit with retired people like you. Always unhappy… always complaining."

A naughty smile playing on her face, his younger daughter Nandini said, "Look, father, how intelligent our Sumitra is! You always considered her a fool. She has taken the help of modern technology and presented herself as a highly educated student from an English-medium school and a university. I strongly believe that if someone comes across her profile, he will be deeply impressed by it. There is nothing surprising if she receives a marriage proposal from a highly educated young man. Apart from inflating her educational qualifications, she has made herself appear attractive with the help of modern make-up. Why should such an 'educated girl' spend her life as a domestic help on a salary of eight thousand rupees a month?"

Contorting his face as if he had consumed something bitter, Sidharth said, "Educated or fool? Earlier, I used to call her foolish but looking at the way she behaved, I now call her imprudent. God save her! Let not her falsehood lead her into some serious trouble."

Aparna, his wife, brought in tea. She only heard the last word of what Sidharth had been saying and quipped, "What trouble are you talking about? You don't know the children of today very well. They will take out your eyes and cut off your nose within the twinkling of an eye."

"It will be seen later whether they decamp with my eyes or ears. Bring your glasses and read the news." Sidharth handed the morning paper to his wife.

"Arey… you have put on your glasses. Why don't you read it yourself?" Looking at Nandini, Aparna said, "My dear, read the news that your father is talking about."

Sidharth, while sipping tea told his daughter, "Read

aloud. Your mother believes that the world is a *'Ramarajya'* but only I consider it a *'Ravanrajya'*."

Nandini read the news story. As she went through the news item her mother sat down and asked her, "What has been printed there?"

Nandini sat down with her head in her hands. She said, "Mother, don't compel me to go through the matrimonial columns. Things were better in your time when newspapers had a limited circulation."

Sidharth intervened and said, "That will be taken care of later. Why don't you tell us about the social media that you are mad about day and night?"

Nandini said, "Mother, the incident took place in Delhi. About two years back, a lady-dentist had selected a boy through a matrimonial site. The young man had given a false name and age and presented himself as an MBBS doctor. After a few days, the lady doctor's parents invited the prospective groom to their house. The forty-seven year old bald-headed conman reached in a Mercedes car, with a wig neatly covering his head. He spoke English fluently. The lady-doctor and her parents were impressed. The marriage was solemnized. The parents of the bride had to spend seventy lakh rupees including twenty lakh cash-present to the groom and twenty-five lakh rupees on the dinner in a posh hotel.

"What happened after this?" Aparna's voice was trembling with anxiety.

"The real name of the conman is Barun Kaul. Many cases of cheating were registered in his name at Delhi, Chandigarh, Goa and Maharastra. But, that's not all. He was going to shoot his wife as she had got wind of his real identity. He had already reached the clinic of his wife at Kirtinagar. Fortunately, the revolver didn't work at the right time. Police have arrested him now."

"Serves him right," Aparna reacted.

"What's good about it? In the meantime, they have a son. Please think of the lady doctor. How will she rebuild her broken life? Think of her parents. Had they imagined this would happen to their daughter after spending seventy lakh rupees?"

Silence enveloped everything. Only the sound of the revolving fan was audible. Sidharth said, "Nandini. Just think of it once. Just as Sumitra has written false stories about her on the facebook, similarly, another young man might have published false things in his profile. By chance, the two cheats get married. Can you imagine what will happen after that? The lac-house of pretence might look very gorgeous, but it is inflammable. Even if a little spark falls on it, it will burn to ashes. Can 'intelligent' Sumitra save herself then?"

Aparna said, "Social media is a powerful tool. Many good things can be spread through it. It can help in creating awareness in society; humanity can benefit from it. But a group of cheats has destroyed it completely. Just mark how some of them have spread a rumour about child-theft and put the entire state government machinery in a fix."

"That's why I was telling you Ram and Ravan, Kansha and Srikrishna are all beneficiaries of the same civilization. The tricks which are available to Ram are also available to Ravana. Using modern technology, Ram constructed a passage to Lanka, whereas misutilising the technology, Ravan created a golden deer and finally his golden Lanka was reduced to ashes."

Aparna said, "Sumitra had left Mani's house without informing anybody. If I had her phone number, I would have asked her why she did something like this."

Nandini objected, "Who will listen to you? Why should you bother? As one sows, so shall one reap."

Sidharth objected, "This is another problem with the young generation. Here, no one is interested in telling anyone anything. What's the harm in telling the truth? She will feel bad… let her do so. But if one day in future you come to learn that her life is in danger, then you will regret not having cautioned her earlier."

Evening had descended while the discussion was on. Aparna got up and switched on all the lights. Bright light spread everywhere.

The Illusion

Sutapa knew that the employees of other departments were jealous of the employees working in the computer department. The signs of jealousy on the faces of the colleagues would be displayed distinctly during summer days. "Yes, you spend time in the air-conditioned room where neither sunlight nor hot air can enter. You enjoy spring weather throughout the year." Some of them, unable to suppress the feelings of the heart, expressed them through the mouth. Sutapa would never say anything. She knew that the air-conditioners were not meant for employees like her. It was thanks to the machines that they got some respite from the heat.

However, this gentleman's behaviour made her aware of the comfortable condition she was in. It made her feel very happy. The gentleman proceeded towards her room bravely. An acquaintance from his village, Sidharth, worked in this office. He sought Sutapa's permission to allow him to take a look at the computer room.

Sutapa noticed that the man had put on a soiled dhoti and a sleeveless shirt. At the back of his shoulder hung an umbrella. She asked, "Do you have any work here?"

While comparing the outside heat with the cool air inside, the gentleman said, "How cold this house of yours feels! You are working comfortably here, aren't you?

Oh! This is called the computer department. If one wants to work in the computer department, one has to work in a cold room like this!

Sutapa smiled. The gentleman had perhaps entered an air-conditioned room for the first time in his life. She was developing a sense of sympathy for this unknown gentleman.

The gentleman looked very excited. But, can a visit to a computer room be the cause of so much excitement? Sutapa continued looking at the man's face to guess the exact reasons for his happiness.

The gentlemen seemed to need a guide. Sutapa could guess this. She raised her head from the keyboard and said, "May I help you?"

The gentleman moved a few steps forward and said, "Yes, my dear. I would like to see some computers."

Sutapa smiled a silent smile. Had it happened a few years ago, she could have made fun of the gentleman for what he had said. Why should one seek anyone's permission to take a look at the computers when he stood right inside a computer room? But she had grown older and wiser. She said, "Yes… these are called computers. These are monitors; these are key-boards; this is called a mouse; that one is a printer…"

Without allowing Sutapa to complete what she was saying, the gentleman said, "Bah! You know so many things." Keen to acquire a little more knowledge about computers, he asked, "Which one is the hardware?"

Sutapa said, "These machines are the hardware."

"And software?"

Sutapa wanted to smile once again. How would she show someone the software? She said, "The command that we give or the information that is stored inside are called software."

It was as if the gentleman discovered some hidden truth. Now he turned his gaze away from the computers, air-conditioners, stabilizers and fixed it on Sutapa and her colleagues. The operators were all sitting on revolving chairs and they could turn to their right, left, front and back with ease. The gentleman looked at them lovingly, and told Sutapa, "Can't I meet the head of the department?"

Sutapa said, "I am the head of this department. Tell me what you want to know."

The rustic gentleman cast a glance at Sutapa and the machines of the computer section, and said, "Oh, you are the head of this department."

Now the gentleman brought his face closer to the ears of Sutapa and asked, "My dear, what salary do you get?"

Sutapa could not believe her ears. This was something very personal. What would the gentleman gain if he found out how much she earned? She had heard that the members of would be in-laws' family secretly enquire about the job and the salary of a girl before marriage. But, she was married for ten years now. Why was he asking about her salary?

The gentleman was rustic but not foolish. He could rightly guess her feeling of discomfort at that question, and raised the question from a personal level to a general one. "I mean … how much do the computer programmers earn?"

"Eight thousand rupees a month", Sutapa answered calmly. She suddenly remembered that if the finance commission had submitted its report, she would have been getting another six hundred seventy seven rupees more per month.

The gentleman appeared extremely delighted and said, "Bah, eight thousand rupees. Are you getting so much?"

This time Sutapa opened her mouth. "Do you think this is a lot? Never mind. Please tell me why you have been asking so many questions."

The gentleman said, "Please don't misunderstand me, daughter. I just wanted to know. My son is reading computer science in Calcutta. I just wanted to find out how much he would earn after he completes his studies."

Sutapa felt depressed. The gentleman's face now looked like that of her own father. How happy her father became the day she had got the job! The past flashed before her eyes.

The gentleman went away. Sutapa thought of the touching faith parents had in their children. These days, many students come out of computer institutes. Young students, without beard or moustache on their faces, wearing ties, flashing glasses, and carrying files moved from office to office looking for jobs. Sutapa was lucky as she had landed that job ten years ago. If she tried these days, she would never get a job. She felt great sympathy for the gentleman. She prayed to God earnestly, "Let his son get a job."

Sutapa was going to have a cup of tea. Sidharth met her on the way and asked, "Has uncle already left?"

Sutapa answered, "Yes. Perhaps his son is doing a course in computer science."

Sidharth appeared glum. He said, "He was. But for the last two years, he is not doing anything. He is looking for a job in Calcutta. He had written a letter to me. He had asked me to tell his father that he would become a programmer by the end of this year. When Uncle heard of this, he insisted on visiting an office similar to the one in which his son was supposed to work. He also wished to collect information about the salary he was going to get."

The world grew blurred to Sutapa. A hopeful father, whose face she had seen a moment ago, had started receding before disappearing forever.

She turned away from Sidharth and went back into the cold room.

The Pain of Loss

Sidharth had been staying in the city for the last few months, after retirement. For Sidharth who was old and experienced, it was not difficult to figure out that the needs of his son and daughter-in-law were more responsible for his stay in the capital than their love and affection for him. He was reminded of what Saratchandra had written in his book *Narira Mulya*. The ever-neglected and uncared-for widowed aunt is warmly welcomed for she would take care of the new-born nephew. Sidharth never thought hard about a world where relationships were valued in terms of needs. Besides, what would he be doing in the village now? After twenty years in the city, he found himself suspended between the city and the village; to expect to be loved for one's own sake in such circumstances would be nothing but vanity.

Sidharth would be found waiting for some time near the school-gate after dropping his grandson Meethun at his school. He would vainly search for his lost childhood among the uniformed tiny tots. He would pour his heartfelt blessings on these little ones, who walked with heavy school bags on their shoulders and plastic water bottles hanging from their necks. He would wave his hands till Meethun disappeared from view. Sidharth would enjoy the brief moment heartily.

Today, the period of waiting had become a long one. Even the young politician, who usually reached and returned late, had gone. His bike was not found parked in front of the betel shop. The gate-keeper of the school had gone somewhere else after locking the gate. The area near the school-gate would be filled with the noise of the crowd, when it opened at eleven o' clock once again. Sidharth should have gone back home, with a packet of milk procured from the milk shop near the *chhak*.

Who was Sidharth waiting for, a ten rupee note in his hand? There was a cemented drain near the main gate of the school. This folded new ten rupee note, lay amidst the grass near the drain. The note might have fallen from the pocket of a careless child. The students of this school belonged to rich families. The 'daddy' or 'mummy' of some child might have handed the note for tiffin expenses. But, due to the negligence of the child, the note lay on the grass.

Of course, Sidharth was sure; no one had noticed him picking up the note. There was nothing exciting happening in the post-retirement life; everything that happened was part of a monotonous routine. The sudden discovery and possession of this ten-rupee note was no less exciting. It was sufficient for a pack of cigarettes, two *paans*, and one box of matches. Gladly, and swiftly, Sidharth pocketed the note.

However, Sidharth was reminded of an incident that had taken place in his youth. Many years ago, one day, Sidharth's father had entrusted to him the task of purchasing a few things from the market. Sidharth went to the shop, with the two-rupee note neatly folded and safely kept in his pocket. But, he had forgotten that the pocket had a hole since long. When he put his hand in his pocket to fetch the note, after the articles were packed at the grocery shop, to his utter dismay, he found that the note had given him the slip. The penniless Sidharth stood sandwiched between the suspicious shopkeeper in front, and a crowd of customers behind him. Tear welled up in the eyes of Sidharth when the cruel shopkeeper emptied the things packed into his bag. That day, the shopkeeper drove him away after heaping upon him insulting words.

The young Sidharth was more scared of the beatings of his parents than the suspicion and abuse of the shopkeeper. He knew his father quite well. For a small mistake like climbing up a tree or swimming in the pond, his father would pick him up and fling him down from a height. This was his method of disciplining Sidharth. Sidharth took four hours to cross a distance of one and a half kilometers that day.

Sidharth had not forgotten his first encounter with the pain of losing something. What a great gulf separated the pleasures of getting and the pain of losing. Losing entails the ill-luck of forfeiting one's own rights; a man is never found ready to embrace such ill-luck. The grief and sighs after losing ten or fifteen rupees that one earns after doing hard work for a day can never be equated with the unexpected pleasure and excitement of finding a piece of gold.

Sidharth had taken out the ten rupee note from his pocket and held it in his hand. This note didn't belong to him. He was waiting for two searching eyes of the person, whose dream of eating *ladoos* or chocolates had been dashed so early in the morning.

No! No one came searching for the note. The child

might have submitted to the routine of the school. He might not have been aware of his loss. Or, perhaps the child of a rich family casually disregarded the loss of only ten rupees. What's the worth of ten rupees today?

Sidharth, who had not forgotten the pain of losing two rupees in a mofussal bazzar about forty-five years ago, was still waiting at the school gate. He was frequently reminded of the hurt caused by slaps landing on his young cheeks.

The Shawl

During the return journey from Koraput to Bhubaneswar they reached Kurli on the way. The place was surrounded by mountains and forests on all sides. The narrow road ran through the jungle like the cascading hair of a woman. Green solemn *salap* trees stood all around. The surroundings looked peaceful and charming.

On the right side, stood the office of the 'Niyamgiri Fruit Growers Cooperative Society'. Sidharth's friend, Ajay shouted, "Stop...stop. I told you about this office. Let's go and see how beautiful the handiworks of *Dongoria Kandhs* are."

For Sidharth, who was born in a coastal district and who had spent half of his life in the city, his knowledge of *Adivasi* culture was confined to the exhibition held in the Adivasi ground or some documentary films. But he could clearly understand the difference between the *harijans* and the *adivasis*. If you uproot the *harijans* from one place and plant them somewhere else, they can prosper, but if you remove the *adivasis* from their roots, they would never thrive. Their life was intimately linked to the mountains, the forest, the streams, the *salap* tree and the *mahua* flower.

Like a plant, they were not independent of their place and surroundings. Their relationship with nature was an integral part of their existence.

The gentleman who was in charge of the office showed them the ornaments and musical instruments used by the *Dongoria kandhs*. He also talked about the importance of Kurli and Chatikona. Chatikona was famous for its waterfalls. The famous Pataleswar temple was situated nearby. The place was under Gunupur subdivision of Rayagada district. Sidharth's friend asked the gentleman, "Where are the special shawls woven by the *Dongrias*? We want to see one of them."

The gentleman opened an almirah and took out five or six shawls. My friend grew extremely excited when he saw the patterns and embroidery work on those. He put one on his shoulders and asked, "Please have a look at me. How do I look? I propose each one of you should take at least one of these. You can use this as a shawl or, if you so wish, you can hang it as a curtain in your house."

Sidharth went on inspecting the shawls one after another. Surprisingly the shawls, though ready for sale, were not even washed and cleaned. There were stains of water and dust everywhere. If one had a close look one would feel as if someone had used it for three or four months before putting it in the almirah, neatly folded. Despite their exquisite colours and design, were they worth purchasing?

Perhaps the official of the cooperative society read Sidharth's mind. He smiled and handed him over a piece of paper which bore some information about these shawls. By the time Sidharth had completed reading the lines, he felt a strange sensation within him.

The shawls have a strange role to play in the tradition and culture of the *Dongoria Kandhs*. Whenever and wherever the *Dongoria* maiden gets a little leisure during the day's hard work, she keeps herself engaged in weaving the shawl. At times, she takes about one or two months to complete the weaving of one shawl. The day the place experiences spells of heavy rain; or a cyclone prevents her from going to work, she sits back at home and weaves the shawl. When the hot sun or exhaustion compels her to take rest in the shade of the dense trees, she thinks of weaving it. When she ties the knots of flowers using red, green, and yellow colour, a delightful dream enchants her. The *Kandh* maiden weaves the shawl for her dear brother, to give it as a present during the latter's marriage. Her brother can drape her sister-in-law with this shawl and can protect her from the jealous eyes of others. What else, other than the colourful garment woven by the sister-in-law, can drape the new bride's soft body like the soft petals of *mahua* flowers? Amidst all this, another dream would stir her young mind, like a playful butterfly. Somewhere else, another *Kandh* maiden like her, would be working hard at weaving a similar shawl; this shawl would come to her through the maiden's brother; and draped in that, she would leave with her husband to start her own family. Such an unending colourful dream scatters thousands of fresh flowers on a white fabric of love, faith and patience. With the unfinished shawl draped around her at times, the *Kandh* maiden would feel exhilarated, at the thought of the absent sister-in-law or the touch of her would-be husband. Even when the needle would pierce her fingers, she would feel thrilled with an aching pleasure.

The official of the cooperative society spoke the language officials use. "They receive no formal training; they have no fixed hours of work. We supply them with pieces of cloth. They take these, and whenever they find the time, they weave the designs on them. So, it's quite natural that they have mud and soil on them. One good thing is that foreigners are looking for such shawls more and more. They want mud and soil stuck to them. They believe such things indicate that these are genuine and pure. Besides, the Kandh maidens are very self-conscious. If one raises any objection, they would throw the shawl away; they would not even receive their remuneration. Oh my God, what pride!"

Sidharth felt a strange sensation coming over him. The stains of soil and mud appeared to him as beautiful symbols of love, faith and patience. He bought two of these shawls. At the same time, he thought that if a *Kandh* maiden got a huge piece of cloth, so lovely and so sweet, she would weave beautiful flowers on those and drape the whole world with it. Then, the world would not rot under the impact of inauspicious planets.

An Unfamiliar World

While approaching the terrace of Rudramadhav's two-storeyed building, Sidharth asked, "Why does the house look so forlorn? Aren't children at home?"

Rudramadhav answered, "Come, my friend. I was waiting for you."

The breeze blew very gently on the terrace. Just as a new bride expresses herself in her new-found family timidly, the southern breeze blew gently to make its existence felt. Asking Sidharth to sit on the chair, Rudramadhav said, "Everybody is present." Then, changing the topic, he said, "I heard that Archana has come. How long is she going to stay?"

"Don't mention her. She has been causing a furore since the day she has arrived. Mother has also reached from the village. The entire house bustles like a market place throughout the day. One finds it difficult to sit in peace and browse the newspaper."

"Where is the need of reading a newspaper? In my house, everybody is an avid viewer of television. We do not purchase a newspaper."

"Back at our home, the television set has been switched

off since the day Archana arrived. She has ordered not to switch on the television. No one will use the mobile phone at least one day a week. All will take breakfast and dinner together at an appointed hour in the morning."

"In that case, your daughter-in-law must be facing a lot of difficulties," Rudramadhav remarked.

"Where is the time for her to realize that she is facing difficulties? She is too busy helping her mother-in-law in fulfilling her demands. Archana has arrived from London with a long list. The list includes *dahikadi, mahuradi* fish fry, paper thin pancakes, and mushroom, wrapped in leaves roasted slowly on cinders. Even I asked her once if she was doing research there or preparing such lists."

"Very good! This will immensely benefit *bhauja*. She will regain her lost skills while cooking all these for her daughter."

The electricity supply to the colony was disrupted. The entire colony was engulfed in darkness.

"See, the supply had been irregular throughout the day. I thought it would not be disrupted in the evening but now there is no electricity," said Rudramadhav complainingly.

The Jagar Amavasya night had fallen a mere five days ago. On the sky now shone feebly a four day old moon.

Rudramadhav's children came to the terrace one after another. They grumbled and looked annoyed as the electricity supply had been disrupted at this odd hour. Even the face of the grandson reflected his intense irritation as he could not watch the cricket match on TV.

Rudramadhav whispered, "Look! Everybody was present at home. Someone was busy browsing through the Facebook on his mobile; another was gazing at the computer screen. Two of them were watching TV. In this house, everybody is lost in his own world. They look for me only when they have some work; otherwise I am conveniently forgotten. My job is to ensure that the lights are switched off at the end of the day and that the gates are properly locked. You can call me the modern Ugrasen."

"Ugrasen… Who is he?"

"I am talking about Ugrasen, the king of Mathura. His son Kansa dethroned him and appointed him as the gate-keeper of the palace. He knew pretty well that none else than his father would guard the gate with dedication."

Sidharth realized that there was a hint of sorrow in Rudramadhav's voice. When Rudramadhav's children saw Sidharth, they said a customary 'namaskar' and went away to another corner of the roof.

Sidharth and Rudramadhav worked in the same office. Five years ago, they retired one after another. Rudramadhav's wife passed away last year. He had two sons, two daughters-in-law and grandchildren living with him. The daughter lived at Bangalore.

Sidharth asked, "Do you remember the childhood you spent in the village?"

"Why talk about it now? The entire house would be filled with noise from morning till night. Besides, there were so many *pujas* organized by grandfather. Since we, many brothers and sisters, lived in a joint family, during Ganesh or Saraswati puja new clothes would be purchased in bulk from the shop. When we all went to the school, wearing the same types of dresses, it seemed as if we were the inmates of some jail."

The lights came on.

Rudramadhav's children went downstairs one by one hurriedly. The noise gradually died down.

Sidharth continued, "I wanted to talk to you about

Archana. But your situation compels me to think that life in India will soon come to resemble that in Britain. The world around us is growing less and less familiar."

Rudramadhav looked up at Sidharth silently. Rudramadhav's elder son Saroj appeared with two cups of tea on a tray. He was leaving when Sidharth called him, "Hey, Saroj. Please come here?"

"Yes… Uncle." He came and stood nearby.

Sidharth said, "I could not believe, at first, what Archana was saying. Do you believe that one day a ministry would be opened to deal with the loneliness of human beings?"

"Loneliness!"

Saroj started and asked.

Sidharth said, "Yes, the British Government has opened a new department which will deal with the problems of friendless citizens. About ninety lakh citizens of that country have to deal with this problem. There are more than two lakh people who have not found anyone to talk to during the last two months."

"Surprising!" remarked Saroj.

"That's true. Just as we need food to satisfy hunger, just as we need water when we are thirsty or a doctor when we are sick, we need someone's company when we are alone. If a man does not get the opportunity to talk to someone for a long time, he would go mad. The British Government has appointed a competent lady as the first minister of this department."

"Uncle, in that respect, we Indians are fortunate. We readily get someone to share our feelings with,"

"But sadly, things are changing," said Sidharth.

"Why did you say this?" asked Saroj.

"The calamity has already struck us. Modern gadgets

like mobiles, laptops, TVs were supposed to serve man but they have started to lord it over him."

"Stop… Sidharth. He is going on a tour tomorrow morning. Don't unnecessarily overburden his mind." Rudramadhav looked at Saroj and continued, "You may go now. This Archana has put all these ideas into your uncle's head. Britain is far away from India."

"No, father… I can understand what he means."

Saroj was going to say something more. The light went off suddenly. Darkness spread everywhere once more. From the roof, he called his younger brother, "Hey… Manoj. Call everybody here. Uncle is telling us something very important."

Rudramadhav heard the footsteps of his children coming onto the terrace. In the enveloping darkness, Sidharth could mark signs of joy on the face of his friend. He prayed to God, "Let the supply of electricity be disrupted for at least an hour."

Treachery

The sudden appearance of Rajanikant in his department like the southern breeze of spring unusually blowing in *Magha*, surprised Sidharth. Rajanikant was a renowned young leader and entrepreneur of Ramachandranagar area. Usually he would not talk to anyone below the level of the Managing Director or Chief Manager. He feared that, if he talked to someone junior in a department, he would demean himself. Sidharth could not figure out for long whether he wanted to climb the ladder of politics through his acumen as a businessman or whether he desired to be an established businessman through his success as a politician. In a manner of divulging a great secret, Rajanikant said once that he was not interested either in industry or in politics; these were the only means of passing time pleasantly. He really wanted to gain name, fame and affluence without hard work.

Raising both his arms in the manner of a politician Rajanikant said, "Namaskar".

Sidharth got up from his chair. To get a glimpse of such a noble person was nothing short of good luck.

Rajanikant said, "A new project is going to be

inaugurated on the thirtieth of this month. I had come to invite the M.D. and the G.M.. Since they are not available, will you please pass these on to them?"

Rajanikant handed two expensive invitation cards to Sidharth. Sidharth, out of curiosity, asked, "Sir, what is this project all about?"

"Arey… don't you know? Ramachandranagar has been declared a tourist destination. In the first phase, fifty houses with thatched roofs have been remodelled as air-conditioned houses. If this is done, foreign tourists will enjoy all the facilities of the city in the village, and this will bring us foreign currency worth lakhs. You will see, the village will be transformed in five years."

Sidharth was going to ask another question. But, the reluctance of Rajanikant to discuss things with a junior official like him brought a premature end to the conversation.

Rajanikant left the place just as he had come—like a storm.

Suddenly, the picture of Ramachandranagar situated by the highway danced before Sidharth's eyes. The village was quiet and beautiful. A canal ran some distance away. Rows of coconut trees adorned the canal bank; on both sides of it spread acres and acres of paddy fields. However, the villagers used these spaces for defecation. The houses with their broken thatched roofs, the damaged tubewell, and the narrow road that led to the village advertised its poverty. Sidharth had visited the place many times. Just as a healthy and charming woman turns forlorn and pitiful under the crushing weight of poverty and advancing age, Ramachandranagar looked similarly forlorn and pitiful. Which foreign tourist will think of spending his leisure in a village writhing in the clutch of painful poverty and squalor?

Sidharth was reminded of a story he had heard long ago. There was a kingdom ruled by a king. One day he went out hunting. He saw a deer. He was going to shoot an arrow at it when he heard the enchanting song of an unknown bird. The king ran after the bird, forgetting everything about hunting. The bird was captured and brought to the palace. The next morning the king waited anxiously for the bird to sing. Despite his best efforts the bird didn't oblige him. The king consulted his ministers. The latter said that the bird needed a tree like the one on which it was sitting in the jungle. The tree was found but still the bird wouldn't sing. This called for further consultations. This time the minister suggested that a spring be created. This too was done; water flowed making a sweet sound; but the bird remained silent as before. The king talked to his ministers once again. The minister finally advised the king to set the bird free in the jungle. It sang there.

If a foreign tourist wants to see a village in Odisha, let him see the real village. If poverty is driven away from the thatched house and an air-conditioner is fitted, it would turn into a cottage of a hotel but not the thatched house of a village. When poverty and squalor spread everywhere which foreign tourist would come to enjoy the divine beauty of the place and spend foreign currency?

Sidharth held the two colourful invitation cards in his hand. They contained the hidden message of the conspiracy to transform an ordinary village by giving it a facelift so that the vulgar image could be traded for money. Sidharth threw the two cards angrily into the drawer.

Uanshi Kanya

Many years have gone by since I left Ravenshaw College.

I have not been able to gather more information about Ravenshaw except some trivial news occasionally published in newspapers.

When I think of Ravenshaw, I am reminded of our 'English Madam'. I can't remember her full name.To us she was 'madam'. After a few days 'English' was prefixed to 'madam'.

'English madam' was thirty-five years old by the time about which I am writing here. But she was not married.

Usually, there is a lot of curiosity among the college-goers to discuss the personal life of their professors; needless to say, we felt the same curiosity about our English madam. Why wasn't madam getting married? Was she a victim of deceit in love? Had she decided to sacrifice her personal happiness for her family? We would discuss all such possibilities at great length. However, no one dared ask madam such a question. It's a feeling of acute embarrassment that prevented us from asking such a question.

One day, only two or three of us attended the tutorial class. Other students had to stay away due to the incessant rain. Madam decided to enquire into our personal life instead of concentrating on our studies. She discussed many topics like, "What would you do after passing B.A.? Whether you would go for P.G. in English? She also talked about how good students were not willing to join the profession." We listened to her, and at times, answered her questions.

Taking advantage of the moment, I boldly asked, "Madam, I wish to ask you a personal question. I'll ask you if only you don't mind."

Madam's face that usually looked solemn like a sky covered with clouds, appeared charming that day. Her eyes reflected an innocent curiosity.

With great boldness I asked, "Madam, Why haven't you decided to raise a family till now?"

English madam was not expecting such a question. She was shocked. But only for a moment. Then she regained her composure and answered, 'I am an Uanshi Kanya—a girl born during the Amavasya. Who would marry an Uanshi Kanya?"

Suddenly, a thunder exploded outside. We could see lightning flashing. The sound of it almost deafened me. It continued raining heavily outside.

Madam went on, "In our society, Uanshi Kanyas are considered ominous. No one comes forward to marry them. Ill fortune befalls those who defy what is written in the scriptures. It is a common belief that the young man who marries an Uanshi Kanya dies an untimely death."

I asked, "Do you really believe in such a superstition? You are a Professor of English. You are supposed to be more progressive than ordinary women. How can you credit such nonsense?"

"Look my dear, this education is only a veneer. Can it bring about social reforms so easily? Who cares whether I believe something? I would not have found a suitable match for myself; it was the responsibility of the people in my family to find a suitable match for me. They have been telling me since childhood, "You are an Uanshi Kanya; you are ill-fated. Who would marry you and destroy his family?" Tell me, will such a girl, who has been listening to such things since childhood ever wish to marry and have a family?"

"But have you never met a man with whom you could have set up a family?"

'Yes, I have. I have met such men. But, I have not been able to gather the courage to propose to them. I have shuddered at the prospect of a noble human being facing untimely death for the sin of marrying me. I dare not play with another man's life for my sake."

Ten years passed in the mean time. I never met English Madam. I lost contact with people associated with my college days.

One day, I met Madam all of a sudden. I and the members of my family were purchasing *mahaprasad* in Anandabazar of Sri Jagannath temple. I noticed a dusky woman clad in a white saree standing some distance away and eating *mahaprasad* from a *kodua*— a clay container.

In the dim light, I could easily recognize madam. However, she couldn't recognize me. Had she even seen me, she could not have done so.

For a moment, my heart overflowed with a feeling of sadness. With me, there were my wife, my daughter and a few friends. Despite being much younger than madam, I had raised a family and become a householder. Madam was superior to me in terms of age, qualification, fame and economic independence but she didn't have a family. No one had stepped into her life and relieved her loneliness.

I didn't like seeing madam standing alone in Anandabazar and licking the *kodua* for food like a female mendicant or widow. It would have been better if I had not met her at all—ever in this life.

Even today,the image of my English Madam, clad in a white saree, floats before my eyes. Her solemn and silent appearance reminds me of a devastated garden that was once in full bloom. In her I also find mirrored the fate of a humble, helpless woman, who unwillingly sacrificed her life and youth in the altar of a superstition-ridden society.

Despite numerous meetings, rallies and protests advocating woman empowerment, many such Uanshi Kanyas must be shedding silent tears in a dark room. Who would revive these Ahalyas who have turned into stone? When?

An Unfortunate Son

By the time Sanjay reached his office, he was late. For the last four or five days, he had been regularly coming late. Sidharth guessed that he must be in trouble; otherwise he was never late in reaching office.

Sidharth asked, "Are you facing any problem? You are late in reaching office during the last few days!"

Sanjay felt ashamed to learn that his Section Officer had noticed his lapses. "Yes, Sir. There was some problem at home. From tomorrow, I will not be late."

Sidharth was the Section Officer of the section, but he had not asked the question in that capacity. He had asked it as a matter of habit. Why should anyone invite trouble by asking another why he was late? Half of the officials think if they have put their signatures in the attendance register, they have done their duty. In that respect, Sanjay was much better. He asked, "Why? What happened?"

Sanjay replied, "Mother had come. She went back to the village today. I had to see her off at the bus-stand."

He could guess from the Sanjay's voice that his mother had not left for the village of her sweet will; but rather, he was compelled to send her against his will. Sidharth didn't wish to interfere in anyone's private affairs. From what Sanjay revealed, he came to know that Sanjay's mother was conservative in her outlook. It was difficult for the mother-in-law and daughter-in-law to stand each other for more than a week. The daughter-in-law was modern and independent-minded. She was not ready to accept the views of her mother-in-law. She was not ready to submit herself to the restrictions imposed on her on *purnamis*, Thursdays, *akadashis, sankrantis* etc. All his attempts to make the two live in harmony had failed miserably. Finally, he was compelled to send his mother back to his village. He was sad because he did not want his mother to return to the village so early. His mother lived alone in the village after his father's death.

Sidharth was reminded of the incidents of his childhood. He was staying in the hostel then. The school was situated twenty-five miles away from his village. He came back home two or three times in a year. The moment his mother saw him, she would behave as if she had found a treasure. But the holidays would come to an end; the time to return to the hostel would arrive. Then his mother would start crying. She would not like her son to go away. His father would comfort mother and prepare for Sidharth's return journey. By the time Sidharth reached the bank of Arjun Babaji's pond with his father through the front gate of the house, his mother would have come out through the back gate and would be standing at the foot of the babul tree on the bank of the pond. Sidharth would tell his mother, "Mother… you go back home… I am leaving. I will come back the moment the school closes for vacation." His mother would say, "You go, I will go back to the house afterwards?"

Sidharth knew when she was a young daughter-in-law his mother had been asked never to go beyond this point. Otherwise, she would have walked all the way to his hostel with him. She had to return from here. Mother's love would make Sidharth emotional and his eyes would brim with tears. Things would turn hazy. He would find it hard to take his eyes off his mother. The mother would find it difficult to say goodbye to her son —it was as if time came to a halt for those two to four minutes. He felt a constriction in his chest. Finally, father would pull him forward saying, "Let's go. It's very hot here." With the end of her saree on her face, mother would burst into tears. Tears would now flow unimpeded. Sidharth would turn back again and again to find his mother standing like a babul tree among babul trees on the bank of the pond. She would keep standing there till both father and son disappeared from view.

Something like this must have happened to Sanjay in the past. Once his world must have revolved round his mother. But today, the affection for his mother has grown less intense. The centre of his world has shifted. Otherwise, he would never have forced his lonely mother to go back.

Sidharth felt only mothers could wait on the banks of a pond, amid village fields. Their eyes never shut; drops of tear never dried on their cheeks; uncontrollable sobs always shook them. They try hard to suppress their feelings, saying, "Go… my dear…make a man of yourself…go, fly into the sky. Wherever the elephant maybe, it belongs to the king. Wherever you go, you are mine, my son."

The elephant returns from the dense forest, but the son never returns from abroad. The hot wind of reality dries up the tears. It shatters the mother's hopes and dreams.

■

An Unknown Friend

To Sidharth, the face of the person seeking compassion looks pathetic like the face of the calf who finds itself lost. A look at the face of this man filled Sidharth with a similar feeling. Sidharth was feeling uncomfortable the way the man was standing in front of them with both hands folded in supplication. He stopped writing and said, "Please sit down first. Please don't keep standing like that. Tell me what has happened."

His colleague, Rameshbabu, who had brought the man with him, had gone. Now, in that room, Sidharth, that unknown man, and Sidharth's friend Umesh were left. The atmosphere around them felt suffocating. Sidharth was mentally preparing himself to stop working and listen to the story of the man. In the mean time, the person finding him busy, had already started telling the story to Umesh.

The man had put on cement-coloured trousers, full-sleeved champak-coloured shirt and glasses. On his round fair face, patches of beard had appeared. Perhaps for the last two days, the man had not shaved himself. He would be around forty or forty-two years of age. From his talk, it was clear that he didn't belong to Odisha. He himself seemed quite comfortable in Hindi but as he wasn't sure they would understand Hindi, he spoke in broken English.

After immersing the bones of his parents at Gaya, the man reached Puri to perform some rituals. After spending two days in Puri, he would have returned home yesterday in the evening. But yesterday evening, his bag containing his clothes and money, was stolen. He had only twenty-four or twenty-five rupees in his pocket. He came to Bhubaneswar from Puri by bus; and because Sidharth's office was very close to the bus stand, he reached here first.

Sidharth came to know that the man belonged to Benaras. If he tried to go there, he would need one hundred and fifty rupees as the train fare. He might need some money for the food. However, he needed the fare first.

The problem that stared Umesh in the face was not the sum of one hundred and fifty rupees but to ensure whether the man had been telling the truth. The crumpled lines on his forehead reflected his worries. Now-a-days, many people try to cheat others on different pretexts. From the bottom to the top, there existed a huge deficit of trust. Some people ask for help, with a rope around their neck and a blade of grass between their teeth. They feign that they have killed a cow and they need to atone for the sin. Once someone came to Sidharth's colony at regular intervals of six months, asking for money for the thread ceremony of his son. If this man was believed to be telling the truth, he would be the proud father of at least twenty-five sons. Some begged for money at the temples of gods and goddesses; some others submitted written requests for money as they were mute; and some sought money for the operation of their close relatives. It was not easy to determine who among these was telling the truth and who was telling lies.

The man sat in front of their table squeezing himself. He had a hand bag by the side of his right foot. Sidharth guessed that he must be having in it his wet towel, tooth brush and old slippers.

Umesh looked at Sidharth once again. He wanted to ask, "What should we do now?" Sidharth was reminded of an incident that had happened with him many years ago. The incident took place in nineteen hundred seventy-seven or seventy-eight. Then he worked part time in the office of a Marwari businessman at Cuttack. Once he had to visit Baleswar on some work. Sidharth boarded the Baleswar-bound bus from Cuttack early in the morning. The journey from Cuttack to Baleswar took four hours. In order to pass time, Sidharth carried a detective novel with him. The novel told an exciting story. After reading through the first three pages, he grew oblivious of the passengers, the road, the electricity poles and the trees around him.

No one sat near him when he had got into the bus at Cuttack. He was seated by the window. In the mean time two or three local passengers had occupied the seat near him and got down at their destinations. By the time the bus reached Baleswar, it was one thirty. He was hungry. In front of the bus stand, he found a tiffin shop. Sidharth got down the bus, went into a shop, and ordered some tiffin.

Sidharth's hunger was satiated only after eating four *samosas*, some *chenapoda* and drinking two glasses of water. He reached the counter of the shop and asked, "How much should I pay?" The shopkeeper answered, "Six rupees". Sidharth, intending to pay the shopkeeper, took his hand upto his pocket, and on discovering that he did not have the money purse in his pocket, felt extremely upset. He felt as if someone had swept him off his feet and he had fallen into a crevice.

On the one hand, the shopkeeper waited for the payment to be made and, on the other, he cursed himself for allowing someone to pick his pocket. After waiting for two or three minutes, he told the shopkeeper what had happened with him, but the shopkeeper was not ready to buy his story.

With much difficulty, and with the help of an unknown student, he had explained his problem to the shopkeeper. He answered various questions of the shopkeeper like 'Where did you read?' 'Who was the principal of Ravenshaw?' 'Who taught you?' With the help of that unknown student, he could lay the suspicion of the shopkeeper to rest. The next problem that faced Sidharth was how to return to Cuttack.

That unknown student, who had rescued him from the shopkeeper, believed in his story. That day, he dropped him at the bus-stand and requested a conductor to help him. Even after the passage of many years, the incident had remained fresh, like dew drops of the morning, in Sidharth's memory, In the mean time, Umeshbabu had paid some money. Sidharth added some more, put the money in an envelope and handed it to the man. The man had not hoped that his problem would be solved so soon. His face now showed great relief.

The man said, "Please give me your address. Once I reach home, I will send you a money order."

Sidharth said, "There is no need of it."

The man was insistent, "No…no… I have to return the money. Please give me your address."

Sidharth asked, "Do you really want to return the money?"

"Yes," the voice of the man reflected his determination.

"Please do one thing. Just as you find yourself in trouble

today, someone else might find himself in trouble tomorrow. If you find someone in that situation, please listen to him and lend him a helping hand. Don't send him away out of suspicion. If you do this, you will repay me."

This time, Sidharth was surprised to hear the sound of his own voice. He felt as if he was not doing the talking, it was that unknown student, who had come to his rescue years ago at the Baleswar bus-stand, speaking.

A Villain

Sidharth felt much relieved after returning from the post office. For the last seven days, he had been spending his time amidst great confusion. He had found it hard to decide whether he should obey the directives of the unknown letter sender or completely ignore it.

One morning, a letter with Sidharth's address written in uneven handwriting on it arrived. Nothing exciting was happening in Sidharth's life those days. He was like a desert island. His children worked far away; they came to him once or twice in a year. The moment they reached they would make plans to return. That's why Sidharth never wished to prolong their stay in the village. In such a life, a letter from an unknown person could have caused enough excitement but for the mysterious and cruel order that it contained. It said, "Great calamity would befall unless ten copies of the letter were made within fifteen days and dispatched to ten different people. A gentleman of Phulbani defied this order and his son went down with an incurable disease. His son got well only when he understood the magnanimity of the deity, made fifty copies of the letter and dispatched them to different people. A penniless man of Bhawanipatna won a lottery of one lakh rupees as he had distributed thirty copies of the letter that proclaimed the magnanimity of the deity. A minister at Bhubaneswar fathered a son fifteen years after his marriage as he had distributed fifty copies of the letter. Those who refused to recognise the magnanimity of the deity unfailingly became the victims of either snakebites or sudden accidents."

Sidharth was completely drenched in sweat by the time he had finished reading the letter. What a cruel order! Sidharth, who had no faith in *babajis*, sages, or gods and goddesses, suddenly grew restless. Thereafter, he had only one thought- whether to do as the letter said or not.

The letter mentioned that those who distributed letters glorifying the deity would find immense wealth. But, Sidharth didn't crave for riches at the fag end of his life; the pension he got was sufficient for him. His only concern was that if he defied the dictates of the letter, would his children be in trouble?

Sidharth blamed himself for the feeling of excitement with which he had opened the letter. Who might that unknown sender be, who dispelled so cruelly serenity from his retired life?

Finally he decided he would send ten copies to his acquaintances; this was the best way to get rid of so much mental agony. This time, he faced another conflict. An unknown cruel-hearted person had disturbed his peace of mind but how could he, knowing full well the message that the letter contained, drive his own acquaintances into deep distress?

No, he can't do anything of that sort.

Last night, he stayed awake for a long time and made ten copies of that mysterious letter. In the morning, he went to the post office and stood near the counter for a long time.

After much hard work, he surreptitiously collected ten unknown addresses from the registration counter. After writing the addresses on the letters, he put them into the post box and heaved a sigh of relief. Oh! What a great relief. Had he done the same thing on the first day, he could have had at least five days' peace of mind.

After opening the lock on the door, Sidharth sat on the bench outside. In his mind, he was reading those mysterious words and the threat that lay lurking behind those. In a day or two, one threat would convert itself into ten threats and reach ten unknown persons. Among them, there might be old people suffering from heart ailments or distressed god-fearing people. What right had he got to harass them? This question suddenly took the shape of a huge moral-shocker and stood in front of him. As if he was able to visualize ten unknown but shuddering human beings! Did human beings keep in store all their anger, jealousy, and cruelty only to aim them at unknown human beings? He visualized ten miserable, frightened human beings busy making copies of that mysterious letter. The number of those letters soon rose to one hundred... thousand... then one lakh.

No, the best thing for him should have been to tear up that letter into pieces the day he received it and read it. But, it was certainly too late for him to do so now.

Where shall I play?

He was lucky that the scooter was not moving at a great speed. Otherwise, Sidharth would have lost control and fallen on the ground. He could not see what hit him—whether it was a small stone or a brick. That thing struck him in the middle of the forehead. He flew into a rage. He stopped the scooter and shouted at the person who had hidden himself taking advantage of the semi-darkness. He shouted, "Who threw it at me?"

After some controlled breathing, he felt as if the pain had subsided a bit. When he raised his head, he found that the culprit stood some distance away looking horrified. The moment his eyes fell on him, his anger subsided. He kept the scooter on its stand and went up to him.

He found a seven or eight year old bare-chested boy by the side of the red-gravel road. Perhaps he was the son of some mason or labourer.

Most of the residents of Bhubaneswar would be unaware of the existence of Rangini Sahi. If one went from Siripur to Baramunda, one would find about thirteen or fourteen houses along both the sides of a narrow road. It is a slum that houses rickshaw- pullers, plumbers, and other daily wage earners.

Sidharth asked, "Why are you throwing stones?"

The child was terribly afraid. If the adversary had been some distance away, he could have run away. But he didn't get the opportunity to run away as Sidharth reached him very quickly.

The child was on the verge of crying. He perhaps wanted to give an answer in many words but, in the end, he was able to utter only one sentence, "I was playing."

Sidharth was feeling a lot of pain in his eyelids. When he touched his forehead with his palm, he felt it was bleeding. Even though he could not see the blood in the darkness, he could feel that the skin had suffered a bruise. When he looked up, he found the electricity wires running from one end to the other. At the foot of one pole, stones were heaped. One day, this road might be converted to a blacktopped one; the heap of stones stood as a solid promise. The child was picking up stones from it and throwing them towards the wires.

Sidharth did not say anything. He returned to the scooter, started it, and rode off.

On the way back home, Sidharth found the innocent words of the child, "I was playing" reverberating in his ears. It was as if the child was asking him, "Where shall I play?"

Sidharth was reminded of his childhood. He was born in a village. The big village garden and field were there for him to run around in; tall trees and wide rivers offered opportunities for his bold expeditions. Gohiri and Badapokhari waited anxiously for stones to be thrown at them. To give him company, he had a large number of carefree friends, young calves, dragon flies and butterflies. But, this place was devoid of most of those charms. When most of the schools in the capital did not have a playground of their own, how could the Rangini Sahi slum dream of having one?

Where will the children and young men of the capital's slums spend their leisure hours? Where will run their swift little feet? Where will they watch the unending interplay of the moon and the stars, and the sunset and sunrise? Childhood never understood poverty, nor did youth heed restraints. Every young man was like a Vishnu in his dwarf *avatar*, for whose two feet the entire world proved too small. However, if there were no playgrounds, what would they do? Where will they go?

Sidharth knew he would be able to bear the pain caused by the boy's stone but he would not be able to answer his question.

Wings of the Butterfly

A few days ago caterpillars had infested Sidharth's garden, the trees there, even his house. Wherever one looked, one found them wriggling. If they stuck to the dresses, they caused great pain. Their bristles caused unbearable itch. Sidharth tried to drive away those caterpillars but he was unsuccessful in his attempt. His wife argued, "If the caterpillars didn't live in the garden, where would they live? Will colonies or villages be constructed for them?"

The caterpillars disappeared. They are not seen even on the trees. All those careful steps which were needed to be taken when they were present, were not required anymore. Sidharth felt relieved.

Yesterday, in the morning, Sidharth was taking a stroll in the garden in front of the house. It was a bright morning of *Bhadrab*. The sky was not clouded. Small dew drops glittered like pearl. Many winter-flowers had raised their heads. Sidharth wished to move around the lawn and caress them. For the last several days, he had not come across such a bright morning. The frequent showers both in the morning and in the evening and the presence of mud everywhere usually made Sidharth gloomy.

While roaming here and there, Sidharth stopped at a place. Among the *haragoura* bushes, he came across a large number of butterflies. Their desire to fly had made them very excited. Whenever Sidharth saw a butterfly or baby-bird learning how to fly, he was reminded of a child learning how to ride a bicycle. Sidharth stood motionless. A big butterfly lay at the foot of the *haragoura* plant with its wings outstretched, not able to fly. It frequently tried to get up and fly but kept falling on its face. The inability of the butterfly to rise pained him. He bent down and picked up the butterfly just as one would pick up a kite stuck to the ground. But lo! The butterfly's wings had grown so big that despite its best efforts it could not fly. The wings meant to support it had turned into a stumbling block; its assets had become its liability.

The butterfly looked extremely beautiful. On its spotted wings shone many colours. The silky wings glistened. But it was not able to rise up. Innumerable small butterflies flew around it and in front of it. They flew about from flower to flower; from flowers to the boundary wall; from the boundary wall to the fencing wire. Flitted from one end of the garden to the other in the twinkling of an eye and rested on the flower of their choice. Only the butterfly with colourful wings could not fly.

Many days ago, Sidharth had seen such a sight in a hotel. A young lady sat at a corner-table drinking coffee. Sidharth sat some distance away and constantly gazed at the lady. She was extremely beautiful. The moment this beautiful lady got up someone handed her two crutches. The young lady was not able to walk on her own. The sight was so painful that Sidharth turned his face away;

but he did not feel like looking away from that helpless butterfly.

Would this colourful butterfly live a worthless deformed life? What can a mere butterfly do when, despite possessing enormous wealth and the magic of science, mankind has not been able to get rid of its infirmities? But why should this have happened? Sidharth tried to lift the butterfly by its wings, just as he did with the kite in the rice fields when he was a child. He placed the butterfly on his palm and waited for it to fly; but the butterfly would fall on the ground, face down, like a kite with a broken thread.

The bright sunlight of the morning fell everywhere. The wings of the infirm butterfly once again reflected their helplessness Sidharth was reminded of the dim figure of that young lady, now almost forgotten. The bright morning had suddenly darkened for him.

The Wound of the Date Palm Tree

Sidharth had never imagined that he would meet Snehalata so suddenly. A decade had passed since they had last met. The thick layer of sand on the market road of Ghanteswar; the cashew nut plants from the Sana Akhada grove; and the mango trees in the school campus had all disappeared. Snehalata was a classmate of his. This girl was well known for things other than her studies. She was noted for her participation in sports, giving pickles and dried mango to her friends, causing offence to the newly recruited Hindi and Sanskrit teachers, and moreover, for hurling verbal abuse at the boys. She belonged to a well-to-do family and was very affectionate. That's why everybody adored her. Besides, she was very beautiful.

But today, Sidharth was not happy when he saw her. At first, he could not recognize her. Where had her plumpness and childishness gone? Her nimble steps and her straightforward talk had disappeared, too! She looked like a living skeleton. Her cheeks had sunken. The bald patch in her oily head looked strange. She now resembled a drought-affected beggar. That she was once the most beautiful girl of a village school was now difficult to believe.

On both sides of Snehalata sat four girls of different ages. On the right hand seat sat her husband, in whose lap sat two more children – one daughter and another son. Her husband was holding the son with both his hands and making it drink either milk or water. The moment Snehalata's eyes fell on Sidharth, the youthful restlessness of the past returned to her face. "Are you not Sidhu?" Sidhu nodded "Yes". But why did Snehalata look so pathetic? Whatever she wanted to say was like this: "She had no role in all this. Her husband wanted a son; before getting a son, she had to give birth to six daughters. Had a child not died, she would have been taking care of seven children now. Her husband was extremely conservative and hard-hearted. In his house, women's wishes were trampled upon. What could she have done in such circumstances?"

Sidharth asked, "How are you, Sneha?"

While getting down from the bus near Dasarathpur with her family, Sneha replied, "I'm alive."

The bus left Dasarathapur. Sidharth, who was compelled to stand at one corner of the bus due to the heavy rush, felt relieved to get a seat. His destination was Sathipur.

On the right hand side of the road that leads from Jajpur town to Sathipur square, and that joins the National Highway number-5 at that place, there runs a canal. Some people called the canal that ran till the Kianal field, Kianali. It had *kia* bushes and wild flowering plants growing on its banks. On the left-hand side, one found empty fields. Sidharth, forgetting about Snehalata, was looking at that canal.

But, he could not sit like that for long. The moment his eyes fell on the date palm trees growing on the banks of the Kianali canal, a gloomy feeling came over him again.

There was something wretched about all the date palm trees that grew between Jajpur and Sathipur square. On the grey trunk, starting from the root to the topmost part, there were marks of axe-blows at almost a thousand places. Those devastating blows, intended to collect date palm juice had rendered the trees weak and diseased; they had not grown the way they should have. The moment these dumb and defenceless trees grew up, they were bruised with thousands of wound marks. Not a single tree was spared this painful experience. How worthless the green dreams of these trees were in the face of man's greed and savagery!

Sidharth was feeling weak. The date plam trees have been regarded as the symbol of uselessness and weakness for ages. But, if the date palm trees had got the opportunity to record their feelings about man's heartless barbarity; or if they had mustered the ability to say that one line; would men bear to hear that terrible naked truth?"

He felt as if it was a mistake for the date palm juice to be sweet just as it was a mistake for Snehalata to be capable of giving birth to children. Snehalata's husband needed a son; the man drinking the juice of date palm needed to be intoxicated. For the sake of fathering a male child, it did not matter if the mother was pushed into a living hell. Similarly, if the date palm trees died of debility and disease while providing their sweet and intoxicating juice, there was nothing to worry about.

Who said infertile women and useless trees were worthless! They must take a look at Snehalata and the date palm trees growing on the banks of Kianala.

GLOSSARY

Aludam-	A delicious dish made out of potatoes and a variety of spices
Annadan-	Offering of food
Asadha-	Month of Hindu calendar corresponding to June and July
Babas-	Indian holy men
Baboo-	A Hindu gentleman; a Hindu title of address equivalent to Sir, Mr.
Bada-	A category of roadside fried snacks
Badichura-	Sundried lentil dumpling and coarse mixture of onion, garlic, green chillies, mustard-oil etc.
Bagudi-	A game played by boys and men during the Raja festival.
Baisakh-	Month of Hindu calendar corresponding to April/ May/ June
Barakoli-	Jujube
Basumati rice-	A variety of long, slender-grained aromatic rice
Bataosha-	Celebrated in Odisha in the month of Pousha (December- January)
Bhadrab-	Sixth month of the Hindu calendar
Bhauja-	Sister-in-law
Bhog-	Food offered to a deity
Biri-	A cheap form of cigarette made from cut tobacco rolled in a leaf.
Bohubohuka-	A traditional game played by children in villages

Chaitra-	First month of the year according to Hindu calendar
Chakuli-	Flat Odia rice-based fried cake prepared using rice flour, refined oil etc.
Chhak-	A village square where many shops exist and where people gather for a chit-chat
Chenapoda-	Roasted cheese-dessert from Odisha
Chuda-	Flattened rice used as snacks
Chullah-	Traditional stove used for cooking food
Dalma-	An authentic recipe of Odisha made using Arhar dal, vegetables etc.
Dalmankudi-	A traditional game played in rural Odisha
Darsan-	The visit of a devotee to the lord
Dharnas-	Sit-in protests
Dholak-	Two-headed hand-drum
Dhoti-	Rectangular piece of unstitched cloth wrapped around waist and legs in Odisha and West Bengal
Diyas-	Lighted earthen lamps
Doob-	*Cynodon dactylon.* Considered auspicious by Hindus.
Dosha-	Cooked flat thin-layered rice batter made from fermented batter
Ekadashi-	Eleventh tithi of Hindu calendar; a day for observing fasts
Gaintha-	Delicate dessert consisting of balls of rice, flour dough soaked in cardamom flavoured milk
Gulabjamun-	Soft, delicious, berry-sized balls made of milk solids, flour, and soaked in sugar syrup
Gotra-	Hindu clan tracing paternal lineage from a common ancestor
Guguchia-	A weed
Gamchha-	A traditional thin, coarse cotton towel
Gudakhu-	A paste-like tobacco preparation
Gunth-	Approximately 1089 square feet
Gurudakshina-	Tradition of repaying one's teacher after a period of studies

Gurudev-   Reverential address to a 'Guru' or 'Teacher' in
                    Hinduism

Guru-brothers-Followers or disciples of the same guru

Haragoura-   Balsam plant

Hokum-   Order or prescription curing a disease by a
                    religious person

Jalebis-   Indian sweet made by deep-frying maida flour
                    batter in circular shape and soaking in sugar
                    syrup

Jyestha-   Third month of the lunar calendar

Kadamba-   *Neolamarckia cadamba*

Kalash-   A metal or earthen pot with a large base and small
                    mouth considered auspicious

Kanika-   Indian food prepared using fragrant rice, ghee,
                    raisins, cashews, black cardamom, and cinnamon

Karanj-   *Millettia pinnata*

Kartik Purnima-Hindu festival celebrated on full moon day of
                    Kartik (November- December)

Khanjani-   Percussion musical instrument found in Odisha
                    and West Bengal

Khata-   A traditional Odia food prepared using tomato,
                    jiggery, and dates

Khir-   Sweet rice pudding

Kirtan-   Narrating, reciting, or telling spiritual or religious
                    ideas

Kitkit-   Game played by two or more players requiring
                    maneuvering through rectangle drawn on
                    ground

Krishnachura- Gulmohar or *Delonix regia*

Ladoos-   Sphere shaped sweet balls made of flour, ghee,
                    nuts and sugar

Luchi-   Bengali puffed deep fried bread made using maida

Magha-   Tenth month of a Hindu calendar

Magha Purnami-Full moon day in the month of Magha (January-
                    February)

Mahantas-   Heads of monasteries
Mahima Bhajans-Songs sung by devotees of an Indian religion
                   founded by Guru Mahima Swamy
Mahua-   A tree whose flowers are used as intoxicants
Manabasa-   Observed by Odias in the month of Margasira,
                   the ninth month of Hindu calendar
Math-   A monastery in Hinduism
Mofussil-   Parts of a country outside an urban centre
Mudhi-   A type of puffed grain made from rice
Mudki-   A delicacy prepared using cheese, sugar etc.
Namaskar-   Derived from Sanskrit 'namas' meaning
                   salutation or greetings
Nolias-   Traditional fishermen living on the sea-shore
Paan-   Betel cones
Pakhala-   Indian food consisting of cooked rice washed or a
                   little fermented in water
Panchamrit-   A holy concoction made from five ingredients and
                   used in the Hindu rituals
Pandas-   Worshippers employed in a temple
Phalguna-   Eleventh month of Hindu calendar
Prasad-   Vegetarian food used as religious offering in
                   Hinduism
Pucca-   Black-topped road
Puja-   The act of worshipping the deity
Purana-   Hindu religious text part of the Vedas
Puri-   Deep fried bread made from unleavened whole-
                   wheat flour
Puspanjali-   Offering of flowers to deities
Raita-   An Indian dish made with yogurt, spice powers,
                   herbs and vegetables.
Rasogolla-   Indian syrupy dessert made from ball shaped
                   dumplings of cheese
Rotis-   A round flat bread
Rudraksh-   A seed that is used as a prayer bead in Hinduism
Ramarajya-   Rule by the divine king Rama

Ravanarajya-   Rule by the demoniac king Ravana
Saga-   Edible fried leaves of certain plants
Salap-   A tree
Samosa-   A fried or baked pastry with a savoury filling
                such as spiced potato, onions, peas etc.
Sandesh-   A dessert created with milk, sugar and cheese
Sankranti-   Transmigration of the sun from one rashi to the
                other; there are twelve sankrantis
Santula-   A vegetable dish cooked using tomato, brinjal,
                papaya first boiled and then fried in oil
Saree-   Garment consisting of a length of cotton or silk
                draped around the body by women in India
Satyagrahas-   Protests
Shalagram-   Fossilized shells worshipped as symbols of God
                VIshnu
Shraddh-   A form of worship; a Vedic ritual performed to
                pay homage to ancestors
Shravan-   Fifth month of the Hindu calendar
Simili tree-   *Bombax ceiba*
Siuli flowers- *Nyctanthes arbor-tristis*; night flowering jasmine
Sufi-   Member of a very spiritual group of Muslims
Slokas-   A couplet of Sanskrit verse
Tandav-   Divine dance performed by Hindu God Shiva
Telingibaja-   A simple drum; a percussion instrument played
                on both sides with canes

About the writer

The writer, Gourahari Das, can be called a traveller. His journeys, both figurative and actual, both inward and outward, have made a writer of him. Born in 1960, in a back-of-the -beyond Indian village, Sandhagara near river Mantei he has come a long way. Real-life experiences acquired while growing up in an impoverished monastery sharpened his skills as a writer and endowed him with a sensibility laced with compassion and humour, which gives his creative being its distinctive character. His first book, Juara Bhatta (High Tide, Low tide), a short story collection, was published when he was only 21 years old. He has now as many as 70 books to his credit, which include novels, short-story collections, vignettes, travelogues, plays and essays. Gourahari has visited many countries across continents and leads a life full of activities. Many of his works have been translated into English, which include The Little Monk and Other Stories, The Nail and Other Stories, Koraput and Other Stories and The Shades of Life. He has received several awards such as Sahitya Akademi (India's national Akademi of letters) Award, Odisha Sahitya Akademi Award, Sangeet Natak Akademi Prize. He was also Senior Fellow of the Ministry of Culture of India and a Writer in Residency of Sahitya Akademi.

Gourahari lives in Bhubaneswar, India.

Manoranjan Mishra

Manoranjan Mishra (PhD) works as an Assistant Professor in the Department of English, Government Autonomous College, Angul, Odisha. He has more than eighteen years of teaching experience. His hobbies include translating short stories from Odia to English and vice-versa. Best Stories of Chandrasekhar Dasburma (ISBN 93-86437-93-7) is his first published translated text. Some of his translated stories and research articles have been published in Galaxy(ISSN 2278 9529), The Creative Launcher (ISSN 2455 6580), The Criterion (ISSN 0976 8165), Langlit (ISSN 2349 5189), Ashvmegh (ISSN 2454 4574), Muse India (ISSN 0975 1815)and Sahayogi (ISSN 2454 6828). ◼